Murder at Bunting Manor

GREG MOSSE is a 'writer and encourager of writers' and husband of internationally bestselling author, Kate Mosse. He has lived and worked in Paris, New York, Los Angeles and Madrid as an interpreter and translator, but grew up in rural south-west Sussex. In 2014, he founded the Criterion New Writing playwriting programme in the heart of the West End and, since then, has produced more than 25 of his own plays and musicals. His creative writing workshops are highly sought after at festivals at home and abroad. His first novel, *The Coming Darkness*, was published by Moonflower in 2022. *Murder at Bunting Manor* is the second book in a new cosy crime series featuring amateur sleuth Maisie Cooper, following *Murder at Church Lodge*, which published in 2023.

Murder at Bunting Manor

Greg Mosse

HODDER

First published in Great Britain in 2023 by Hodder & Stoughton
An Hachette UK company

1

Copyright © Mosse Futures Ltd 2023

A CIP catalogue record for this title is available from the British Library

Paperback ISBN 978 1 399 71516 4
eBook ISBN 978 1 399 71518 8

Typeset in Monotype Plantin by Manipal Technologies Limited

Printed and bound in Great Britain by Clays Ltd, Elcograf S.p.A.

Hodder & Stoughton policy is to use papers that are natural, renewable
and recyclable products and made from wood grown in sustainable forests.
The logging and manufacturing processes are expected to conform to the
environmental regulations of the country of origin.

Hodder & Stoughton Ltd
Carmelite House
50 Victoria Embankment
London EC4Y 0DZ

www.hodder.co.uk

For Rosie

Cast of Characters

Maisie Cooper
Alberta Tinker, a stranger
Ernest Sumner, landlord of the Dancing Hare
Jenny Brook, village shopkeeper
Alice Spragg, retired librarian and organist
Phyllis Pascal, owner of Bunting Manor
Zoe Richards, orphan
Mr & Mrs Beck, foster parents
Commander Kimmings, retired naval officer
Canon Dander, vicar of Bunting & Harden
Sergeant Jack Wingard of the Chichester police
Bert Close, stablehand
Maurice Ryan, Stephen's solicitor
Charity Clement, Maurice Ryan's assistant and wife
Florence Wingard, Jack Wingard's grandmother
Police Constable Barry Goodbody of the Chichester police
Gordon Stock, failing farmer
Archie Close, Phyllis Pascal's estate manager, Bert's brother
Mr Singer, builder
Inspector Fred Nairn of the Chichester police
Steve Weiss, a social worker
Sergeant William Dodd of the Chichester police
Canon Dander's cleaner

PROLOGUE

It was a crisp autumn day on the cusp of winter, November 5th, 1971. In a village hidden in a fold of the Sussex Downs, preparations for Guy Fawkes Night were almost complete, watched by a stranger, a woman dressed in several layers of ill-assorted clothes – almost rags. She had walked to Bunting along the pilgrim way, across the hills.

The bonfire field was beside a lane that led up to an untidy failing farm. For an hour at least – she had no watch – the stranger observed the villagers stacking prunings from overgrown hedges and fallen trees. Then the publican arrived – a little unsteadily – with the 'Guy', a pair of old striped pyjamas crammed with straw. The village shopkeeper brought the head, an upturned paper bag stuffed with newspaper and decorated with black wool for his long stringy hair, the face drawn on with a thick felt-tip pen – dark eyes, heavy brows, an ugly mouth with blacked-out teeth. The stranger watched the shopkeeper sew the head to the pyjama collar with a darning needle. It lolled to one side, grinning foolishly in the failing sun.

Finally, a strongly built woman in a worn wax jacket drove up in a tired Land Rover with an enormous box of fireworks. Her labouring man began setting the rockets in the ground, the Catherine wheels on the fence.

Earlier, a little before 'last orders' for the lunchtime service, the stranger had gone to lurk at the back door of the pub, the Dancing Hare, begging for scraps. A kind young woman with wide-set eyes, clear skin and nervous hands had given her a piece of quiche left over from someone's plate and told her she might come back at evening opening time, at five-thirty, for something else.

The gift had made the stranger feel warm inside. She had eaten it 'out of her hand', as the country people said, standing on the village green, watching a drab couple teaching two smallish boys – one English, one brown-skinned with dark brows – how to wash their tiny car, an off-white Hillman Imp with rust peeking through the paintwork round the wheel arches. Then, the four of them had gone back inside their ugly salmon-pink house, leaving their buckets and sponges and chamois leathers on the front step. The girl from the pub had turned up and was shouted at to 'bring in the things' and 'not make another mess like this morning'.

The stranger's cold feet were sore from her trudge over the hills, so she left the bonfire field and went to sit in the porch of the church, looking out at the gravestones. Then, after a while, looking at nothing at all.

Time passed. Day became dusk, dusk became almost night.

From a smart-looking converted worker's cottage on the far side of the green, a red-faced overweight man, encased in a grey three-piece suit, picked his way through the puddles around the green, a sheaf of music in his hands. Seeing the stranger, he screwed up his piggy face in a sneer of contempt and went inside. Discreetly, she followed him, sitting quietly in a rear pew, almost out of sight beside a pillar, while he practised Christmas hymns at the organ.

Soon she heard footsteps and there was the girl from the pub again, looking reluctant and unhappy.

'At last,' said the red-faced man, heaving himself off the organ stool and lumbering towards her. 'What's this I hear about you not singing the solos at Christmas, Zoe?'

'I'm sorry, Mr Kimmings, I don't want to.'

'Don't want to?' he spat. 'What's that supposed to mean?'

'I'm very sorry,' said the girl.

'You need to learn that life isn't about what you want to do,' he told her. 'It's about doing your damn duty. That's what young people don't understand. I'm surprised you haven't a better sense of your obligations. What are you? An orphan with no family, living off the kindness of Mr and Mrs Beck, off the kindness of the state.'

'Yes, Mr Kimmings.'

'I'll thank you to give me my rank and call me "Commander". Someone should take a slipper to you, you little minx.'

'In school,' said the girl, truculently, 'they tell us it's rude to call people names.'

Quick as a flash, he lurched forward and slapped the girl's face with the flat of his meaty hand. The stranger stood up in her pew. The girl ran towards the door. Just then the vicar – a tall man with a bland unremarkable face – stepped inside, catching her in his arms, clutching her to his chest.

'Now, what's the matter?' he asked, his eyes wide.

The girl pulled away, taking a couple of stumbling steps.

'Stop it. I hate you. I hate you both.'

She sounded like a small, broken child. The stranger wanted to say something to comfort her, but she didn't have time, because the girl ran away and the two men disappeared into the vestry.

The stranger shuffled outside. A hundred yards away, she could see the girl disappearing into the Dancing Hare. The church bell chimed and a car pulled in – a Triumph Herald. Its occupants came tumbling out, a happy family looking forward to the fireworks but keen to get into the pub nice and early for their quiche or 'fish-in-a-basket' beforehand.

The stranger made her way to the back door and stood in a corner, away from the lighted rear window, through which she could see children with parents who loved them, a wife who respected her husband, a husband devoted to his wife. At least, that was how it seemed.

She wondered if the girl would remember her promise, but soon the door opened and the pale face looked out.

'Are you there?'

'I'm here,' said the stranger, her words only just louder than the breeze.

The girl stepped outside. The slice of quiche was warm in her hands, steam rising in the chilly air.

'If you want, there's room to sit down in the woodshed.'

'No one will be coming out for logs, then?'

'We'll not be needing any more. We shut early to go up to the bonfire and the fireworks. You should stay for the display.'

The girl went back inside and the stranger did as she suggested, perching on a heap of cut beechwood in the log shelter, pulling her rags around her for warmth.

Maybe I will stop on, she thought. *There's no one who'll miss me.*

Once she had finished eating, wiping her oily fingers on her clothes, the stranger crossed the road and took the path through the woods towards the untidy gravel drive of Bunting Manor. From the shadow of the encroaching trees, she paused to peer in through tall leaded windows, seeing the firework woman in the worn wax jacket, opening a trapdoor in the floorboards. She descended to her basement, returning a few moments later with a dusty bottle of wine.

The stranger moved on. At the corner of the building, a cold moon revealed steps that led down to the outside door of the wine cellar, half concealed by overhanging leaves.

That might be useful, thought the stranger, *when I come back.*

I

JUSTICE

ONE

It was ten in the morning on a bright and blue-skied Saturday at the beginning of March, 1972. A week had gone by since Maisie Cooper had solved the puzzle of her brother Stephen's murder. The grief and the loss were still raw. With distressing frequency, memories of all she had seen and learnt came unbidden into her mind, robbing her of sleep, unsettling her days. She was tormented by regret that she hadn't been present enough in Stephen's life to save him from his cruel fate. She felt sickened by all she had discovered about human depravity. She tried to hold on to her sense of satisfaction at having solved the puzzle – the idea that she had, at least, been an agent of justice.

Yes, she had solved the mystery of his murder at a cost of turning her own life upside down.

Feeling rather sluggish, Maisie dressed in the cold bathroom of Church Lodge, brushing her teeth with pink Eucryl tooth powder, running damp fingers through her short curly hair. Downstairs, in the kitchen, she found the Aga was still slightly warm from the previous evening. She had sat up late with Jack Wingard, a sergeant in the Chichester police, talking over old times and, at rather depressing length, the trials that she would soon be obliged to attend.

'You'll be a crucial witness,' he had reminded her.

'I know that,' she had replied, more snappishly than she meant. 'Do you think I'll be criticised for interfering in the investigation?'

'I wouldn't be surprised,' Jack had replied, sympathetically. 'You may have "invited censure".'

That had made Maisie cross and put a dampener on things, despite both of them trying not to let it. Maisie had tried to lighten the mood with memories of their shared school days. Finally, Jack had left, driving away in his white Zephyr police car, a look of frustrated regret in his lovely warm eyes.

I wonder, thought Maisie, *if we'll ever get past this.*

Maisie stoked the fire box of the Aga with a good shake of coke from the scuttle, leaving the cast-iron door ajar to draw new flame. She felt conflicted, unable to accept Jack's declarations of affection – of love? – but aware that she was deeply drawn to him as well.

She made herself a cup of double-strength instant Maxwell House coffee, improving it with gold-top milk and demerara sugar, and drank it sitting on a tea towel on the back step, looking out at the orchard garden.

She would soon have to leave her late brother's rented home. She had been given a week's dispensation to stay on by the owner, but that was now over. Her open return ticket for the boat train to Paris was in her handbag. If she left that very night, she could wake the next morning at the Gare du Nord and take the *métro* to her shabby apartment under the mansard roof of a building on the Place des Vosges. Then, back to work in her role as a high-class tour guide. Were it not for the preparations for the trial, she might already have left.

Were it not for Jack, too.

Maisie drained her cup and went back inside. The Aga had drawn up nicely and the room was beginning to warm up. On the table was a copy of the local newspaper. On the front page was a drawing of the celebrated Tudor prayer book, stolen from Chichester cathedral crypt and central to her investigation of Stephen's death.

Maisie shut the firebox and set about the task she had allotted herself – cleaning and dusting the large cold house, determined to leave it better than she found it. She worked for almost two hours: Duraglit wadding on the brass door handles; Vim cleaning powder on the porcelain in the bathroom and kitchen; Vigor liquid on the chequer-board hallway floor. As the nearby church clock chimed twelve, still she hadn't attacked the cobwebs high in the double-height ceiling.

She decided to give herself a break and opened the front door. The sky was a limpid blue. Birds were singing in the trees. Last year's fallen leaves, blackened to mulch, smothered the untidy borders, but snowdrops and dwarf narcissi were poking through, like upright green swords. A rabbit came lolloping out from under the evergreen choisya, sniffed the air, looked left and right, then disappeared beneath the dark, waxy leaves of the rhododendron.

'Well, Maisie,' she told herself out loud. 'I think it's time.'

She put on an old quilted anorak she had found hanging in the hall and went outside, walking briskly, crossing the road to the small car park in front of the pub, the Fox-in-Flight. She paused to look in and was surprised to see Maurice Ryan, her late brother's solicitor, sitting in the window with a young woman wearing a rather ratty Afghan coat. They seemed to be discussing something private. The girl kept glancing round the bar to make sure they weren't overheard.

If that's a client, thought Maisie, *I wonder what sort of legal advice she can possibly be seeking.*

She walked on, past the blacksmith's forge then along a right turn leading to an uninspiring red-brick close, a small U-shaped council estate of eighteen cheap houses surrounding a tatty green. A girl of about fourteen years old was sitting on the solitary bench, her left hand gently

9

moving a pram back and forth. Maisie made her way to the last house on the left, apparently identical to all the others but, for her, imbued with special memories.

For the two weeks she had been back in Framlington, Maisie had avoided even looking at her old family home. It was here that she and Stephen had been raised by loving parents. It was here that she had first tasted tobacco and found the taste disgusting and the after-effects depressing. It was here that she had first made herself sick with alcohol – a particularly ripe local apple scrumpy – and her father Eric had sat with her until she had managed to drink a pint of cold water, then let her sink into grateful sleep. It was also here that her mother Irene had taught her and Stephen their first useful words of French, kick-starting their love of languages.

But those loving parents had died a decade before, in a road-traffic accident in one of the last London pea-souper fogs. And now Stephen was gone, too, and she was alone.

What did looking at the house make her feel? Nothing much. It was just a rather mean council house where some unknown new people were pleased or disappointed to live.

A curtain twitched in an upper window and Maisie turned away, not wanting to have to explain herself, trying not to feel disappointed. There was one other place she couldn't fail to find her parents. For the first time in ten years, she would look at Eric and Irene's shared resting place – a memorial she had avoided for the grief it would undoubtedly cause her to feel.

For a minute or two, in the graveyard at the end of Church Lane, she was frustrated, unable to locate their stone. She felt a kind of panic that it had been removed for some reason, as a kind of punishment.

Why a 'punishment'? Because she had paid it no attention and because the unconscious mind is a harsh judge.

Yes, she had been miles away in the West Country when they had been run over by a London bus. No, their deaths had been nothing but a stupid accident. But they were dead and she was alive. And, now, Stephen was dead as well, burnt to ashes at the dismal Chichester crematorium.

That was the problem. Stephen and Eric and Irene were gone while she still lived. And what was she going to do with her life, with all of its myriad possibilities? What did she want – the hustle and excitement of Paris or the reassurance of rural Sussex?

And Jack.

At last, she found the grave, beyond the yew tree on the southern edge of the graveyard, a modest upright stone in black basalt. She read the confident inscription, the words seeming hollow, though she knew they were well meant.

Eric and Irene Cooper, their love will endure.

It wasn't fair. Why had they been taken? The world was full of people who didn't deserve to live, but Eric and Irene were not among them.

She sighed.

'It's not fair,' she said aloud.

She left the graveyard and trudged back up Church Lane, barely lifting her feet. She saw Maurice Ryan go past in his rather ostentatious bottle-green Rover car, driving back into town. When she turned in at the drive of Church Lodge, she was delighted to find Jack waiting for her, off duty, looking immensely handsome in jodhpurs and tweed hacking jacket. He smiled and she smiled back.

They didn't kiss or even touch one another – there had been just one moment during the investigation into the murder at Church Lodge when he had taken her in his arms, relieved to know she was safe, angry that she had walked into danger – but the next two hours passed in a blur of laughter at the stables and up across the gallops on the Downs, by turns breathless and delighted. When, at last, their horses were tired, they walked them back to the yard and brushed them down in companionable silence, helped by Bert Close, the elderly stable lad.

Once they had finished, Jack asked Maisie what else she had to do, then added, with sadness in his lovely warm eyes: 'Before you leave for Paris?'

'I haven't gone yet,' she told him. 'Oh, and Charity asked me to drop in.'

Charity Clement was wife and assistant to Maurice Ryan, Stephen's solicitor.

'I'll give you a lift. I have a surprise for you, too.'

'You do?'

'It will give you a kind of resolution, I hope,' he told her.

Maisie wondered what it could possibly be.

'Are you sure I'll like it?' she asked.

'I believe you might,' said Jack, in his steady way.

'Then, yes,' said Maisie, lightly. 'I accept your kind offer of a lift.'

Two

Back at Church Lodge, Maisie felt a frisson of unaccustomed intimacy as she washed and changed upstairs in her bathroom, knowing that Jack was doing the same in the warm kitchen. When she came down, flushed and smiling, she felt embarrassed to find him waiting by the door, looking adoringly up at her.

'So, what's next?' she asked.

'You'll see,' he said with a wink. 'And don't forget, Grandma is expecting you for dinner this evening.'

That, too, would be a new level of entanglement of their lives. Would she welcome it? Yes, she would.

They drove into Chichester, across a stretch of arable land then through the woods. Everywhere Maisie saw evidence of quickening new life – buds beginning to open on the trees, early lambs in a field, daffodils on the verges.

Jack parked outside the cathedral and led her to the impressive west door. They went inside.

'Why are we here?' Maisie asked.

'I hope this is the right thing to do,' he told her, frowning. 'I thought it might help to lay a few ghosts to rest.'

'I don't understand.'

Jack seemed unusually tentative.

'I'm sorry if it turns out to be a mistake.'

Maisie wondered what it could be.

'We're here, now,' she told him. 'Why don't you just tell me?'

At that moment, they were joined by a small man in a dusty shapeless suit, carrying a leather-bound ledger. Maisie had briefly met him once before. He was the cathedral's curator of historic objects.

'Er, good afternoon, Sergeant Wingard, Miss Cooper. All is ready. Would you follow me?' The curator led them to a flight of narrow stone stairs in the north transept of the cathedral. They followed him down. 'A modest ceremony of rededication,' said the curator, 'will be conducted tomorrow lunchtime after the sung eucharist, but Sergeant Wingard has prevailed upon me to grant a private preview. Here we are.'

The curator unlocked a heavy wooden door and led them into the crypt, a surprisingly roomy space comprising several chambers, each with its own vaulted ceiling. Jack was hanging back but Maisie was drawn to the centrepiece of the well-lit display – an ancient devotional book, resting on a velvet cushion, open at the illuminated page for Justice.

'Would you put on these gloves, Miss Cooper?' He offered her a pair in white cotton. 'I will leave you for a few minutes. Will you excuse me?'

He bustled away to a far corner of the crypt as Maisie stepped up to the cushioned lectern, a flutter of anxiety in her chest. She reached out a gloved hand and touched the thick pages.

'I thought you should be able to see it properly,' said Jack quietly. 'I hope I did the right thing.'

Maisie wondered if the fact that it was open at the page for Justice might have been deliberate. She turned the pages, finding the other virtues depicted with skill and respect: Patience, Temperance, Hope, Charity, Faith and Courage.

'You were right,' Maisie replied, matching Jack's low voice. 'I'm glad to see it back in its rightful place.'

Jack came close, standing just behind her. He reached out a hand and placed it gently over her own.

'Please don't go,' he murmured.

'I can't . . .' Maisie began.

She wasn't sure what she wanted to say, how she wanted to finish her sentence. Time slowed and her mind became almost blank. All she knew was that she didn't want this moment to end. But, at the same time, she felt an awful ache of loneliness and loss. Would Jack's affection always be tainted by her grief?

'I don't know what to—'

'Now, er, I am a little pressed for time,' interrupted the dusty curator and Jack snatched his hand away. 'Perhaps you would like to attend the rededication tomorrow?'

'No, thank you,' said Maisie quickly. 'I'm very grateful for your time, today.'

She gave him a bright but, she felt, brittle smile and climbed back up the narrow flight of stone steps, emerging with relief into the huge nave of the cathedral. She led Jack out through the west door and turned her face up to the weak March sun, closing her eyes, breathing deeply.

'It was a stupid thing to do,' Jack told her, a deep frown creasing his regular features. 'I'm sorry.'

'No, it wasn't,' said Maisie. 'I think it will help, you know.'

'Do you really believe that?'

Maisie sighed. 'I hope so, Jack. I honestly do.'

'Good,' he said with relief. 'Now, when I say "dinner", I mean tea. Grandma eats at five-thirty, like the farmer's daughter she is.'

'I'm looking forward to it.'

'She's a character. I do hope you get on. And she's interesting, too. You know she was born at the beginning of the century, in 1903?'

'I'll be there, Jack. Don't worry. You get on with catching criminals.'

'All right.'

He smiled and turned away and Maisie knew that his presence was central to how warmly she felt towards this provincial market town with its overblown cathedral and carefully cultivated history. As she watched him go, she was grateful that he had the good manners not to look back and see her gazing after him.

Once Jack had gone, Maisie took out her purse and counted her money – a few pound notes and a handful of coins. If her Paris flatmate, Sophie, hadn't been very kind and sent her some traveller's cheques in the post, she would have been down to her last ha'penny.

She put the purse away, gave herself a shake and walked the short distance round the corner onto West Street to Maurice Ryan's solicitor's office. Both Maurice and Charity were there, despite the fact it was a Saturday, doing some decorating. Maisie felt a little guilty. It was she who had pointed out how scruffy the place looked when she had visited to go through her brother's papers.

'Don't feel bad, Maisie,' said Maurice, a delicate fitch brush in his hand for painting the narrow mullions of the sash windows. 'If I'm going to sell the business, this can only help. You know my dream is to retire to the sun.'

'You should go, Maurice,' said Charity to her husband. 'You'll be late.'

'God, yes, I will,' said Maurice in his flamboyant way, leaving the fitch on a piece of newspaper and casting around for the keys to his Rover. 'No peace for the wicked.'

The keys were on the corner of Charity's desk. He snatched them up and left.

'What's Maurice up to?' Maisie asked.

'Nine holes of golf with a client.' Charity smiled. 'He will lose very gracefully.'

Maisie wondered whether she should ask her friend what Maurice had been doing at the Fox-in-Flight with the girl in the Afghan coat, but Charity continued, a look of concern in her eyes, speaking French, faintly accented from her childhood in Guadeloupe.

'*Tu as beaucoup encaissé, ces derniers temps. Tu dois prendre soin de toi.*'

You've had a lot to put up with recently. You need to look after yourself.

'You're right,' Maisie told her. 'But I feel fine. And I'm very grateful to you and to Maurice for all you have done. Do we have a date for the trial?'

'No, not yet. But I had a message for you, something quite unexpected. I sent it on to Church Lodge in the week and now the lady has rung to say she has had no reply.'

Maisie felt guilty. She had neglected to open her post for fear of finding more of Stephen's bills that she couldn't afford to pay.

'What's it about?'

'I'm not exactly sure,' said Charity, with a frown. 'Her name is Phyllis Pascal. She wants to meet you so that you can conduct an investigation on her behalf.'

'She does?' asked Maisie, surprised.

'She promises "generous remuneration",' said Charity, encouragingly.

'Well, that wouldn't go amiss. Do we know why she was in touch – a stranger, appealing out of the blue on the strength of . . . Well, on the strength of what, exactly?'

'I suppose that will form part of your discussions,' said Charity. 'She is a powerful woman, in her way.'

'Powerful how?'

'How is any woman powerful? She has money. She is connected to several of Maurice's most important clients. And your brother's murder was widely reported, not just in the local papers but in the nationals, too. She says she read about it and learnt of the role that you played in uncovering the facts.'

Maisie felt pride in her achievement but was private enough to hate being 'talked about'.

'Jack and I agreed that we should play that down.'

'Sergeant Wingard was not the source of the . . . What is the English word?'

'The leak?'

'That's it, although you must remember, Maisie, these things are a matter of public record.'

'All the same, someone must have spoken to a journalist.' An idea came into her mind. 'You remember Police Constable Goodbody? Barry Goodbody, the one who looks like a ferret?'

'A ferret?'

'*Un furet.*'

'Oh, yes, he does.' Charity laughed and the sound was a delightful counterpoint to Maisie's rather sombre mood. 'An angry ferret.'

'He hated me from the very first,' said Maisie.

'Because you conducted your own freelance investigation in parallel to the police,' said Charity, reasonably. 'Anyway, it doesn't matter. The point is, she read about you, this wealthy woman, and she also learnt of our connection – I mean to Maurice and to me, as Stephen's solicitors. Don't mistake me. Maurice was interviewed by the press and said almost nothing – he fears a connection with scandal as one would the plague – but he said his almost-nothing so beautifully that it was reported all the same.'

Maisie smiled. 'I can imagine that.'

'Do you want to meet Mrs Pascal?'

Maisie considered.

'Could you invite her here, to your office? If she turns out simply to be a nosy gossip, it will be easier to get rid of her.'

'On Monday, perhaps? You must soon leave Church Lodge, I believe?' Charity reminded her.

'Yes,' said Maisie, feeling her heart sink. 'Especially as I'm not paying any rent. I'm meant to find something for Monday and you say there's no trial date yet and I'm running out of money.'

'We've had another bill for your attention, by the way,' said Charity. 'For the coke for the Aga.'

Maisie sighed. Back at Church Lodge, she had seen the delivery truck and almost run into the coalman, hanging back so as not to give him the chance to present his account.

'I'll sort it out. But this Mrs Pascal, could you invite her in as soon as possible? First thing Monday, even?'

'I will call her now.'

Charity put her paintbrush alongside Maurice's narrow fitch on the sheet of newspaper protecting her desk and dialled, the rotary mechanism tinkling as it spun from her forefinger. Maisie heard the distant ring then a loud voice at the other end.

'Two-nine-eight-nine.'

'Mrs Pascal? Miss Clement, speaking, Mr Ryan's assistant. I have spoken to Miss Cooper. Would it be convenient to come into the office on Monday at nine-thirty?'

'It would,' said the voice on the other end of the line. 'Thank you.'

Maisie heard the click and the dial tone.

'That was very abrupt.'

'It was.' Charity shrugged. 'The other day, she wanted to know your address and phone number in Paris, in case you left. I refused on grounds of professional discretion. She is probably still angry.'

Maisie sighed. 'Perhaps it's a mistake to meet her.'

'It's done, now. Meet me in the café opposite beforehand to fortify ourselves? I'll pay.'

'Oh, that reminds me. Could I please use your phone? I must call Madame de Rosette.'

Stephen had allowed the phone at Church Lodge to be disconnected.

'Go ahead.'

Charity went back to her painting, applying gloss white in long smooth strokes to the skirting board. Maisie sat at her friend's desk, steeling herself for a difficult conversation. Her Paris boss was tricky.

She dialled and Madame de Rosette replied after two rings with a curt: '*Allo.*'

Maisie announced herself and got straight to the point.

'I am very sorry,' Maisie told her. 'I cannot return to Paris quite yet. I have been called as a witness, as we both knew I would be.'

'And the solicitor says you must present yourself in person.'

'I am central to the case. My testimony will be cross-examined.'

'And what shall I do?' complained Madame de Rosette. 'Your calendar is full. Only this morning, I had two requests for you very particularly.'

Maisie knew this might well be true. She had an excellent reputation as a high-class Paris tour guide and could, of course, speak to clients in several languages.

'I can only apologise,' Maisie assured her. 'I will return as soon as I am able.'

'Your holiday entitlement is almost exhausted,' Madame de Rosette replied brusquely. 'After that . . .' She left the thought hanging.

'I understand,' said Maisie.

They said goodbye to one another, then hung up.

So, on top of everything else, thought Maisie, *Madame de Rosette is threatening to give me the sack.*

THREE

Because it was still a lovely early spring day, Maisie spent the rest of the afternoon window shopping, then sat for nearly an hour over a pot of tea-for-one in the St Martin's Tearooms, reading a rather sombre novel she had bought in the Paris branch of W H Smith's on the Rue de Rivoli. It was by an important literary novelist and politician called André Malraux, entitled *Les Chênes qu'on abat* and had only recently come out. If the title was anything to go by, it would eventually have something to do with cutting down oak trees – a storyline that would chime quite well with her unexpected return to rural south-west Sussex.

Eventually, Maisie realised she had allowed the whole afternoon to drift away. She closed the book and put it away in her handbag, a vague smile on her lips.

Yes, despite her years of working abroad, her cosmopolitan outlook, her multilingual friends, she had never shaken the dust of her home town off her feet. This unremarkable place was still important. It was where, as Philip Larkin said in his poem 'I remember, I remember', she had her 'roots'.

And it was where Jack lived and worked, too.

She paid for her tea and went outside into the narrow city-centre lane. She didn't dawdle because the early evening was chilly and because she didn't want to be late.

She turned onto Parklands Road and found the pink bungalow just a hundred yards away on the right-hand side. She walked quickly up the path to the front door. It opened before she had time to knock and there was Jack

Wingard's grandma, small and rosy-cheeked, smiling and welcoming.

'Well, I never did,' said Grandma Wingard. 'This is a lovely surprise.'

'It's a treat for me, too,' said Maisie, beaming back.

'Can it be sixteen years?'

'I suppose it is,' said Maisie, feeling a reassuring connection to her own childhood and a deeper intimacy with Jack's life. Did she want that right now? She thought she did. 'But we were never actually introduced?'

'I noticed you when I came in to sports day, the year you and Jack left school.'

'Why did you notice me?'

'Jack pointed you out because you were so good at everything, dear. And you were very pretty. You still are.'

All this was said with such disarming candour that Maisie laughed. Grandma Wingard was speaking as if sixteen years ago was yesterday – but perhaps it really was nothing when you had been born early in the century and experienced two world wars.

'Come in,' she urged. 'I've laid the table.'

Maisie went inside and found the bungalow rammed with things, the accumulation of fifty years' occupation. The narrow corridor to the kitchen was lined with hooks, all of them groaning under the weight of hangers supporting suits and dresses and overcoats. Maisie recognised the bell-shaped winter cloak worn by girls at Westbrook College.

'Jack told me you still do tailoring?'

'I do. It's mostly mending, buttons and zips, blemishes, torn linings and so on. I keep myself busy.'

'I'm sure you do.'

They arrived in the kitchen, a small square room in which Jack Wingard seemed to Maisie to take up quite a lot of space, not just because of his wide shoulders. He opened his mouth to say something but his grandmother rattled on.

'A nice man from Oxfam comes to get them,' said Grandma Wingard, 'and then he sells them in the charity shop to buy rice for Bangladesh, though why they had a civil war when they didn't have enough to eat is beyond me.'

'Not just Bangladesh, Grandma,' said Jack, smiling, 'and not just rice.'

'Goats, then?' she said, unconvinced. 'Now, get out of the way. Let me see if it's ready. I hope you're both hungry.'

With surprising suppleness, Grandma Wingard bent down to open the oven and inspect an old-fashioned iron roasting dish. The aroma was intoxicating – rich and flavoursome.

'It's brisket, isn't it?' asked Maisie.

'It is,' said Grandma Wingard, straightening up, 'and it's ready. If you two go through, I'll make the gravy, then Jack can come back for the dishes.'

'Thank you, Mrs Wingard.'

'How old are you now, Maisie?'

'I'm thirty-four.'

'Then you can call me Florence.'

'Can I?'

'I wish you would. It's one of the small miseries of age that no one calls you by your first name any more.'

***

The traditional English meal was delicious and hearty and precisely what Maisie needed. She attacked it with gusto and, when she had finished, asked for seconds. Once their plates were empty, they stayed where they were, sitting up

23

at the dining table in the crowded living room. Soon, more than an hour had passed in pleasant reminiscence of how life had been when Maisie and Jack were children, then the private secondary school where Maisie had been a weekly boarder and Jack had been a scholarship day student.

'You must know, Maisie, that Jack is very clever?' said Florence.

'Oh, for heaven's sake,' said Jack lightly.

'I do,' said Maisie.

'Don't you think he should have been promoted by now? Fred Nairn joined up at the same time and he's an inspector already.'

'I agree,' said Maisie, smiling. 'Jack should definitely be in charge.'

'He's been offered more than once but he won't take it.'

'Because it would mean moving to another station in another town,' Jack replied, 'maybe as far away as Crawley or Southampton, and leaving you on your own.'

'But I'm quite all right on my own.'

'Are you?' he asked, raising an eyebrow.

They discussed Florence's social life, made up of church and Women's Institute, a shared allotment and whist drives and cake sales and so on – and how she sometimes needed help getting about.

'You have a busier social life than I do,' said Maisie.

'If I wasn't here,' said Jack, 'or within easy reach, Grandma would miss out on three-quarters of all that and then—'

'Yes,' interrupted Florence with an ironic smile. 'Then I'd be lonely and sad, a poor little old woman living isolated on the edge of town, looking out of her window over her sewing machine, wishing someone, anyone, might come to call.'

Jack laughed. It was a lovely warm sound.

'Now you're showing off for our guest. Sixty-eight is no age.'

'Never mind my years,' said Florence. 'There's a bit of cheese in the pantry if anyone wants it to finish.'

'No, I couldn't,' said Maisie. 'That was delicious.'

'Then I'm going to my chair. I'll let you two young things tidy up.'

Maisie helped Jack clear the table, leaving Florence to move to her easy chair by the fire, knitting. Together, they washed up at the large white sink, chipped here and there from years of use, stacking the plates in a chrome drying rack on the wooden draining board, leaving the roasting tray till last. Maisie felt comforted by the brief episode of domesticity.

After a while, the dishes and plates and cutlery were all put away in their proper places and the drying-up cloths draped over the backs of the kitchen chairs. Still, she and Jack discussed everything and nothing: the weather; Maisie's Paris friends; the Rotary Club that Jack supported as his contribution to local charity. Then, as Maisie had feared, Jack grew serious.

'I'm so pleased you came this evening, Maisie,' he said, meaningfully. 'I wish you wouldn't go away again.'

'Do you mean back home to Paris?'

'I mean ever.' He put his hand on hers and Maisie felt oddly coy, as if worried that Florence might come in and tell them off for 'canoodling'. 'Don't you feel that, too?'

'Don't spoil it, Jack,' she told him, quietly. 'You know I can't separate my feelings for you from all that's happened. Just for this evening, can't we keep things as they are?'

His face fell. He withdrew his hand and she felt unkind.

'What does that mean, exactly, "things as they are"?' he asked, unhappily.

'I can't make any big decisions until after the trial,' said Maisie. 'It's all fine as long as nothing changes and we keep things on an even keel.'

'Everything changes,' said Jack, 'but not how I feel about you.'

'That's exactly what I mean. How do you expect me to reply to that?'

He looked at the floor. 'Would you prefer not to see me?'

'Of course not. I'm grateful that you're going to make time to prepare me for the witness stand. It's just . . .' Maisie hesitated. What did she want to say? That her emotions were simply too raw. 'Just until it's all over and done with, could we simply behave like old friends?'

'Of course, we can,' said Jack after a moment's hesitation. He put his arms around her and, briefly, held her close. Maisie felt herself melt and was on the point of changing her mind, rejecting all her qualms, when he pulled away. 'Let's see what Grandma is up to. I expect she'll want her bedtime sherry.'

Maisie followed him along the crowded corridor to the crowded living room. Florence was winding up her knitting and was on the point of going to bed.

'I can fetch my own glass of sherry,' she told them. 'Jack says you're going to come over again on Monday to talk through your evidence.'

'That's right,' said Maisie.

'Well, that will be nice. I'd say let's have fish and chips but Monday's not a good day for that. You always worry it won't be fresh.'

'You certainly don't need to cook for me again,' Maisie protested.

'Well, we'll see,' said Florence. 'Now you run along.'

Maisie said her goodbyes and she and Jack left. He drove her back to Framlington, keeping up a steady conversational rhythm with funny stories from his police work: a cat that refused to come down from its owner's loft; a grown man who got stuck in the kids' climbing frame in Priory Park;

Constable Barry Goodbody's comical inability to grasp the difference between 'imply' and 'infer'.

'What will you do tomorrow?' he asked her.

'First of all, I'll finish cleaning the house. Stephen left it very grimy.'

'I'd come and help but I'm on Sunday duty.'

'I'll do a bit of hand laundry, say goodbye to a few neighbours.'

'Will you go to a hotel until the trial?'

'I haven't decided.'

They arrived at Church Lodge and Jack's manner remained so brisk that Maisie found herself out of the car and waving him goodbye before she knew what had happened.

As his tail lights receded, she stood on the gravel drive in the moonlight, thinking to herself: *What have I done?*

FOUR

A few miles north of Framlington, tucked in a frost pocket in a fold in the Sussex Downs, the village of Bunting was a very desirable place to live for those with money, a dead end for those without. At its centre was a quartet of public spaces: the green through which a stream merrily trickled; a poorly stocked shop; a warmly welcoming pub; a Norman church whose roof seemed always to be in need of repair. It was surrounded by sweeping green hillsides whose grass was cropped by livestock, cows and sheep bred for the butcher's knife. In the woods were flocks of pheasant and partridge, bred for the hunter's gun. Apples and pears grew in damp orchards.

Phyllis Pascal was Bunting's richest resident, an abrupt, self-important woman whose wealth was inherited through marriage to – then divorce from – an unloving husband. A country woman by birth and by inclination, Phyllis Pascal knew she looked as though she had everything. In reality, many years before, she had lost what Hollywood calls 'her heart's desire' and behaved abominably as a consequence.

How long had she carried the burden? Thirty years? No, more than that. And no one knew. There was no longer anyone left alive who needed to know.

Except, perhaps, one other.

Phyllis's mightily ancient manor house – in whose rustic kitchen she was currently sitting – was tucked away on rising ground in the trees, away from the floodable village green. It had been built during the lifetime of Shakespeare for the

28

richest person for twenty-five miles in any direction. Phyllis's elderly estate manager, Archie Close – brother of Maisie's friend Bert who looked after the stables in Framlington – always referred to it as the 'Big House', which reminded Phyl of how gangsters in American films referred to prison. Over time, she had allowed the woods to encroach on her gardens, pushing the mansion further and further into shadow – a circumstance that she had done nothing to remedy.

It was Sunday. Phyllis had been to church, listened to Canon Dander's half-hearted sermon, joined in the hymns in her loud alto voice, then stomped home along the woodland path. Her fridge and her vegetable basket were empty, but she couldn't face the pub and more company, so she sat at the large scratched kitchen table covered with unanswered post, unread newspapers and unwashed crockery, eating salty Ritz crackers from the box.

Eventually, Phyllis picked up and skimmed a letter from a charity she supported. Being rich, she was courted for what her money could buy – social prestige, political or business advantage. In a sense, charity was a way to make amends, but she had reached a point where she wanted to do something bigger, something more . . . meaningful.

She picked up the local newspaper, the *Chichester Observer*, with its front-page article on the 'Framlington murder' and the priceless illuminated book of sins and virtues. The journalist suggested that, in the end, 'justice had been done'.

She picked up a Roneo'd copy of the parish council newsletter, noticing its astringent odour. She was chairman, a rewarding but often difficult role. Bunting was a tight-knit community, but not always a happy one.

Though Bunting Manor was outside the heart of the village, Phyl had recently taken two unexpected decisions, surprising herself by weaving her life much more tightly into those of her neighbours. Both involved the acquisition of responsibility for another human being. Neither the girl nor the woman had any legitimate call upon her. They weren't relations, close or distant. They hadn't ever been dependants or employees. But each one's desperate circumstances had broken down her defences.

Phyl abandoned the parish council newsletter. When she needed to think, she preferred standing to sitting, so she went outside to have a rummage through her walled kitchen garden, pulling up weeds and herbs with indiscriminate inattention.

Had she done the right thing, making an appointment for the next day, Monday, at nine-thirty in Maurice Ryan's office?

She decided to take herself out for a trudge through the village. She emerged from her woods not far from the pub, the Dancing Hare, a nicely symmetrical building in flint and red brick, the roof and windows in good repair – as Phyl knew only too well because she owned the property. The trouble was, the publican was a soak.

That wasn't to say that Ernest Sumner was an alcoholic in the sense that word is sometimes meant. He didn't go out in the street, embarrassing himself by shouting at the moon. He didn't climb the narrow stairs to his upstairs apartment at closing time and wet his bed. But, every day, without fail, he drank more than was good for him.

The Dancing Hare was a tied house, beholden to its brewery for a certain level of financial performance. Phyl had to believe that, somewhere, a clock was ticking on Ernest's management. Would it end in an explosion, like a bomb, or would it be an anti-climax, a quiet whimper? Time would tell.

Next to the pub was an ill-maintained stretch of potholed gravel, ineffectually filled with bits of broken brick – the car park. Beyond that was the shop, a utilitarian prefabricated building from the late Forties, almost a definition of the term 'Jerry-built', derived from the post-war practice of using forced labour from German prisoners of war as part of the reconstruction effort. It resembled a converted car garage whose up-and-over door had been replaced by a large cold window of plate glass. Through the window, Phyl could see the unhappy shop owner, Jenny Brook, pottering about between the meagrely stocked shelves, using her Sunday to dust and clean.

Phyl wanted to support poor Jenny, but to shop there was to be transported into a fug of apathy and lost dreams: Jacob's Cream Crackers soggy from sitting for too long on the shelf; Daz soap powder caked together in its cardboard packaging by incipient damp; bland 'products of last resort' from the cheapest shelves at the cash-and-carry in Chichester.

Because Jenny had seen her through the window, Phyl knocked and went in and – just to be kind – bought a bottle of bleach and left. She was aware that, in his moments of sober clarity, Ernest Sumner was courting Jenny Brook – or perhaps it was the other way around – but their schedules were incompatible. Jenny was always up with the lark, busy opening up, taking delivery of bread and eggs and milk and newspapers, while Ernest slept off the previous evening's overindulgence. At the other end of the day, as Ernest became expansive – leaning lazily on the polished counter in the Dancing Hare while his young barmaid kept glasses full and tables tidy – Jenny was pulling on her bedsocks and mixing a milky, malted Ovaltine drink for bedtime.

Their only shared time was afternoons, when Jenny closed the shop and came into the pub to help bake pies and pastries and quiches and tarts. She had a lovely hand for pastry. Some local people, including Canon Dander, were in the habit of taking delivery of her wares to eat at home. That morning, Phyl had seen Jenny and Ernest sitting chastely alongside one another at the eleven o'clock service in a rear pew.

She walked on, the bottle of bleach heavy in the poacher's pocket of her disreputable waxed coat, and came upon a drive, deeply rutted by farm vehicles. It led about a hundred yards uphill towards a charming but unkempt farmhouse, lodged comfortably in a cleft in the hills. Phyllis paused at the gatepost.

When its current owner, Gordon Stock, had taken over, it had been prosperous. Phyllis had known his parents, a skilful farming couple who ran it scientifically, rotating the arable fields, season on season, through wheat, barley, oats, peas, beans and brassicas, seeing the livestock into the barns when snow covered the ground, then back out in spring to enjoy the lush new grass.

But Gordon's parents had retired to a bungalow on the beach at West Wittering and were said to be delighted with long days of blissful inactivity. Meanwhile, their son – only nineteen years old because his conception had been an unexpected 'accident' with his mother past forty – worked endless hours, trying to be attentive to the rhythms of his livestock and his fields but, inexorably, failing. To make ends meet, he was thinking of selling one or two parcels of his land to his neighbours, robbing his future to pay for the dilapidations of the present.

The rain grew a little heavier so Phyl stomped up through the graveyard to sit in the porch of the church, also set back from the road, musing on how millennial wisdom had placed all the older buildings a little uphill, away from the stream that ran through the valley. It was a winterbourne known as the Bunt. For much of the year it flowed underground through chalk and flint, emerging only between November and April or May, often flooding the green and some of the newer houses. Despite Phyl's strongly argued objections, a planning application had been made for part of Gordon Stock's lowest field. If successful, four new red-brick houses would stand, as old Archie Close was fond of saying, 'with their feet in the wet'.

Rain dripped from the clogged gutter of the church porch and Phyl's thoughts turned to the incumbent of the stolid Norman church, Canon Dander, a tall man with a lovely tenor voice whose bland features and unenergetic manner undermined his ministry. He had been moved on from his stipend at Framlington for reasons only a few people knew but others, perhaps, guessed at. He was well connected in the hierarchy of the church, with strong ties to the local cathedral in Chichester, sometimes officiating in a minor role at unimportant services.

Canon Dander was good friends with another local resident, a retired naval officer known as Commander Kimmings. The red-faced ex-sailor lived as a bachelor in a sensitive conversion of two adjacent workers' cottages. They had been part of Phyl's estate and she had sold them on when she was much younger and didn't know that property was for keeping.

Knocking the two cottages together gave Kimmings plenty of room for his knick-knacks and mementos of a life spent at sea – first in the Royal Navy, later the merchant marine – for his baby grand piano and his volcanic temper. He had, at one time, used the instrument to teach local children the rudiments of keyboard music. Then, something had happened to make his pleasant home no longer a welcome venue for such appointments – an explosion of anger from Kimmings and the child running outside, frightened, to its parents waiting in the car. He seemed to learn some kind of lesson because, for a year or two, there had been no further unpleasantness – until the unfortunate incident on Guy Fawkes Night.

The rain began to ease and Phyl's eye moved to the third worker's cottage, inhabited by Alice Spragg, a grey-faced retired librarian. Like Commander Kimmings, Alice Spragg lived on her savings and her pension. But, while he seemed comfortably off, she looked on impotently, nervously, as both her capital and income were eroded by inflation. Also unlike Kimmings, Alice Spragg's cottage was a single dwelling, not two knocked through, and its Spartan refurbishments had gone no further than replacing rotting windows with cheap new ones and repainting the front and back doors. Nothing had been done about their poor fit or the draughts. No insulation had been added, no central heating installed.

Phyl frowned. She was the owner of the property and should have done more, not least because her inattention provided fuel for Alice Spragg's violent class-consciousness. The woman was a communist.

Phyl got to her feet, shaking off a few beads of rain that still clung to her waxed jacket. The sun was trying to come out. She walked down through the graveyard to the road and on to a more modern house, also part of her estate, built in the mid-Fifties – an arrangement of slabs of utilitarian concrete, painted an unpleasant shade of salmon pink. She shook her head, leaning on the inappropriate picket fence, paint peeling from every strut.

The house was empty with a faded note pinned to the front door, giving a telephone number in Portsmouth. The demoralised couple who had rented it from her for the previous decade, Mr and Mrs Beck, had made an unlikely living by taking in foster children. What, Phyl wondered, had they taught their sad charges? A way of understanding the world from the point of view of an isolated Sussex downland valley without prospects and with a regimented social structure . . .

Mr and Mrs Beck had left four months before, soon after Guy Fawkes Night, taking with them two younger foster children, but leaving behind their older ward, Zoe Richards, who helped out Ernest Sumner at the Dancing Hare. Phyl supposed they considered Zoe an adult, putatively independent. But the girl was only just sixteen and had been left homeless.

How had it come to pass that Phyl had scooped Zoe up and given her a place to live in the Big House, Bunting Manor? That was a question that Phyl was sure everyone in the village would like an answer to.

Not long after Phyl had welcomed Zoe to Bunting Manor, Alice Spragg had come to inform her, 'as a neighbour, with her best interests at heart', that she had a low opinion of Zoe's morals. Phyl had told her she was not fond of gossip and sent her on her way. Soon after, Jenny Brook had come to call with news that 'a little bird had told her' that she should watch out for Zoe shoplifting and 'someone should tell poor Ernest Sumner', the publican for whom she nurtured a damp passion. Phyl dismissed both Jenny and the slanderous idea, certain that the 'little bird' must have been Alice Spragg.

Phyl turned away from Mr and Mrs Beck's empty, salmon-on-pink house, brushing her hands on her waxed jacket to get rid of the flecks of peeling paint from the fence, and turned for home. There was a path back to Bunting Manor through the woods. It avoided walking along the road through the bottleneck with no pavement just by the pub. As she plodded through the trees, she thought again about young Gordon Stock, the failing farmer. More recently, he had come to call and she had invited him into the library where he stood, irresolute, by the open trap-door to the wine cellar, burbling about Phyl being 'in local parental', mistaking the Latin phrase.

'You mean "*in loco parentis*",' Phyl had replied.

'A farmer ought to marry,' he'd told her. 'You see where I'm heading?'

Phyl had feared she did and didn't like it.

'Go on, Gordon.'

'Well, here 'tis. I'm the farmer I'm talking about and I've a mind to marry the prettiest thing I've ever seen in this village.'

He'd given her a meaningful look, wanting her to complete the thought. Phyl had chosen not to.

'Spit it out.'

'Well, if you're in a position of being a sort-of parent to the lass, I thought it would look well on me to ask you for permission to pay my addresses.' He'd stopped and, when Phyllis still didn't indicate that she knew what he meant, he'd almost shouted. 'To be courting young Zoe, there.'

'Gordon, I want you to listen to what I say very carefully,' Phyl had told him, not too unkindly, she hoped. 'Put it out of your head. She's only just sixteen and has recently been abandoned by her foster parents. She's in no state to be thinking of anything of the kind.'

His face had reddened and, in an explosion of resentment, he had bellowed: 'We'll see about that!'

He'd slammed out of the house and Phyl, shaken, had simply watched him go, certain he would hold a grudge, nurturing his sense of injustice.

Phyl trudged up the side of Bunting Manor, past the library windows and up a slippery lane to a squalid encampment in her woods. She stopped at the edge of the ring of trees. There was the shanty dwelling but the homeless woman who had been living there for the last ten days seemed to have gone.

Phyl moved closer, looking at the cold ashes in the ring of stones that had served as her cooking stove. Just the other day, Phyl had crept up to spy on her, sitting on a fallen tree trunk, swaddled in multiple layers of drab clothing, skinning a rabbit, poached from a burrow somewhere on Phyl's land, probably with a wire set in a loop that tightened as the poor little creature pushed through. Phyl had watched her make an incision with a wooden-handled knife with a short wide blade. The rabbit had writhed and made an awful sound, somewhere between a cry and a squeak. Phyl had flinched and the woman had changed her grip to the back legs and given the animal a swing and a flick, smacking its head sharply on the tree trunk.

Phyl shuddered to dispel the memory and walked away, wondering once more why she had allowed the woman to build her awful camp under her ancient trees.

Back in her cold kitchen, she put the bleach on a shelf under the double sink, behind a scrap of tatty floral curtain, then went to the fridge and found an open bottle of white wine. It was almost the only thing in there. She sat down, damp and regretful, alone in her magnificent Jacobean mansion.

Oh, well, she thought, pouring the wine into a tumbler. *Perhaps it will all come right in the end.*

II

PRUDENCE

FIVE

On Monday morning, Maisie said goodbye to Church Lodge with regret and relief, standing on the chequerboard tiles of the cold double-height hallway, wishing Stephen were still alive.

She took the early bus from Framlington into Chichester and got off on West Street, outside the post office. Her suitcase – albeit small – felt very heavy at the end of her arm. She had seen some Paris tourists with bags with built-in wheels and decided she must invest in one of those if she was to make a habit of travel.

Except, if truth be told, she could afford neither the travel, nor the time off work, nor the new suitcase.

At Morant's, the large department store opposite the cathedral green, the manager – in dark suit and old-fashioned collar – was unlocking the glass doors. It was just nine o'clock. She went inside and found herself in a forest of cosmetics and perfumes – Revlon, Max Factor, Yardley – eight or ten branded cubicles, none of which held any interest for her. The over-made-up ladies who ran them weren't ready, in any case.

She sidled through into glassware, worried at every step that she might knock something down with her suitcase, then found the stairs to the tearoom on the first floor where she and Charity had agreed to meet.

Maisie was the first customer and was able to choose a nice table at one of four tall sash windows overlooking the street. She ordered lemon tea that came quickly in a tall glass in a stainless-steel frame, served by a pinch-faced waitress. She drank it thirstily with plenty of sugar, then discovered she was hungry. She was pleased to find that the kitchen was able to send her some toast and jam. If she waited ten minutes, bacon and eggs would be available.

'No, thank you.'

She was just scraping the last of the strawberry jam from the cruet when Charity arrived, drawing a double take from the waitress. Was Maurice Ryan's wife the only dark-skinned woman in the whole of Chichester? Surely not. All the same, she was noticed wherever she went. Maisie wondered what it was like to live under that kind of permanent scrutiny.

'Have a seat. Shall I order more tea, more toast?' Maisie asked.

'Nothing, thank you.'

With a tinge of regret, Maisie gave Charity a bunch of five keys to Church Lodge, the ugly village house where her brother had lived and died. Maurice Ryan represented the owner.

'Thank you. I will return them.' Charity put her head on one side. 'This might be an opportunity, Maisie.'

'This Mrs Pascal? Somehow, I can't quite believe it.'

'All the same—' Charity began.

'Let's wait and see.'

Maisie drained her tea and Charity insisted on paying the bill.

'Look after the pennies – the pounds, they look after themselves,' she said, looking pleased with the vernacular phrase.

'Thank you,' Maisie agreed, feeling rather touched. 'Let's go.'

They let a cream-and-green double-decker Southdown bus trundle past, then crossed the road. As Charity put the key in the lock to open the office door, Maisie heard someone calling her name.

'Maisie, Miss Cooper. My dear Maisie, is that you?'

On the opposite side of the street, a heavily built woman in moleskin trousers and a waxed jacket was climbing out of a muddy Land Rover, badly parked, almost obstructing the turn into Tower Street. She lumbered across the road, holding up a bandaged hand to apologise to oncoming traffic – or, rather, Maisie judged, to insist the traffic made way for her to pass.

Surely this can't be the wealthy Mrs Pascal, she thought.

'Come here, my dear little girl!'

To Maisie's great surprise, Mrs Pascal embraced her, putting her long arms round her back and squeezing her tight. What was more, Mrs Pascal stood half a head taller, so Maisie's face was pressed into the unsavoury sludge-green coat and she was unable to reply.

Just as abruptly as she had taken hold, Mrs Pascal let Maisie go.

'You'll have to forgive me. I am so terribly sorry. I don't know what came over me, but it's been so long.'

She took a step back and, for the first time, Maisie got a good look at her face. Something clicked – a combination of early memories and ancient, small-format family photographs. Another double-decker bus rumbled by.

'Auntie Phyllis?'

'Oh, do you remember me?' said the woman, a look of astonishment and gratitude on her ruddy face.

'But . . . I don't understand,' said Maisie.

'I'm sorry,' said Mrs Pascal. 'I should have warned you.'

'No, that's all right.' Maisie shook her head. 'This is extraordinary . . .'

'Shall we go inside?' asked Charity.

Maisie was grateful for a moment to collect her thoughts and, once they were indoors, further discussion was interrupted by the arrival of Maurice Ryan and, with him, a good deal of suave chit-chat – plus, of course, the inevitable

43

making of tea. Whether or not it was wanted, tea was always, it seemed, required.

Finally, they were all installed in Maurice's office. Maisie and Mrs Pascal took the pair of leather club armchairs he used to welcome clients, while he sat behind his desk in a spinning office chair. Charity perched primly to one side on a velveteen-covered bench, a shorthand notebook on her knee.

'My car is badly parked,' said Mrs Pascal in a voice characteristic of someone used to giving orders. 'Will you find a better space for it, please, somewhere close at hand?'

She held out her keys, certain that one or other of them would accomplish her request. Maurice Ryan stood up.

'I would be glad to,' he said, smoothly. 'Miss Clement, shall we leave the ladies to it?'

They left and Mrs Pascal's expression seemed abruptly to melt – so much so that she needed to take a grubby handkerchief from a pocket of her worn coat and dab her eyes.

'Auntie Phyllis, are you all right?'

'I'm sorry I was rude to your friends. I just needed to speak to you in private . . . After all these years!'

The following fifteen minutes passed in a blur of reminiscence. The more Mrs Pascal – previously Auntie Phyllis Smith – spoke, the more concrete Maisie's childhood memories became. And, of course, there was the close resemblance between Auntie Phyllis and her mother, Irene Cooper, née Smith. Auntie Phyllis was taller and heavier, of course, but there were the same strong cheekbones and deep-set eyes, the same thick mouse-brown hair with a natural curl – not so different in style from Maisie's own, though a couple of shades darker.

'But why have we not met more recently?' Maisie asked. 'I barely remember you from when I was little. After Mum and Dad died, you were at the funeral, but then I got the impression that you had moved away again and . . .'

44

Auntie Phyllis fiddled with the dirty bandage on her right hand. 'Yes, I regret all that very much.'

Maisie felt something stir, some question she did not quite know how to articulate. 'What do you regret? What do you mean by "all that"?'

'Losing touch,' said Mrs Pascal vaguely. 'But you can't do everything.'

'In life, you mean?'

'Exactly, but it's a long story and this isn't the place.' She stood up. 'I don't think we can reasonably keep that rather ingratiating man out of his office all morning. Can we go somewhere and talk?'

'There's a rather sombre tearoom in Morant's,' she said, 'the department store opposite?'

'Yes, I know it. That would be splendid.'

***

The pinch-faced waitress eyed Maisie with interest, recognising her arrival for a second time that March morning.

'I'm afraid the same table is not available.'

'We'll sit over there,' said Auntie Phyllis, prudently choosing a discreet, distant corner at the far end of the tearoom, separated from the rest of the space by a pillar. 'That will do nicely.'

'We only use that corner when we're busy.'

'All the same, that is where we choose to sit.'

'Very well,' said the waitress. 'I'll lay up.'

She slouched away and Auntie Phyllis nodded.

'For privacy, my dear Maisie,' she said.

They took their seats and, as the waitress brought cutlery and doilies and crockery, Maisie reflected on the fact that the community of people she knew well in Sussex was growing: Jack, obviously, and his charming grandmother; a dozen people in Framlington; Charity and the 'ingratiating' Maurice; now, most surprisingly, her mother's sister.

'What did you do to your hand?' Maisie asked, gesturing to Auntie Phyllis's bandage.

'I caught it on something. What will you have?'

'Just a glass of water. I was in here off the bus before you arrived.'

'Well, I'm having hot chocolate and a bun.' Auntie Phyllis placed her order and there was a pause while she gathered her thoughts, then she spoke with determination: 'I want you to investigate something for me.'

'You waste no time,' Maisie replied with a smile.

'Oh, God, I haven't even asked you about Stephen, have I?' Auntie Phyllis cried, holding her hand up to her face.

'That's all right. I . . .' Actually, it wasn't all right. Every time Maisie thought about her brother, she felt a wave of guilt that she had done too little, too late. But she carefully avoided sharing that sort of intimacy at this early stage of finding out what sort of person her aunt really was after all these years. 'I'll be happy to talk about it another time,' she said, politely.

'Family brings responsibility, whether we ask for it or no,' said Auntie Phyllis. 'But this is not a favour or an obligation I am asking of you. It's a job.'

'You mean a paid job? Because that's important, too,' said Maisie. 'All the time I'm here waiting for the trial, I'm not earning and Stephen's debts just keep emerging.'

'I thought that might be the case. Your clothes are good, but well looked after, as if you need to make them last.'

'I do.'

'What do you live on? In the newspapers, it didn't say.'

'I'm a tour guide, in Paris.'

'Is it your own company?'

'Good heavens, no, someone else's.'

'Any prospect of ownership, of shares, that sort of thing?'

'None whatsoever.'

'So, not much of a future?'

'I'm content with it at present,' said Maisie, and realised she sounded defensive.

'Well, I would like to pay you for your time – and pay you better than this tour-guiding thing, I'll be bound. I tell you what, I'll double your wages and give you board and lodging, too.'

Maisie pursed her lips, wondering if this was all too good to be true.

'I should probably know what it's all about first?'

'Yes, you should.'

The waitress arrived with the hot chocolate, the bun and the glass of water.

'I will need to lay up this table for luncheon at twelve o'clock.'

'Thank you,' said Auntie Phyllis. 'We won't want anything else from you until then.'

The waitress looked uncertain whether she had been snubbed, but she slunk away without further comment.

'That was very crisp,' said Maisie.

'The cheek of it, telling us what to do . . .' said Auntie Phyl, huffily. She buttered her bun, dipped it in the hot chocolate and began chewing. 'Had you ever before,' she said, indistinctly, 'had any involvement with murder or a police investigation of any kind? Before Stephen's death?'

'No.'

'Then how did you manage it?'

'Well, I think, had I not known Sergeant Wingard from school, I might have very quickly been sidelined by the police.'

'Told to mind your own business?'

'Exactly.'

Auntie Phyllis swallowed and took another bite.

'Yes, I see that, but I meant how did you go about it? I mean, you couldn't take fingerprints and make plaster casts of footprints or identify a strange and exotic tobacco only smoked by the murderer.' She frowned. 'Your mother hated smoking.'

Maisie felt herself becoming alert, as if about to be told a secret. She thought about the tombstone she had visited, her parents' last resting place.

'Could we talk about her for a moment?'

'About Irene?'

'Yes.'

Auntie Phyllis swallowed the last of her bun.

'Irene was cleverer than me at school, but she had no drive. I expect she might have said that I was dumb as a tree and had no manners.'

'She thought you were very impressive.'

'Did she?'

'She never spoke of you except to say how remarkable you were, to celebrate your achievements and . . .'

Maisie paused. What exactly were Auntie Phyllis's achievements, she wondered. She didn't think her mother had actually said.

'She was younger, of course,' explained Maisie's aunt, 'so it was annoying when I had to ask her for help with my science homework.'

'She was very grateful to you.'

Auntie Phyllis looked surprised. 'What for?'

'I am grateful, myself. You paid for our education, Stephen's and mine. That was very generous of you.'

'No, I didn't,' she replied.

'At Westbrook College,' Maisie persisted.

'Not me.'

Maisie didn't know what to say. The idea that their wealthy aunt had paid for her and for Stephen to attend a local private school as weekly boarders was a foundation

48

stone in how she saw herself, both good and bad. And it was where she had met Jack. On the credit side, she was grateful to have been given a broad, classical education. On the debit side, she resented being made to feel a 'toff', spoilt even.

'Your father had a good job,' said Auntie Phyllis.

'He sold cleaning products door-to-door.'

'Only to keep himself busy – and he was very good at that, too. Earlier on in life, he sold insurance.'

'I know that, too. Also, door-to-door.'

'Yes, well, it doesn't happen so much now, but it was how people used to save, and he was very convincing, very good at it, collecting up people's weekly subs in cash and coin and investing them. What was the company called?'

'Target.'

'That's right. Target Insurance. And he was paid on commission plus a long-term interest in the growth of the savings policies. He went out to work at fourteen when he left school. He was thrifty. Things were different then – no foreign holidays or new cars every three years. He never spent much except on the two of you.'

'But we had nothing. We lived in that tiny house in Framlington on the council estate. When they died, there was almost nothing.'

'Because they spent all they had on your schooling.'

Auntie Phyllis seemed to have forgotten that she had asked for a more or less private table. Her loud voice was of interest to four mimsy-looking ladies sitting just beyond the pillar. Maisie replied quietly, hoping to bring the volume down by osmosis.

'This is all very surprising, but why would they have lied?' she asked, feeling a pang of disloyalty.

'I don't know. Because they didn't want you to know that paying for Westbrook College was the reason you had to make the jam last?'

Yes, perhaps, thought Maisie, trying to reconfigure her father as a successful salesman and her mother as a woman with secrets. Then she saw that Auntie Phyllis was waiting for her next question.

'Can you tell me what it is you want me to "investigate"?'

'You've not yet answered my question.'

'What question?'

'How you solved it.'

'Oh. That was easy,' Maisie told her. 'I just talked to people.'

'That's all?'

'Well, yes.'

'Tell me how it worked.'

Maisie smiled, enjoying the memory of her success.

'At first, I think I was helped by the fact that I didn't know he'd been murdered, so I talked to people quite innocently, if you see what I mean. They were obliged to answer out of a sense of duty, because he was my brother. Then, there was the fact that they wanted to talk to me because, although they knew more than I did, they assumed that I knew more, if you see what I mean.'

'I do.'

'But it really was just that – talk to everyone, ask them questions. Eventually, a pattern seemed to emerge.'

'Like a proper detective.'

'I don't know about that.'

'And you're prepared to do it all again?'

'I've not said yes, yet.'

'No, you haven't,' said Auntie Phyllis. 'I'd noticed that. What if I ask nicely?'

'You're not telling me there's been a murder in your life, too?' said Maisie quietly, glancing at the eavesdroppers at the other table. 'Is that what we're talking about?'

'Yes, we are,' said Auntie Phyl. 'That's precisely what I'm saying.'

Six

They left the department store soon after this revelation, heaving Maisie's suitcase into the rear of Auntie Phyllis's filthy Land Rover, driving at imprudent speed out of Chichester, north-west into the countryside, crunching the gears. Maisie began to have qualms. Was this really such a good idea? She hadn't said yes, but she had agreed to be shown round.

'Are we going to Framlington?'

'To and through,' said Auntie Phyl. 'And on.'

Maisie found it a hair-raising journey. Everything Auntie Phyllis saw seemed to constitute a glorious distraction: a horse in a field; a muck-spreader; the bright-green leaves on the earliest trees; the number of cars outside the pub in East Bitling; the shapes of the clouds; the farrier at work outside the forge in Framlington. They swung right, past the council houses where Maisie had grown up in a kind of schizophrenic double life between apparent poverty and the riches of her posh school.

The Land Rover twitched on some gravel, washed onto the road by heavy rain from a gateway into a field. Then the road dipped down to a junction where the driver of a red Massey Ferguson tractor politely slowed to let them take the right of way ahead of him.

'It's Archie, my estate manager. Open the window,' said Auntie Phyllis. Maisie did so, winding the stiff handle round and round. Phyllis leant across, shouting out: 'Morning, Archie, or afternoon, is it?'

The tractor driver mimed not being able to hear.

Auntie Phyllis laughed, crunched the Land Rover back into gear and drove on between tall hedges of hawthorn and beech. The air was cold and damp. Maisie rolled up the window as they turned right towards Harden and Bunting, a gentle valley that soon felt lonely and lost in the Downs.

'Is this where you live?'

'That's right.'

'How long for?'

'All my adult life.'

Maisie was shocked.

'It's so close. Why did we never see you? You were my mother's sister. I mean, you are, but she's gone. And we hardly ever met.'

'You saw me now and then.'

'No, I don't think so. Did you know about Stephen's cremation?'

Auntie Phyllis sighed.

'I didn't. I live quite an isolated life in the village. It's a long story.'

Maisie wondered if she should probe further. She summoned a few memories of childhood, blurred and indistinct, like leafing through a water-damaged photograph album. The more she thought about it, the odder her mother's attitude to her older sister appeared. How would she describe it? Respectful but not warm? Shadowed by some tension?

'Nice people round here?' Maisie asked, lightly.

'Not so as you'd notice.'

'Would you like to tell me about them?'

'Better if you form your own impressions, perhaps.'

That was true. It had served Maisie very well investigating Stephen's murder.

'Fair enough.'

'That said,' said Auntie Phyllis, unexpectedly, 'I walked through the village yesterday and I peered in all their windows and I made a mental checklist of the web of resentments and . . .' She paused. 'No, I don't think I should tell you yet. It wouldn't be just.'

'Did you write it down,' asked Maisie, 'your checklist?'

'I could.'

'It might be useful.'

'Then perhaps I will.'

The Land Rover splashed round a bend where a ditch had overflowed onto the tarmac then accelerated. Auntie Phyllis struggled to find third gear, over-revved and slammed it into fourth.

'How did you get to be rich,' Maisie asked, 'if you don't mind me asking?'

'I'm not so rich, not compared to some.'

'You do mind? You don't want to talk about it?' asked Maisie.

'Not at all, but we're here now. It'll have to wait.'

They were just entering the village of Bunting. Maisie gazed a couple of hundred yards ahead to an untidy green, a few muddy parking places, a trio of older cottages and some newer houses, one salmon-pink monstrosity with a piece of paper pinned to the front door flapping in the breeze, a charming-looking pub, a Norman church. But Auntie Phyllis gave a tug on the steering wheel and Maisie was thrown against her door as they lurched to the right, onto a gravel drive between two impressive pillars mounted with stone acorns. She changed down from fourth to second gear and ground up a lumpy sweep through a bank of hydrangeas, loose flints crunching beneath her tyres, the centre of the drive overgrown with a miniature forest of dandelion and henbit and chickweed. Then, all at once, the trees seemed to part to reveal a Jacobean mansion in

all its rust-red glory, just as the seventeenth-century architect and landscape gardener had intended – dark bricks
almost the colour of blood, small leaded panes of glass in
the narrow windows, tall chimneys reaching up through
the bare canopy.

'Here we go,' said Auntie Phyllis. 'The Big House, as
Archie calls it.'

'Good heavens,' said Maisie. 'And this is yours.'

'All mine.'

'What a lovely old pile.'

'Glad you think so.'

Auntie Phyllis brought the Land Rover to an abrupt stop
in an unnecessary slide of gravel, hard up against three wide
stone steps that led up to the front door.

'Is money a motive in what you want me to investigate?'
asked Maisie.

Auntie Phyllis turned off the engine. 'Murder for money?'
she said, as if she hadn't thought about it. 'I have no idea.'

Maisie pointed through the windscreen to a small yellow
moped. It looked rather bedraggled, with a couple of dark
wet leaves clinging to its leather saddle.

'You don't ride that?'

'I got it for Zoe, but she doesn't like using it. She's a
timid creature, in some ways.'

'Zoe?'

'All in good time. We'll go round to the kitchen door.'

Auntie Phyllis heaved herself out of the Land Rover with
a wince and a grunt. Maisie tried to calculate how old she
was. Older than her mother Irene would have been, had she
lived – fifty-six or fifty-seven, perhaps?

'I was just wondering how old you are?'

Auntie Phyllis stopped and looked Maisie in the eye.

'I know how old *you* are. You were born on 23 April and
you'll be thirty-five in a little over a month. And when you

were eighteen, instead of going to university, you joined the Women's Royal Army Corps and served two tours of three years each. When Irene and Eric died a decade ago, you were working in hospitality in the West Country. Then you moved to Paris. Is that right?'

'All that was in the newspaper.'

'It was.' Auntie Phyllis waved a hand. 'Remember the moped. That could be important. Later on, I'll show you why.'

They made their way through a gateway in a high, red-brick wall to the right of the house – Maisie lugging her suitcase – leading to an untidy kitchen garden, strewn with planks, broken clay pots and sad, rusty tools. Nevertheless, a few useful edible plants were pressing on with preparations for spring.

Auntie Phyllis pushed the kitchen door open – it didn't seem to have been closed, let alone locked – and led Maisie into an unadorned, functional space with a stone-flagged floor and a huge battered table surrounded by mismatched wooden chairs. At the far end of the table was a lovely escritoire – a sloping wooden letter-writing box, like a small desk without legs. Two wine bottles sat in the centre, one empty and one unopened, surrounded by newspapers, circulars, several copies of the parish magazine, and quite a lot of unopened post. There was a double sink and wooden draining board beneath a pair of windows with stone mullions, an unused Aga and a greasy cooking stove, connected by a rubber tube to a large Calor Gas cylinder. In the far corner of the kitchen was a rather inviting doorway into the rest of the house.

'Will you show me round?' asked Maisie, glad to put her suitcase down. 'This is wonderful.'

'I have a plan. Drink first, then yomp outside, then tour of the ancestral dwelling. Fetch me those glasses.'

Maisie followed her gaze and found two tumblers on the draining board.

'These?'

'Perfect.' Aunt Phyllis took a Swiss Army knife from a pocket of her worn waxed jacket and used the corkscrew to draw the cork from the unopened bottle. She filled both tumblers almost to the brim. 'Bottom's up.'

'Cheers,' said Maisie, taking a sip. When Auntie Phyllis put down her glass, it was half empty. 'So,' Maisie prompted. 'Tell me all about it.'

'Not here. I have to show you something first.' Auntie Phyllis drained her wine. 'Ready?'

Maisie took another careful sip. She wanted to keep her wits about her. She was worried about getting caught up in Auntie Phyllis's rather wild energy. On the other hand, if she stayed one or two nights, it would be a great help in stretching out her meagre funds.

'All right.'

Auntie Phyllis put one of the unopened letters – a brown envelope from the Inland Revenue – on top of Maisie's glass.

'Change into wellingtons. There are four or five pairs on the rack. It's muddy in the lane.'

Seven

The borrowed wellingtons Maisie chose were too big for her feet and she felt her socks being dragged down as they plodded up the lane between the trees. They heard a distant, metallic racket and Maisie looked back down the track through an opening like a window in the dark trees. At the end, close to the house, she saw the red Massey Ferguson tractor with a big scoop at the front, creeping along.

'Do keep up, Maisie,' said Auntie Phyllis. 'It's not far.'

'Where are we going?'

'To meet my lodger. Or, at least, to see her remains.'

'Her remains?' repeated Maisie. 'You don't mean—'

'No, not her corpse. The remains of where she lived. I came looking for her yesterday and she was gone.'

The path was steep and, though she usually enjoyed outdoor exercise, Maisie felt tense and breathless. Auntie Phyllis was used to it, clearly, and spoke easily.

'I hated my name growing up. I expect your mother did, too. What am I talking about? I know she did. Phyllis and Irene. So old-fashioned. I expect you know what Irene means?'

Maisie racked her brains. She had been told more than once.

'Peace.'

'That's right, from the Greek. Did you do Greek?'

'Yes, but I can't remember much of it.'

'And my name? That's Greek, too.'

Maisie searched her memory for a clue to Phyllis.

'Is it "green", like chlorophyll in leaves?'

'The money Irene and Eric lavished on your education was well spent. In the Greek myth, Phyllis dies for love and is turned into an almond tree.'

'Why almond?'

'No idea.'

Maisie felt a pang of heartache for her dead brother and parents. This was exactly the sort of sprightly conversation – pointless but erudite – that they would all have enjoyed. She stayed quiet and Auntie Phyllis seemed aware that her mood had changed and respected her silence. In any case, they had arrived at the top of the brief lane, by a clearing in the woods.

'It's along here.'

'What's along here?' said Maisie.

'Where my lodger lives,' said Auntie Phyllis. 'Or lived.'

'Up here in these damp woods?' asked Maisie. 'And she's dead?'

'Missing. You'll see,' said Auntie Phyllis.

Maisie thought she heard doubt behind the words.

'You're not sure?'

'Not entirely sure, no.'

They stepped into a clearing about the size of a tennis court. Birds were singing enthusiastically in the trees, glad to see the spring sun piercing the bare canopy. The air smelt fresh. However, at the centre of the clearing was an appalling shanty dwelling. Maisie could see a length of corrugated iron, some salvaged fencing, two tarpaulins and a forklift truck pallet. It was just about possible to make out the canvas of a tent that had been incorporated into the dreadful structure. There were scraps of rubbish all round on the ground.

'What on earth is this?'

'She likes mess, I suppose,' said Auntie Phyllis. 'Or liked.'

'How long has she been here, building this?'

'Ten days. Can you see the entrance?'

Where was it, Maisie wondered? Was it behind that dark-green tarpaulin that hung down over the tent? Or was it behind that forklift truck pallet, stuffed full of twigs and leaves to make it windproof?

'I suppose I'll have to bury her,' said Auntie Phyllis. 'If we find her, I mean. Just find a quiet corner to put her in the ground and not tell anybody.'

'I don't think that's a good idea,' said Maisie. 'There must be laws.'

'No one knows who she is,' said Auntie Phyllis simply. 'The rule of law is often an inconvenience imposed on common sense, rather than its systematic – though imperfect – expression.'

The wind changed direction and the air was no longer quite so fresh.

'What's that smell?' said Maisie.

'Her open latrine.'

'Of course. And why do you think she's been murdered, if you haven't found her body?'

A cunning look came into Auntie Phyllis's eyes. 'Look there.'

Auntie Phyllis pointed to a substantial heap of ashes in a wide, rudimentary fireplace – a ring of heavy stones on the bare ground. Beside the ashes was a circle of beechwood – a thick disc cut from a mature trunk, used as a low table. In the centre, where the close-grained timber was oldest, was a handful of dried-out mushrooms with white stalks and gently curved tops. The domes of their caps retained a lemon-yellow tint.

'Should I know what they are?' Maisie asked.

'*Amanita phalloides*,' said Auntie Phyllis. 'And yes, everyone should.'

'*Amanita phalloides*?' said Maisie. 'In plain English?'

'Death caps.'

'Oh.' Maisie glanced around, as if there might be more growing about her feet. 'Are they hard to find?'

'They account for more or less all the mushroom fatalities you'll ever hear of so, no, they are reasonably easy to find.'

Maisie glanced at the cold ashes of the fire.

'Wouldn't cooking have removed the poison?'

'The toxins are thermostable.'

'You know a lot about them,' said Maisie, wondering why.

'They like oaks and beeches – damp darkness generally. Also, hazel, conifers, chestnuts – more or less every tree I own.'

'And how many would one need? To kill someone?'

'Sometimes just half a mushroom will do.'

'Good heavens.' Maisie looked a little more closely at them. 'Should they be allowed to proliferate? I wouldn't be able to tell them from edible fungus.'

'But you might have the sense to ask advice of someone who can.' Auntie Phyllis looked up at the sky, through the bare canopy. 'Anyway, she was a country woman. She knew how to catch and skin rabbits, perhaps how to survive a cold spring up a lane in the woods. It isn't a mistake she would have made, I don't think. Anyway, they're not in season. She can't have just found them growing. Someone brought them here.'

'You mean someone left them here for her to eat? But you think she would have rejected them. Or what if there were more and these are just the ones she didn't eat?'

'I don't know,' said Auntie Phyllis, shrugging. 'But where is she? I've not seen her since Saturday. People will tell you, I'm not an overly generous person. I don't generally find myself doing things for other people. I live my life. I join in with the village. I spend my money at Ernest Sumner's pub and in Jenny Brook's village shop, even though she very seldom has what I want.' Auntie Phyl paced the clearing. 'She turned up, my mystery lodger, not two weeks ago, pushing her shopping trolley of things. You can see it there.'

Maisie looked. It was true – a shopping trolley formed part of the shanty.

'With all her worldly goods on board?'

'I suppose so.'

'And you let her go about building this?'

Auntie Phyllis sighed again.

'I surprised myself. Do you think I'm getting old?'

Maisie smiled. 'I don't know, Auntie Phyllis.'

She made a face. 'Don't call me that. Call me Phyl, please.'

'All right,' said Maisie, feeling a little cast adrift by not being allowed to use the term of endearment.

'At first, I was just interested to see what she was up to. I thought I would eventually get Archie to move her on – my estate manager, the tractor driver we saw earlier? But the weather was cold and wet and I'd seen her before and . . .' Phyl stopped.

'And what?'

'Like I said, I surprised myself.'

'In what way?'

'I didn't have the heart.'

Maisie wandered round the shelter, thinking about how awful it must be to be homeless, condemned to a precarious life on the road. Was this better, this squalor? Perhaps, yes. She knew that she would have felt grateful if someone had let her set up camp, somewhere to call home.

'It was very kind of you.'

'Out of character,' said Phyl decisively. 'Anyway, will you investigate?'

'I'm not sure how. Or what, come to that.'

'Do what you did before? Talk to people? Act innocent and trusting?'

'Or why.'

'Because she's disappeared.'

'Couldn't she have just moved on? It will soon be spring. Wouldn't that be the way, to move on with the seasons?'

'It's complicated. It isn't just her. There's more.'

'What does that mean?'

Phyl wouldn't meet Maisie's gaze. She looked sly.

'What if, though, someone had actually killed her?' Phyl asked.

In the damp clearing, redolent with the foul odours of the open latrine, the birds had gone quiet. There was no wind. Everything seemed still, expectant.

'Have you contacted the police?' asked Maisie.

'For what reason?'

'You should notify them that she's a missing person.'

'She was a homeless itinerant. How can such a person be missing? Their whole life has gone missing.'

'But she existed. You saw her and spoke to her.'

'No.'

'Not once?'

'I never thought she wanted human contact,' muttered Phyl. 'Perhaps I was wrong.'

'And someone brought her deadly mushrooms and left them for her. How do you explain that?'

'Maybe she made a mistake?' Phyl protested, sounding exasperated. 'Maybe she thought the mushrooms were a kindness, a gift from a hiker or a walker. Quite a few come through this way because it joins up with the pilgrim path over the tops.'

'Like giving alms to a hermit?'

'Now you're being fanciful.'

'No,' said Maisie, 'I'm just trying to imagine. Imagination is how you work things out that you weren't present to witness.'

Phyl frowned and scuffed the toe of her boot in the leaf litter.

'I haven't persuaded you, have I?'

'I'm meeting Sergeant Wingard this evening. He's an old schoolfriend.'

'Are you now?' said Phyl, raising an eyebrow.

'Nothing like that,' once more questioning her determination to remain 'just friends'. 'He's coaching me in what to expect under cross-examination at the trial.'

'Will it be all very chaste and above board?'

Maisie smiled. 'I'm not sure an auntie should be asking that sort of question.'

'Please stop calling me "auntie",' Phyl snapped.

'Sorry, I forgot. Meanwhile, what should we do with the death caps?'

'Nothing.'

'We can't just leave them here.'

'Why not?'

'Someone else might come along.'

'You can't legislate for stupidity,' said Phyl. 'Anyone who comes across a death cap and thinks "yummy, breakfast," deserves what's coming to them.'

'But they might not know.'

'Then they should find out.'

'But they've been harvested and laid out, clearly for consumption or cooking—'

'What's a person doing, living in the country, if they don't pay attention to it?'

Yes, thought Maisie. That's a good question. What had brought Phyl's unexpected lodger to this damp corner of Sussex?

'In any case,' she insisted, 'we shouldn't leave them here for just anyone to find.'

'Oh, all right.' Phyl scooped up the mushrooms in her ungloved hand.

'What are you doing?' said Maisie.

'They are quite safe to touch.' Phyl tossed them away into the undergrowth. 'They're only dangerous if you eat them.'

Maisie made a mental note of where the death caps landed, thinking she might dispose of them more prudently later on.

'Now, what?' asked Maisie.

'Pub,' said Phyl, decisively.

EIGHT

As they trudged back down the lane to the magnificent Jacobean mansion, Maisie wondered what she was doing, letting herself be drawn into Phyl's mystery. The story didn't really hang together. But this, for her, as far as family went, was it. No more parents a decade before. No more brother a couple of weeks before. What else did her life amount to? Her job, her prospects and ambitions? Actually, no, not really. Madame de Rosette's patience was clearly almost at an end. But was that a bad thing? Behind the worry about earning a living, she was beginning to feel a kind of relief. Of course, she enjoyed being successful. She liked it when the customers praised her knowledge and enthusiasm, her fluency and charm, but the pleasure was fleeting. Being a tour guide – however 'high-class' – was not what she wanted her life to amount to.

'You're very quiet,' said Phyl.

'I was thinking, that's all,' she said, more sharply than she meant. 'Tell me, why are we going to the pub? Or is that another mystery?'

'So that you can meet people.'

'You mean the possible suspects?'

'Yes, Maisie,' said Phyl, though she sounded uncertain.

They reached the kitchen door and Maisie began changing back into her own shoes, pulling up her socks.

'What are you really worried about, Auntie?'

'Please don't call me that.' Phyl ran her hands through her hair. 'This business has made me feel unsafe.'

'Unsafe? Surely not.'

'Yes, and . . .'

'Go on?'

'Like I said, it's not the only thing.'

'So, tell me. What else has happened?'

'I'd rather you heard it from the horse's mouth.'

'And that would be at the pub.'

'Yes.'

Masie contemplated her rediscovered relative.

'You really are worried, aren't you?'

Like most country women, Phyl's face was deeply lined but healthy-looking, wind-burnt and tanned. At this moment, however, she seemed pale and tired.

'I am.'

It turned out that there was a shortcut through the trees, avoiding the long curving drive, on a well-made path without mud, leading to the church and the shop and the pub – the Dancing Hare – at the heart of the village. They went inside and stood at the bar, Maisie's forehead almost touching a heavy ceiling joist. It took a couple of minutes before they could be served by a young woman in denim dungarees. Maisie watched her, busy with other customers, all of whom she addressed by name. She wondered if the girl was related to the publican. She seemed clearly under age – perhaps only sixteen years old. Did she recognise her from somewhere?

Eventually, the girl brought Phyl a half-pint of draught ale in a glass branded with the insignia of Harvey's, the local brewery.

'Thank you.'

The girl looked enquiringly at Maisie. She had very pale skin and good bone structure with wide-set brown eyes. Maisie asked for a pineapple juice.

'Shall we eat?' said Phyl. 'They have an excellent ploughman's lunch.'

Maisie realised how hungry she was. It had been hours since her toast and jam at the department store. 'Yes, let's.'

'Two, please, Zoe. Put it all on my tab.'

The girl nodded, spoke briefly to a tall thin man in a white apron who disappeared through a door behind the bar to prepare their meals. Maisie and Phyl took their drinks to a table not too far from the open fire and sat down. The table wobbled on the stone flags of the floor. Maisie used a Skol Lager beer mat folded over to wedge under one of the legs.

'You're very practical,' said Phyl. 'You get that from Eric.'

Maisie smiled. 'Dad was never happier than when he was making or repairing something.'

'Yes,' said Phyl, and Maisie thought she heard something like regret behind the simple word.

'Tell me about who we've come to see. You called the barmaid Zoe. She's the one who lives with you. Is that right?'

'She does.' Phyl shuffled her chair round so that she was sitting beside Maisie, close to her ear. She pitched her voice unusually low so that what she said would remain private. 'Where shall I start?'

'Do you actually have suspicions?' asked Maisie, quietly.

'Oh, look, there's Archie. You need to hear his story.'

Abruptly, Phyl stood up and eased herself through the tables to the far end of the pub where Phyl's estate manager was perched on a stool, reading the *Chichester Observer* in his calloused hands. Maisie watched them speak then move slowly back towards her. She felt uncomfortably like she was being evaluated by Archie's calm eye, as if she were a goose that might or might not be ready for the table.

'This is my niece, Maisie Cooper,' said Phyl.

As was normal in Paris, man or woman, Maisie stood up and held out a hand to shake. Archie declined, murmuring something about not having had time to wash.

Zoe brought their two plates of food. The ploughman's consisted of a spoonful of Branston, three pickled onions, a wan tomato, a sad-looking leaf of lettuce, a limp stick of celery, a generous pat of butter, a hunk of delicious-smelling warm bread and a huge lump of strong cheddar cheese. Phyl started eating as soon as it arrived, encouraging Archie to tell his tale.

'But the lady's eating,' protested Archie. 'It won't do for eating.'

'Don't worry,' said Maisie. 'I have a strong stomach.'

As it turned out, her confidence was misplaced.

***

Archie was an idiosyncratic storyteller. Things that were central to his recollection of the facts weren't necessarily central to understanding what had happened.

'I was up on top field, just after teatime, and getting dark. Good sky, apricot sunset. Thirsty, I was, and the lights not on in the pub for a while yet. I heard it first and I knew it was trouble for one of them poor old sheep.'

'Why "poor old sheep"?' Maisie asked.

'Well, they are, aren't they? Sheep's a magnet for trouble.'

'Fair enough.'

'I was walking in,' Archie resumed, 'because I'd need the tractor up top the next morning and, that way, I wouldn't be waking the whole village at the bang of dawn. There's no need, is there? Then I came to the stile and what did I see?'

'I'm assuming a sheep?' said Maisie. Her attention had wandered a little. Apart from the weary salad, the other elements of the ploughman's were delicious. 'Go on.'

'It were a lamb. There was some birthed early, up indoors, in the barn, and the weather's mild enough for them to be out.'

'Was it caught in the fence?' Maisie asked.

'Poor little thing,' said Archie, shaking his head. 'No, it wasn't caught in any old fence, although it was up against, hard by the post. I saw it was dead and I got down on my hands and knees, to look at it up close.'

'And?'

'Now, I didn't touch it, not straight away. I gave it some thought. There are all sorts of things can take off a lamb. Some of them just die where they stand and that's the way of it. Then there's things you have to tell veterinary.'

'Notifiable diseases,' said Phyl, quite at ease with Archie's roundabout style. 'There's bluetongue, foot-and-mouth, scrapie, brucellosis. If any of those are discovered, they have to be communicated to the authorities. Tell Maisie how long it had been there, Archie.'

The thought of all the possible sheep diseases and their disgusting medical details made Maisie queasy. She put down her knife.

'I'd like to offer my sympathy for your brother,' said Archie, unexpectedly.

'Oh. Thank you. Did you know him?'

Archie shook his head. 'I seen him when he come up to Bunting, but not so as to talk to. He was here with young Gordon Stock. But I know what happened from Bert. He told me about it when he came through for a couple of bales of hay for the stables down Framlington.'

'You know Bert Close?'

Phyl had finished her bread and cheese. 'Archie is Bert's brother,' she said.

'Oh, I'm sorry,' said Maisie. 'I didn't know.'

'No reason you should,' said Archie. 'No reason to be sorry. Bert speaks very highly of you.'

'That's kind of him.' Maisie looked from Phyl to Archie. Neither seemed in any hurry. 'The sheep?'

'Well, I didn't know just there and then how that poor old lamb had died,' Archie resumed. 'The little heart wasn't pumping. There wasn't no wire around its throat. It was cold, though, to the touch. Then I lifted him up a bit and saw underneath where the blood had gone down into the soil. Not much, though. That was a teaser, especially when I found the wound.' Archie looked at Maisie's unfinished meal. 'Don't you want that?'

'I'll just wait till you've finished your story.'

'I do like a pickled onion.'

'Go ahead.'

She pushed her plate towards him and he took one, pushing it into his cheek with his tongue, crunching it as he spoke.

'The knife went in under the ribs into the heart, but there wasn't much blood because the lamb was smothered beforehand. I used to do it myself when I delivered the halal to the Muslim butcher in Portsmouth round the mosque.' He swallowed. 'Nice people.'

'Why would someone do all that and then just leave the poor thing by the stile?' asked Maisie.

'That's what I wondered,' said Phyl.

'And?'

'Clear as day, isn't it?' said Archie, looking from one to the other. 'Someone funny in the head.'

'Funny how?' said Maisie.

Archie pushed his chair back. 'I can't stop here gossiping. Soon it'll be dark and then where will we be?'

'Work left undone,' said Phyl. 'All the same, come on, tell us what you thought happened.'

'Well,' Archie said, judiciously, 'if someone smothered, it would be for one of three reasons I can think of. First, for the meat, but that only counts if you take the beast away with you to butcher and it was left, wasn't it, out

70

on the field? Chalk that one off. The second would be for quiet, but I don't see that because, up there on the Downs, there's no one about to be listening. In any case, they're always jabbering and bleating so who would notice, even if a person was out for a tramp on the hills and not far away? Third . . .' He nodded. 'Well, I don't like it, but that's where my mind goes.'

'Where does it go, Archie?' said Maisie, leaning in.

'The only reason I can see for someone to do those two things, then leave the carcass where it lay and pay it no more mind, is because they were—'

Frustratingly, that was the moment the adolescent bartender decided to come over and interrupt, asking if she might clear the table.

'No, not just now, Zoe,' said Phyl, shortly. The girl went away, empty-handed. 'Go on, Archie.'

'The thing is, the two parts don't fit together, do they? Smothering, then a blade in the heart? It only makes sense if it was someone trying things out,' said Archie, as if that made everything clear and obvious.

'I don't follow,' said Maisie.

'He means,' said Phyl, 'that whoever did it was practising.'

'Practising for what?'

'Yes, well, that's where 'tis,' said Archie, sounding just like his brother Bert.

'I still don't see. Practising to do what?' asked Maisie.

'Murder,' said Phyl.

***

The crowd in the pub was thinning out. Archie left them without another word, just a nod of thanks for his pickle, leaving his chair askew. Maisie wanted to stand up and straighten it but Phyl was asking her what she thought.

'I don't know,' said Maisie.

'Neither do I,' said Phyl, 'but I don't like it.'

Maisie pondered.

'Isn't this all a bit gothic, a bit far-fetched?'

'I know what you're thinking. "Something out of nothing." But that's not all. Come on, let's go.'

She pushed her chair back.

'Aren't you going to introduce me to more people?' asked Maisie.

Phyl looked round the bar.

'Well, there's Gordon Stock who inherited from his parents and is very likely going to run his farm into the ground.'

'Which one?'

'There.'

Maisie saw a surprisingly young man, leaning on the bar, wearing a very loud suit. Phyl read her thoughts.

'He goes into the charity shops in Chichester and comes back with the most extraordinary clothes. The other day, the vicar had him mowing the village green in a yellow shirt with ruffles all down the front like a lounge singer. He's not long taken over.'

'From his parents?'

'Moved away to the seaside. He's ridiculous,' said Phyl, breezily.

'You don't like him?'

'But then we're all ridiculous, aren't we, each in our own way?'

'You mean in the village of Bunting or people in general?'

'People who live cheek by jowl. We get to know one another well – too well, perhaps. Everyone learns everyone's foibles in the end. You can put on an act for a while, but not forever.'

'I know what you mean,' said Maisie. 'And there?' With a nod of her head, she indicated a grey-faced customer, a narrow woman with a severe, pageboy haircut, dyed an unlikely raven black. 'She looks like a librarian.'

'You *are* good,' said Phyl. 'Alice Spragg, retired librarian, class warrior. But we have to go. I want to show you something else.' Phyl noticed Maisie's look of regret for her unfinished ploughman's. 'You can bring that.' Phyl picked up the hunk of bread and wrapped it round the remaining cheese. 'There you are.'

Maisie took it without enthusiasm. Phyl's hands weren't completely clean.

'Thank you,' she said, politely.

They left the Dancing Hare and took the path through the trees but, when they reached the drive, Phyl led Maisie away from the house and stepped off the gravel into the undergrowth.

'Here, look.' There was a wire, wrapped around the smooth trunk of a beech tree. 'Now come over here.' She crossed the gravel drive. Maisie followed. 'Look here.'

Around the trunk of a youngish oak was more wire, wound tight into the bark, the loose end hanging in a coil down at the roots.

'It was stretched across the drive?' said Maisie, shocked.

'Exactly.'

'Did you hit it and break it in the Land Rover?'

'No. Anyway, that's not the issue. The real danger would be for someone on two wheels.'

'Zoe's moped,' said Maisie, remembering the little yellow two-wheeler with damp leaves stuck to its leather saddle. 'You said she doesn't often use it. Does anyone else come up here on a motorbike?'

'No one.'

'It seems too dangerous to be just a prank.'

'As it happened,' said Phyl, 'it was me who almost had my head taken off. The Land Rover gearbox keeps playing

73

up. I expect you noticed. I'd taken the moped to go down to the garage in Framlington. I was very lucky.'

'When was this?'

'A few days ago. Then I wrote you a letter via the solicitor.'

'And you'd already read about me in the paper by then?'

'Yes,' said Phyl warily. 'Why is that important?'

'I like to have a clear sense of the sequence of events,' said Maisie.

'Fair enough.'

'And the wire was pulled taut between the trees? How did you see it?'

'I didn't, but there was a robin, perched in mid-air – at least, that's what it looked like – singing away, very pleased with itself. I slowed down to make sense of it, how it was perched on nothing.'

'The robin was on the wire.'

'It was – a wire put there to take my head off.'

'Or Zoe's head.'

'Or Zoe's head, yes.'

'By someone who wants one or either of you or both of you hurt or dead.'

'Precisely. What do you think of that?'

'I think,' said Maisie, 'that we should be very careful.'

NINE

They returned to the kitchen and sat either side of the big rustic table. Maisie had dropped her bread and cheese – folded over by Phyl's grubby, bandaged hand – discreetly in the woods. She was now regretting it as she felt obliged to finish her glass of white wine on an almost empty stomach.

'When I was a girl,' said Phyl, leaning back in her chair, 'I had a French teacher called Miss Thistle. Actually, that was just what we girls called her. I can't remember what her real name was. She had short grey hair that stood up straight from her forehead, hence her nickname. She was all angles, narrow shoulders and long, simian arms.'

'She sounds a character,' said Maisie, thinking that Phyl was becoming more expansive as she drank.

'In French conversation, Miss Thistle would say, "a judiciously placed idiom will go a long way to convincing a native to treat you, if not as one of them, at least as a friend". Then she would purse her lips and push them forward, shaping her mouth to produce the foreign sounds. "*Jamais deux sans trois.*" You see what I'm saying, Maisie?'

'Never two without a third.'

'Exactly. My lodger, well, that's number one. What's happened to her? Where's she gone? The poor lamb is number two, smothered and stabbed. And three, a wire stretched across my drive where no one comes but me and . . .'

Phyl's voice trailed off, as if she had thought of an explanation but wasn't ready to share it.

'Not even a postman?' asked Maisie.

'Box down by the stone gate pillars, you know, with the acorns on top.'

'Milkman?'

'I fetch it myself from Jenny Brook's shop or from Gordon Stock's farm gate.'

'I thought you said he was running the farm into the ground?'

'That doesn't prevent him having some fine cows. He's all right with his beasts and his crops. It's business he doesn't understand.'

'I see.' Maisie considered. 'Do you have any enemies?'

'People tolerate me,' said Phyl, complacently. 'What do you want me to say?'

'The name of someone who wishes you ill? If you say there's no one, I'll believe you.'

'There's one or two I've upset,' said Phyl, grudgingly.

'Oh, yes?'

Maisie watched as Phyl lifted her tumbler of white wine to her lips, her eyes unfocused, draining the glass. Maisie thought there was probably a kind of rogues' gallery of potential enemies passing through her imagination. Phyl put down her glass and grinned.

'One or two or three or four.'

'And you say you haven't been to the police?'

'No.'

'Why on earth not?'

'If I go to the police, whoever it is could learn of it.'

'That might make them think twice, reconsider.'

'It might. That's exactly what I'd be worried about. It might make them think again.'

'That's what I mean,' said Maisie.

'No, not think again and dissuade them. Stop practising and take decisive action.'

'Oh,' said Maisie, grasping her aunt's concern.

'Quite. "Oh." If I go to the police, whoever it is will have good reason to—'

'To finish the job?' interrupted Maisie.

'Yes,' said Phyl. She picked up the wine bottle. 'So, I've got your attention. Do I have your support?'

Maisie thought it over. This was the moment of decision, a kind of point of no return. Obviously, she had to help her auntie. In the end, she thought it unlikely that Phyl was in danger. She was fairly confident she would discover a better – more innocent – explanation for the unconnected events. It was just a question of working out what that explanation must be. The homeless woman might have wandered off of her own accord and the story of the lamb was peculiar but perhaps not actually threatening. The wire across the drive, on the other hand, was definitely a kind of assault.

'You don't think it could have been a prank,' she wondered aloud. 'The wire, I mean?'

'How could it be a prank?'

'Well, if you struck it with the Land Rover, would it do much damage?'

'Probably.'

'But not to you, just to the windscreen.'

'I was out on the moped when I saw it, though. Whoever put it there was close enough to see the Land Rover was home, maybe even someone who knew it was playing up and I was using it less often.'

'Because everyone knows everyone's business,' said Maisie, completing the thought. Plus, she was considering her options. She was obliged to stay in Sussex until the trial and it was tempting to reconnect with family, having thought that she was the only one left. And it would give her a new reason to spend time with Jack. 'I'll talk it through with Sergeant Wingard,' she said, decisively.

'No—' Phyl began.

'Hear me out,' Maisie insisted. 'I will swear him to secrecy. He won't like it but I think he will agree. Those are, if you like, my terms – plus I need somewhere to stay. I had to give back the keys to Stephen's place, Church Lodge.'

Phyl poured herself another glass of wine. The bottle was now empty, Maisie noticed.

'All right. It's a deal.'

'And you meant what you said,' Maisie insisted, 'about covering my lost salary in Paris? I can make myself useful about the place, washing and cleaning and so on.'

'There's no need for you to do that.'

'And I'll try and find out what's going on. Agreed?'

'Agreed,' said Phyl, warmly. 'I'm so glad. Thank you.'

* * *

Later, thinking back on this 'point of no return', Maisie regretted not trying to draw her aunt out further. There were bound to be additional details Phyl hadn't yet shared, but any more conversation was prevented by the unexpected – to Maisie – arrival of the young woman in denim dungarees and a scruffy, furry Afghan coat. It was the bartender from the pub, the Dancing Hare, the one Phyl had called Zoe. Maisie was struck by her gaze – very direct, with extremely dark eyes, accentuated by her pale skin. Almost mesmerising.

'Is this a private party or can anyone join in?' said Zoe, eyeing the empty wine bottle.

She threw her Afghan coat over the back of an upright kitchen chair and Maisie realised where she had seen the girl before – in the Fox-in-Flight in Framlington, consulting with Maurice Ryan.

'Zoe,' said Phyl, 'this is Maisie. She's visiting from Paris.'

'I'm Phyl's niece,' said Maisie.

'You never told me you had a niece,' complained Zoe.

'Didn't I?' asked Phyl.

'Or that you knew someone from Paris.'

'We've not seen one another for many years,' Phyl replied neutrally. 'Would you like to introduce yourself?'

'No, you do it.'

There was a rather ugly little pause. Maisie thought she saw Phyl working hard to retain her temper. The young woman, on the other hand, seemed to be enjoying herself in a sad, bitter way – a kind of unhappy enjoyment that Maisie recognised as characteristic of thwarted adolescence.

'Zoe lives with me,' said Phyl carefully. 'We rub along.'

'I'm her charity case,' said Zoe. 'She's taken pity on me and has given me a place to sleep for some reason I haven't yet discovered. Perhaps it's money from the foster people?'

Zoe was smiling – but not with her eyes. She had a very pretty face and bright white teeth, but it was hard to focus on that, hidden behind the veil of bitterness.

'That's just Zoe's little joke,' said Phyl.

'Is it, though?' said Zoe. 'By the way, what were you doing up at the bang of dawn, rummaging about in the barn?'

'I'm sorry,' said Phyl. 'Did I wake you?'

'I'm pleased to meet you,' said Maisie, smiling brightly to defuse the tension. 'I like your coat. I would have loved one like that when I was your age.'

'How old do you think I am?' asked Zoe, putting her head on one side.

'Sixteen?'

'Just sixteen, actually. My birthday is the same day as Guy Fawkes Night – at least, that's the date I was abandoned at the hospital.'

'How awful,' said Maisie. 'I'm very sorry for you.'

'Yeah.' For a fraction of a second, Zoe looked like she might accept Maisie's kindness, then her expression closed down once more. 'And you must be nearly thirty?'

'Zoe,' rebuked Phyl, quietly. 'Really.'

'Thirty-four, actually,' said Maisie.

'You don't look it. How long have you lived in Paris and what did you do to get there? I suppose you're rich. Do you live in squalor like Mrs Pascal, even though you can afford not to? I've been thinking of going and taking over the tramp's encampment in the clearing at the top of the lane.'

'No one's impressed by your bad manners, Zoe,' said Phyl.

The young woman widened her eyes. 'I'm just asking a question? Isn't that allowed in grown-up society?'

Maisie was beginning to feel silly, just a bystander in Phyl and Zoe's sparring. She decided to take the initiative.

'My parents died ten years ago,' she said, calmly. 'And my brother died a few weeks ago. He was murdered. Apart from Auntie Phyl, I have no living relatives. I have no family money, if that's what you mean, and I live in a small shared apartment in a dusty old building with my friend Sophie. I have to be careful every day. I settle my bills by working. I only eat out when my job pays for it. In my purse there is a grand total of twelve pounds, but that's for me to live on for as long as I'm in England and, all the time I'm here . . .' she hesitated over the white lie '. . . I'll not be earning. I owe nothing to nobody and that's how I like it.'

At the conclusion of this speech, Zoe met Maisie's eyes frankly for the first time and Maisie felt a rush of sympathy for her. The bravado was just a thin shield for a damaged heart. What was the rest of her story, Maisie wondered?

'Sounds lovely,' said the young woman, dropping her gaze, and Maisie thought she meant it. 'Thank you for putting me in my place.' She made for the door into the main part of the house. 'I'm sorry.'

Despite her apology, Zoe managed to slam the door behind her as she went. Ten seconds later, Maisie heard another door slam, quite faint, on an upper floor.

'You were asking about enemies,' said Phyl, wryly. 'Zoe gets overexcited, as you can see.'

'The girl? You're not serious?' said Maisie.

'No, of course not.'

'Who is she? What's her story? Why does she live with you?'

'Would you mind,' said Phyl, 'if we put off the Zoe question for the time being?'

It was the second time Phyl had asked that, clearly finding the tale a painful one, so Maisie let it go.

'Not at all.'

Phyl was turning her empty tumbler between her fingers. Maisie wondered if she was going to suggest opening another bottle. Then Phyl picked up first one then another of the unopened letters.

'When you have money,' said Phyl, 'I mean more money than you need, there's an unexpected problem.'

'The problem of choice?' Maisie wondered aloud.

'Of direction.'

'Wanting to do the right thing?'

'There is no right thing,' said Phyl, pouting. The expression on her face reminded Maisie of Zoe. 'No ideal scenario.'

'But there's usually the "better" thing,' said Maisie. 'That's good enough, isn't it, when there's no perfect solution?'

'Maisie, do you . . .' Phyl began, then seemed to change her mind and heaved a great sigh. 'It's Monday. It's my day to open the post. I do it once a week. It's very boring. Do you want to leave me to it?'

'If you like, but where would you like me to go? Oh, and soon I'll need to get a bus or something into Chichester. I have an arrangement to see Jack Wingard, remember?'

'You can take the Land Rover. You must have driven one of those in the army?'

'Yes, but I don't have English insurance.'

'I expect you're covered by mine,' said Phyl, unconvincingly. 'Go carefully. Third gear's a bugger.'

Maisie thought about what Zoe had said about Phyl having money but not knowing how to spend it for a comfortable life.

'Thank you. Perhaps you would show me before I set off?'

'You'll manage.' Phyl got up rather ponderously, like a beast of the field rising from soft grass, then gave up and flopped back down. 'Push that escritoire along a bit would you?' Maisie slid the sloping letter-writing box from the far end of the table. 'And pass me a dinner knife?'

There was some good-quality old-fashioned cutlery on the draining board that had been allowed to air-dry, leaving the metal mottled and tarnished. Maisie passed a knife and Phyl used it to begin opening her post.

'Can I help?'

'No, I don't expect so.'

'Shall I go to my room?'

'Top of the stairs, first on the right. I laid in a fire.'

'But you didn't know I was coming?'

'I hoped, though,' said Phyl, simply.

'I feel very lucky,' said Maisie, trying to lighten the mood, 'to have met you again after all this time. But I have so many questions to ask about you and Mum and Dad and . . . Well, you know, family, the past, how things used to be.'

Phyl nodded, her face rather closed off.

'Come down for the car keys in a bit. I must get on.'

Maisie picked up her suitcase and carried it through into an impressive hallway, panelled in sombre wood. The March afternoon was progressing. The tall windows with their impressive stone mullions were made up of many tiny diamond-shaped panes of glass, divided by strips of lead, impeding the light. Beyond them, the house was encroached on by trees, deepening the shadows. A different owner, Maisie thought, would probably have kept the woods at a distance, to encourage sunlight into the building. Not Phyl, though. Why was that?

A grandfather clock chimed the quarter hour as Maisie climbed the stairs, running her hand along the sticky banister. Was it damp or was it polish that hadn't been properly buffed away?

On the landing, she could hear faint music from the floor above – presumably Zoe playing vinyl records in her room. She thought it was David Bowie's 'Hunky Dory'.

The 'first room on the right' was lovely, overlooking the drive, nicely proportioned and smelling slightly of woodsmoke. Maisie thought Phyl must have lit a fire the previous day to remove the chill from what was usually an unused part of the house. The hearth was compact and already laid with a small wigwam of kindling hiding a handful of scrunched-up newspaper. There was a mesh fireguard to one side.

Maisie checked her watch. Was it worth lighting the fire, even though she would quite soon have to go back into Chichester? She wondered how she would get on with the Land Rover. It looked like it might come on to rain and she hadn't driven for . . . how long? Two years, perhaps? No, a little less. She had hired a car for a trip out of Paris to Reims and its champagne houses. But, of course, that had been a much smaller vehicle, a Renault Quatre, with the steering wheel on the 'wrong' side.

She put a match to the newspaper then unpacked her carefully selected travel clothes, hanging everything in a tall mahogany wardrobe on an assortment of wooden hangers, some of them inscribed with the names of hotels from which they had been purloined. She put the two books she had packed on the bedside table, both recent publications, last-minute purchases from the bilingual bookshop on Rue de Rivoli. As well as *Les Chênes qu'on abat* by André Malraux that she had been reading in the St Martin's Tearoom, there was a rather odd story entitled *Fear and Loathing in Las Vegas* by Hunter S. Thompson. She drew back the counterpane and blankets, testing the springs of the mattress with her hand.

A little lumpy but not bad, all things considered.

Maisie sat on the bed, found the page in the Malraux novel marked with a paper St Martin's serviette, but she found it hard to concentrate, thinking again about Zoe's remark about Phyl being rich but not wanting to spend. What was the story there? Come to that, what was Zoe's story? Was she really a foster placement that Phyl had taken in return for cash? Did that mean that Charity Clement and Maurice Ryan were wrong – or had been misled – that 'Mrs Pascal', despite her Jacobean mansion, wasn't rich at all? Did she have capital but no cash, obliging her to be thrifty – what the country people called 'careful'?

And, if that were the case, why would Phyl feel the need to lie?

TEN

At the police station in Chichester, Sergeant Jack Wingard was busy with a series of complaints, petty thefts of food and clothing from kitchens and clothes lines out in the village of West Dean. Someone's shed had been broken into and 'everything turned upside down'. Jack had been to see the shed in question. It looked pretty clear. A poor person with nowhere else to lay their head had used it for shelter from the March rain.

Jack was sitting at his desk in the untidy open-plan office area at the heart of the station, wondering if the complaints were connected. Probably. They formed a kind of sequence and could therefore all have been carried out by the same person. He called Constable Goodbody over to his desk.

'What are you up to, Barry?'

'I've got the road safety posters drawn by the kids from the school. You asked me to have a look-see and suggest which ones should get the prizes.' Barry looked at his boots. 'Is that because you don't trust me to do any proper policing?'

Jack smothered a sigh. Barry had made several serious mistakes recently – above all in relation to the theft of the valuables and the devotional book from the cathedral. Now, he was always on the defensive.

'Good work. You'll come into the school with me in the morning. Community policing is an important part of our responsibilities.'

'Do I have to?'

'Why on earth not?'

'There'll be kids there know me from before I left – and teachers.' Barry didn't meet Jack's eye.

'What's wrong with that?'

'They said I wouldn't amount to nothing and, with the mess I've been making, I reckon they're right.'

Jack stood up. 'Come with me,' he ordered.

Jack led Barry out of the open-plan office into a corridor lined with interview rooms. He marched to the end and opened a panelled door onto a small, rudimentary gymnasium – a bench, a few barbells and a punchbag hanging from the ceiling.

'Take off your jacket.'

'What?' said Barry.

'Come on, take off your jacket.'

Barry removed the top half of his dark blue police uniform, his thin frame all knobs and angles beneath his regulation white shirt.

'Now what?'

'Make a fist and hit it.'

'This is stupid.'

'Barry,' said Jack with an edge of frustration, 'you should try and get out of the habit of thinking anything you don't understand is stupid. Just do it.' Barry gave the punchbag an ineffective thump. 'Harder than that,' Barry hit it again, his knuckles leaving a slight dent. 'That's better. Now again – and put your weight behind it.' Jack saw Barry wavering, torn between following orders and flouncing out of the room. 'Imagine the leather is full of the mistakes you've made,' he said quietly. 'Give them what for.'

It turned out these were the right words. For Police Constable Barry Goodbody, something clicked. Awkwardly at first, then more powerfully, more rhythmically, the unfortunate young man pummelled the heavy punchbag, leaning into each blow, grunting and gasping in air.

'Okay,' said Jack, after a minute or so. 'That's enough now. You don't want to skin your knuckles.' Barry took a step back and sat down on the bench, breathing heavily. 'Stop here for a bit,' Jack told him. 'Get your breath before you come back through.'

'Thank you, sir.'

'Good lad.'

Jack returned to his desk, thinking about how much of his own professional credit he had invested in Barry Goodbody. Too much, perhaps? More than was prudent? But Jack had a soft spot for awkward teenagers without direction, probably because he had once been one himself.

He checked the time – half past four. Soon the street lamps would come on and he would leave the station and go home to perhaps find Maisie already there, waiting for him. Wouldn't that be grand?

He frowned. No, that wasn't the right way to think. Maisie was coming round to be coached in answering counsel's cross-examination. Whether or not justice was ultimately done in the case of her brother Stephen's murder rested largely on her shoulders. There was nothing romantic about their rendezvous. It wasn't what the young people called a 'date'. He needed to remember that and behave accordingly. Above all, he needed prudently to silence the urge to tell her, every time they met, that he wanted to be with her.

Perhaps, when the trial was over, things would change? That was what he hoped. The trouble was, she might simply depart as suddenly as she had come, back to France on the boat train, leaving behind all the upset and grief, glad to resume her – no doubt – glamorous life surrounded by attractively sullen Parisian gentlemen.

Jack shook his head and returned to his sequence of petty crimes. There was a reason for them, he was sure. If he studied them carefully enough, he would find it.

ELEVEN

Maisie put down her book and crossed the bedroom to put the mesh fireguard in front of the hearth. She picked up her purse and left her temporary bedroom to find Zoe on the landing. She was dressed for out of doors in her Afghan coat with a loud Indian scarf round her neck. She had put on mascara and lipstick and seemed a little more grown-up.

'It's tipping down,' Zoe said, without preamble. 'I can't take the moped because Mrs Pascal worries. Would you give me a lift into town?'

'And back?' asked Maisie.

'Well, yes.'

'I won't be late,' Maisie warned.

'Me neither. What I have to do won't take long.'

'All right, then.'

They went downstairs to find Phyl in the hall with a handful of letters. She put them down on an occasional table by the front door.

'I have to go into Chichester,' said Zoe shortly.

'Don't you have work at the Dancing Hare?' Phyl asked.

'Evening off.'

'Not on the moped, though,' said Phyl with real concern.

'No, Miss Cooper is giving me a lift.'

'Who are you going to see?'

'Someone.'

'Oh, please, Zoe.'

'It's private,' the young woman insisted.

'How will you get back?'

'I can bring her home, too,' Maisie piped up. 'I'll be with Jack until seven.'

'So,' Zoe said, decisively, 'that's all organised and you don't have to think about it.'

Was there – finally – a tinge of kindness in Zoe's voice, Maisie wondered, as if she genuinely didn't want Phyl to worry? Glad of the lowering of tension, Maisie chipped in again. 'Do you know where Parklands Road is?' she asked. 'It's a pink bungalow at the top, number 147.'

Zoe nodded.

'I'll be outside at five-to.'

'Make sure you are,' Phyl insisted, her eyes anxious above her thin smile.

★★★

It was getting darker. Dusk was turning down the light of day, slowly but inexorably, rain streaking down the sky.

Maisie and Zoe were in the Land Rover, on their way into Chichester. The headlamps showed as two orange pools on the wet, uneven tarmac. Maisie was driving, now and then struggling and failing to get the gearbox to accept third gear. They were following the tail lights of a Mini that pulled away on each corner, with a high-pitched whine from its tiny engine, then came back towards them on the straights. The rain was heavy enough to collect, here and there, in puddles at the side of the road.

Maisie looked at her watch. She could just catch Charity before she left her office and still be on time to meet Jack.

'Did you ever make a mistake?' said Zoe, abruptly. 'Like, a really big mistake?'

'Dozens,' said Maisie, smiling. 'Why?'

'I mean misjudge somebody – someone you thought you could trust?'

'No, not often. I'm usually a good judge of character.'

'Lucky you.'

'Why do you ask?'

'No reason.'

Maisie kept her eyes on the road, but she could observe Zoe in her peripheral vision. Leaning her head against the window, the girl sighed. At the junction in Framlington, Maisie braked and brought the Land Rover to a halt.

'The Fox-in-Flight is a nice pub,' said Maisie, giving Zoe an opportunity to mention her conversation with Maurice Ryan.

'I suppose.'

They waited for two cars to pass.

'Do you know it?'

Zoe didn't answer. Maisie turned left, past Church Lodge.

'Is that where your brother died?' Zoe asked.

'That's where he was living. He actually died – I mean, he was murdered – nearby.'

'Did you love him?'

'Yes, of course.'

'Did you see him much? Write to him?'

'No, not much,' Maisie admitted, sadly. 'After our parents died, we drifted apart.'

'Would you say having a family is a blessing or a curse?'

'That's an odd question.'

'I read it in a novel.'

Zoe became silent again. Maisie wondered what she had been getting at, if anything. She wondered about asking the girl point-blank what legal matter she had been discussing with Maurice Ryan, but decided to wait.

'I'm going to West Street first. Can I drop you there?'

'Fine.'

'You'll have an hour and a half. Is that all right?'

'Easily . . .' Zoe yawned. 'You know what I'd really like to be doing right now?'

Maisie yawned as well. It was catching. 'Sleeping?'

Zoe laughed and the sound was unexpectedly innocent and charming, like a spring flower pushing through a frosty border.

'Exactly, sleeping.'

They came into Chichester from the north, passing the end of Parklands Road. Maisie slowed to point out the pink bungalow.

'Who is he again?' asked Zoe.

'Sergeant Wingard is an old schoolfriend. He lives there with his grandma.'

'Sounds like a catch,' said Zoe, dismissively.

'Appearances can be deceptive,' said Maisie. 'I'm making no snap judgements about you, otherwise I wouldn't have offered to be your chauffeur.'

Zoe gave her a very direct look. 'All right. I'm stupid, you're clever. Is that what you mean?'

'I didn't say anything of the sort.'

'No, but you put me properly in my place.' They drove in silence for a few moments. 'Rightly. People think I'm too fragile to be taught how to behave. You don't seem to agree.'

'I really know almost nothing about you.' They had arrived outside the solicitor's office near the cathedral, finding a parking space opposite. 'Do you want to tell me something about yourself?'

'Not much.'

Zoe had closed herself off once more, but she didn't get out of the car. Was there some confidence she wanted to share, Maisie wondered? What was Zoe going to do in town?

The rain was slowing to a fine drizzle. Zoe swung her door open.

'Thanks, Miss Cooper.'

They both got out.

'You can call me Maisie,' she said, but Zoe was walking away, her Afghan coat swinging round her knees. 'Please don't be late,' Maisie called after her.

Zoe replied without turning round. 'I won't. I'm sorry.'

Maisie watched her go, wondering what precise experiences had shaped the girl's odd personality – by turns formal, rude, angry and apologetic. She hoped Phyl would tell her the whole story the next time she asked.

★★★

Maisie opened the door to the solicitor's office without knocking. The hallway was almost blocked with boxes.

'Hello?' she called.

'Come through.'

Maisie found Charity at her desk, typing. There was an impressive pile of envelopes beside her, each one with a similar letter tucked under the adhesive flap, waiting to be signed. There were more document-storage boxes round her desk.

'What's happening?' asked Maisie.

'I was here all Sunday. I didn't have time to tell you the other day,' said Charity, with a resigned smile. 'Maurice has been successful.'

'He has sold the business?'

'A serious enquiry. He would retain a consultancy role. It's what he wants.'

'But not what you want?'

'Oh, I think it will work out.'

'You will go with him to live in the Caribbean?'

'He's my husband, after all.' Charity shrugged. 'And I have never been accepted here.' She waved a hand to indicate all of Chichester. 'I've always been an outsider and, you know, in the end it's very tiring.'

Maisie knew that Maurice Ryan had been working all hours, schmoozing the great and the good – losing to them at golf, admiring their crass interior-decorating choices – in order to sell up and retire. She knew that his plan was to move to Guadeloupe, the French overseas territory where Charity's family originated, and buy a villa above the beach.

'Is he in his office?'

'He's meeting a *pro bono* client at the pub by the station, the big one, the Globe, where they can speak in public but in private, if you see what I mean.' Then she asked: '*Comment tu trouves Madame Pascal?*'

'How do I find her?' Maisie mused. 'Actually, I wanted to ask you, how well do you know Auntie Phyl?'

'Less well than you, surely?'

'No, not at all. In fact, it turns out it's rather a mystery. My parents told me that she married a Frenchman and moved away to live, I assumed in France. I remember them saying that her husband was only interested in horses. I remember thinking how romantic that was – the idea of living on a French stud farm, raising and training livestock, attending the great meetings at Longchamp or Auteuil. But now it turns out she lives in Bunting, just up the road and . . . Well, I wondered if you knew anything?'

'I will ask Maurice. He knows the ins and outs of all the wealthiest residents.'

'Thanks.'

Maisie frowned and became lost in thought. Charity paused before asking what the matter was.

'*Qu'est-ce qu'il y a?*'

'I'm sorry. I was just thinking – things don't add up.'

'What things?'

'I've been trying to get it all straight in my mind. When I was a child, I was told that my aunt, who was rich, paid for me to go to Westbrook College.'

Charity smiled. 'Where you met the handsome policeman.'

'You think he's handsome?'

'Do you deny it?'

'All right. No, I don't.' Maisie smiled. 'Anyway, Auntie Phyl, Mrs Pascal, she told me that my father was a successful insurance salesman and he had income, beyond selling door-to-door cleaning products, which was what I understood to be his occupation. So that was a surprise. But what possible reason could there be for never seeing her again? I mean, there was the war but . . .' Maisie stopped. 'Well, that's it. I don't really know what I'm asking and I don't know who to believe.'

'Your parents or your aunt.'

'Exactly.'

'Again, we should wait and find out what Maurice thinks.'

'But you're packing up.'

'We are. *Tu m'excuses . . . ?*'

Charity went back to organising the post. Maisie hung around in case Maurice came back. She remembered this morning, when she had been so pleased to see Charity, warmed by the idea that she had a friend in Chichester where she, too, felt out of place, despite having grown up within a few miles of this very spot. She had been confirmed by the local bishop in the cathedral, had sat her O levels and A levels in the local minor public school, had bought clothes in the local jumble sales.

And now, her friend was leaving.

'I think you're going to have a wonderful time,' said Maisie, despite her disappointment. 'How soon do you leave?'

'Tonight.'

'What?' said Maisie with shock in her voice.

94

'Not for Guadeloupe. We're going to London to tell my family.'

'Oh, that's a relief.' Maisie checked her watch. 'I'm afraid I can't wait for Maurice any longer. I must get off.'

She and Charity air-kissed one another *à la parisienne* and Maisie left, climbing up into the rather damp Land Rover and driving back across town. She parked outside the pink bungalow on Parklands Road. As she did so, she realised she was fantasising about finding her own tropical villa above a white sandy beach, coconut palms casting narrow strips of shade, fresh fish just pulled out of the water, cooking *al fresco* over hot, grey embers.

She got out into chill drizzle and went to the front door. Jack greeted her politely with his hands full. Florence had prepared delicious sandwiches from the leftover brisket.

'Where is she?' Maisie asked.

'At her whist drive,' said Jack.

They ate and, to Maisie, their conversation felt stilted. She didn't want to talk about emotions and Jack was trying to be 'just friends'.

When they had finished eating, he cleared the plates. Maisie went through to the kitchen to help, but he put them to one side and told her: 'We should get on.'

The process of practising for cross-examination was rather punishing. Jack was patient and kind, but also disappointingly stand-offish, as if he had taken on a different personality. Time passed and she felt a steadily increasing tension. Oddly, it brought to Maisie's mind an image of the wire strung taut between the trees on Phyl's drive and she realised, with a pang of guilt, that she would soon have to leave, without having told Jack anything about the smothered sheep or Phyl's disappearing lodger. She was about to ask his opinion when the moment was broken by a loud banging on the door.

Maise looked at her watch. It was ten past seven.

III

TEMPERANCE

TWELVE

'You didn't have to go banging on the door like a mad person,' Maisie gently chided. 'I don't know what Sergeant Wingard must have thought. And his poor grandmother.'

'I thought you said she was out,' Zoe retorted.

They were driving back through the countryside towards Bunting. There was very little traffic and, only now and then, a few street lamps, just one or two in each village they passed.

'She might not have been,' Maisie replied, realising how pious she sounded, advocating the holy virtue of temperance. 'What did you suppose had happened?'

'You were late.'

'Barely,' said Maisie.

Maisie thought it through. She had insisted Zoe shouldn't be late and then, when the girl had arrived, the poor thing had become worried because she had been made to wait and . . .

And what, though? The Land Rover had been right outside.

'Didn't you see the car? Didn't you just think I'd be out in a minute?'

'I told you I don't know. I was . . . I got worried.'

'About what?'

'I don't know. Just worried.'

Maisie glanced over at her passenger. There were tears on Zoe's cheeks. Maisie felt awful, realising she had been unfairly taking out her own frustration.

'Never mind. I'm sorry I sound cross. It's my fault. It doesn't matter.' Maisie took a moment to recalibrate her ideas. Zoe was perhaps much more damaged than she had imagined. She wondered if she could try and draw her out – for the girl's sake and to help Phyl. The cold, clammy cab of the Land Rover felt a little like a cave – a place to hide and, perhaps, to confess. 'I suppose I should be grateful,' said Maisie. 'You know?'

For a few seconds, there was no reply, then Zoe wiped her nose on her sleeve and sniffed.

'Why's that?'

'I was having a bit of a crisis.'

'Oh.'

There was another pause. Maisie tried again. 'You know, with my friend Jack.'

'I've met Sergeant Wingard.'

'Oh, yes?'

'I haven't been in trouble with the police, if that's what you're thinking. But he came into the school a couple of times before my mum and dad . . .' Zoe took a deep breath. 'I mean, he came while I was living with Mr and Mrs Beck.'

'They left a few months ago. Is that right?'

'Something like that.'

'Weren't you very young to be left alone?'

'Maybe.'

'How did they think you were going to manage?' Maisie insisted. 'You were only sixteen.'

'*He* gave me a pound note and said he hoped I would be all right. *She* never looked back.'

'How awful.'

There was a pause, then Zoe asked, provocatively: 'Was the handsome policeman trying to seduce you?'

Maisie laughed. 'No, nothing like that. We have a history and I don't know if I want to . . .'

'Rekindle it?'

Maisie slowed down for a bend, glanced at Zoe and smiled. 'You think he's handsome, too?'

'Oh my God, but he's so old,' said Zoe. 'Anyway, I don't want a boyfriend . . .'

Maisie felt the banter had touched a nerve, but she seemed to have been successful in drawing Zoe out and decided to share some more.

'Things are odd between us because he investigated Stephen's death, my brother's murder. Now, I have this reluctance . . . I don't know how to explain it.'

'There's an ugly connection,' said Zoe, perceptively. 'You can't think of him without remembering grief and loss.'

'Yes,' said Maisie. 'That's very insightful of you.'

There was another, longer pause. Zoe wound her window down a couple of inches, letting the breeze ruffle her hair. Again, it was Maisie who broke the silence.

'How did you get on?' she asked, breezily. 'In town, I mean.'

'Fine, but I don't know if there's any point. Are you asking what I was doing?'

'No, I was just making conversation.'

'Good, because it's private.'

'Don't tell me, then.'

'I won't. And I'm sorry I came banging and spoilt the moment.'

'You didn't and it doesn't matter. It's all fine.'

'Of course, it is,' said Zoe, sarcastically. 'Everything's fine. Nothing matters.'

Maisie turned onto the valley road. Zoe wound up her window and there was another unhappy silence. An owl flew up out of a hedge, the white underside of its chest and wings like a ghost against the dark of the night.

'Would you tell me how you come to be living with Phyl? I don't like to pry but I feel like I will keep putting my foot in it otherwise.'

'I don't mind but she might.'

'You mean it ought to be her who tells me?'

'I don't know.'

'Oh, for heaven's sake,' said Maisie, losing patience, 'whether you tell me or you don't, at least have a reason, Zoe, please.'

Maisie's eyes were on the road but she felt the young woman looking at her. She wondered if she had gone too far, if Zoe would definitively clam up.

'All right,' said Zoe. 'I was born, I assume, out of wedlock, a bastard. I was left at the hospital, a foundling, healthy but unwanted, so I was taken into care. It doesn't take long before you're old enough to understand that you're different from other children, the ones with families whose parents wanted them and wanted what was best for them. Thanks to the "generosity" of the welfare state, I was raised by a succession of foster families – "bounced around", as they call it – all in Sussex, a burden on the county services, as they seemed to enjoy telling me any time I answered back or ran away. I knew, anyway. Then, the last family I was placed with, when I was nine, they lived in the village, in Bunting, and by then I'd learnt that however bad things were, they could easily be worse, so I stuck it. Perhaps *she* preferred younger kids or she just didn't like me growing up. I don't know, I suppose they thought it was their duty, they were doing good, or I was filling a hole in their sad lives or something. But, in the end, they changed their minds and . . . He wasn't so bad. She was a bitch. She made me leave school before my exams so I could go out to work. I helped on the Stocks' farm, Gordon's parents, before they retired, then at the pub.'

'Isn't the school leaving age sixteen, now?' said Maisie.

'That doesn't come in till later this year. My old social worker tried to get her to let me stay on. Later, he got the sack and the new one didn't care. He told me: "What will be, will be, you know?" Stupid hippy . . .'

Zoe's voice drifted into silence. They were nearly home.

'But then the Becks left?' Maisie insisted.

'They told me that Mum—' She stopped and corrected herself. 'Mrs Beck got cancer, so they had to move to Portsmouth to be near the hospital and they couldn't take me with them.' Zoe hesitated, then asked in a small voice: 'Do you think that was true?'

'How could I possibly know?' asked Maisie, kindly.

'Well, anyway, they went.'

'Just like that? Without you?'

'Just like that.'

Maisie couldn't think what to say. Eventually, she murmured: 'You poor thing.'

'Or they didn't want to,' said Zoe. 'I wouldn't blame them. Yeah, probably, they'd had enough of me. I have.'

Of course, that was what any child would believe, thought Maisie, that it was their fault. Six years old or sixteen years old, it made no difference. Poor Zoe was a child inside.

'How awful.'

'Yeah,' said Zoe, miserably. 'Not much like living your perfect life in Paris, is it?'

Maisie didn't argue. She turned in between the two stone gateposts, surmounted with stone acorns, and up Phyl's drive. She took it slowly, wary of what Phyl had shown her.

'What did you think of the wire?' she asked.

'The what?' said Zoe.

'The wire stretched across the drive?'

'What wire?'

'Between those two trees.'

Zoe's eyes grew wide. 'What for?'

Maisie pulled up at the front door. Zoe threw the door open and leapt out of the car, running round to the gate in the red-brick wall that led to the kitchen garden.

Maisie got out and followed her. The back door was open. Zoe had thrown herself down on the floor by Phyl's chair, her head in her arms on Phyl's lap, sobbing like a small child.

Maisie felt awful.

Of course, Phyl was trying to provide Zoe with some small security.

Of course, Phyl wouldn't have told Zoe about the wire.

And now she, Maisie, had made Zoe think that her small security was in doubt, that Phyl was in danger.

She and Phyl exchanged a glance.

'What did you tell her?' Phyl mouthed.

'I'm sorry . . .' Maisie began.

Phyl shook her head, then looked towards the door to the hall, indicating that Maisie should go.

Maisie nodded apologetically and slipped past them, feeling foolish and cruel. She fumbled in the dark, unable to remember where to find the light switch. She climbed the stairs by touch, turning right on the landing, finding her door.

She went inside and found the fire still burning with the fireguard pulled across in front of the hearth. Phyl must have added a few logs. She sat at the end of the bed, looking into the flames, feeling that she had carried upstairs with her an enormous, unfathomable desolation – not her own sense of loss and loneliness, but that of poor Zoe, a foundling, 'bounced' from one foster parent to another, unable to accept that here, in Phyl's extraordinary, grubby mansion, she might finally have found a safe harbour.

And now, because of Maisie's indiscretion, Zoe had once again lost all sense of proportion and was desperate that she would lose it all.

THIRTEEN

Maisie slept late, then enjoyed lying quietly in bed for half an hour, watching the sun weave bright magic through the branches of the beech and ash and oak trees, glinting on the damp bark and the first tight leaf buds of spring. Eventually, her thoughts turned to the previous day's adventures. Looking back, she felt she had let tiredness and a sequence of shocks and surprises make her a little overwrought.

Not just her. Zoe, too, of course.

But wasn't it normal for teenagers to have mood swings?

Yes, obviously. It was more or less what made teenagers teenagers.

She sat up, following another train of thought. Was it really likely that Phyl or Zoe were being targeted by a murderer?

No, of course not. Murder was not an everyday occurrence. It was like lightning – capable of striking twice in the same place, but the odds were against it.

She got up and went looking for the bathroom. It was at the end of the corridor, above the kitchen. The window was open a crack, presumably to avoid damp, and the room was chilly. She turned on the taps of an old-fashioned iron tub, very cold to the touch. The hot water ran out quite quickly, giving her only just enough for a shallow, tepid wash, probably because the immersion heater was set for much earlier in the day. The time was nearly ten o'clock. It was better than nothing, however.

Because there was no shampoo, she washed her short hair with some Radox bath foam and rinsed using a plastic jug she found on the wooden bath rack. Then she got out and half dried herself, keen to get back to the relative warmth of her bedroom. Wrapped in a towel, as she passed the top of the stairs, she glanced down and saw Jack Wingard.

'Good heavens!' she blurted, without thinking. 'What are you doing here?'

He glanced up, his eyes taking in her semi-naked form. She laughed as he reddened and quickly averted his gaze.

'I'm sorry, Maisie,' he said, panic in his voice.

'It's all right,' she told him, partly shielding herself behind a post of the landing. 'Don't worry. What are you doing here?'

'Perhaps you'd better come down.'

'Just a minute.'

He disappeared into the kitchen and Maisie's smile faded. Why was Jack here? What had happened? Was it Phyl? *Oh, please don't let it be Phyl.*

Maisie went back to her bedroom, rubbed herself vigorously and threw on some clothes. She felt another pang of guilt at being so wrapped up in reminiscences and the ambivalence of Jack's company, last night in Florence's kitchen, that she had failed to mention anything about Phyl's lodger or the smothered lamb or the murderous wire stretched across the drive.

Maisie pushed her feet into her shoes and ran down the stairs without doing up the laces. She almost tripped over them on her way into the kitchen.

Surely not. Surely Phyl couldn't have been . . .

'Oh,' she breathed. 'Thank God.'

Phyl was standing with her back to the double sink. Her face was very white and her hands bunched into fists. Jack Wingard was by the back door.

'Archie found her,' said Phyl, her voice tight.

'Found who?'

'A body,' said Jack.

If Phyl was safe, was it Zoe?

'Who, though?' Maisie heard herself shouting.

'She hasn't been identified,' said Jack.

'Auntie, why won't you tell me?'

'But I did tell you,' said Phyl, her eyes glazed and uncertain. 'It's my lodger. I knew it. And now there's no getting away from it. She's dead, like I said she might be. Like I said she would be, almost like I made it happen. Oh, God.'

★★★

Maisie, Phyl and Jack were on the slippery uphill bridleway behind the house. Maisie was wearing a different pair of wellingtons from yesterday in a slightly smaller size – ones that didn't drag her socks down under her heels.

'We go the same way as before, up to her camp, then over the top,' said Phyl.

They were the first words she had uttered since they had left the kitchen. Jack Wingard was almost equally taciturn, apart from a second apology for surprising her in her towel at the top of the stairs.

'I should have minced by without attracting your attention,' said Maisie, trying to make light of it.

'Anyway, I'm sorry.'

'It really doesn't matter.'

They trudged on. Beneath the trees on either side, the undergrowth was still sparse. Soon, it would be bursting with life, perhaps a carpet of bluebells reaching up for the light, taking advantage of that brief window of opportunity, until the trees came into full leaf and completed their shady canopy. Then they reached the shanty.

'How far?' Maisie asked.

'A bit further,' said Phyl. 'Down to the stream.'

Maisie glanced around, trying to remember in which direction Phyl had thrown the poisonous mushrooms. Should she mention them to Jack? They wouldn't be too hard to find.

Beyond the squalid encampment, the track narrowed to a bridleway that ran across the south side of the wood, traversing the steep slope rather than going straight down. Soon, Maisie heard the sound of water trickling across stones.

'This would be where she came for a drink?' asked Jack. 'She didn't come to the house?'

'That's right,' said Phyl, tersely.

'How old would you say she was?' Jack asked.

'Thirty, maybe a little more?'

They came upon Archie, sitting on a tree stump, rolling a cigarette from a packet of Golden Virginia tobacco. There was ash on one knee of his corduroy trousers where the pile had been worn smooth by use. He looked like it was the most normal thing in the world, for him to be standing guard over a corpse.

'Down-along,' he said, tilting his head to give the direction. 'That's where 'tis.'

'I think I've changed my mind. I don't want to look at her,' said Phyl.

'I do need a positive identification,' said Jack Wingard in what Maisie thought of as his 'constabulary' voice. 'Could you help, Mr Close?'

'I never saw her nearby, not to memorise,' said Archie. 'She fled me like a fox. I mean, like a vixen. Afeared I'd turn her off, I reckon.'

'But you've not moved her?' Jack asked him.

'Not a whisker. I just checked her pulse to see she didn't have one and left her where she was with her face in the water.'

'Oh, God,' said Phyl. 'I shouldn't have insisted on seeing her, Sergeant Wingard. I'm sorry. I can't face it now.'

'But there's no one else can do this,' said Maisie patiently. 'It will be over in a moment.'

'Now you're here?' said Jack, encouragingly.

'Best to get it over with,' said Maisie. 'Let me help. This is difficult going.' She took Phyl's arm and could feel her shaking. 'You'll be all right.'

Phyl took a deep breath.

'Okay. I'll try.'

Maisie could see the tiny stream, glinting through the tree trunks, sparkling with life, cutting its narrow channel in the chalk and flint, no more than one long stride across. They followed Jack along it, picking their way, holding on to the tree trunks for balance as they went. Then he paused, a few yards ahead of them, and Maisie and Phyl stopped. There was a dark, sodden shape, half in and half out of the stream. Jack was hanging back, examining the ground.

'Are you looking for footprints?' Maisie asked.

Jack turned his head and gave her an odd look. It took her a moment to realise that he must be remembering how she had 'freelanced' her own investigation into Stephen's death, against his wishes. And now, here she was, already interfering.

'I know you know what you're doing,' she said, quietly.

'There aren't any footprints,' said Jack. 'Most of the bank is flint and the fringe of the trees is all leaves and twigs. There's no reason why I shouldn't go closer and just lift her face out of the water.'

'I can tell it's her,' said Phyl. 'Those are her awful clothes. You can see, with how the water is making them cling, that she wasn't as fat as she seemed. It was just all the dirty layers . . .'

Maisie could feel Phyl trying to pull away, as if that was it and she had done her duty and identified the corpse already.

'Are you ready?' said Jack, carefully stepping in closer to the body.

'Do I have to?' asked Phyl in a tense undertone.

'No, but you say no one else in the village knew her?'

'She kept her distance. Zoe gave her leftovers from the pub kitchen, but she would sneak round when no one else was looking.'

Maisie explained to Jack in a few brief words who Zoe was.

'She's at work,' said Phyl. 'At the Dancing Hare.'

'Should we go and get the girl, Mrs Pascal,' Jack asked, 'if you can't do this?'

'No,' said Phyl. 'I'll not have the child put through it.'

'You can manage,' said Maisie, touching Phyl's arm. 'Just a moment, then it will be over.'

Phyl took a deep breath.

'All right. Go on.'

Keeping a strong grasp on an adjacent sapling, Jack took a long stride forward to plant his regulation left boot on a solid lump of stone, close by the dead woman's head. With his free hand, he leant over and took hold of the shoulder of the dreadful coat. He pulled up and towards himself. There was a sound of releasing suction, revealing a white-blue, bloated face, exposed to the bright sun that dappled through the almost-bare trees.

'That's her,' cried Phyl, shrinking away. 'That's my lodger. Oh, what have I done? Please, Maisie, help me get away from here.'

Fourteen

Maisie wasn't sure if they should leave, but Jack explained that, not far away, beyond the water, was a wide woodland track suitable for vehicles. He explained that would be the easiest access for the scene-of-crime team and the mortuary van. She and Phyl left Jack and Archie by the stream in the trees, struggled back up and over the hill to the house of blood-red brick in the shadowy woods.

'And you never knew her name?' asked Maisie.

'I never asked,' said Phyl in a tone of regret.

They went round to the kitchen. Phyl picked up the empty wine bottle from the table. She put it in a cardboard box on the floor with four or five others, presumably returns for the shop. Maisie thought she looked shaken, but was determined to put a brave face on things.

'Different mood, I think,' said Phyl, in a brittle voice. 'Let's have a different colour.'

Phyl didn't explain further so Maisie had to follow her across the dark-panelled hall and through another doorway into a library room with tall windows on the south and west sides, two-thirds of the walls lined with books, three or four overlapping rugs and a few sagging sofas and armchairs. Two of the armchairs had built-in bookshelves under the armrests and Maisie immediately wanted to sit in one and lose herself in fiction and forget the awful experience of going to identify the drowned woman.

'This is a wonderful room,' she said, taking it all in.

'It is. Would you like to see the cellar?' Phyl gestured to the floor. There was a trapdoor in the boards, just poking out beyond the edge of a gorgeous – though grubby – Persian rug.

'You seem much better now,' Maisie told her. 'But shouldn't we both sit quietly for a bit?'

'The walk back did me good.' Phyl raised an eyebrow. 'You didn't seem too bothered.'

No, thought Maisie. *But then, this isn't my first dead body.*

Phyl pulled back the Persian rug, revealing the whole trapdoor.

'Give me a hand.'

'It really shocked you, didn't it?' Maisie insisted. 'Can't I make you a nice cup of tea?'

'Let's get ourselves a proper drink, then I'll tell you the whole story.'

'Oh,' said Maisie, looping back to Phyl's cryptic remark about moods. 'You meant a different colour of wine.'

They each took hold of a brass ring, recessed in the polished timbers. The trapdoor wasn't heavy and moved easily on well-oiled hinges, going just past vertical, where it was held in position by a chain. Maisie peered into the hole.

'It looks very spidery.'

'Down we go,' said Phyl enthusiastically, then descended a set of steep steps, not much more than a wooden ladder. Maisie followed.

In the cellar, there was natural light from two dirty slot windows, protected with metal bars, just beneath the low ceiling. Everything was grimy and cobwebby, a place to store things no one wanted but which seemed too good to throw away: two pairs of skis and ski poles; three tennis rackets in stretcher frames to prevent the wood from warping; a ramshackle pram; two saddles and some other horse leathers and rugs; an open suitcase of unwanted clothes; seven or eight empty wooden wine crates piled on top of one another, the top ones containing useful household objects including polish, boot brushes, Windolene, Brasso, Three-in-One Oil and light bulbs. Beyond the heap of crates was a dark doorway into a further space with a dusty dirt floor strewn with newspapers.

'The white wine I buy from the village shop,' said Phyl. 'Jenny Brook gets it in on the quiet. She doesn't have a licence, obviously, and the stuff she used to choose was almost vinegar. But I put her in touch with a dealer I know and came up with the idea that she simply coordinates purchases for the village, placing bulk orders for about a dozen of us, charging a little on top for her trouble.'

'Is that entirely legal?' Maisie wondered, smiling.

'Not precisely, but perhaps not illegal either. Anyway, I was saying, reds are different. They must be carefully chosen and aged, personally nurtured. That way, one isn't tempted to overdo it.'

'Temperance,' said Maisie, lightly. 'A holy virtue.'

'Moderation, not abstinence,' said Phyl. 'Know your limits.'

The wine rack was in the darkest corner of the cellar, well away from direct light from the high slot windows. Maisie thought it must contain at least a hundred dusty bottles and felt she must be in the presence of a small fortune's worth of esteemed vintages. She ran her fingers along the top row, just touching the dusty wax that encased each cork.

'Are they all very old?'

'Not at all. Some of them I bought only five years ago. How about a nice Burgundy?'

'Yes, splendid,' said Maisie, wondering what the time was. There wasn't enough light to see the face of her small lady's watch. 'To have later, with lunch, you mean?'

'*Apéritif*,' said Phyl, choosing a bottle and drawing it tenderly from the rack. 'Do you think we'll need two?'

'No, I don't.'

'As you wish.'

They climbed back up the steep steps and Phyl gave Maisie the bottle to hold horizontally in her hands like a baby while she closed the lightweight trapdoor and replaced the corner of the Persian rug.

'Don't shake it.'

'I know,' said Maisie. 'I'll be careful.'

Phyl opened a glass-fronted cabinet and took out a crystal decanter. She used the corkscrew on her Swiss army knife to carefully draw the cork, pouring the wine very slowly, leaving about half an inch in the bottom of the bottle.

'I've had a couple of these before. They both had quite a lot of sediment. I want it to stand and clarify for a few minutes before we drink it.'

'Of course.'

Maisie checked her watch. The longer they left it, the happier she would be.

'Well,' said Phyl, 'is it a permissible hour for alcohol?'

'It's not yet midday so I'd say not quite.'

'Sun not over the yardarm?'

'I don't know what that expression means, but no, I reckon not.'

'Shame.'

Maisie thought Phyl was using the ceremony of preparing the wine as a way of recovering from the shock of identifying the body. Beneath her abrupt bonhomie, she was still shaken, trying to find ways to not talk about it.

'Glasses?' said Phyl.

Maisie took the empty bottle across the hallway to the kitchen and put it in the cardboard box with the other returns. She washed up yesterday's two tumblers, drying them on a crumpled tea towel. As she did so, a hint of suspicion began growing in her mind. Had Phyl really looked at the terrible bloated white-blue face? She wasn't sure. She had been holding on to her auntie's arm and had felt Phyl turn away, just at the moment that Jack had heaved the body out of the stream and the head lolled back. She was pretty sure that Jack hadn't been watching closely because he was busy making sure he kept his balance on the slippery bank.

Phyl followed her into the kitchen.

'Did you definitely recognise her, Auntie?'

'What's that?' said Phyl, vaguely, holding the decanter up to the sunlight through the window.

'I mean, if you barely knew her, can you be sure of your identification?' Maisie asked. 'It's a serious legal question, after all. You wouldn't want to have made a mistake?'

'Who else could it be?' said Phyl.

Yes, thought Maisie. *Who else could it be? Good question.*

FIFTEEN

Ten minutes later, the grandfather clock in the hall struck midday – a few minutes early, Maisie thought. Phyl poured three fingers of Burgundy into each of the two tumblers. They said cheers and drank.

It was a magnificent wine, complex and . . . What was the word? Nourishing. It tasted like a meal, all on its own.

As they drank, Maisie noticed that all the papers on the table – the parish news and the circulars and the post – had been organised into three separate piles. Phyl must have made good progress on her fortnightly 'business Monday'.

At just that moment, Zoe appeared in the doorway to the sombre hall. She was wearing faded flared jeans and a granddad shirt with no collar, rather like a smock, over something closer-fitting underneath. Her clothes looked a little shabby but she had an energy, a vibrancy about her. She held a tatty gentleman's black umbrella in her hand.

'Ernie dropped his coffee while we were prepping the lunches and it went all over me so I came back to change.'

'Before you go—' Phyl began.

'I have to get back,' Zoe interrupted, already leaving. 'I put a couple of slices of the game pie in the fridge. If you run out of wine at home, come and have a chaser at the pub.'

'Keep my table,' said Phyl, quickly.

Maisie heard the front door slam but, again, she thought it was just hurry, not an adolescent strop or anything like that.

'How was she last night, after I went up?' she asked. 'I'm so sorry I told her about the wire. I ought to have realised it would upset her.'

'I let her cry. She wasn't worried for herself, just for me. Once she'd wept it all out, she left with barely a word.'

'She didn't mention what she'd been doing in Chichester?'

'That remains "private", as she said before the two of you left.'

'No explanation for her tears?' Maisie asked. 'No "thanks for listening"?'

'Would that be in character, do you think?' asked Phyl, wryly.

'I don't really know her well enough yet. She's rather a closed book, though she did tell me a little about her background.'

'It may be much worse than she lets on, Maisie. When you think about it, she has every reason to be difficult and no reason to trust.'

'I understand that. Poor thing.' Maisie thought for a moment. 'Does she have anything she's good at?'

'How do you mean?'

'Something to give herself purpose, something that belongs to her and to no one else. I had languages for that, even when our parents died. I was already working, of course, making a living, but speaking other languages was something else, something I could do that most people couldn't.'

'I see what you mean,' said Phyl, nodding. 'You had something to validate you.'

She drained her glass and refilled it. Maisie cautiously kept her own out of reach.

'Yes,' she agreed.

'But the things that validate us,' said Phyl, carefully, 'they aren't always as neutral or as innocent as a passion for irregular verbs and the subjunctive voice.'

'True,' said Maisie, wondering why wariness had crept into Phyl's tone. 'But she's bright and intelligent and she's soon going to grow into an attractive young woman.'

'Not so different from you,' said Phyl. Maisie didn't reply. Phyl was looking into her glass. Eventually, she went on. 'I'll give it a think but, poor Zoe, I'm not sure she's got anything very special to anchor her.'

Maisie held her peace. She had an odd feeling that there must be something unique about Zoe, if only she could discover what it was. She thought about her own childhood with two loving parents and all the advantages of West-brook College. What did it mean that Phyl hadn't paid for it? Was her aunt right, that it was a way for Eric and Irene to keep from her and Stephen the reason they were rather poor?

There was a knock at the back door.

'Come in,' called Phyl.

It was Jack Wingard, his waterproof cape dripping wet, water running from the peak of his helmet. While they had been talking, the rain had returned. Maisie stood up to greet him but he looked past her to Phyl.

'Please forgive the intrusion,' he said, politely. 'I won't come in and drip all over the floor.'

'Don't be silly,' said Phyl. 'Flagstones are made for drip-ping on.'

'Fair enough,' he replied, but he stayed where he was on the rubber doormat and told them that the body had been removed, that no one should go to the encampment and disturb anything because the forensic team was going to go through the whole insalubrious heap tomorrow.

Maisie told him about finding the poisonous mushrooms – she hadn't liked to mention it on their way to view the body – warning him that Phyl had tossed them away into the undergrowth 'to be safe'. While she was talking, Phyl looked rather pained. Jack replied neutrally that he was glad to know and that he would warn the forensics team straight away.

Politely, he went outside to make the communication on his radio.

'What did he say when you talked to him last night about everything that's been going on here?' asked Phyl.

'I'm so sorry, Auntie. I didn't get around to it. Time ran on and we were talking about the trial and then Zoe was there and . . . Well, I missed my chance,' said Maisie, lamely.

'And you couldn't get your thoughts in order, so busy were you admiring his handsome features?' asked Phyl, with a hint of humour.

'The wine is loosening your tongue,' said Maisie with a grin. 'Stop it.'

Jack came back in.

'Will you have a drink?' said Phyl, indicating the decanter. 'No, of course you won't. But Maisie can make you coffee or tea.'

'I'll be needed at the station.'

'Ah, but we have a tale to tell, don't we, Maisie?'

'We do. Would you stay for ten minutes, please, Jack. I meant to share all this with you last night but, well, it didn't seem to be the moment.'

'In relation to the discovery of the body?'

'Perhaps,' said Maisie.

Jack hesitated and Maisie watched with a kind of dismay as what she thought of as his 'constabulary' persona took over. He took off his cape and hung it on the back of the door, pulled one of the wooden chairs away from the table and sat down with his palms on his knees.

'Of course. We're always grateful for information received. Don't trouble to make tea.'

★★★

Maisie found it hard work putting all the information in order. Partly, this was because it wasn't really her story to tell. She was just the conduit. Also, because Phyl insisted on interrupting with her own observations, not always to the point. Finally, Jack knew everything that they knew.

'So, what do you think?'

'I think the idea that the sheep – I mean the lamb – was killed for practice sounds very far-fetched.'

'But can you think of another explanation?' Maisie asked.

'Hang on,' he told them. 'The wire across the drive could have been a prank by someone who didn't realise quite how dangerous it would be. I mean, I don't suppose you drive very quickly up there, do you?'

'But it's not just the Land Rover, Jack,' said Maisie, not liking the rather whiny sound of her own voice. 'Everyone knows Zoe goes buzzing about on her moped.'

'And me too, sometimes,' said Phyl.

'Yes,' said Jack, 'you made that point.'

'So?' said Maisie, surprised that he didn't seem as concerned as she was. 'Put it all together with Auntie Phyl's lodger and the death caps—'

'What I was about to say is this,' he interrupted. 'Though there might be individual rational or coincidental explanations for all these things – and it does no one any good to imagine all kinds of fanciful connections – there is quite clearly reason to be cautious and to keep an open mind. I think you,' he said, looking at Phyl, 'should be very careful and get back in touch if anything else happens to worry you, however slight.'

'Well, good, bravo,' said Phyl. 'And I should hope so too, but it's a fat lot of good that advice is going to do me.'

'Did you expect the police to mount a permanent guard?' asked Jack, mildly.

'I wouldn't accept it anyway,' retorted Phyl.

'So, you're not worried like we are?' insisted Maisie. 'I feel there's something wrong, Jack. I can't exactly say why.'

Speaking the words out loud, Maisie realised it was true. She did feel a knot of tension just beneath her diaphragm.

'Let's just say,' replied Jack, 'that I'd rather not jump to conclusions either way.'

'And a fat lot of good that does, as well,' said Phyl.

He stood up and retrieved his cape.

'I've given Mrs Pascal my advice, Maisie. Meanwhile, I would prefer it if you,' he persisted, looking meaningfully at her, 'could remember where your responsibilities as a private citizen end and where those of the police begin.'

Maisie was about to protest when she noticed the smile on his face.

'Yes, Sergeant,' she told him, demurely.

The little triangle broke up with Jack promising to ring later on with any early results of the post-mortem examination. He made an official note of Phyl's full name, address and phone number and left. For Maisie, the kitchen felt suddenly empty.

'What do we do now?' she asked. 'Just wait?'

'That doesn't sound much fun,' said Phyl. She replenished her glass very slowly, to make sure any further sediment stayed at the bottom of the crystal decanter. 'Are you sure you won't?'

'Oh, go on then,' said Maisie, but she lifted the rim of her tumbler when it was half full to stop the pouring. 'That's enough.'

They drank, each lost in their own thoughts. Finally, Maisie came to a decision.

'I'm here. You've given me a place to stay and I'm determined to repay you by trying to find out if there is anything behind all these upsets.'

'Thank you,' said Phyl, her eyes wide. 'I've been so worried you were going to abandon ship and go and stay in a hotel or something. You can't know how much this means to me—'

'But I need to get on,' interrupted Maisie, caught up in her own train of thought. 'I need to meet people.'

'What people?' asked Phyl, smiling broadly.

'People in the village. People who know you.'

Phyl didn't answer right away. She searched the pile of fortnightly parish magazines – six or seven of them, one so old it had a Christmas message on the front page. She found the one she wanted.

'This is the most recent.' She turned to the inside back page. 'Here we are, "parish announcements".'

Her finger, still grubby from grappling with the trees to help keep her balance on their awkward walk, pointed to a notification of the date and time of a parish council meeting.

'This evening?' said Maisie. 'But that won't work. I'm an outsider. I can't go.'

'Who's to say you're an outsider?'

'Well, I am.'

'Not if you're my only blood relative, you're not.'

Maisie hesitated. She didn't know why, but the idea made her uncomfortable.

'Do we want that to be common knowledge?'

'Everyone knows everything about everyone in the end.'

'Not everything, surely, or there'd be nothing for me to discover?'

'No, all right, not everything, but that's a new mystery because my lodger was a stranger so that doesn't count.' Phyl shook her head, tapping the notice of the parish council meeting. 'Anyway, I have an idea. Are you hungry? Let's wander down to the Dancing Hare and I'll have a word with Archie.'

Maisie checked the time. It was just after twelve-thirty.

'Lunch will be in full swing,' she said. 'But that's not what I meant. I meant that I need to meet people on my own.'

'Because?'

'Because then people are more likely to be themselves.'

'Rather than?'

'The person they are when they talk to the wealthiest woman in the village.'

Phyl nodded.

'You make a good point.'

'Is that right, Auntie Phyl? Are you "the wealthiest woman in the village"?'

'I wish you'd stop calling me that. "Phyl" will do.'

'I'm sorry. But are you?'

'Ask people. See what they say if you don't believe me.' Maisie was about to argue, but Phyl ploughed on. 'I'm hungry and I've got nothing to eat at home.'

'What about Zoe's slices of game pie?'

'We'll have those later. If this idea of mine works, you'll have a chance to observe the key players as a group this afternoon. Then, maybe tomorrow, you can choose your moment to confront each one of them alone, as and when you feel like it. Do we have a deal?'

Maisie thought about it.

'All right, Phyl. Yes, we have a deal.'

SIXTEEN

Maisie and Phyl went back out, down the path through the woods to the heart of the village. Maisie was thinking about Jack and barely noticed how lucky they were with a gap between rain showers. They crossed the road and Phyl pushed open the low-lintelled door. The public bar of the Dancing Hare was grey and smoky.

They each ordered a repeat of yesterday's ploughman's lunch from the man in the white apron: Ernest Sumner, the publican. Maisie thought he had a rather distinguished military air, like a throwback to some 1940s feature film designed to maintain wartime morale. His narrow face had a hint of derring-do and, perhaps, steadfastness under fire. She wondered if it was genuine or merely a pose.

Sumner addressed Phyl by her first name, but with a nicely judged deference to a valued customer. He passed on the order to Zoe, who had overheard in any case. As she disappeared through the door behind the bar into the kitchen, Maisie thought she looked very much better than the previous day – more grounded, mistress of her emotions. She supposed it was the result of the previous evening's weeping, a kind of release of tension.

Ernest served Phyl a half-pint of the local Harvey's ale and Maisie ordered another pineapple juice. Archie came in, passing close by, smelling of damp and the fields. Phyl went with him to his stool at the end of the bar. Maisie saw him listen attentively then nod as he took in what Phyl had to say.

Maisie sipped her juice, wondering about the couple who had abandoned Zoe. When was that? Just after Guy Fawkes Night. Just after Zoe's birthday, too. Was that part of their reasoning? Was she no longer a source of income if she came of age? But did a child come of age, according to the care service, at sixteen or, as was more common in law, eighteen?

Phyl came back, retying the bandage on her hand, and Ernest Sumner initiated an involved conversation about horses, making a big thing of it, very keen to know her opinion. Apparently, they shared an interest in flat racing and were both looking forward to attending the spring meetings at Goodwood race course, not far away on an awkward, north-facing slope of the Downs.

Maisie stayed silent, trying to remember Zoe's exact words about her foster parents. What had she said? That the wife, Mrs Beck, was 'a bitch', that she had been diagnosed with cancer, that they had had to move to Portsmouth to be near the hospital?

Was that true? Was Portsmouth hospital a cancer centre of some kind? It ought to be possible to find out. What sort of cancer was it? An immediate life sentence or something that would grow over many years, inexorably in the background? Either way, Maisie could accept that being stuck out in the sticks, away from good healthcare, could make even a slowly progressing diagnosis all the more oppressive. Unless one liked the countryside, of course, in which case it might be a final solace?

Perhaps the reality was that the Becks had simply had enough of raising a difficult teenager and made up the cancer story as a pretext? That would be a very cruel thing to do, especially if the truth ever came out.

Zoe emerged from the kitchen with two large white dinner plates.

'At my table, please, Zoe,' said Phyl.

Phyl led the way to the same small table, close to the open fire. Zoe put down the plates and a small wooden box containing cutlery and condiments and cleared away the small plastic 'reserved' sign that had kept it free.

'Anything else?'

'No, thank you,' said Phyl.

Maisie recognised the tone of voice they were both using – one that meant: 'We've had an emotional moment, but we don't have to let that change everything.'

Maisie and Phyl attacked their bread and cheese, tucked in between the heat of the hearth and a cold draught falling from the ill-fitting window. The warm bread and strong cheese and pickles were as good as before, and the salad was much improved. Presumably yesterday had just been a bad moment in the cycle of supply and demand – the last few wilting remnants from a previous delivery. When they had finished and Zoe had cleared the plates, Phyl told Maisie what she had planned.

'Normally the council meeting is held in the parish room.'

'Where's that?'

'It's a lovely toy-town sort of building on the road out. It used to be the edge of the village but a few modern houses have been built beyond it. That's not important. The point is, I've asked Archie to turn off the water to the WC and tell the vicar the parish room can't be used, that there's a problem, so they will have to all come to me.'

'But I still can't be present.'

'Perhaps not at the deliberations, such as they are, but you can be there before and after and sort of mill about and bring in the tea and biscuits, being helpful, that sort of thing.'

'Okay,' said Maisie, trying to picture it. As she had said, it would be much more useful talking to people one-to-one. But the one-to-one meetings might be easier to arrange if she had been introduced as Phyl's guest. 'It'll be a start,' she said.

'Once they're all gone, you can tell me what you think,' said her aunt.

'If I think anything at all,' Maisie warned.

'Yes, but people are interesting, aren't they, in any case?'

'Even without a suspicion of murder hanging over them?' said Maisie quietly. 'I've never before been in the habit of thinking like this. All my life, I've been the sort of person to take others at face value, to simply believe they are as they say they are. Not any more.'

'No wonder you've never got anywhere,' said Phyl abruptly, then she reddened. 'Oh, I'm sorry, Maisie. That was rude. It's living on your own. It makes you very dismissive. It's easy to let the voice in your head become bitter and self-righteous.'

Maisie thought that was probably true. She sometimes had to curb her own tendency to being judgemental.

'And you want to tell them we're related?' she asked.

'You think it would be better if you were simply a friend?'

'Perhaps?'

'I don't know. That would just be creating a lie we would then have to maintain.' Phyl yawned. 'This won't do. Food on top of that excellent Burgundy is making me sleepy.'

Ernest Sumner sidled over with Phyl's bill, but she told him they were in a hurry and to 'chalk it up with the rest'. They trudged back to the house, this time taking the long way round, through the village, along the road and in at the stone gate, in order, Phyl said, 'to wake me up'. As they came up the unweeded gravel drive, Maisie saw that the remnants of wire had been removed from the two trees. She mentioned it to Phyl.

'Sergeant Wingard took them to dust or powder or whatever it is for fingerprints.'

'Of course. I wonder if it can be identified.'

'He's already been beetling about. He says it was from my tractor shed, cut from a roll of fencing.'

'Your shed?' said Maisie, astonished.

'Yes, the barn behind the kitchen garden wall. There're all sorts in there.'

'Don't you think you should have told me that?'

'Yes, perhaps I should have, but he's the forensic man. You're more . . .'

'Yes?'

'You're the people person.'

They came round the bend in the drive, revealing the mansion. Annoyed as she was, feeling there were probably more fragments of information that Phyl had not shared, Maisie couldn't help voicing her admiration for the building.

'It really is impressive. Did you choose it?'

'No, my husband.'

'You didn't have a share in the decision?'

'He wasn't that sort of man.'

'How on earth did you marry someone who told you what to do?'

'Times were different,' said Phyl. 'I was different.'

'Different how?'

'I did something I regretted. I was looking for a new direction, a new life. He provided it. Accepting he was in charge was part of my escape route.'

'Do you want to tell me what it was?' Maisie asked, thinking that was a very surprising admission. 'This regret that meant you needed an escape route?'

They had arrived at the three steps to the front door. Maisie noticed the barred windows to the cellar, set low in the wall, just above ground level.

'No,' said Phyl, pushing open the front door. They went in. 'Not yet.'

'Don't you ever lock up?' said Maisie.

'You think I should?'

'Well, yes.'

'I'll have a look for the keys.'

'You don't even know where your keys are?'

'Not so as to lay my hands on them straight away.'

'Auntie Phyl!'

'That's the second time you've called me "auntie" today.'

'Well, that's accurate, isn't it?'

Phyl didn't answer. She looked cross – no, not cross, exasperated. Then, unexpectedly, she laughed.

'I think I've genuinely worried you, Maisie. Am I right?'

'Well, someone has to worry – and a woman has died, after all.'

'Someone I took in.'

'Exactly.'

'Or, rather, allowed to live on my land. I never did anything for her. I regret that now.'

'Another regret? When we first met, I had no idea you would harbour so much self-doubt.'

'When we re-met,' said Phyl, with an anguished glance. 'We weren't strangers, were we? Anyway, that's enough for now, don't you think?' Maisie followed Phyl into the library, the room with the cellar beneath. 'Let's lay in a fire.'

Maisie helped arrange paper and kindling in the open hearth. 'Tell me more about how it happened.'

'What?'

'Your lodger. When did she arrive? How did you come to notice she was there?'

'The first time was last year.' Phyl struck a match. 'Guy Fawkes Night.'

'The fifth of November, Zoe's birthday?'

'That's right. I was coming back from delivering the fireworks for Archie to set up in young Gordon Stock's lower field, just after the parish room on the edge of the village. Everyone takes their autumn garden rubbish and prunings . . . Well, that doesn't matter.'

'The more detail you give me the more I like it,' said Maisie.

Phyl put her match to the fire just before it scorched her fingers. The paper burnt up brightly.

'The point is, she turned up some time in the afternoon and was standing outside the pub at three o'clock, closing time, all swaddled up in layers and layers of clothes, a scarf pulled across her face. The pub was busy and people were leaving. Four people came out – not wealthy people, just comfortable – two couples, dressed by Marks & Spencer, visitors to the village, probably going off for a tramp in their wellies on the pilgrim trail then back for a few drinks and the fireworks. They looked at her like she was something they didn't want to step in.'

'How horrible.'

'Yes, people are horrible. Anyway, I felt sorry for her and went into the pub and asked Zoe to give her something from the kitchen.'

'Zoe was still living with her foster parents then?'

'Only just. Her foster parents, Mr and Mrs Beck, they told everyone who would listen what a trouble Zoe was, but I never believed them.'

Maisie wondered why Phyl was so sure.

'What kind of trouble exactly?'

SEVENTEEN

Once the kindling was burning strongly, Phyl added some thicker logs and they both sat back in the two delightful armchairs with bookshelves built under their armrests. Maisie reflected on the fact that emotions in the village of Bunting seemed to run very high. And everyone drank, it seemed, at every opportunity – the holy virtue of temperance seemed a stranger.

'You said Zoe was causing trouble?' Maisie prompted.

'Two separate people told me she was not to be trusted – you know, shoplifting or some other nonsense. Then poor Gordon Stock came . . . You know, that farm is all too much for him. His parents had him late and couldn't wait to retire, but just nineteen is too young to carry the responsibility all alone.'

'How is that important?'

'Again, you'd better make up your own mind.'

Maisie dropped her gaze, wondering about what Zoe had been doing in Chichester the previous evening, while she herself was practising for cross-examination at Stephen's murder trial and wondering if she had finally succeeded in exhausting Jack's patience. Could Zoe's rendezvous have also been romantic – but more successful than her own, an innocent 'date' with a suitable boy close to her own age? If so, why not Gordon Stock?

'Okay, back to your lodger?' she prompted.

'She wasn't my lodger then. She was just a stranger. But she was still hanging around when I drove over with the fireworks.'

'For Archie to set up.'

'Standard is the best brand. They cost a pretty penny.'

'I expect they do.'

'You know the jingle on the radio: "Light up the sky with Standard Fireworks"? And you must have heard of Bunting Bonfire Night?'

'I have a vague memory . . .'

'Lots of people come,' said Phyl, proudly. 'The road through the village has to become one-way, in from the west, out to the east. That's how popular it is. And there's a march with candles in jam jars, singing local songs, you know, "Sussex by the Sea" and all that. I expect it sounds very silly and rusticated.'

'It sounds charming. But go on. You saw her again later?'

'She spent the whole evening mooching around, near Jenny Brook's cake stand, over by the choir, right up against the bonfire but with her face hidden by a scarf and a soft hat pulled down over her eyes. I could see the steam rising from her wet clothes. It had been raining in the afternoon.'

'And no one knew who she was?'

'I didn't go asking everybody.'

'But you were interested in her?'

'Stop interrupting, Maisie. Let me get you up to date, then you can ask what you like. So, there she stood, up against the bonfire, steaming away, and I wondered what she wanted and if she was going to try and scavenge a living here. She didn't have the trolley or any of the stuff she built her shanty from later – just the clothes she stood up in.'

'You felt sorry for her.'

'I did. Jenny Brook from the shop told me later that she'd noticed her in the afternoon, eating leftovers out of her hand and then sheltering in the church porch. After the fireworks I saw her again myself, out of my bedroom window. I'm on the back of the house and I have quite a good view up through the woods and there was a good moon. She was mooching about under my trees. So, I got myself shod again and trundled up there to see what was going on.'

'She was building her encampment?'

'No, not yet. She was just looking round, traipsing about, as if she was reconnoitring.'

In the library, the fire was burning down. Phyl leant in to add two more logs from the basket.

'Did you speak to her?'

'I approached her but she fled.'

'Where?'

'Away over the hills on the pilgrim trail.'

'Where does it go?'

'The trail? West towards Leigh and Havant, east towards Kingley Vale and West Dean. Anyway, for several months I didn't give her a thought. Then, she was back, at dusk about ten days ago, this time with her trolley of gear, in the same place, building her encampment. I suppose, back in November, she'd done her recce and found it to her liking for her spring jamboree.' Phyl's forehead became deeply lined, as if she was trying to solve a difficult maths problem. 'I'm trying to remember the exact date but it's all a bit vague in my memory. The days tend to merge into one another when you don't have a job to give structure to your life.'

'I feel that, too,' said Maisie, 'since I've been back in Sussex.' Phyl didn't answer, giving Maisie a moment to remember another question that had been bothering her. 'You know I asked you earlier, when we looked at her body in the stream to give an official identification? I wondered if you could be absolutely sure.'

'Who else would it be?'

'Yes, you said that, but did you actually look?'

Phyl gave Maisie a crooked smile. 'You're a sharp one, aren't you?'

'Am I?'

'You are. No, I didn't look. I saw death in the war and . . .'

'Go on,' said Maisie.

'I didn't like it.'

'You shouldn't have done that,' said Maisie, thinking about Phyl's idea of simply burying the woman somewhere in the woods without even informing the authorities. 'Why did you insist to Jack that he should allow you to view the body in the first place?'

'I felt I owed it to her,' was all Phyl would answer.

***

They remained in what Maisie thought of as the living room – but which Phyl referred to as the library – for the remainder of the afternoon. Phyl said she had things to do and couldn't 'carry on chatting', so Maisie fetched the Malraux novel from her bedroom. When she got back, Phyl had brought the escritoire through from the kitchen so she could complete her letter writing with it balanced on her knees. Before she sealed each envelope, she made a note of the contents in a ledger that she called her 'day book'.

'Otherwise, I would forget what I'd said and where I was up to.'

'Is that all business correspondence?'

'Business, charity, you know.'

'No, I don't – not really.' Maisie frowned. 'I mean, I don't know much about you at all.'

'Read your book. I haven't finished.'

For twenty minutes, Maisie remained quiet, finding it difficult to concentrate. Then Phyl folded another letter and she took advantage of the hiatus.

'What will Zoe be doing now?'

'In the kitchen at the pub, preparing the pies and things. Jenny Brook shuts the shop and comes in to bake and Zoe helps. She often doesn't come home in the afternoon.'

'Does she like cooking? Is that her thing?'

'You really want her to have a "thing", don't you?' Phyl thought about it. 'No, I don't think so. It's just a job.'

'And when she's not working?'

'Hiding out in her room.'

'Does that worry you?'

'Everything worries me just now,' said Phyl.

'That doesn't seem in character for you.'

'It isn't. Now let me concentrate.'

Periodically, the fire burnt down and one or the other of them built it back up. The window glass became dark and, finally, Phyl sighed. 'I'm afraid this charming interlude is over.'

As if to confirm her words, there was a knock at the door. At a gesture from Phyl, Maisie went to answer it.

The hall was cold after the warmth of the library. She opened up. A damp wind came whistling in and, with it, the failing farmer, Gordon Stock. He had changed since Phyl had pointed him out in the pub, but not for the better. He was improbably dressed as if for a discotheque or a wedding, in a burgundy three-piece suit and his lemon-yellow shirt with ruffles, looking very young and tired.

'Is young Zoe in?' he asked, dragging his feet out of his wellington boots, the nails on his big toes protruding through his threadbare socks.

'No, she's at work.'

'She's by way of being my only friend,' he told her.

'That's nice,' said Maisie, foolishly, feeling rather sorry for him. 'I'm Mrs Pascal's niece, by the way. She's in the kitchen.'

Gordon nodded and walked past her. Maisie heard a crunch of gravel and turned back to find a tall man with a large, unremarkable face on the step.

'I'm Maisie Cooper,' she said, brightly.

'Very glad to meet you. I've heard so much about you – your intelligence and bravado.'

'You have?'

The man wore a university scarf wrapped high under his chin.

'Yes, from my colleague in Framlington,' he told her. 'Please accept my deepest sympathy for your loss.'

'Thank you.'

Was he a policeman, Maisie wondered? Was that the colleague he mentioned? No, there wasn't a police officer who lived in Framlington, was there?

Another guest arrived, pottering up the drive on foot with a lever-arch file clutched to her chest. It was the woman that Phyl had pointed out in the pub, the retired librarian with the black pageboy haircut. As the tall man unwound the university scarf to reveal his dog collar, she came and stood very close to him, speaking in a low ingratiating tone: 'Do let's go in, Vicar, or shall we stop outside until we all catch colds?'

'Forgive me, Miss Spragg.'

The vicar stepped to one side. The grey-faced Miss Spragg gave him an adoring glance, sidled in, took off her galoshes and revealed a pair of tartan carpet slippers.

'I'm Maisie Cooper.'

'Are you new to the village?' said Miss Spragg, clearly desirous of a label with which to arrange Maisie on the correct shelf in her mental Dewey Decimal system.

'She's with me,' said Phyl, bustling into the hall. 'I've put the gas oven on and left the door open to warm up the kitchen. Come through.'

They did so and, at a word from Phyl, Maisie set about making tea for four. As she waited for the water to boil, eavesdropping on the conversation between Phyl, Gordon

Stock, Alice Spragg and Canon Dander, she realised that her aunt had very different ways of being, depending on who was present. With Maurice Ryan, Charity Clement and Ernest Sumner at the pub, she adopted a kind of patrician demeanour, looking down on those whose role, she clearly felt, was to serve her wishes. Maisie, Archie and Zoe were granted a kind of warm-hearted indulgence. The murdered lodger, too, and perhaps even Gordon Stock? Phyl spoke of him with a kind of disappointed pity, whereas she was consistently short – even cold – with Canon Dander and Alice Spragg.

The kettle boiled and Maisie poured the hot water on the loose tea leaves.

'Where's Kimmings?' asked Phyl.

'I'm afraid I cannot say,' replied Canon Dander. 'Is your neighbour quite well, Miss Spragg?'

'He told me he has a sniffle,' said Alice, as if the idea was inexplicable to her. 'He is not robust, like you are, Vicar.'

'So, he isn't coming?' asked Phyl.

'We are a little early,' said Canon Dander. 'Shall we allow him a period of grace?'

He said it with a smirk, as if to indicate that it should be taken as an ecclesiastical witticism. Alice tittered.

Maisie put four unmatched cups and saucers on the table.

'Three without sugar and one for you, Mr Stock, with.'

'Very kind, I'm sure,' said the farmer.

'Thank you, Miss Cooper,' said Dander. 'Did Gordon say you were related to Mrs Pascal?'

'I don't know,' she replied pleasantly. 'Did he?'

Gordon Stock slurped his tea, sucking it in with air to cool it down.

'I told you she was a niece.'

'A niece?' asked Alice Spragg. She turned to Phyl. 'I thought you told us you had no close relatives?'

'Nieces aren't close,' said Phyl.

'You used to serve in Framlington, Vicar?' said Maisie, innocently.

'It was my second stipend and might have been my last. I could have ministered there my whole career, I don't doubt. But the bishop saw fit to request my presence in the parish of Bunting and Harden of which we are custodians.'

He looked round the table. Gordon Stock looked baffled, Alice Spragg impatient and Phyl bored.

'Do you remember my family?' Maisie asked.

'No, I don't. You were not regular churchgoers?'

Maisie paused. Everyone else was quiet, aware perhaps of an unspoken undercurrent to the apparently affable exchange. Should she go on?

'My parents preferred the cathedral,' she told him.

'Miss Cooper, listen to this,' said Gordon Stock, unexpectedly. 'Here's something maybe you don't know. Your brother came to see me about veggies.'

'Stephen? Did he?'

'He had a plan for taking freshest veggies up to London for supplying the best restaurants at top prices, just the cost of the little van to deliver.' He laughed. 'But I wasn't taken in by him. I reckon he just wanted me to stump up for the little van to run about in.'

Maisie knew Stephen to be a chancer – his deceptions had, after all, been the motive for his murder – and she felt a certain respect that the young farmer hadn't been 'taken in'.

'But he was a friendly chap,' said Gordon. 'I'll give him that.'

'Are we going to begin?' said Alice. 'It must surely be time.'

'We are,' said Phyl.

'Without Kimmings?' asked Gordon, looking lost. 'I want him to know what's what.'

'We are quorate at four council members,' said Canon Dander.

'He won't be here to back me up,' Gordon complained.

'You can make your point without him,' said Phyl. 'Now, the minutes of our last meeting – have you all read them?'

'We cannot begin with a stranger present,' said Alice.

'None of what we have to say could possibly be deemed confidential,' argued Phyl.

'It's a matter of principle,' said the retired librarian. 'You agree, don't you, Canon Dander?'

'Of course,' said Maisie before the vicar could speak. 'I'll slip away.'

She went out into the hall.

'Could we fully shut the door?' Alice called after her.

Maisie did so and, alone in the hallway, stood very still, wondering if she might be able to overhear. But the heavy door fitted snugly in its frame and absorbed all sound and, sadly, she could make out only a faint murmur of their parochial deliberations.

IV

HOPE

EIGHTEEN

Jack Wingard was a keen supporter of the Rotary Club, a charitable organisation and an important social network, knitting together various communities within the town. As the Bunting parish meeting began, he was preparing to give the results of the school poetry competition on the theme of 'Hope'. It was his role, as judge, to read aloud the works of the winners in an impressive panelled chamber in the assembly rooms in the centre of Chichester, the children all delighted and smiling to hear their words spoken with authority and respect.

That would be later on. For the moment, Jack was sitting at a raised desk at one end of the chamber, looking through the entries, checking if there were any names he would have to ask how to pronounce. He got to the last page – a rather clever sonnet by a fourteen-year-old girl with a clear talent for wordplay – then put the poems aside.

He was looking forward to the ceremony to give him a lift after a long and disappointing day. Among other routine tasks, he had made modest progress with his sequence of petty crimes. Some of the clothes stolen from the washing line had been discovered, discarded in the garden of a large empty house in the village of West Dean, then traced back to their owners using the name tags sewn in the collars. He intended to visit but, so far, he had been unable to track down anyone who could brief him on the large building that was, in the police records, listed as a 'bail hostel for released prisoners'. He had an idea that was out of date and the place had been taken over by social services.

Tomorrow, he decided, he would look into it further. It was a real head-scratcher. Was it possible that bureaucracy had utterly failed and there would be no records of who had ended up living there?

The janitor of the assembly rooms came in, asking if it would be convenient for him to put out the chairs.

'Of course. Go ahead, Mr Eames. Do you want a hand?'

'No, ta, Sarge. I've got my system.'

Jack went down the impressive wooden staircase and out into the street. He didn't smoke, otherwise this would have been the perfect moment of inactivity between one task and the next, time to reflect and ponder.

Ponder what?

Whether he might still be entitled to hope.

Jack sighed. A Dunnaways cab went by and then a South-down bus. In the Co-op supermarket window opposite he could see an advert for Cadbury's 'Smash'. He wondered how life had got too busy for people to make their own mashed potatoes. Then he thought the answer was perhaps to be found in the shop next door, Radio Rentals, suppliers of television sets to people of all classes. How much time was spent, gazing at their bulbous screens? Now colour televisions were becoming available – albeit at a price – how much more attention would they demand?

On the other side of Radio Rentals, Mr Chitty came out of his bicycle shop, glanced up at the sky, then called out across the road. 'A fine evening, Sergeant Wingard.'

'At last, sir,' Jack called back, nodding.

He watched Mr Chitty moving four bicycles back inside from the pavement. One of them was the Raleigh Chiltern ladies' model Maisie had borrowed to get out and about, investigating her brother's murder. Jack's expression darkened. He had warned her against it and she had persisted, throwing herself into danger. Was she now about to do the same again?

He'd had a brief chat with his friend and colleague Inspector Fred Nairn, and Fred had expressed the same worry, nodding his prematurely balding head and pronouncing, sagely: 'Your Miss Cooper should probably try to rein herself in a bit.'

'She's not my Miss Cooper,' he'd replied, grumpily.

An image came into Jack's mind – Maisie in her towel at the top of the impressive stairs in Bunting Manor, her hair and shoulders wet from her bath.

Somehow, his imagination transformed the picture, transporting it somewhere more modest – a 'starter home', perhaps, on the edge of town where he and Maisie might live together, happy in one another's company, for the rest of their days.

That was his hope.

Would it ever become a reality?

NINETEEN

Maisie's brief conversation with Canon Dander stayed with her as she wandered through to the library and stoked the fire. She gazed into the flames, thinking about the small council house on the tiny estate in Framlington where she and Stephen and her parents had lived. On reflection, she thought she had always known there was a reason why her parents – committed Christians, after all – didn't attend Sunday service in the local parish church. As a child, though, she hadn't known what that reason might be.

Her mind turned to a tale Jack Wingard had told her. The conversation had taken place in an interview room at Chichester police station and didn't reflect well on Canon Dander. He had made no attempt to help a young woman about whom it was public knowledge that she was trapped in an unhappy home with an unkind father.

The logs in the fire settled. Maisie took another from the basket, unseasoned, heavy with sap and covered with moss. She bridged two fragments of burnt timber, suspending the new log over the hottest embers. It spat, a spark shooting out of the hearth, landing on the large Persian rug. Maisie snatched up the fire brush, sweeping the ember into a small ornamental shovel and dropping it back into the flames. She pulled across the fireguard.

What next?

She went back out into the hall and, shamelessly, pressed her ear against the kitchen door. This close, she could hear the tone of the discussion, but nothing more. It sounded like an argument, at least three of them interrupting one another, but the substance of what they were saying was unclear.

She went upstairs with a vague idea she might lie down on her bed until the meeting was over and she and Phyl could debrief. On the landing, however, she remembered what Phyl had said about having a view from her window, up the lane into the woods.

She found Phyl's bedroom door ajar and went in, groping for the light switch. After the gloom of the hall and stairwell, the bare 100-watt bulb was painfully bright under a beaded shade. It was plain to see, however, that the room was a perfect match for her aunt – old-fashioned, incoherent and not quite clean. There was a heavy counterpane on the iron bed, decorated with a pretty pattern of wild flowers, but crumpled and unironed. Against the far wall was a teak dressing table, almost black in colour, with a three-part mirror. In the window alcove were two low padded chairs, upholstered in buttoned and faded velvet, the kind of thing you might expect to see in the lobby of an unpretentious hotel. Against the nearest wall was a glass-fronted dresser, full of lever-arch files, photograph albums and scrapbooks.

Maisie went to the window. Of course, it was too dark to see anything up the lane. She wondered where the homeless woman had found the forklift truck pallet that she had stuffed with twigs and leaves as a windbreak. Scavenged from Phyl's barn, perhaps? She tried to imagine how her aunt must have felt, seeing for the first time the ugly encampment being assembled by her unexpected visitor – erecting her tent, pushing the pegs into the soft ground, tying the guy ropes, lashing the tarpaulin between.

Surprise, of course, but generous, too.

Maisie wondered if there was more to it than that. Could there be something that Phyl hadn't told her about her lodger, something that made it impossible to turn her out and move her on? And might that be connected to the fact that Phyl couldn't bear to look at her poor drowned face? Or might the whole thing have taken a wrong turn because the woman in the stream wasn't Phyl's lodger after all?

More worrying still, perhaps, when Jack found out that Phyl had not given a proper identification, would that be another black mark against Maisie?

She turned away from the darkened glass and looked more closely at the room. Three make-up pots and an unidentified tube were lying about on the dressing table, two of them without their lids. A tissue from a 'man-size' box was discarded on the floor. The bed was unmade, the covers drawn back into position but not straightened or tucked in. Next to the bed was a nightstand with a couple of books, one of them on top of the other, open, face down, straining their spines. Maisie picked up the top one, interested to know what it was her aunt was reading.

It was an illustrated field guide to edible and non-edible fungi.

She turned it over in her hands, looking to see the page that Phyl had left open. The list was alphabetical based on taxonomic names. The page was near the beginning.

Amanita phalloides. In plain English, death cap.

Extremely interested, Maisie scanned the gruesome litany of symptoms. They generally appeared ten or more hours after ingestion, depending on quantity and the general health of the victim, starting with stomach pain, vomiting and diarrhoea, continuing for a day or two, followed by apparent recovery. Then, on days three to five, a recrudescence of intestinal disturbance was accompanied by jaundice and kidney failure, with coma and death about a week later.

Blimey, thought Maisie. *How's that for bedtime reading?*

Of course, it was only natural that Phyl would look up what she had found at the tramp's encampment, if only to be sure. Or perhaps in order to show Maisie a picture if she hadn't been convinced? Looking closer, she realised there were indentations on the opposite page, as if someone had leant a sheet of paper there to copy their own notes. Who had done that?

Maisie put the book aside on the pretty floral counter-pane and picked up the second volume. It was a smallish hardback in a dull paper dust jacket: *Phytotoxicology: a field guide* by Owen P Royburg, an American professor. Beneath the author's name was a subtitle: 'Poisonous plants and how to recognise them'. The top few lines on the open page were a warning:

> *Identification is often a tricky first challenge; worrying symptoms demand immediate contact with a physician; better never to eat an unknown item; never turn them into potions or tinctures; never to allow dangerous prunings within reach of humans or animals.*

If the reason for the first book had been the identification of the death caps, what would be Phyl's reason for the second? Wanting to know whether any of the 'common poisonous plants' could be found easily in and around the village? In her own woods, even? Or had she learnt of somebody – perhaps her lodger – doing what the learned professor said they shouldn't?

> *Never turn them into potions or tinctures.*

How would one go about that, anyway? Soaking, boiling and reducing? Drying and grating to a powder?

Maisie also wondered where Phyl might have found such books. She checked inside the front covers. Each carried the library stamp and a rectangle of lined paper, gummed onto the half-title page, with a list of names and dates, written in a clumsy hand.

How many of these borrowers, she wondered, *might have wanted the book because they feared or even contemplated murder?*

As she replaced the two books, trying to make sure that the nightstand looked exactly as it had before she disturbed it, she noticed the penultimate name on the library list. It was hard to read, but could it be 'Jennifer Brook'? She was so shocked by this possibility that she knocked a chemist's bottle to the floor. Like the items on the dressing table, the lid wasn't on and half a dozen small white tablets spilled out onto the grubby carpet.

She knelt down and collected them up, looking carefully at the label. It was a word she did not recognise: Benzodiazepine. Was that a trade name or the actual chemical compound? She had no idea. Alongside was the simple instruction: 'One when required.'

What did that mean? That the patient was to decide when the medication was and wasn't necessary? What sort of prescription was that?

Maisie returned the bottle to the nightstand and wondered how long she had been absent from downstairs. She went and stood quietly on the landing, listening. She could see down into the hall where the kitchen door was still firmly closed. Should she go and offer to make more tea? Would that be a good pretext for further eavesdropping?

She turned back to the overbright bedroom with its powerful bulb hanging in a beaded shade on a braided electrical cable. Perhaps she should continue snooping, while she had the chance? It made her feel rather ashamed but she was sure, too, that Phyl hadn't yet been entirely frank.

The glass-fronted dresser was a good candidate with its many files and photograph albums and scrapbooks. It was locked but the key was in the keyhole. She turned it and swung the door open, scanning the three shelves.

Two-thirds of the contents – the top two shelves – were filled with business folders with labels that she supposed Phyl found tiresome but which seemed, to Maisie, to be full of charm: 'Forestry', 'Arable', 'Livestock', 'Farm Management'. Four others were titled 'Accounts' with a note of the period they covered, several years within each. Three more were labelled 'Day Book', again with sequential dates.

Maisie had been thinking about how the Land Rover was on its last legs and how Phyl had put off Ernest Sumner when he sidled over wanting payment for lunch, asking him to put it on her tab. She opened one of the most recent files, hoping to find out the exact state of her aunt's finances. The trouble was, the information was all quantities and dates, not actual pounds and new pence.

She turned to the contents of the bottom shelf. On the left, piled horizontally on top of one another, were three photograph albums – recognisable from the gold-tooled lettering on the spines – and two scrapbooks. The top album was titled 'Our Wedding Day'. Maisie sat down on the rumpled counterpane of the bed to turn its thick black pages.

TWENTY

The wedding day album was, simultaneously, one of the most hopeful and one of the saddest things Maisie had ever seen. There were only twelve dismal photographs, all of them formally posed, in the small square format of the 1940s – different combinations of the same four people in every one.

Maisie recognised the location. It was the registrar's office on North Street in Chichester and the photographs had been taken in wartime. She could tell because she could see paper was glued to the window glass to prevent it shattering in the event of bombing.

She recognised Phyl in a narrow wedding dress, the sort of thing that a bride of the 1930s rather than the 1940s might have worn, straight and austere. She held the album up to catch the light. Phyl was wearing her hair quite short and had an expression of reserved amusement. It gave Maisie a jolt. She recognised it as an expression she sometimes surprised on her own face – a kind of detachment from life, not taking things quite as seriously as perhaps she ought.

Standing next to Phyl was a shortish, round man with a dome-shaped head and a dark goatee beard, hiding what Maisie thought was probably a weak chin. His wedding suit was a kind of tailcoat. He held an unlikely top hat in his pudgy hands. The other two people looked like guests and, Maisie supposed, witnesses. The man was in uniform and the woman wore a lady's matching narrow jacket and ankle-length skirt suit in some heavy fabric – it was impossible to tell what colour because of the black-and-white process.

Shouldn't the witnesses have been her own father and mother, Eric and Irene? That was right, wasn't it? Maisie squinted at the sparsely filled pages. Might they have looked different then?

No, try as she might, she couldn't persuade herself that the other couple was her parents.

She turned the pages of the dismal album and found the final entry after the twelve photographs. It was an undated formal invitation, pasted onto a left-hand page, printed on thick cream card with an embossed ink. It was for a wedding reception at an address just outside Paris, in the suburb of Auteuil. The reception was due to last for an entire weekend, with celebrations of different kinds on the Friday evening, the Saturday afternoon and the Saturday evening, followed by a church blessing on the Sunday. Underneath, someone had written, in a clear, firm hand: 'When this damn war is over!'

Of course, thought Maisie, that was why the invitation was undated. Phyl had married her Mr Pascal in England, without any kind of ceremony, but had a gorgeous three days of feasting planned for later on. The male witness was probably a friend enlisted in de Gaulle's Free French Army, waiting impatiently for D-Day.

Checking back through the photos, she found no date anywhere. Maisie counted back through the years. If her memories were correct, Phyl had married when Maisie was two or three years old. She leafed through the thick black pages all the way to the end. There was nothing else, no photographs from the French weekend wedding reception – not in this album, in any case. Perhaps it had never happened?

She returned the album to the shelf and drew out another. This one was different – chock-a-block from first page to last, full of treasured two-dimensional memories, some of which Maisie thought she recognised. Hadn't she seen copies in her parents' albums?

It was an entire history of the Smith family, beginning with Phyllis and Irene as children and young women, then two pages that included her father, Eric. The final one was a tiny shot of herself at a few months old with a two-year-old Stephen in a paddling pool.

Maisie smiled, feeling a little less alone in the world, a little less disconnected from what were, after all, treasured happy memories of family life.

She pulled out the final album and opened it with a gasp. It was entirely taken up with her own childhood. Of course, Eric and Irene appeared, and Stephen too, but it was mostly lots and lots of pictures of her – learning to walk, to run, to swim, to ride a bike, to ride a horse, to cook, to build a fire, to plant out spring flowers, to load a shotgun, to dance . . .

It gave her an odd feeling, looking at so many images of her own past, many of which she couldn't remember ever having seen before. Why did Phyl have them? Could she have taken possession of the album when Eric and Irene died? She wished she knew precisely when she had last seen Phyl – or, rather, when Phyl had seen her, before she had begun to form memories of her own.

She turned back to the front of the album. Written in pencil on the inside cover, almost illegible on the soft dusty paper, was a message. She angled it to get more light from the bare bulb.

'Because you couldn't be there.'

Underneath was a signature of some kind, but it was impossible to say what it was, just a squiggle, really, with a flourish at the end that might have been an X for a kiss.

What did that mean? Was it the reason why Phyl had the album or was it a red herring?

Promising herself that she would ask Phyl for permission to look through the albums together, she returned it to the shelf and took out one of the two scrapbooks. Someone had written 'Blaise One, Two and Three' on the front.

Maisie opened it and turned the pages with delight, discovering it was a record of the triumph of hope over experience.

On each of the thick soft pages were race-cards, betting slips, clippings from *Sporting Life*, and dozens and dozens of photographs of three horses, successively named 'Blaise', each with a 'blaze' of white on its forehead, though they had different coats and different builds, insofar as thoroughbreds can be said to differ. In only a couple of early photos did her aunt appear.

Maisie glanced at her watch. She was beginning to worry that she was pushing her luck, that surely Phyl would soon be sending her guests packing, but there was still no sound from the hall. In any case, she couldn't tear herself away. She revelled in piecing together the ups and downs of the three horses' careers.

It was clear that Blaise Two was the most successful. There was a delightful large-format photo from a newspaper of the weak-chinned Mr Pascal in a winner's enclosure, standing alongside a sweating horse, a hand proprietorially on the animal's neck. It was captioned: 'Owner, Mr Pierre "Blaise" Pascal, with his winning two-year-old "Blaise Two" and his Irish jockey, Mr Patrick Cavan.'

So, thought Maisie, 'Blaise' was Phyl's husband's nickname – presumably for the French seventeenth-century philosopher and mathematician Blaise Pascal – and he had named his horses using the same conceit.

The idea made Maisie smile, but then she wondered – where was Phyl in all this racing history? The dates made it clear that the scrapbook was from the period of their marriage, and Phyl was knowledgeable in the field of horseflesh, as she had shown the other day, chatting to Ernest Sumner.

Out of the entire album, there were only two photos that included her.

What had happened to alienate her from something clearly very close to her husband's heart?

Maisie opened the second scrapbook and discovered the pages were empty. No, not empty, exactly. They had once been full of memories and text. That much was clear from the many marks left behind by glue and Sellotape. But their contents had been removed.

Maisie wondered when and why. To transfer to another volume of mementos or, perhaps, to destroy them? That would make sense if something had happened to drive Mr and Mrs Pascal apart. If that were true, what had alienated them one from another? And where was Pierre 'Blaise' Pascal today? Maisie had assumed he was dead, that Phyl was a widow. Hadn't Charity said that was the case?

Maisie rummaged through her memories. No, on reflection, she thought she was wrong. Charity hadn't said that. She had simply assumed.

But, if Pierre Pascal wasn't dead, could he be the reason that Phyl felt herself to be in danger, because her husband wanted to take revenge for some unknown insult or slight or crime? If that were true, why would he have waited so long?

Could he have been in prison? Had he emigrated and only recently returned? And how could Maisie investigate without knowing the full story of Phyl's past, when she had a pretty strong sense that the past was something Phyl didn't want to discuss?

TWENTY-ONE

Maisie almost jumped when she heard the door from the kitchen to the hallway open and the sudden increase in volume of conversation. She put everything back on the shelf, fairly certain she had returned it all in the correct order, then shut the glass door and turned the key. For a moment, it stuck, then locked with a satisfying click.

She went out onto the landing, leaving the bedroom door ajar, as she had found it, moving swiftly along towards the bathroom. Phyl saw her from the hall as she shut the door on her departing guests.

'Did you get lost?' Phyl asked, a curious expression on her face.

'I just ran up to use the loo and went the wrong way,' said Maisie, caught on the hop. 'I'll be down in a minute.'

Maisie went into the bathroom and wet her face at the cold tap. Her heart was beating very quickly. She felt guilty and sneaky and hated it. She really had no reason to be rummaging in her aunt's past. That wasn't her job – if, indeed, there really was a job.

Unless, of course, the past was crucial in understanding how it shaped the present.

She looked at her reflection in an ancient mirror whose silvering had begun to peel away behind its glass. She felt a fraud. Wouldn't it be better if she simply got a lift into Chichester to catch a train and return home – home to Paris and her uncomplicated life and uncomplicated job?

If, that was, she still had a job.

She sat on the edge of the iron bath, giving herself a few moments to collect her thoughts. In reality, putting aside the shock of almost being caught snooping, she actually felt quite at home in Bunting. And there was so much she might be able to find out and add to her own childish memories of family life.

She dried her face on the hand towel, glad that she hadn't used eyeliner or mascara. When she emerged onto the landing, Phyl was still lurking.

'Are you all right?' asked Maisie, descending the staircase.

'Any one of them might want to kill me after that,' she said.

'I'm not sure we should be joking about that sort of thing.'

'I'm not. The trouble is, I could end up needing their support for my own project, once I get the necessary permissions.' She waved a hand. 'I have plans for this monstrous old mausoleum.'

Recognising that Phyl seemed to be in the mood to talk, Maisie suggested they sit in the library. Together they lifted the slender trapdoor and Phyl went down to fetch another bottle of red wine.

'Just in case we need it,' she said. 'And we'll leave the trap open and let the basement air out. It isn't a bad thing for a wine cellar to be damp, but not too damp. All this rain . . .' Phyl drew the cork, looking critically at the fire that Maisie had neglected while she was snooping upstairs. 'Why didn't you look after it?'

'I did my best. Do you think it's gone out?'

'No, it's fine,' said Phyl, adding some smaller sticks. 'This will help.'

She held a double sheet from a broadsheet newspaper across the opening. The hot updraught sucked it in and Maisie heard the flames draw behind the sheet. Then the newspaper blackened and began, in its centre, to smoke and burn. Phyl let go and it shot up the chimney.

'When did you last have that swept?'

'I don't know, 1666?' joked Phyl, referring to the Great Fire of London.

'Soon after the house was built, then.' Maisie smiled. 'Being serious, though, do you feel a responsibility to preserve it, not to make changes, to respect the original Jacobean architect's vision?'

'I have enough responsibilities without preserving this damp manor house as if it were a national treasure.'

'Don't tell the heritage people you think that.'

'I'm not talking about a ghastly redevelopment,' said Phyl.

Maisie expected Phyl to go on, but she lapsed into silence and they both sat for a couple of minutes, their chairs opposite one another, at right angles to the hearth. Finally, Phyl raised her head from examining the Persian rug beneath her feet.

'I suppose I should fill you in, you know, on the people involved.'

'You said you wanted me to find everything out for myself, not to influence me.'

'I know, but I've changed my mind. It means I can't talk to you, tell you what I think. It's frustrating.'

'Don't worry. I can wait.'

'I'm going to describe my recent walk through the village,' Phyl insisted. 'It will help with the layout and the "dramatis personae", the cast of ugly characters.'

'They weren't all here this evening, were they?'

'Kimmings was absent with his sniffle.' Phyl frowned. 'Oh, that reminds me, what was going on between you and Dander?'

'You noticed that? I happen to know he left Framlington under a cloud and I wanted him to know that I know, if you see what I mean.' Another question had been nagging at Maisie's consciousness, one that might be linked to Phyl's lie about identifying the body in the stream. 'Earlier on,' she said, 'you told me you'd seen death in the war and that you didn't like it.'

'Who would?' retorted Phyl.

'No, of course,' said Maisie, with a sympathetic smile. 'But I wondered what the circumstances were?' Phyl frowned and Maisie thought perhaps she had gone too far. 'I'm prying. I'm sorry. I hate nosiness, too. Forget I asked.'

'No, it's fine. I drove an ambulance in World War II, in Portsmouth. The city was a target for German bombs, being an important naval port. The devastation was terrible. People talk about the East End, but the working classes in Pompey saw a terrible lot of destruction. Parts of the city are still in a dreadful state.'

'Did you have a medical training?'

'First aid. Not much use when someone's been buried under a ton of rubble or lost a limb to shrapnel.'

'How awful.'

'Pierre was a military doctor. My husband, I mean, Mr Pascal.'

Maisie realised she had almost given herself away by not asking who Phyl meant by 'Pierre'.

'Oh, yes,' she improvised. 'I think you mentioned his name.'

'Did I?' asked Phyl, vaguely. 'Well, he was Free French, fled the Nazi advance, came to England with nothing but the clothes he stood up in. Back home, if the war ever ended, he would be as rich as Croesus. At least, his family was and he was the only son. Because he had trained as a doctor, he rode in the ambulance with me and . . .' Phyl looked rather grim. 'Well, what was bound to happen, happened.'

'A love affair, you mean?' asked Maisie, lightly.

'A catastrophic error of judgement.'

'Oh dear.'

'You have to remember, at that time, all hope was gone. The war looked like it could only end one way: with a Nazi victory. I think Pierre calculated that marrying an English-woman might confer some advantages in such a scenario.'

'He didn't love you?'

'He wasn't the loving kind.'

'Poor you.'

'And I betrayed him,' said Phyl, surprisingly, 'as they say in popular fiction.'

'Well, I never did,' said Maisie, surprising herself by using Grandma Florence Wingard's old-fashioned phrase. 'You found love elsewhere?'

'I did.'

Phyl was slumped in the armchair and the expression on her face, in her eyes, was impossible to read. Maisie felt the silence become an uncomfortable, almost threatening presence. She wanted to break it but hesitated, not knowing what it was that oppressed her. Was it guilt at snooping, or was it the unaccustomed intimacy of Phyl's unexpected, unguarded confessions?

'You were going to tell me about a walk,' she said finally, 'and the "cast of ugly characters"?'

'I was, wasn't I.' Phyl yawned.

'Not if you're tired,' said Maisie.

'There is little prospect of me sleeping, so why not.'

Before she began, Phyl insisted on serving the two generous slices of game pie that Zoe had brought from the pub. She warmed them through by lying them on a piece of clean newspaper on the coal shovel and balancing it over the flames. The newspaper darkened as the fat melted out of the meat and pastry, sending wafts of delicious flavour into the room.

'Made by Zoe?' asked Maisie.

'Under instruction from Jenny Brook.'

'Yes, you said, the woman who runs the shop.'

'It's very inconvenient. She's almost always closed when you want her open, but she's a wonderful cook.'

Maisie's mind wandered to the books on Phyl's nightstand, especially the second one, about common poisons found in nature. She wished she could mention them, but didn't want to admit having been nosy. Wasn't it problematic, though, and typical of an isolated English village, that someone with murderous intent might find it beyond simple to introduce some hedgerow toxin into their victim's food?

From the same cupboard where she had found the decanter, Phyl fetched a couple of ornamental side plates with gold paint – or possibly genuine gilt – around their scalloped edges. She slid the two slices of pie off the shovel.

'Is that mushroom in there?' said Maisie, inspecting the filling.

'I hope so,' said Phyl, attacking hers hungrily.

Despite herself, Maisie couldn't help watching her aunt for a moment or two, wondering if this was what the Roman emperors or the Borgias felt like as their food tasters risked their lives, eating first to ensure that their masters' and mistresses' meals were untainted. Phyl didn't seem to notice her scrutiny and, in any case, showed no ill effects, so Maisie tasted her own. It was delicious, peppery and full of flavour.

'So, this walk you took?' she said, her hand over her mouth. 'I don't really know what you meant by that.'

'Let me tell you.'

TWENTY-TWO

Phyl's story took Maisie back to Sunday, when her aunt had apparently trudged alone through the village on a drizzly afternoon, looking in windows, peering over hedges, gazing up drives and contemplating her neighbours.

'There are people who mean well and others who don't, in Bunting as elsewhere. I'm talking about those who don't.'

'One of whom tried to decapitate you with a wire stretched across the drive,' Maisie insisted.

'Never mind that,' said Phyl. 'It's not important.'

'And may have given your lodger a handful of dangerous fungi that you then tossed away into the undergrowth beside the entrance to her encampment.'

'I've been reading up on poisons, by the way,' Phyl admitted. 'Those mushrooms aren't the only option in these woods.'

'And let's not forget the someone who tortured and smothered the poor lamb – or the body in the stream.'

'You do interrupt, don't you?'

'Sorry,' apologised Maisie. 'Go on.'

'Where are we now? Tuesday evening. So, it was two days ago. I was fed up, disappointed. I'd been in touch with Maurice Ryan via his rather austere secretary, Miss Clement, trying and failing to get hold of you. They said they would pass on my message. I'm very happy they did.'

'So am I.'

'Are you? Are you really?'

'Of course,' said Maisie with a smile. 'You're all I've got left.'

She meant it to sound light and friendly but Phyl did not at first answer and, just for a second, Maisie thought that there were tears in her aunt's eyes. She wanted to ask what was the matter, but Phyl abruptly gave herself a little shake and went on.

'Anyway, Sunday afternoon. Out I went, looking in at the windows of the Dancing Hare, thinking about how Ernest Sumner is a soak – not an embarrassing one, but drinking his way to oblivion all the same. And I don't trust an alcoholic. It shows they have a weakness. It makes them vulnerable.' Maisie raised her eyebrows, questioningly. 'I mean,' said Phyl, 'that it's easy to get a hold over them. I'm not saying they're all monsters.' Maisie nodded. 'You're interrupting without even speaking,' said Phyl, crossly. 'Are you going to finish your supper?'

Maisie had eaten only three-quarters of her game pie. She passed Phyl her plate and her aunt greedily demolished the rest.

'So,' she continued, her mouth full, 'I walked on, beyond the car park, into the shop.' She swallowed and wiped her mouth. 'Jenny Brook. You've not met her, vicious little wasp. I went in and bought a bottle of bleach, just to be kind. I'm her landlord and only charge a peppercorn rent, but she still thinks I'm exploiting her like Peter Rachman – you know, the notorious Notting Hill landlord?'

'Would that be enough to turn her against you?' asked Maisie.

'Not just against me, remember. Against me and Zoe, both of us together or each of us separately. Anyway, I don't know.' She wiped her mouth on her sleeve. 'After the shop is the lane and the farmhouse up-along. The rain was getting heavier so I went to have a sit in the porch of the church. I had a good view of Gordon's lower field where we have the bonfire and where he wants to build some horrible cheap houses and I'm opposing him. He has an idea Kimmings will come in with an investment. That was why he wanted Kimmings at the parish council meeting so badly, because I've told him I'm against him and he wanted Kimmings to help him and gang up on me.' Phyl snort-laughed. 'Fat lot of good it would do them. I'll not let it happen.'

Maisie thought back to what Phyl had said in the hallway, about the meeting giving each of the council members a reason to murder her. It was all a bit thin at the moment, but there was a definite crescendo. If the story went on in the same vein for much longer, perhaps it wouldn't seem so far from the truth.

'Of course, sat in the church porch, I got to thinking about the vicar. There are enough kids in Bunting and Harden and but it's been a long time since there was a Sunday school or beetle drives or any of that sort of thing at the vicarage. So, why's that?'

'Because there's no Mrs Dander?'

'Perhaps, but he's very high-handed with the little ones.'

'But no actual unpleasantness?' Maisie asked.

'Not that I know of.' Phyl pursed her lips. 'Kimmings is different. He's got a horrible temper and, when he plays the church organ – I forgot to tell you, he and Alice Spragg share duties as church organist – some of the choir children find reasons not to come.'

Maisie heard a sort of scuffling sound below them.

'What was that?'

'Rats in the cellar?' suggested Phyl, unconcerned.

'You have rats?'

'Everyone has rats. This is the countryside.' Phyl shook her head. 'Look, I don't like speculating and I only want to give you the incontrovertible truth. But be quiet again. I'm nearly done.' Phyl leant back in her armchair, putting her thoughts in order. 'Oh, yes. He used to teach a bit of piano. Kimmings, I mean, in his own home. He's got two of my workers' cottages knocked through. I sold them when I didn't know any better. Anyway, he got volcanically angry with some poor mite and word got about and he doesn't do any teaching of youngsters any more.'

'I see.'

Phyl's careless matter-of-factness was beginning to grate on Maisie. Perhaps that showed in her face.

'Yes, I know what you're thinking,' said Phyl. 'I should take this sort of thing seriously. But people don't want to talk about it, you see? They sidle away and whisper in corners but no one says anything out loud.'

Maisie thought about Jack, whose job and whose character made him always steadfastly face the truth.

'I agree.'

'Good. Moving on. I've been making a mental list. Stock and Kimmings want me to let them build houses where the stream – the Bunt, the winterbourne – is likely to flood. I won't let them. Jenny Brook resents the fact I'm her landlord. I'm Ernest Sumner's landlord, too, freeholder on the bricks-and-mortar of the Dancing Hare, so perhaps one or the other thinks I might want to get a publican in who doesn't drink his own profits. Then we come to Spragg, first name Alice. She lives on a meagre pension in a cottage I should have done up years ago but never got round to.'

'That doesn't sound like much?'

'And Spragg hates me because I'm rich. She's a class warrior.'

'Yes, you said.'

'She once called me "feudal mistress" because I wouldn't support the idea of a bypass round the village, cutting a swathe in my woods, taking the through-traffic away from her front door. "What through traffic?" I asked. "No one comes through but locals." She wasn't having that. "You wouldn't know, up in your ivory tower," she told me.'

Maisie nodded. Perhaps that might be enough to create ill will and malign intentions. But she doubted it was enough to make an insipid, retired librarian resort to actual violence.

Was Alice Spragg insipid, though? She had been very sharp and sure of herself in the prelude to the parish council meeting in Phyl's kitchen.

'So,' Phyl resumed, 'I walked past the workers' cottages, two nice ones knocked through for Kimmings and a shabby and draughty one for Spragg. Then I'm looking at the Becks' place – again, it belongs to me. It's an awful thing built by the previous "feudal mistress" in the hope that her married son would set up home there, but he died in the war and she decided to sell up and leave. By this time, Blaise had come into his inheritance and he decided to buy the manor house and the woods and the land and quite a bit of the village. When we separated, he tried to leave me with nothing, but I'd taken the precaution of having him followed by a private detective and had all the evidence I needed. In the end, he let me keep the real estate if I accepted that he would never pay alimony. I bit his hand off, as they say.'

Maisie thought that was a deal that a man might come to regret and resent.

'Did you call him "Blaise"?' she asked innocently. 'I thought you said "Pierre" before.'

'His nickname,' said Phyl shortly. 'Where was I?'

'You own the village and everyone resents you, but you've not told me much about the Becks – just where they lived.'

'I never much liked them. They moved in eight years ago, was it, with their fostering? Not long after Dander, though I don't think those things are connected in any way. The place didn't need to be smart and I hoped I was doing a good thing, letting them have it, like Jenny's shop, for a peppercorn rent.' Phyl smiled. 'I used to get Archie to take the two boys out on the tractor and show them farming life and fresh air and good food and all the rest.'

'The fostered children came from the cities?'

'From Pompey – Portsmouth – where the Becks originated. It was a good plan, to look after slum kids in the countryside.'

'You make them sound like very devoted people.'

'But then they abandoned Zoe.'

'I wondered about that. Wouldn't she have been under age?'

'She was sixteen on the fifth of November. The next morning, I found her weeping in the church porch with her little suitcase on the ground next to her, not knowing which way to turn. I went and found the Becks to give them an earful and found them all packed up in their little Hillman Imp with the removal van waiting. That's when they told me about the cancer and all the rest of it. I took Zoe in because she had nowhere to go. Later, I consulted my lawyer and signed up as temporary guardian to prevent her from ending up in a home and you won't believe the hoops I had to jump through for a social worker who barely knew Zoe's name.'

'So, someone did come to ask about her?'

'No and yes. The social worker responsible had recently been sacked for some kind of professional indiscretion which, in my experience, is pretty typical. The new one, a stringy little hippy, came and signed it all off and tried to persuade Zoe to rejoin the church choir.'

'Why?'

'To be "integrated in the community",' said Phyl with a sneer. 'As if she was still a child.'

'But you wouldn't call her an adult?'

'No, not really,' said Phyl, with a sad shake of her head.

'Is there more? Who's left?' Maisie asked. 'Gordon Stock. Did your walk take you up to his door?'

'Gordon has two reasons to resent me. First, opposing his planning application. The second thing is more recent, from just a week ago. Gordon turned up, assuming because I'd taken Zoe in that I was *in loco parentis*. He wanted me to authorise him to ask Zoe to marry him, for "permission to pay my addresses". It gave me quite a turn.'

'Poor boy, though,' said Maisie. 'What's his story?'

'His parents left him in the lurch, swanning off into retirement. He's only nineteen and she must have had him at forty, at least. It's hard for him, shouldering the farm alone. He's just joined the parish council in his father's place and, if you ask Zoe, he's been a friend to her and I'm afraid that means he's developed a bit of a crush that she absolutely does not reciprocate.'

'You told him so?'

'I've not had to fear violence from a man for many years, but I did that day.'

'Surely not?'

'He told me he didn't need my permission. I told him I'd have him thrown off his land. That was an empty threat. He owns it, even if he is digging himself deeper and deeper into debt.'

'And then? Did he touch you?'

'No,' said Phyl. 'He just sort of simmered in silence, without boiling over completely, then he shouted, "We'll see about that," and slammed out of the house. I know I sound callous, but I'm not.'

'I know, Auntie Phyl.'

'Stop calling me that.'

'Sorry.' Maisie pondered. 'You're different with Gordon Stock.'

'I am?'

'Not different, exactly. But you seem to feel some . . . I want to say pity.'

'I can see how it makes sense in his head. You know the old rhyme? "The farmer wants a wife. The farmer wants a wife. E-i-addio, the farmer wants a wife." I think it goes no further than that.'

'But you're also opposing his planning permission and he's broke.'

'Going broke. Not broke yet.'

'There's a sort of indulgence in how you talk about your lodger, too. Where does that come from?'

'Yes, I've wondered that myself. I think it was the first time I saw her, damp from the rain on Guy Fawkes Night. I remember thinking that she shouldn't stick around in a lonely downland village all winter – that she would have fared better in a city with dustbins to scavenge in and warm corners to sleep.'

'There's nowhere she could have found shelter here?'

'Like where?'

'A barn, for example?'

'Like in an Enid Blyton story?' Phyl shrugged. 'I suppose, but she'd be turned out. And what would she eat? She couldn't expect someone to be fetching her quiche every day from the pub.'

'But then she came back ten days ago and you approached her when she was putting up her tent and so on?'

'I didn't talk to her but I felt something shared,' said Phyl, looking like it was an idea she was articulating for the first time. 'I thought she had lost something and it was painful to her, that she couldn't get over it, get past it.'

'Like an unhappy marriage?' asked Maisie.

'No, something much deeper than that.'

Maisie waited a second then probed a little further.

'Like something else that has happened to you?'

'Something I thought could never be put right.' Phyl had slumped down in her armchair once more and her voice was very low. Maisie had to lean in to hear it. 'But, now, perhaps I'll have another chance.'

'Do you want to tell me about it?'

'Yes. But I won't, not yet.'

'Can you tell me why?'

'If I told you "why", you would know "what".'

Maisie heard the front door open – Zoe coming home from work. The girl put her head round the door, looking rather pale and exhausted, wished them both a polite 'goodnight' then disappeared.

'We should all go to bed,' said Phyl.

Maisie insisted on Phyl finding her house keys – they were in the drawer of the occasional table in the hall – and, together, they went round locking all the external doors and making sure the windows were properly fastened. Eventually, they bid one another 'sleep well' on the landing.

★★★

It took Maisie quite a long time to go to sleep and she soon rewoke and lay tossing and turning. Eventually, she went downstairs for a glass of water from the kitchen.

Perhaps it was the eeriness of the ancient house at night, perhaps it was all the stories of upset and dashed hopes, but she felt frightened, sure that something evil was close at hand.

She took her glass of water into the library to stand in front of the remnants of the fire. There was nothing left but a handful of warm ashes. In the darkness and silence, she thought she heard movement, a kind of scuffling.

Rats, again, perhaps?

Spooked, she bent down to grasp the poker. It clanged against the other fire irons and the scuffling stopped. Maisie waited, counting her rapid heartbeats, until she knew at least a minute had gone by. She noticed the dark shadow of the trapdoor to the cellar, still standing upright. Immensely carefully, she took hold of the two recessed metal rings and lowered it to horizontal, taking care not to let it bang and wake Phyl and Zoe. Finally, it was done. Was there a click of a mechanism locking as it fell into place? She wasn't sure there was.

She returned the poker to the rack and ran back upstairs, putting her bedroom chair against her door. She was thinking about something Phyl had said much earlier that day.

'But that's a new mystery because my lodger was a stranger so that doesn't count.'

Why had the phrase come back to her so clearly? What was it that felt so wrong about it?

She crawled into bed and, this time, through sheer exhaustion, she fell into an unsatisfying slumber and a sequence of unpleasant dreams of chasing and being chased, questioning and being questioned, crying and hearing cries. At one point she almost woke with a sense that somewhere in the ugly Jacobean mansion there was a broken heart and hopeless muffled weeping.

TWENTY-THREE

Maisie woke up, once again, rather later than she meant. Her tongue was furry and her head thick, as if she had been breathing all night through her mouth.

Oh no, she thought. *A cold. What a bore. Was it Kimmings's 'sniffle' on its way round the village?*

She got out of bed and washed and dressed, brushing her teeth for two minutes precisely. As she came down the stairs, she saw Phyl opening the front door, already wearing her waxed jacket, on her way out.

'I'm going into Framlington and, when I come back, the fridge will be full. I'm ashamed of myself.'

'Could you buy cold medicine?'

'I'll see what they've got.'

She left with characteristic abruptness and, ten seconds later, Maisie heard the crunching of reluctant gears as the Land Rover pulled away.

Maisie stood for a few moments, exactly where she was, halfway down the stairs. The house was very quiet, not like after dark when it seemed to creak and groan. Perhaps it was something to do with the damp of the night, or the abrupt fall in temperature after sunset or . . .

Maisie's mind was drifting back towards sleep. She roused herself to go and drink a large glass of water in the kitchen. It tasted stale, though it was fresh from running the tap.

Her cold, again.

She didn't feel like eating anything. She opened the back door and looked out at the untidy kitchen garden. Was it her imagination or were things beginning to grow? The air felt milder, too – no, not mild, exactly, but not chilly, either.

She decided to look through the parish magazines and other bits and pieces of local print on the kitchen table and found it was quite interesting, learning about the life of the village of Bunting. The parish included the neighbouring hamlet of Harden that she and Phyl had driven through on the way over. She turned the pages, glancing at black-and-white, hand-drawn advertisements for logs or manure, the programme at the Granada cinema in Chichester and the Savoy cinema in Petersfield, two taxi services, planning notices and the news column of the rambling club. There was also a copy of the *Chichester Observer*, still interested in details of the 'Framlington murder'. She wondered if Jack had attended the rededication service for the Tudor devotional book of sins and virtues.

Maisie sighed. What did it make her feel, immersing herself in all this random local news? That she would rather have something concrete, something more satisfying to get her teeth into – a clue that took her to the public library, for example, where she could look something up and think: 'Yes, that's the motive.'

Maisie got up from the table to make herself a cup of tea, drinking it sweet and black. It all seemed so unlikely, so unreal, but she had a plan – to talk to people and try, through conversation, to find out about their hidden motivations and, perhaps, their hidden misdeeds. She should begin with the ones she hadn't yet met – Commander Kimmings, for example, who had been noticeably absent from the parish council meeting, or Jenny Brook in the dismal village shop.

Maisie finished her tea and rinsed the cup in the big porcelain sink. She knew she wasn't really a detective, but she did have a system and a method, backed up by intelligence and, she thought, intuition.

She found a coat on the back of the kitchen door – a padded anorak with mud round the cuffs. It would do. She went out into the hall. Phyl had left the front door unlocked, obviously, despite Maisie's insistence on better security. And she had taken her keys with her, on a bunch with those for the Land Rover, so Maisie couldn't lock up behind her. Feeling she was contradicting herself, she went outside and simply pulled the door to.

It was quite a nice day, the sun was almost warm through the trees. Maisie realised she hadn't looked at the time or put on her watch. She had simply got up and gone about her business as if time didn't matter. Which, of course, it didn't, not really. She had no appointments, no meetings, no timetable to respect – just the days unfolding in front of her and her vague mission.

'Come on, now. Buck up,' she told herself.

She heard a car coming up the drive, grinding its tyres in the untidy gravel. She waited and soon it swung round the corner – a white Zephyr with police markings. Maisie smiled.

Jack.

However, it wasn't Jack who got out of the vehicle. It was Constable Barry Goodbody, the ferret-faced junior police-man who had taken against Maisie and who she had then made a fool of – not intentionally – with her freelance investigation. Half aware of what she was doing, she remained in the doorway, on the top step of three, looking down on him as he got out.

'Mrs Pascal in?' he asked truculently.

'Good morning, Constable Goodbody. No, she's out.'

'Sergeant Wingard asked me to tell you he'll be up the lane with forensics, coming at it from the other side of the hill, there.'

So, Jack is close by, thought Maisie. *Good.*

'Thank you. I'll mention to him that you told me.'

Goodbody looked at her as if he wanted to tell her to be on her way, that there was 'nothing to see here'. After a moment's hesitation, he just nodded, got back in the car, made an incompetent five-point turn, and drove away.

Now there's a man who deserves to have his head taken off by a taut wire stretched between the trees, she thought.

Her eyes widened.

Maisie, she told herself. *What sort of person are you becoming?*

Though she had intended to go and talk to the other villagers, seeing Jack was much more enticing. She set off for the shanty encampment, round the side of the house, past the library windows. At the rear corner of the building, she noticed a set of steps, leading to a low door below the level of the garden. The steps were overhung by the thickly leaved branches of an evergreen tree, casting them in deep shadow.

Maisie went down the steps and grasped the Bakelite door handle. It turned easily and the door swung outwards, scuffling across a few leaves and twigs that had collected at the bottom of the steps. The sound reminded her of something, but she couldn't place what it was.

She took a step inside, brushing a cobweb away from her face. The floor was slightly uneven and, as she stepped forward, her foot struck something that moved and rolled away. As her eyes adjusted to the darkness, she saw it was a log from a pile of dry timber. She was also able to make out bags of coal against one wall and a stack of old newspapers, presumably for lighting fires, lots of them spread out untidily across the dirt floor. Ahead of her was an opening through which she could see the high barred windows that let light into the wine cellar. She was in the other, darker part of the basement.

Then it came to her – the scuffling sound she had heard in the middle of the night.

Not rats but newspaper or kindling, disturbed by movement. Someone had been in here.

Hiding in here? Sleeping in here?

She visualised the trapdoor in the library floorboards, under the Persian rug. Was there a catch of some kind or had they just pulled up on the rings? It wasn't heavy. If there was no catch, anyone who could get into the wine cellar would also have access to the house.

Maisie grimaced with frustration. Was there danger or wasn't there? Should she take Phyl's stories seriously, or shouldn't she?

She made a mental note to ask Phyl if there was a key to the outside cellar door and, if not, whether they should put some substantial item of furniture on top of the trap to prevent it being used from below.

Then, with a feeling of relief, she climbed back up the steps to the overgrown garden and set off to find Jack, hoping he would greet her kindly.

TWENTY-FOUR

Maisie got rather breathless trudging up the hill – much more so than on her previous visit. She found her handkerchief and dabbed at her nose. It was beginning to run and her eyes felt scratchy.

'Damn,' she said, aloud.

She plodded on and found Jack and two other police officers at the scene of the tramp's encampment. They must have been there for some time because the place had been entirely dismantled, the different elements set out in tidy piles. One of the policemen was taking photographs of individual items, using a camera equipped with a powerful flash. Jack was crouched down by the remains of the fire in its ring of stones. The second officer was working alongside him with a sieve to remove unconsumed objects, setting them aside in a cardboard box.

Jack must have heard her because he looked up and smiled. Just for a second, Maisie felt it was only the two of them there, smiling at each other. Then he spoke, gesturing to the scene.

'Don't come too close,' he told her.

The spell was broken.

'I won't,' she replied.

He stood up, moving lithely towards her, as if he had been up for hours and was full of the energy of the day. Maisie felt weary just watching him.

'Jack, I think I have a cold. Better to keep your distance, perhaps,' she told him. 'Are you finding gruesome things?'

'No,' he said, raising an eyebrow. 'Did you think that we would?'

'I don't know.' Maisie sneezed.

'Whisky, hot water, lemon juice, honey,' he told her.

'Good idea.'

'And back to bed.' Maisie felt a jolt. There was something rather too intimate in his suggestion and she didn't know how to reply. Happily, Jack went on: 'I was going to drop in on you both shortly. Is Mrs Pascal in?'

'No, she's gone out to the shop in Framlington. I don't imagine she'll be very long.'

'I wonder . . .' He stopped, looking at her meditatively. 'I did promise, I suppose.'

'Promise what?'

'To bring you the preliminary results of the post-mortem examination.'

'Yes?'

'But do you really want me to tell you? Wouldn't you rather wait for your aunt?'

'Because she'll hold my hand and make sure I don't cry?' asked Maisie, more abruptly than she meant.

'No, I just thought we . . .' He frowned. 'Never mind. You're not yourself.'

'I'm quite myself, thank you. I just have a cold. I'm not a wilting flower.'

'No,' said Jack. 'You're not that.'

There was a moment of awkward silence.

How does he keep doing this, Maisie thought, *making me feel unsure of who I am and what I want?*

'Sir?' said the officer who was sieving the remains of the fire. 'I think that's everything.'

'Excuse me.' Jack walked away to look at all the objects in the cardboard box. Maisie followed him.

'It's what we thought it was, sir. And also, there's this.'

With a pair of oversized tweezers, the officer held up the remains of a knife with a short wide blade, the handle entirely burnt away.

'Is that the weapon used to kill her? Was she stabbed?' she asked.

Jack glanced round. He seemed surprised to see her so close. 'Didn't I tell you to keep your distance?'

She was about to argue but she saw he was smiling.

'Sorry. I won't interfere. Or could it be the one used on the sheep?'

'We will try and find out.'

'How will you do that?'

'The carcass is in Mrs Pascal's freezer.'

'It is? I didn't know.'

Another secret, thought Maisie, annoyed.

'Without the head and feet,' said Jack. 'Archie Close skinned it and put it by. Waste not want not.'

Maisie nodded. 'Can I . . . ?' she asked.

Jack stepped aside and she looked down onto the box at a collection of blackened objects, some small and round, others more like writhing metallic worms.

'It's the buttons and poppers and zips of burnt clothing, isn't it?' she said.

'Yes, that's exactly what it is. Why would our homeless lodger be burning clothes?'

'To hide something? Perhaps there was blood on them?'

'Perhaps,' said Jack. 'And another question we're asking ourselves is this. Why would a normal woman – a woman with reasonable dental care, good hygiene, unbroken fingernails, general good health – dress up as a homeless person and come and hide out in Phyllis Pascal's woods? The woman found dead in the stream, according to the pathologist, showed none of the markers usually associated with vagrancy.'

For a second, Maisie thought about telling him that Phyl hadn't properly identified the body, but she bit her tongue, hoping it wouldn't ever have to come out. It was a crime, wasn't it, misleading the police?

'You mean she wasn't homeless at all?' she asked him, just to fill the gap in their conversation.

'And now there's evidence of clothes having been burnt on her fire.'

'I don't understand.'

'No, Maisie,' he said, rather intimidatingly. 'Neither do we, but we will continue to accumulate facts until we do.'

***

Promising to pass on what she had learnt to Phyl, Maisie trudged back down the hill to the house. As always, when she met Jack and he was busy with his duties, she left disappointed and unsatisfied, like at the end of the practice session for giving evidence. It wasn't fair to want more, though, was it, when she had told him that – for the time being, at least – she had nothing to give in return?

She went in at the front door and stood in the hall, once again listening for creaking and rustling. There was a new sound, coming from the second floor.

She climbed the stairs carefully, attentive to any movement of the treads. At the head of the second flight, the floor above her own room, she stopped on a dark landing, the only light coming from a narrow slot window, like others in the house, glazed with tiny rhomboid panes of glass.

The sound was someone singing – a voice of exceptional purity and strength. It came from behind a heavy wooden door set into a frame whose top corners were cut off at an angle to follow the roof line – the entrance to an attic bedroom.

Without stopping to question what she was doing, Maisie turned the handle and stepped silently into a long narrow space with a bed at the far end. In the middle of the room was a record player with a vinyl 33 rpm disc on the turntable, playing at moderate volume. Zoe had her back to the door and was singing along, her beautifully rounded voice almost covering the original – something about losing her sight and no longer needing to cry. It was very touching, to see Zoe lost in the music, but also in control.

Then, annoyingly, Maisie felt a tickle in her nose. She scrunched up her face, determined not to sneeze and ruin the moment. She backed out silently, pulling the door to. As she did so, the song came to an end and Zoe stopped and Maisie hoped she hadn't given herself away.

She padded quickly but carefully back down the stairs, arriving on the ground floor to see a face at the window beside the front door, obscured by the old-fashioned glass, trying to peer in. She went and opened up.

'Can I help you?' she said, with a frown.

It was a stringy-looking man with long hair and an earnest unshaven face.

'To whom do I have the pleasure?' he asked.

'What do you want?' insisted Maisie. 'Why were you trying to look in? This is private property.'

The man clutched a leather document wallet to his chest, as if to protect himself.

'I, er, I hoped to speak to Mrs Pascal . . .' He fumbled for an official form from his document wallet. The paper was headed 'Social Services'. 'I'm Steve Weiss.'

A number of ideas competed for prominence in Maisie's mind. The man was almost certainly here to ask about Zoe, and Maisie was sure that neither the girl nor Phyl would welcome the attention of the authorities. Zoe had called her social worker a 'stupid hippy' and Phyl had complained at the 'hoops' he had made her jump through. She hoped Zoe wouldn't take it into her head to start singing again. Her voice was easily strong enough to be heard through the window of her attic bedroom.

'I'm afraid,' Maisie told him, smiling broadly, 'Mrs Pascal is absent today. Perhaps you would like to call again another time, perhaps later in the week?'

'She's gone away?' asked Steve Weiss.

'I don't know, I'm afraid. I'm staying with her but – isn't it frustrating? – I've only just arrived and we didn't have time to speak before she left.'

A calculating look came into the eyes of the social worker. Maisie wondered if she had gone too far with the ingratiating tone.

'I would like to speak to someone else,' he said, 'a young woman. You may have met her? Zoe Beck – or rather Richards? Would you happen to know if she might be in?'

'There's nobody here but me.'

The social worker looked up at the house. Maisie listened. All was quiet.

'You like singing?' he asked.

'I do,' said Maisie.

'I could hear you right out here.'

'Well, it's one of my favourite songs.'

'What was it?' Weiss asked.

What was it Zoe had been singing? Luckily, it came to her.

'Cat Stevens, "Moon Shadow".'

'Of course, it was,' he said. 'A very spiritual guy.' There was a small hesitation, as if Weiss was wondering whether to believe her, then he seemed to relax. 'I'll leave you my card.' He took one out of the fob pocket of his embroidered waistcoat. She took it. 'Later in the week, you said?'

'Or next week,' she replied, breezily.

He smiled and nodded.

'I understand,' he said, then turned off, slouching away down the drive.

Or never, thought Maisie.

She returned to the kitchen, placed the social worker's card on the table and put some water on to boil in the whistle-kettle on the gas stove. Might there be a lemon in the fridge?

Happily, there was – at least, three-quarters of a lemon, a wedge having been cut out, probably for a gin and tonic. In a cold cupboard set into an outside wall she found pickles and jams and marmalades and other preserves and, to her delight, a jar of set honey from a local producer.

She washed up one of the cups from the parish council meeting – Phyl really was extremely inattentive to household chores – and mixed her ingredients, then through to the library and found a bottle of Bells whisky in the cabinet where Phyl had located the wine decanter.

She sat down, and the hot whisky, honey and lemon did her a lot of good, improving her mood as well as her symptoms. The sun had come out, too.

She heard footsteps on the stairs and called out. Zoe appeared in the doorway, looking drawn.

'Has he gone, Steve-the-Sneak?' Zoe wrinkled her nose. 'Bit early for Scotch, isn't it?'

'I have a cold and I'm drinking honey and lemon.'

'And whisky.'

'That was in my prescription as well,' said Maisie, trying to lighten the mood. 'Is "Steve-the-Sneak" your social worker?'

'Not *my* social worker. Just *a* social worker. What did he want?'

'To speak to Phyl. To speak to you.'

'I don't want anything to do with him. Do you think he'll take me away? I'm an adult, aren't I?'

'I don't know. Do you become an adult at sixteen or eighteen as far as the welfare state is concerned?'

Zoe didn't reply at first, then she complained: 'There's nothing in the fridge.'

'Phyl went out to the shop. Did I hear you singing?' Maisie asked.

Zoe flopped down in the other bookcase armchair. 'Maybe.'

'It was very lovely. I mean, you have a lovely voice.'

'I saw him coming, looking out of the window, so I stopped. My mum and dad – I mean, Mr and Mrs Beck – made me join the choir and Steve-the-Sneak thought it was good for me to be "integrated into society". Idiot.'

'You didn't enjoy it?'

'You've met them, haven't you?' she replied, bitterly.

Maisie tried to catch up with Zoe's jerky thought processes. 'You mean the vicar.'

'Slimy Dander.'

'And Miss Spragg, the organist?'

'She hates me. And Dander's friend, the fat boy from the Royal Navy.'

'Kimmings?'

'Angry Kimmings,' said Zoe with a kind of smile, but one that hid something deeper.

'So, you left the choir so as to no longer come into contact with them?'

'What would you have done?'

'The same thing as you,' said Maisie, sitting down at the table and deciding to change the subject. 'Is the house noisy at night, in your experience?'

'What?'

'Creaking, rustling?'

'Maybe.'

'I mean, are there rats or pigeons in the attic, scuffling about, or juddering pipes?'

'It's a house. I'm usually listening to records.' Zoe shrugged. She got up and hovered by the door, as if at any moment she might bolt. Then she asked, unexpectedly: 'Can anyone go and live in Paris? Do you need a passport or something?'

'More or less anyone but, yes, you need a passport and, when you arrive, if you're going to work, you need other papers issued by the police.'

'You have to talk to the police? Why?'

'Well, they run the registration of immigrants. That's reasonable, isn't it?'

'I suppose.'

'Would you like to go to Paris?'

Zoe was looking at the floor. 'Passports are expensive, aren't they?'

'That depends on how much money you've got.' Maisie smiled. 'Nothing's expensive if you can afford it.'

'I've been saving up.'

'Good for you. And I imagine Mrs Pascal would help you if you wanted to—'

'How did you do it?' Zoe interrupted.

'Well,' said Maisie, carefully, wondering if she was doing the right thing. 'Like I told you, my parents died and I had a tiny inheritance and I used that to get myself set up and then I found a job and then it became routine, you know? Life just took on its own momentum.'

'But you had no help.'

'No.'

'Because you're an orphan.'

'I am, but that doesn't define me.'

Zoe at last met Maisie's gaze. 'Do you think that's better than your mother not wanting you?'

'I think both are very difficult, but life is what you make it, whatever cards you are dealt. You have to hope for the best.'

'Can I have some of that?'

'My cold mixture? Do you feel unwell?'

'No, I just want a drink.'

'You're joking, aren't you?' asked Maisie, light-heartedly.

'Am I, though?' Zoe demanded.

And with that, she was gone.

With an uncomfortable feeling that she had made things worse, Maisie took the precaution of pushing one of the bookcase-armchairs over the trapdoor.

V

CHARITY

TWENTY-FIVE

Maisie felt very sorry for Zoe, despite the girl's habitual rudeness. Maisie could still hear the tone of self-contempt as Zoe had bitterly derided herself as Phyl's 'charity case'. She decided it was time she took matters into her own hands. She had spent long enough waiting to be told things, looking for the right moment to probe what Phyl really believed or to wheedle official information out of Jack. It would be better to be active and to fulfil her promise and employ her conversational method, starting with the man Zoe had referred to as 'Angry Kimmings'.

Revived by her hot toddy, she strolled down to the village, taking the woodland path, thinking things through.

Because of the wire, she had to believe someone was intent on harming either Phyl or Zoe or both – it was far too dangerous to do as a prank. A dead body had been found in the stream on the far side of the woods, possibly not Phyl's homeless lodger – because the pathologist maintained she was in good health and Phyl hadn't properly done her duty – meaning there might be a missing woman to find as well as a dead stranger to identify.

She emerged from the path close to the pub, with the trio of converted workers' cottages over to the right, near the green, on slightly rising ground. It was clear which was which. The one inhabited by Alice Spragg was tatty – paint peeling from the window frames, a poorly maintained border under the front window, a scraggy lawn, a flagstone path slippery with green winter slime. The two knocked through to form Commander Kimmings' retirement dwelling were completely different – beautifully maintained with matching window boxes stuffed with winter-flowering pansies, and nicely proportioned herbaceous borders enclosing a bright green lawn. The path to the off-centre front door was paved in rough brick and not a danger to the postman.

Nor to Maisie, come to that.

Maisie approached the front door, composing her opening speech in her head. She had decided to go immediately on the offensive. But the door opened before she reached it, revealing a red-faced man of average height, but seriously overweight, dressed in a well-cut three-piece suit in good-quality grey wool. In fact, it was so well cut that it seemed to encase him, like the skin of a sausage, giving his corpulence shape. He wore a monocle on a black silk ribbon and was carrying a wicker shopping basket.

'Good morning, my name is Maisie Cooper. I'm Mrs Pascal's niece. I wonder if you might have a few minutes to spare me. You were too under the weather for the parish council meeting yesterday. I hope you feel better?'

Her voice had surprised him and he had half-turned, his right hand on the key, his left hand raising the basket involuntarily, like a shield.

Well, thought Maisie, *that's the second inadequate man I've frightened this morning.*

'I'm sorry, I didn't quite catch that?'

Maisie repeated herself, concluding: 'But I don't want to share my cold. Could we talk as you walk to the shop in the fresh air?'

'To the shop?' he asked, as if she had said something absurd.

'Isn't that where you're going?'

'Good heavens, no. I want eggs and milk.'

Maisie remembered something Phyl had said.

'Ah, not from the shop. From Gordon Stock's farm? I met him yesterday evening. You know him well, don't you?'

She left a pause. Finally, he turned the key and properly faced her. There was a definite wariness in his piggy eyes, a flush to his florid skin. Was it high blood pressure or alcohol, or just an outdoor life spent at sea?

'I know Gordon Stock fairly well, yes.'

'Then I'll walk with you. I need to speak to him, too.'

He looked like he wanted to refuse and glanced down at her shoes. 'You will find it muddy.'

'I'll pick my way,' she assured him.

'All right. If you wish.'

'Your garden is lovely. Do you look after it yourself?'

'Yes, I do. I'm not made of money.'

'Who is?' asked Maisie, cheerfully, holding out a hand for him to shake.

'Uh, well, some people . . .' he began. His hand was limp like a rag. 'Shall we go along, er, Miss . . .'

'Cooper.' Maisie was fairly certain he was pretending not to remember her name. She had an idea her arrival in Bunting would have been fairly widely discussed. She had appeared twice in the pub, after all. She decided to find out for sure. 'You may have read in the newspapers about what happened in Framlington, to my brother.'

'I did, I think, see something.'

'You know I helped the police?'

Was there a tiny pause before he replied?

'I read a little in the local paper.'

Maisie was feeling much better – the combination of her home-made medicine and the fresh air. They stood to one side as a battered Ford Cortina drove past, followed by a Volkswagen Beetle. She thought perhaps she might find something out if she goaded him a little as she had done Dander.

'It made the nationals, too,' Maisie told him, complacently. They crossed the road. 'It taught me a good deal about criminal investigations and, of course, when Mrs Pascal rang out of the blue . . .' She left the thought hanging.

'Yes, she rang?' he asked.

'To ask that I look into one or two events in Bunting.'

They had come to the bottom of the lane to Gordon Stock's farm. The yard and farmhouse were a hundred yards up the hill in a cleft in the Downs. The track was muddy so they separated either side, each walking on their own verge of clean grass, but Maisie could still hear Kimmings' laboured breathing.

'One or two events?' he asked.

'Odd things,' said Maisie, without explanation.

'Such as?'

'Why Mr and Mrs Beck should pack up so suddenly, for example,' she told him. 'Brutal for the girl, wasn't it?'

'I understand there was illness.'

'All the same – devoted foster parents by all accounts. What was the girl's name? My memory is awful.'

'Zoe,' he said, reluctantly.

'That's it. She sang for you in the choir, didn't she?'

He didn't answer. They came to a gate, tied back with a chain. He looked very red in the face.

'The yard is extremely mucky,' said Kimmings. 'We needn't walk in. Stock will come down from the house. He's expecting me.'

'Anywhere one goes,' she told him, 'one finds upset and deceit, don't you think? It always comes back to people, doesn't it? You must have broad experience of dealing with human beings and their foibles – as a naval officer, I mean.'

'Of course. The management of the men is the single most important aspect of command.'

194

Maisie recognised the tone of someone repeating something they had said many times before. Kimmings' eyes were fixed on the door of the farmhouse, as if he believed he could make Gordon Stock emerge by force of will. Thinking about his reputation as a bully, Maisie tried another tack.

'I spoke to Zoe's social worker this morning – and to a friend of mine, Sergeant Wingard. Do you know him?'

'I don't have any acquaintances in the police.'

'Why would you?'

'Indeed.'

'Why did you stop teaching piano in your home?'

'It was a service,' he mumbled, without looking at her.

'You mean you did it for free? I understood you charged the parents.'

'It became a burden, in the end.'

Gordon Stock came striding across the mucky yard, carrying a two-pint metal milk pail and a box of eggs.

'Here you go, Commander. Are we still going to the council, then?' he asked.

'Later, Stock. Just give me my things.' Kimmings held his basket over the gate and Stock put the box of eggs and the sealed metal churn inside. 'Thank you. Good morning, Miss Cooper.'

He left them and walked away, the fold on the back of his neck damp with sweat, despite the chilly March day.

'Anything I can do for you, Miss Cooper?' asked Gordon.

'I beg your pardon?' she replied vaguely, wondering if Kimmings' temper and guilty conscience could be connected with the body in the stream.

Gordon laughed and it sounded very natural and innocent.

'Well, here you are still.'

He wiped his hands on the jacket of his extraordinary suit – the same one he had worn for the parish council meeting. Under it, he wore a thick Aran jumper that had yellowed with age.

'Yes.' Maisie pulled herself together. 'Are you busy?'

'A farmer's always busy.'

'Could we speak while you work?'

He gestured to a fenced enclosure on the right-hand side of the yard. 'I could be feeding my chickens.'

'How interesting. I'll come with you.'

'Gladly. It's a poor life with only the beasts and the fields and I'd be happy to share a moment with company.'

He unwound the chain from the gate and pulled it open. Maisie made her way round the very edge of the yard, avoiding the worst of the mess, while he strode to a rickety shed, splashing through the muck in his heavy boots. She came to a tall fence, more than double her own height, presumably to keep foxes out. Here and there it was shored up with diagonal struts where the main posts weren't properly secured in the ground. At the foot of the chicken wire were bricks and fallen branches, placed to secure the bottom edge. It all looked very amateurish.

Gordon emerged from his shed and recrossed the yard, carrying a bucket of feed – some mixture of grains. Thirty or so laying hens were already at the fence, clucking and fussing, flapping their clipped wings.

'Away!' he shouted in a loud voice, pushing open a panel of wire on a flimsy timber frame. 'Away, now!'

He kicked several of the birds out of his way with his boot, hurling a handful of feed onto the untidy ground beyond them. They all turned and squawked and fought for it. Maisie found the scene unpleasant. The chickens resembled nothing so much as prisoners, desperate for their rations.

Gordon wandered about, hurling handfuls of grain in every direction. The hens began to calm down and the riot of clucking gave way as they realised that there was enough for all of them to concentrate on eating.

'They don't like their feet in the wet,' said Gordon with a sigh. 'I'm doing my best. I built them those coops for roosting.'

He nodded towards a set of four chicken coops, all different shapes and sizes, cobbled together from recycled timber – an old door, some cherry-wood fencing, a couple of forklift truck pallets. The coops were covered with sheets of tarpaulin secured with binder twine poked through holes in the corners and tied to the frames. It made Maisie think of Phyl's lodger's shanty. Indeed, one of the tarpaulins was brand new.

'Have you had storms, strong winds?' Maisie asked. 'Did you have to replace that tarpaulin?'

'I don't know what happened there, but it went, all the same. New one wasn't cheap, neither.'

Maisie wondered if the homeless woman might have stolen the tarp. She could imagine her, though they had never met, creeping about in the pitch-black night. There were only three street lamps in Bunting, by the pub and the green. The countryside lay in utter darkness beyond.

'When did you lose it?'

'Last week, was it? Bit more maybe.' He paused in broadcasting the feed. 'Did the wind take it down-along or have you seen where someone's pinched it?'

'I'm afraid not,' Maisie lied. 'Don't you have a dog to bark if anyone comes up here who shouldn't?'

'Used to. My parents' dog. It died.'

'And you wouldn't want another?'

'I can't afford one,' he said miserably. 'Anyway, no one's coming up here thieving a few eggs and I've precious little else.'

Maisie felt more and more sorry for young Gordon, burdened with a business he neither enjoyed nor understood.

'I believe you want to build on the lower field. Aren't you worried about the houses flooding?'

'We'll see the council about that and they'll tell us how to protect them.'

'That sounds reasonable, but can't you build somewhere else?'

'Got to be there. There were sheds before so that makes it a brownfield site so we're in our rights to ask for permission. You can see the old stones on the ground.'

'The foundations?'

'There weren't no foundations. It was just built straight on the dirt.'

'I see.'

Maisie wondered if there really had been sheds there, back in the mists of time. It sounded unlikely that there would have been cattle shelters on a floodable bit of land. Cows didn't like their feet wet any more than chickens did. Had Gordon – encouraged by Kimmings – come up with the obvious ruse of placing a few salvaged stones from somewhere else on the farm to give the impression that the lower field had been built on in the past?

Gordon emptied his bucket, tipping it upside down on the damp ground. There was an odd sort of pause. The sun had become much weaker, caught behind a veil of white cloud that covered the sky, the hens all busy pecking among the grass and grit. She wondered if he knew what he ought to do next on his failing farm, then remembered that Phyl had felt physically threatened by him.

Maisie took a couple of steps away, trying to give the impression that she was thinking something through.

'Why would someone smother a lamb in a field,' she abruptly asked him, 'then stab it in the heart?'

He answered quite naturally. 'I heard about that from old Archie Close. Some nutter.'

She tried again. 'Do you know anything about poisonous mushrooms?'

'I don't like mushrooms.'

'But would you recognise a deadly mushroom if you saw one?'

'I know what's not to touch, if that's what you mean.'

'You heard about the body that was found?'

'People talk,' said Gordon. 'Did she poison herself, then? Was it deliberate?'

If it's not the homeless woman, thought Maisie, *that is indeed another possibility.*

'We'll have to wait for the police to pronounce,' she said.

He stood looking at her, placidly. She hadn't succeeded in shaking or shocking him. There had been no real reaction to her questions – nothing to indicate that she had touched a nerve or persuaded him that she knew that he had something to hide. Perhaps he was telling the truth?

'Is the commander well off?'

'Old Kimmings? He seems all right.'

'And you and he will be in business together. Do either of you have experience in construction? It sounds like quite a risk – a lot of money up front in the hope of future sales.'

He looked at his chicken coops and Maisie thought for a ridiculous moment that he was going to give them as examples of his prowess.

'There's builders, aren't there, builders who can take charge if we get our planning permission.'

'If you do.'

'Happen we won't, though, not with Phyllis Pascal against us. I've been wondering about getting Zoe to speak up on my behalf, but I can't seem to find a moment to get her to myself.'

Maisie was shocked by the naked anger on his face. Affecting nonchalance, she repeated something she had said to Kimmings.

'I was talking to my friend, Sergeant Wingard, of the Chichester police. Do you know him?' Gordon didn't answer so she went on: 'I was telling him all about Bunting – everything I've seen and learnt since I've been here. He was very interested.'

'Are you warning me off or something?' he asked her, his eyes wide.

'Actually, yes,' she told him. 'Thank you for your time.'

TWENTY-SIX

Hoping she hadn't done the wrong thing, Maisie left Gordon Stock without looking back, thinking how she was using Jack's name as a kind of shield – like Steve-the-Sneak with his document wallet and Angry Kimmings with his shopping basket. She was more and more sure that there was danger – for Phyl, for Zoe or for both. If Kimmings or Gordon constituted a threat – again, one or the other or both – she felt she had at least given them a reason to hesitate.

She picked her way back down the farm lane, once again sticking to the verge. She had a brief vision of herself in uniform as an enterprising police constable, making brilliant deductions to impress handsome Sergeant Wingard.

In another life, she thought.

Her eyes were running – she wasn't sure if it was her cold or the chilly breeze – but she was reasonably satisfied with what she had achieved. Her intention had been to pressure Commander Kimmings and find out if he seemed guilty about something. She was certain that he had, but she didn't know exactly what. The pretext of walking with him up to the farm had been a bonus, giving her a way of following up straight away with Gordon.

She hesitated, her steps slowing.

Though the young farmer's anger had been disconcerting, she hadn't felt frightened. Was he combustible but, in the end, unlikely to lash out?

She walked on.

If Kimmings had a guilty conscience – about the wire, perhaps? – could that be the hidden reason why he had avoided the parish council meeting?

She reached the road as a small builder's van pulled up over by the converted workers' cottages. A man in a beige overall got out, carrying a clipboard, and walked up the slimy flagstones to Alice Spragg's front door. Maisie quickly followed, arriving just as the retired librarian answered.

'I'm sorry to intrude,' Maisie said quickly, stepping in front. 'Could I come and speak to you, perhaps later today?'

'I expect so,' said Alice Spragg, looking confused to see the two of them together on her doorstep. 'What might it be in connection with?'

'I'll be along before you know it,' replied Maisie with a bright smile. 'Thank you.'

She turned away, not moving too quickly, so that she could eavesdrop on the start of the builder's conversation.

'Miss Spragg? My name is Singer. Mrs Pascal requested a quotation for some remedial works. I have a list . . .'

So, thought Maisie, Phyl had acted quickly and charitably, taking it upon herself to put right one of her wrongs – the lack of maintenance to Spragg's rented cottage.

There was a board for parish notices on the corner of the green. Maisie stood beside it as if interested in what it had to say, hoping still to be in earshot, but she couldn't hear anything else. Then the builder went inside.

Maisie was left quite alone. The green was empty with not even a starling patrolling the wet grass. The air was fresh and, yes, carried a hint of spring. There were a few snowdrops poking through and, at the roadside, a handful of colourful crocuses. She blew her nose and took several deep breaths, closing her eyes, aware that she had accumulated quite a burden of stress from her conversations with Commander Kimmings and Gordon Stock.

She opened her eyes. Beyond the green, up the narrow road, just beyond the village, she caught a glimpse of a sludge-green vehicle, swinging up Phyl's front drive – the unreliable Land Rover.

Maisie set off, keen to get back and discuss her progress with her aunt, but there was Jenny Brook, the lady with the failing shop, standing on her front step, looking at her with undisguised curiosity. She decided to seize the moment and changed direction. The turf was spongy beneath her shoes as she crossed the green.

'I'm Maisie Cooper, Mrs Pascal's niece,' she called out. 'I'm very pleased to meet you. This must be your lovely little shop, is that right?'

'Oh, is that who you are?' said the shopkeeper, warily.

Maisie came closer and dropped her voice to a normal conversational level. 'It is, yes.'

'Did you want to buy something?'

'Yes, I did – I mean, I do.'

'You're the first,' she said with self-pity.

'I beg your pardon?'

'It's getting on for lunchtime and you're my first customer. I saw you with Kimmings, going off to buy eggs and milk direct from the farm. They all do that. Well, almost all. How am I supposed to make a living?'

'Awful for you,' said Maisie with a sympathetic smile.

'Did you get anything?'

'From the farm? No.' Maisie showed her empty hands. 'Can I come in?'

'A shopkeeper,' Jenny Brook insisted, 'has to be regulated and inspected and that all costs money. But the farmer just sells things out of his back door from who-knows-where.'

'From his own livestock, I suppose?'

The shopkeeper sighed. 'Yes, probably.'

'People like his produce, do they?'

'Seem to,' Jenny Brook replied grudgingly.

'Have you thought about buying it yourself and selling it on for a profit?' Maisie suggested. 'It would be much more convenient for people than traipsing up the muddy lane. For him too, surely, not being disturbed in his work every time someone wants a pint of milk?'

'I've never thought of that.'

'He might like the plan.'

Jenny Brook chewed her lip then surprised Maisie with a question: 'What do you think of him?'

'Gordon, you mean?' Maisie considered her answer. Jenny was a surprising character. From the way Phyl had described her, Maisie had formed an impression of someone angry, vengeful, vindictive. In real life, she just seemed defeated. 'I suppose he's the salt of the earth,' said Maisie, thinking that was a safe, charitable judgement.

'He moons over Zoe,' said Jenny with a sigh. 'He's just a kid, really. Do you think they'll get married?'

'I think it very unlikely.'

'I suppose he's lonely. I expect he means well. Bunting's a terrible place without money.'

'Is that true? It seems lovely,' said Maisie, smiling. 'Anyway, I'm not going to try and persuade you. Did I say I'm Mrs Pascal's niece? I'm Maisie. And you are . . . ?'

'Miss Brook.'

'Of course. That's right,' said Maisie, beaming, trying to make it seem that she had been told many kind and complimentary things about the miserable shopkeeper. 'Jenny, isn't it?' The woman nodded. 'Well, I'm very pleased to meet you at last.'

Maisie left a pause for Jenny to return the conversational ball, but she just stood there, limp and unengaged, like a housecoat hanging on a hook.

'Oh, well,' said Jenny, at last. 'Are you coming in?'

'I'll just have a look round, shall I?'

Jenny stepped aside and Maisie went in.

'What do you want?' said the depressed shopkeeper. 'I might not have it.'

Good question, thought Maisie. *I suppose I'd better buy something.*

'Washing powder, for hand washing?' she suggested.

'Oh, that's good. I can help with that.'

Jenny took Maisie round the dismal displays, finding a cardboard box of Daz on a low shelf. The contents were suspiciously firm, as if they had coagulated to form a homogeneous block. The suspicion must have shown in Maisie's eyes.

'If it's caked, you can scrape it out with a spoon,' said Jenny, quickly. 'It still works.'

Maisie paid, needing change from a pound note. Jenny scrabbled about in the till, unable to find the right coins.

'Round it up,' said Maisie, charitably. 'That will be fine.'

'Are you sure?'

'Of course. Or give me one of those.'

There was a display of Dobson's Traffic Light lollipops on the counter.

'Oh, yes, they're lovely,' said Jenny.

'By the way, did I see one of your library books at Mrs Pascal's house? Are you a big reader?'

'Why would she have a book of mine?'

'I mean it had your name on the little list gummed in the front. It was about mushrooms and things.'

Jenny shrugged. 'Not me.'

Maisie left the depressing village shop carrying the most expensive box of washing powder she had ever purchased and a hard lollipop, like a red, yellow and green marble on a stick. The sky had darkened a little but the clouds were moving quickly across the sky so she thought it would soon brighten up again. Glancing back, she saw

Jenny out on her doorstep, looking out for non-existent customers, unpeeling her own lollipop. Then Maisie saw her drop the cellophane wrapper on the ground and Maisie lost all sympathy for her.

A couple of cars went by in each direction, then a farm lorry that had to wait to pass at the bottleneck just after the pub. Maisie crossed the road and hurried back through the woods to Bunting Manor. As she emerged from the trees, Phyl was outside talking to Archie Close, the door of the Land Rover open, her shopping bags around her feet on the ground.

'Where have you been?' Phyl called. 'I got you some Anacin aspirin. I was about to send Archie to search after you.'

'Just out and about,' Maisie replied, negligently, 'but I have a lot to tell you.'

Archie put a finger to his brow in a kind of salute and disappeared beyond the kitchen garden towards the barn. Maisie helped Phyl carry the shopping indoors to spare her aunt's damaged hand. As she came back for the second trip, she grimaced as Archie came thundering past, his diesel engine incredibly loud between the trees.

Once all the shopping was away, the fridge was packed full of Danish bacon and Wall's sausages, Fray Bentos pies and pasties, Mr Kipling tarts and cakes, as well as three different hard cheeses. Phyl was leaning on the edge of the double sink, looking out of the window, her eyes vague.

'I'm going to mix another honey and lemon and take two of those aspirin,' said Maisie.

'Who are we, Maisie?' asked Phyl, wistfully.

'What's that?'

'I was just thinking, are we who we really are, underneath, or are we who we pretend to be, who we show to the world?'

'That's an odd thing to be thinking as we put away the shopping.'

There was a pause, then Phyl said: 'No one knows me, Maisie. No one at all.'

'Can that really be true?'

Phyl didn't answer.

The phone rang in the hall, shockingly loud. Phyl went to answer it, leaving Maisie rather baffled.

'That was Zoe,' said Phyl, coming back. 'Ernest Sumner is plastered. She wants to know if I can help. She has a shooting party at twelve.'

'Help what?'

'Plating up, serving, you know.'

'Have you done it before? Do you know what you're doing?'

'Yes, and how hard do you think it is?' Phyl opened the back door. 'You should take your medicine. How do you feel?'

'I don't think it's going to hang around. Do you want me to come?'

'I don't know, Maisie,' she said in a colourless voice. 'I don't know what I want.'

Phyl left. Maisie closed the back door and ate one of the pasties, sitting at the kitchen table, wondering what had happened to alter Phyl's mood. Then, taking advantage of the empty house, she decided to go back upstairs to have another look at Phyl's photograph albums and scrapbooks. To her surprise, the glass-fronted cabinet was locked and the key had been removed.

Oh dear, she thought, Phyl must have noticed her things had been moved. But why hadn't she said anything?

Maisie crept away, hoping Phyl wouldn't get the wrong end of the stick and blame Zoe rather than her. She also wondered if this could be the reason why Phyl was thinking about pretence and reality, because she realised someone had been looking – literally – into her past. Did that mean there a secret in those albums and scrapbooks that gave the lie to what Phyl appeared to be? And was that lie somehow connected to Maisie or to Zoe or to the body in the stream?

Maisie's mind began wandering, creating an unlikely scenario in which Phyl was actually Zoe's birth mother and had been obliged to give the child up by a cruel husband, Pierre 'Blaise' Pascal, who . . .

No, that didn't work. The ages made that unlikely. Phyl was probably too old, Zoe too young.

She tried to imagine a family connection between the homeless woman and Phyl herself but couldn't think of one that made sense.

Maisie went back downstairs to the library. Phyl's 'day book', in which she made a note of all her correspondence, was still there, balanced on the wide arm of one of the bookcase-armchairs. Maisie picked it up and took it through to the kitchen where the natural light was better. She mixed her honey and lemon and took her Anacin aspirin, without whisky this time, and sat down to leaf through the pages, starting at the most recent entry, then backwards through time. On each page was a letter Phyl had received and a note of how she had replied.

Maisie learnt that Phyl was on the board of a charity called 'Every One Counts', an organisation that attempted to help orphans and children in care to find accommodation, training and employment. She had recently signed up for a large annual donation and was expected at a board meeting in London the very next day. Maisie wondered if her aunt intended to go.

Phyl also supported at least three local charities. One provided support for the homeless. Another was trying to establish a nature conservancy in Chichester harbour. The third, called 'Stables Disabled', used horse riding as a therapeutic practice for handicapped children.

Maisie was impressed by the range of support Phyl gave and rather shocked by the demands placed upon her.

She found several letters from each organisation, asking for additional payments for special projects and requests to attend lunches and dinners, schmoozing other possible donors. Phyl seemed always to answer in the affirmative.

Maisie frowned. Did that make sense? Hadn't the divorce left her with property and land but no cash or alimony? Of course, there was rental income from properties in the village. Could there be some outside the village, too? And the awful salmon-pink house where the Becks had lived with Zoe was still unoccupied. How long had that been? Several months – from early November, in fact. Did that mean rents were depressed? And what was the paper pinned to the front door? It wasn't a repossession order, was it?

Thinking of income and expenses, Maisie wondered how much turnover Archie's labour could possibly generate. She remembered the categories in the accounts: 'Forestry', 'Arable', 'Livestock' and so on. How did that work? Could one fairly elderly man stay on top of all that? If not, where were the other labourers?

Maisie turned a few more pages, looking backwards for the moment when the Becks had departed around Guy Fawkes Night. There had to be correspondence of some kind.

She found it almost at the beginning of the 'day book', a letter from Mrs Beck confirming that they were leaving without notice. There was no mention of Zoe or the cancer, but there was a forwarding address in Portsmouth, near the cathedral in the oldest part of the port city. It was a place Maisie knew well from singing there in school choirs.

Here, she thought, *is my opportunity.*

She made a note of the address in her diary and returned the file to the library, putting together a plan in her mind.

TWENTY-SEVEN

Once the forensic investigation in Bunting was complete –
at least, the part of it that would take place at the scene of
the crime – Jack returned to the police station. He spoke
briefly to Inspector Nairn who was also a big supporter of
the Rotary Club charity.

'What did you think of the kids' poems, Fred?'

'Very good,' replied his colleague. 'When you were reading them aloud, their little faces lit up. Did Barry make any
progress on the West Dean establishment?'

'Shut down two weeks ago.'

'Who were the residents?'

'Long-term care, psychiatric disorders. Only three of
them left when it closed. The local health authority had
been running the place down for a few years.'

'Where did they go?'

Jack frowned. 'That's the thing. Barry hasn't located
the official records. You know how slow the local health
authority is to respond. And, apparently, the social worker
in charge isn't what you might call assiduous. It's going to
be a family house, now. There's already builders in.'

'So, they're simply missing? That's a scandal the *Chichester Observer* will soon be putting on its front page. Is the
house connected to the estate owner, Edward James? He
has some funny connections with his poems and his jazz.'

Jack shook his head. 'None at all. I'm considering sending Barry for some door-to-door.'

'You'll not drive out there yourself?' said Fred, sounding surprised. 'Barry's inclined to miss things. You remember the Tudor prayer book in the Church Lodge murder? That was virtually under his nose. Or is it by way of a test?'

'An opportunity,' said Jack, decisively. 'You never know, Fred. Maybe Barry will come up trumps.'

Jack went to his desk and made sure that he had a complete record in his notebook of all he had seen and done in the woods above Bunting Manor that morning. He came to the pages where he had jotted down a dry official record of his conversation with Maisie.

Why had she come trudging up the path under the trees? Oh, yes. Because he had sent Barry to tell her he was there.

Jack tried to force his mind to focus on the facts of the case, but it was difficult. He put down his pen, lost in memory, caught in the moment when he looked up and their eyes met and she smiled, as if she and he were alone and connected to one another. Then, like an idiot, he had told her not to come too close and the spell was broken.

He returned to his notes. The knife discovered in the ashes looked very much like it would correspond to the wound on the sheep found stabbed with a short wide blade by Archie Close. It was a bonus that the carcass had been retrieved from Mrs Pascal's freezer. But what did he now think of Maisie's idea that someone had been practising murder? Far-fetched but, incredibly, it seemed she might be right. After Maisie and Phyl had left, he had seen the wound to the woman's chest through her sodden ragged clothes.

Jack sighed. It really wasn't fair. Just as he had begun to believe that the repercussions of Maisie's brother's murder were beginning to fade, Maisie had to go and get involved in this new drama and . . .

No, that wasn't fair. Maisie hadn't gone looking for more trouble and upset. Mrs Pascal had come to her.

He ran his finger down another page of his notebook. Had Maisie understood the significance of the burnt clothing? He regretted letting her see what the forensics officer had found. He didn't want her to go off 'freelancing'. Foolishly, he'd drawn her in with his rhetorical question.

'*Why would a normal woman, a woman with reasonable dental care, good hygiene, unbroken fingernails, and in general good health – dress as a homeless person and come and hide out in Phyllis Pascal's woods?*'

He'd gone too far, there. He wished he could take the words back. Now he was certain that somewhere in this tangle of unexplained events there was danger and evil intent, he wished he could pick Maisie up and put her down somewhere safe, far away from Bunting Manor. He didn't think she'd yet seen the significance of the dead woman being in good health, but he knew she would, in time.

She hadn't, however, caught a glimpse of the dirty scrap of paper, found inside the tent, with a couple of paragraphs copied out of a book on hedgerow poisons. He had kept that to himself.

Police Constable Barry Goodbody came in from beat duty in the city centre. He looked cold. He'd probably forgotten to put on a vest beneath his shirt and woollen uniform jacket. Jack gave him his instructions, concluding: 'So, this is important – top priority. Go door-to-door in West Dean, round the neighbours, the public house, the forestry manager, Edward James himself in his stately home – anyone who might know what became of the residents of the halfway house.'

'Can I have a cup of tea first?' asked Barry.

'No, you can't. I want this done by close of play. Take the car. Put the heater on. You look shrammed. I'm going to the post-mortem.'

Jack got up and went through to the front desk. Sergeant William Dodd – an elderly officer in a tired but well-kept uniform – was having a leisurely read of the *Chichester Observer*.

'I saw you at the cathedral on Sunday, Jack. You were with the VIPs in the crypt, weren't you? A lot of fuss for a funny little book,' said William.

'A very special book,' said Jack. 'Anyway, see you later.'

He went outside and set off. The walk to St Richard's Hospital would only take ten minutes. Waiting at the level crossing, he reflected on the fact that the 'funny little book' was the reason Maisie had come back into his life.

It was the most important book in the world.

Twenty-Eight

In the kitchen at Bunting Manor, Maisie began to feel guilty that she hadn't offered to help Phyl and Zoe at the pub. She looked round for the house keys and, eventually, after increasingly frustrated searching, found them in the fridge where Phyl, in her distracted state, must have put them by mistake.

She checked all the doors, remembering at the last moment that she had forgotten to ask Phyl about a key to the exterior door to the basement.

Oh well, she thought. *It's been unlocked all this time, a few more hours won't hurt.*

She went outside, thinking about all the charity work Phyl was engaged in – hadn't she said she had big plans for Bunting Manor itself? – then realised she was barely paying attention to the beauty of the countryside on the pathway through the trees. How quickly it had become routine, a part of her everyday life – yet so different from the hustle and bustle and honking traffic of Paris.

When she got to the Dancing Hare, she found a tractor and trailer in the car park with a dozen men climbing down – the shooting party Zoe had mentioned. They had mud on their boots and gaiters, noisy and excited from their morning's sport, several of them swigging from hip flasks. They carried their shotguns broken over their arms for safety.

Maisie recognised Archie, stringing up several brace of dead birds by their feet along the outside rail of the trailer, heads down, blood dripping onto the panelling and the ground. Did that mean the shoot was on Phyl's land? Were they Phyl's birds? That might be a lucrative sideline in the proper season.

One of the men, very tall with grey hair brushed back, asked for a moment of quiet and Maisie realised he was about to make some kind of pre-lunch speech. She decided to take advantage of the pause to slip into the Dancing Hare ahead of them.

Zoe was behind the bar. There were only five customers indoors, none of whom Maisie recognised. She supposed that village people kept away when they knew the pub would be taken over by noisy outsiders.

'How's Mr Sumner?' Maisie asked.

'Everything's plated up, but Ernie's hopeless,' said the girl, looking frustrated.

Maisie was interested to learn that Zoe called her boss 'Ernie', as if he was a friend.

'Can I do anything?'

'Maybe talk to him, make sure he doesn't get in the way?'

'Okay, where do I find him?'

'Through the kitchen, up the stairs.'

The front door opened, banging clumsily against the wall, and the shooting party tumbled noisily inside. Zoe skipped quickly out to welcome them and show them to their tables.

Maisie went behind the bar, through the door to the kitchen and found Phyl with two plates expertly balanced on each arm, ready to serve.

'Zoe asked me to keep an eye on Mr Sumner?' she told her aunt.

At that moment, the landlord appeared at the foot of a set of narrow stairs, leaning against the wall, both hands wrapped around the banister, as if he was on a lurching deck at sea.

'Thank you,' said Phyl, in an undertone, 'he keeps coming down and interfering.'

'Understood,' Maisie whispered, then she brightened her voice. 'Mr Sumner, how lovely to meet you. Shall we go upstairs?'

***

It wasn't easy to get Ernest Sumner settled in his crowded first-floor sitting room. Maisie didn't enjoy drinking to excess herself, but she knew there were many and complex reasons why someone might. Ernest was drunk enough to lose the thread of what he was talking about, but his state of inebriation was sufficiently recent that he hadn't forgotten he had a gang of happy men in his bar with whom he wanted to share his expansive thoughts.

'Don't you think I should go down?' he slurred.

'No, much better not,' Maisie insisted. 'Everything is under control downstairs. Shall we have a sit-down?'

For a second nothing happened, then Ernest flopped into the nearest chair, a low, two-person sofa with a fabric cover that had been several times repaired with hand-stitching. His hands lay palms up on the cushions either side of his thin thighs.

'Important customers,' said Sumner. Then he frowned. 'Aren't they?'

'They're making speeches,' Maisie told him, embroidering the truth. 'They won't want anyone else there. It's really quite formal.'

'I like speeches,' said Ernest, his eyes unfocused. 'Another time, perhaps . . .'

'Can I get you anything?' Maisie asked.

'Might you bring me a glass of water?' he said, vaguely.

'Of course.'

The low-ceilinged room was horribly over-furnished, with three bookcases of different sizes in different woods, a small dining table with three upright chairs, a television on an old battered chest, a radiogram, a chest of drawers almost the same height as Maisie, as well as the sofa and a matching armchair. On a tall table behind the sofa was a tray with glasses. Maisie took one and went to fill it at a small wash-basin in the corner.

'Run the tap, would you?' said Sumner. 'Lead pipes, you know.'

Maisie made sure the water was properly clean and cold and gave him the glass. He drank it down.

'Another? Would you mind? You are very kind, Miss . . .'

'Miss Cooper, I'm Mrs Pascal's niece. Do you remember?' Maisie refilled his glass.

'I do, of course,' he said, unconvincingly. 'How interesting. What a life you lead.'

Do I, wondered Maisie, *or are you confusing me with someone else?*

She sat down opposite him on the fabric armchair. As she did so, it released a puff of dust. Looking around, it was apparent the crowded room hadn't been cleaned for some time.

Ernest Sumner drained his second glass and twisted round to put it behind him on the sofa table. When he turned back, his eyes were closed.

Maisie wondered if she should let him drift off to sleep. She had accomplished her mission and got him out of the way of the busy pub. She could hear the happy voices from downstairs, shouting and laughing. Then, abruptly, his eyes snapped open and he sat up straighter.

'What were we talking about?'

'We weren't, actually.'

Maisie smiled. Ernest had a nice face. He was a little thin and his complexion was compromised by a fine web of broken blood vessels, but Maisie thought he looked intelligent behind the haze of alcohol.

'No, it was Zoe I was talking to. She's a lifesaver.'

'I suppose she's a sort of unofficial cousin to me,' she told him, 'now that Mrs Pascal is looking after her?'

'I thought she had a mother?' said Ernest, his eyes vague.

'We all have mothers, don't we?'

'Mrs Beck.'

'That's right. She moved away.'

'Oh, yes. But she came back.'

Maisie felt her attention quicken. 'When did she come back, Mr Sumner?'

'Oh, recently, you know.'

He waved a hand but it was impossible to know if it meant in the last ten minutes or the last ten weeks.

'Did she come in to see you? Is that how you know?'

'She came in with another lady. They sat in the nook by the fire.' He yawned. 'Where you sat the other day, you know?'

So, Sumner's memory isn't that bad, thought Maisie.

'How long ago was this? A week? A month?'

'Oh no, not that long.'

'Days?'

'Yes, days.'

'And who was the other lady?'

'She was the one who comes,' said Ernest, yawning again. He leant over, resting his head on the arm of the sofa. 'I'll be more use if I have forty winks. Must be ready to . . .' his eyes closed and spoke in a sing-song voice '. . . wash up and dry, wash up and dry . . .'

'Mr Sumner,' said Maisie loudly, 'who was the other lady who comes? Is she local?'

'I think so,' he said, his voice very faint. 'She was at the bonfire, wasn't she?'

'What does she look like?'

Ernest Sumner said something so low and quiet that Maisie had to lean in and ask him to repeat himself. He smiled without opening his eyes.

'Two people,' he said.

'What do you mean?'

'She looks like two people.'

***

Maisie tried to get Ernest Sumner to talk some more, but he was gone, lost, profoundly asleep. Now and then his lips moved, as if he was dreaming of speech, but the words – if there were any words – were indistinct. There was nothing more to be gleaned.

She found a blanket in a small adjoining bedroom that smelt of his John Player Special cigarettes, Old Spice after-shave and lavender talcum powder, and brought it through to drape over him. Then she left Ernest Sumner to his dreams.

Downstairs, the members of the shooting party had all emptied their plates. Zoe was clearing and Phyl was giving them each a bowl of treacle sponge. There were already blue-and-white jugs of hot custard on the table. Maisie found the noise oppressive so she went to stand outside.

As she had anticipated, the clouds had blown through. Sheltered from the breeze, the sun was warm on her face. Still, she was glad of her padded anorak with dirty cuffs and felt her cold medicines were taking good effect.

What had Sumner meant, she wondered? Two people? Did he mean someone whose job requires that they wear a uniform while in civilian dress they seem like a different person? Jack often seemed different out of uniform, unless circumstances obliged him to use his 'constabulary' voice. Or was it more subtle, that the unknown woman was a different person depending on who she was with? That was quite common. Look at Phyl. She was harsh and autocratic with some people, warm-hearted and forgiving with others.

Maisie sat down on a stone bench under one of the pub windows, tucking the tail of her threadbare anorak under her bottom. She breathed deeply, enjoying the scent of spring.

She tended to think it was the first idea, someone who appeared in different guises. Someone who had been at the bonfire, as well. Was that important? The bonfire was months ago. Why did it ring a bell? Because of the story Phyl had told her about the homeless woman having turned up for the first time on Guy Fawkes Night.

Maisie wished she could go back upstairs and question Sumner more closely, but that would have to wait for him to sober up. And he hadn't seemed completely sure about whether the woman was local. He'd had a vague look as he reminisced about the bonfire.

What about Mrs Beck, Zoe's foster mother, who Sumner said had recently come back? Did that have something to do with the social worker, Steve Weiss, poking around? Could Maisie trust Sumner's vague guess that it was just a few days ago? Maybe, maybe not, but surely it had to be recent, no longer than a week at the most?

She was glad to hear that he considered Zoe a 'lifesaver'. She thought about how she would describe Phyl's ward – spiky, damaged, changeable, challenging? For 'Ernie', she was clearly hard-working and personable, a godsend when imbibing his own wares got the better of him.

The pub door opened and the shooting party came tumbling back out, like a pack of happy dogs finally allowed outside after five minutes' scratching at the door. They trooped round to the car park and began hauling themselves up onto the trailer, taking their seats on the hard benches down either side. A moment later, Archie emerged, rolling a cigarette in his stubby fingers.

'Archie,' said Maisie, abruptly, 'could I ask you something?'

The man flinched. 'Here, you did make me jump.'

'I'm sorry. Tell me, are pheasants in season just now?'

'Mrs Pascal gets a special licence.'

'Of course. One other thing – I wanted to ask you about the homeless woman, Phyl's lodger?'

'Go on, then.'

He licked the Rizla paper and put the slim cigarette in his mouth.

'What did you think of her?'

'What I told your pal, Jack Wingard.'

'And what was that?'

'That she wasn't what she pretended but that didn't mean I knew what she really was.'

On the trailer in the car park, several of the men of the shooting party called out to Archie and banged their feet on the floor, good-humoured but anxious to get going and shoot more defenceless birds.

'All right, gents, I'm coming,' Archie called. Then he surprised Maisie by saying: 'You're good for Mrs Pascal. She's right glad you came.'

'So am I,' said Maisie with a smile.

She wasn't certain that she meant it, though. She was beginning to feel uneasy. What really was Phyl's motivation? And why had she been absent from Maisie's life for so long?

'I hope you have a good afternoon,' she told him.

'They're worse and worse shots as time goes by and their flasks get emptier. Let's hope they don't hit one another.

They're precious unlikely to hit many more birds.' He tutted. 'Well, there 'tis.'

Archie wandered away, raising a hand. The men on the trailer whooped and cheered. Maisie grinned, despite herself.

How happy they were, escaping from their lives, having a jolly adventure out in the countryside with their deadly toys, their guns. She was glad they were unlikely to hit any more defenceless pheasants.

She watched Archie haul himself up into the cab of the tractor and expertly reverse the trailer out into the road. He pulled away, past the green and the cottages and the church. Watching them go, Maisie reflected that she hadn't yet spoken to Canon Dander one-to-one. She wondered if the vicar might be available right then, or if he might be out and about, ministering to the elderly and sick in their homes, or on important business at the cathedral in Chichester.

She went back inside the pub, glancing at the clock above the fireplace. Zoe was behind the bar, washing up glasses. It was almost three o'clock, the end of lunchtime opening hours. Last orders had been called. Soon the pub would lock its doors, allowing her to make good on her promise to drop in on Alice Spragg.

'That went well,' said Maisie. 'You're very good with them.'

'They like me,' Zoe replied.

'Too much?' asked Maisie, lightly.

'They were all right. I've seen worse.'

'Good – I mean, it's good that they were all right. I'm sorry that you've seen worse.'

The final customers, a youngish couple with open country faces, got out of their chairs and made towards the door. Maisie stepped aside to let them leave.

'Shoot the bolts top and bottom, would you?' said Zoe.

Maisie did so.

'Do you have to stay and prep the evening service, Zoë?'

'No evening meals tonight. Just serving behind the bar later.'

'Is that legal – at sixteen, I mean?'

'I don't drink, do I? No one's said anything.'

'Do you like your job?' Maisie asked.

Zoe shrugged. She hung up half a dozen wine glasses on a rack above the counter. Maisie admired Zoe's dexterity and efficiency and tried another tack.

'Just before the social worker came, I heard you singing.'

'You said.'

Zoe had finished washing glasses. She dried her hands methodically on a tea towel branded by the local brewery, her eyes down.

'I was upstairs, you see.'

'He didn't hear?'

'I made him think it was me. Is that important?'

'No, I just didn't want him to know I was in.'

'Surely you can't be taken back into care?' Maisie waited for Zoe to reply, but the girl seemed frozen, the tea towel scrunched up in one fist. 'You have a lovely voice. I was very impressed.'

'What do you know about it?'

'Well, I'm not an expert but I did sing in choirs to quite a high level when I was around your age, school then city then county then South of England. You have talent and good tone and you could take it further if you wanted to, if you found the time and the right opportunities.'

'Out here?' said Zoe, vaguely gesturing.

'You mean in Bunting?'

'Stuck out here where there's no one but petty old men and jealous old women.'

'They're not all old,' said Maisie. 'Though I suppose they seem that way to you. And life has a way of surprising you. Good things sometimes happen without any warning.'

'And bad things, too.'

'Yes,' Maisie agreed.

Zoe threw down the tea towel and sighed.

'Why couldn't they have taken me? I'd have been all right in Portsmouth. I would have been better in a city where I had things to do and could make friends and have a normal life.'

Maisie sympathised. As a teenager, she had hated being trapped in Framlington.

'I don't know, Zoe.'

'I mean, I wasn't perfect, but how did they expect me to behave if they kept me prisoner and made me look after the kids?'

'Do you mean the other foster children?'

'The two little ones, Bruce and Arif. They were all right. Mr Beck was all right. But she, Mrs Beck, should have tried to be their mum, not me.'

'You're right. That wasn't your responsibility.'

'But they didn't have to just leave, did they?'

Maisie hesitated. There was a lot to consider – to do with Zoe's admission of bad behaviour but also the way Mrs Beck in particular had treated her.

'So, they would have been all right if they'd given you some freedom, if they hadn't made you their skivvy?'

'No.' Zoe sighed. 'She was always shouting.'

'At you or at everyone?'

'Just me.'

Maisie felt a surge of sympathy for Zoe.

'What about Gordon? He likes you.'

'I know, but that just makes it worse,' Zoe complained. 'It was all right when we were just friends, when we were just kids, but now he keeps talking about love and marriage and everything's spoiled.'

'That is awkward. Has he actually come out and proposed?'

'No, but he told Mrs Pascal he was going to.'

'Did you know my aunt well before she took you in?'

'Of course. We'd been years in the village.'

'Do you mind me asking why you think she did it?'

'Pity.'

Maisie visualised the story Phyl had told, of finding the girl in the church porch with her sad little suitcase, weeping.

'Maybe she did it because she saw something in you, something strong and worthwhile? How about that?'

Behind Zoe, Maisie realised that Phyl was standing in the doorway that led through to the kitchen. She caught Maisie's eye and nodded, encouraging her to continue.

'I don't know—' Zoe began.

'I can see great potential in you,' Maisie interrupted. 'Life is long. There's no telling all the things you might achieve. The people in this village, maybe they haven't got much ambition or drive. Maybe some of them have been unkind to you – are still being unkind to you. Maybe there's truly nothing for you here. But they've led their lives, haven't they? Maybe they've done all they set out to do. Maybe this is just where they've ended up.'

'If that's all life is, I don't know if I even want it,' said Zoe fiercely.

'No,' said Phyl suddenly. 'Don't joke about that sort of thing.'

Zoe swung round, surprised. 'I'm not joking,' she said, almost shouting. 'You don't know what it's like to be trapped.'

'Yes, I do,' said Phyl, sharply. 'I know what it means to be trapped by something, not by circumstances, but by my own actions, and it's taken me thirty years to face it.'

There was something in Phyl's tone that made Zoe calm down.

'I'm sorry, Mrs Pascal.'

'I'm going to look after you, Zoe,' Phyl insisted, 'however much you kick against it. I will help you and try to make sure you find direction and happiness.'

'You said that already,' said Zoe, truculently, but with less ferocity. 'Lots of times.'

'That's all right, then. Everything's tidy in the kitchen. You remember you promised to come with me this afternoon? Maisie will accompany us.'

'Yes, I remember.'

'And you promised to change your clothes?'

'All right,' said Zoe wearily. 'I said I would, didn't I?'

The three of them exited through the kitchen, shutting the door on the Yale latch, Maisie wondering what it was they had to do.

They walked back together to Bunting Manor, through the woods, none of them saying a word. Two-thirds of the way there, Maisie was struck by the idea that the snib of the Yale lock on the door of the Dancing Hare hadn't quite clicked home.

TWENTY-NINE

To Maisie's surprise, it turned out that Phyl had insisted that the village turn out for a remembrance service for her lodger. There was, in any case, a midweek evensong at four o'clock, so Phyl had asked Canon Dander to insert a suitable passage of scripture, inviting the congregation to pray for the woman's soul.

Maisie, however, was beginning to think that the question of who the woman was had become more important than how she died. And, of course, what she had been looking for in Bunting. Did Phyl know?

Maisie was sitting between Zoe and her aunt on a kind of platform to one side of the nave. Phyl explained that the platform belonged to the Big House, built by a seventeenth-century lord of the manor to give a semblance of privacy and class segregation to their worship. It gave them a view over the whole church.

The nave wasn't full at first, but the congregation built quickly to thirty-five, to forty, to more than fifty. It included every one of the people that Maisie considered her 'dramatis personae', her cast of characters, plus the fresh-faced youngish couple from the pub, plus others, so Phyl said, from the neighbouring village of Harden and beyond.

Phyl hadn't changed her clothes but her mood was much brighter. Zoe was wearing a black dress from Phyl's wardrobe, plain and straight, covered by a long woollen cardigan in soft cashmere.

To Maisie's astonishment, given she had left him unconscious in his upstairs rooms only a little more than an hour
before, Ernest Sumner was present. He looked reasonably
in control, his hair mussed from sleeping on his sofa, his
eyes bloodshot. Jenny Brook was sitting next to him, presumably having closed her shop for the duration of the
service. Commander Kimmings came in with Alice Spragg,
speaking in low urgent tones. Kimmings took a seat in the
congregation and Alice Spragg went to her seat at the organ.
Gordon arrived, dressed improbably in an ill-fitting dinner
jacket, presumably his only decent 'black'.

Just before the service began, a cluster of choirboys from
the cathedral school in Chichester arrived, processing up
the nave in their red cassocks and white surplices, not one
of them more than four feet tall.

'They come out into the sticks,' whispered Phyl, 'on
a sort of rota round the parishes for sung vespers. They
really are rather wonderful. Next week they might be in
Framlington, then Bosham, then Southbourne. That's
why there's so many people in the congregation. I couldn't
miss this opportunity.'

'You mean for a memorial?'

'Not just that. To get the word out. You'll see,' said Phyl,
cryptically.

Maisie saw Jack Wingard arrive, in uniform, with Constable Barry Goodbody. They found a space at the back,
giving her a flashback to her brother Stephen's cremation
service. It made her realise how far she was from a solution
to this new mystery.

Was there even a mystery? Yes, Phyl's lodger was dead
but . . .

Maisie frowned, struck by a possible solution to several of the unexplained ideas that she had been collecting
and turning over in her mind. What if Mrs Beck was the

perpetrator? What if it was Zoe's foster parent who had come back to Bunting and killed the poor homeless woman? Why? Because Ernest Sumner seemed to think he had seen them together in the pub and then . . .

Well, that was it, really.

And where did she have the information from? From a drunk who thought for some reason of his own that Phyl's lodger was two women – or that Mrs Beck was two women. She pursed her lips, lost in thought.

The two women had apparently been seen together and that meant—

Maisie's reflections were broken by the beginning of the service – a few chords from Alice Spragg on the organ and then the extraordinary voices of the six choirboys, raised in song. The pace of the music was very steady, allowing for an echo from the vaulted architecture to add an extra layer of polyphony, their clear tones weaving in and out of one another in sweet harmonies and satisfying cadences.

Delightful as it was, Maisie's mind soon wandered. She had, in her head, made a vague plan to borrow the Land Rover and go to Portsmouth the next day to visit the Becks, having copied their address from the letter preserved in Phyl's 'day book'. She wanted to know more about Zoe – how she had been nurtured or neglected.

The choral singing stopped and the organ accompaniment faded. Canon Dander's voice was raised in a beautiful *a cappella* tenor chant. The choir sang the formal responses, together with those members of the congregation who knew them. Dander let the reverberations fade before he continued with a prayer for the dead. After the 'amen' he paused before inviting Phyl to speak. The congregation of fifty-odd all turned their faces towards where Maisie, Zoe and Phyl all sat on the raised platform. Phyl stood up and took a step forward to a low, wrought-iron rail.

'Thank you, Canon Dander. Thank you all for being here, if only to hear the voices of these marvellous choir-boys. Forgive me for my intrusion. I hope, when I have finished, you will understand why I wanted to address as many friends and neighbours as I could.'

Phyl left a pause and Maisie reflected that this was yet another version of her aunt's personality – sober, consid-ered, too self-assured to be completely charming but, all the same, authoritative. She wondered if this would be how Phyl would choose to appear in the charity boardroom in London the next day.

'A woman came to us for refuge,' said Phyl in a carrying tone, 'and we paid her no attention. It was last November. We fed her scraps from our table and let her warm herself by our bonfire, then gave her no more thought than the squirrel that we see running along the garden fence before disappear-ing into the woods. We assumed that her life was elsewhere, that she could fend for herself, that she was not our respon-sibility. But she could have been our responsibility, had we only been charitable. To prove it, she came back, cold and damp, nearly a fortnight ago. Many of you will know that she built a shelter up the lane behind my house, in a clearing on the pilgrim trail.' Phyl paused, looking around the politely expectant faces. 'She had no permission or right to build there, but build she did and I let her. Why?' Again, Phyl left a beat. 'Because I saw her, looking out of the window of my warm, dry bedroom, through the glass that protects me from the wind, under the roof that protects me from the rain, and I thought: "What right do I have?" That's why.'

Maisie could see Phyl was having quite an impact on the congregation. All eyes remained turned towards her.

'At the parish council meeting yesterday evening,' Phyl resumed, 'I put forward a plan – one that, I am pleased to say, my fellow councillors were happy to endorse.'

Maisie's eyes flicked round the church, picking out Canon Dander in his ceremonial chair beneath the pulpit, Alice Spragg at the organ, Commander Kimmings in the front pew, Jenny Brook sitting next to Ernest Sumner and Gordon Stock just behind. Was it true, what Phyl had said, that the parish council had been in agreement? Maisie remembered only upset and raised voices. Plus, Kimmings hadn't been there . . .

'My plan is to endow a new charity to provide respite to the homeless in nature. To this end, I will be seeking permission to convert Bunting Manor to become a reception centre, fully equipped, with a permanent staff, trained in appropriate domains of medicine and welfare. In the coming weeks, I will deliver to each of your homes a letter laying out my project. I hope that many of you will support it. I hope, above all, that none of you will object to what you must agree is a mission of Christian charity.'

Phyl sat down. Zoe leant across Maisie and whispered excitedly to Phyl: 'This is so wonderful. Why didn't you tell me?'

Phyl shook her head. Canon Dander rose and invited the congregation to join in the Lord's Prayer, then the choir completed their part with a sung psalm, before Dander closed with a recitation of the evensong prayer of dismissal.

'Lord, you have brought us through this day to a time of reflection and rest. Calm us, and give us your peace to refresh us. Keep us close to Christ that we may be closer to one another because of his perfect love. In his name we pray.'

The congregation replied 'amen', the choirboys filed down the nave and that was that. As the people made their way out of the west door, Phyl descended the two steps from the platform and crossed the church, following Canon Dander and Commander Kimmings into his vestry. The door closed behind them.

'What a lovely thing to do,' Maisie said. 'Do you know where she got the idea, Zoe?'

'From me, actually,' she shyly replied.

'Really? It's a wonderful plan. I'm so impressed.'

'She was a nice woman, really,' said Zoe, 'but she always looked like she was about to cry. I gave her leftovers, in the afternoon, when she came to the back of the pub at closing time. I used to talk to her.'

'Phyl's lodger?'

'Don't call her that,' Zoe scolded.

'Well, the homeless woman, you mean?'

'She wasn't homeless. She just . . .'

Maisie waited. She got the impression that Zoe was holding something back, that she had been sworn to secrecy. It was just a feeling, but she was sure she was right.

'It's fine. I don't want you to break confidences.'

Zoe was sitting very still, looking at the door to the vestry.

'What are you thinking about?' asked Maisie.

'Nothing.'

'I suppose we should wait for Mrs Pascal?'

'I'll have to go back to work soon.'

'Will you come home and get changed again?'

'No. And it's my home, not your home,' said Zoe.

'I know that,' said Maisie, patiently.

Zoe was still staring at the vestry door. Maisie could almost feel her anger and insecurity.

'You hate him, don't you?'

'I'm going to get him,' said Zoe, quietly.

'You're going to do what?'

Zoe got up, went quickly down the steps from the platform to the nave, up the aisle and out into the twilight. What had Zoe meant? That she was going to go and talk to the vicar? Or she was going to get him back for something he had done?

Or that she was going to kill him?

No, that was ridiculous.

Or had she actually meant Kimmings?

Night had almost fallen while they were inside the church. Left alone, Maisie shut her eyes and allowed the silence in, breathing slowly and deeply. She thought about her parents and how much she missed them still, a decade on. She thought about Stephen and how much she regretted being too late to save him – from himself and from his fate.

She heard footsteps and, opening her eyes, saw Phyl coming towards her. She went down to meet her.

'Where are Dander and Kimmings?' she asked.

'The vicar's gone home. Kimmings is on his way up to see young Gordon. I do feel sorry for that boy, in a way.'

'I hope they support you in the end. What an amazing project,' she said with enthusiasm.

'I'm not convinced any of them will.' Phyl sighed. 'Anyway, I should have told you in advance. I'm very sorry. One day Bunting Manor will be yours. I have no other family.'

'That's a very generous thought but you're going to live a good many years yet and, in any case, you must follow your dream.'

'There are things . . .' Phyl stopped and shook her head.

'There are what?' Maisie asked, hiding her frustration. 'Things I don't know? You only have to tell me.'

'You are sharp, aren't you?' Phyl seemed to come to a decision. 'Perhaps you're right.'

'Well,' Maisie encouraged her with a smile, 'there's no time like the present.'

For a second, Phyl's face – usually lined with thought or worry – seemed to relax, as if a burden was about to be lifted and that would be a good thing. Then Jack Wingard came striding up the aisle.

'Oh, good, I thought I'd missed you. Could I have a word?' He stopped, looking from one to the other. 'What is it? Have I interrupted something?'

'Not at all,' said Phyl.

But Maisie knew that he had.

***

Jack, Maisie and Phyl returned on foot to Bunting Manor, leaving the white Ford Zephyr parked outside the three converted cottages, and Zoe walked back to the Dancing Hare for evening service. Phyl led Maisie and Jack along the road, up the drive, round the side of the house and in through the kitchen garden to the back door. It wasn't locked, although when Zoe had got changed Maisie had asked Phyl to do so.

'I thought you promised to be more careful,' Maisie chided her aunt.

'I've a lot on my mind,' said Phyl, shortly.

They sat down around the scratched kitchen table, almost as if they had been carefully placed in such a way as to leave the maximum space between one another.

'I agree with Maisie, Mrs Pascal,' said Jack. 'You should take more care. Particularly in light of what I have to tell you.'

Maisie thought again about the outside cellar door and whether it had a key.

'Go on, then,' said Phyl.

'Two things. Firstly, the knife we found in the fire.'

'What's that?'

Maisie explained what Jack had shown her when she visited the forensic examination.

'The knife is the same shape and size as the one that was used on the lamb.' Jack left a pause. Maisie knew what the second thing would be before he said it. 'It may also have been used on the body that Mr Close discovered face down in the stream.'

'Used in the same way?'

'Thrust upwards under the ribcage into the heart,' said Jack.

'Because someone practised on the lamb,' said Phyl with a sigh. 'Was she smothered as well?'

'No.'

'Any connection to the death caps?' asked Maisie.

'There was no poison in her system, no evidence of having ingested mushrooms in her stomach.'

'Anything else?' asked Phyl.

'The wire that was strung across your drive. I told you it came from a coil used for fencing and was stored in the tractor barn – your tractor barn.'

Phyl was picking at the grubby bandage on her right hand. 'You did,' she said.

'There were no fingerprints but there was blood on the wire. We hope to establish a blood group.'

'I see,' she repeated.

Maisie chipped in again. 'Do you have any idea of motive, Jack?'

Jack frowned. 'It is a poser – a woman of about forty-five years old in perfectly good health. We have a possible lead.'

'What is it?' Maisie asked quickly.

'Barry has been doing some door-to-door. I'm going to have a word with Zoe's foster parents. They may have seen something when they were still in Bunting. I'll tell you if we find anything concrete.'

'Meaning you don't want me to know,' said Maisie, her hackles rising. 'What are you worried about?'

'You know what I'm worried about,' Jack told her quietly.

'That I'll stick my nose in?' she guessed, hating how petulant she sounded. 'Is that it?'

Jack smiled at her. 'That's precisely it.' He put his hand over hers and she was too surprised to argue any further. 'You look tired. You should have a quiet evening in. Don't you think, Mrs Pascal?'

'Hm?'

Jack took his hand away. 'Miss Cooper should take it easy.'

'Yes,' said Phyl, distractedly.

'What's the matter?' asked Maisie.

'I don't know if I've done the right thing,' said Phyl.

'You mean your respite home for homeless people?' said Maisie. 'It's a wonderful project and incredibly generous.'

'No, that's not what I'm talking about.'

'What do you mean, Mrs Pascal?' asked Jack in his official voice.

'I can't tell you.'

'You can speak to me in confidence,' he told her.

Phyl shook her head. 'No, I can't.'

THIRTY

A little earlier, on the road west towards the neighbouring village of Harden, Canon Dander had set off home from the sung vespers. It was an odd set-up, obviously, the parish church in one village and the vicarage in the other, the reason for it lost in the mists of time. But he liked it. He knew he wasn't without sin and to walk the Sussex byways gave him, he felt, a connection to an age-old tradition of itinerant preachers, taking the Word out into the community – devoted servants, pillars of rectitude, bearers of Good News.

Dander walked three-quarters of a mile along the twilit road on the side facing the traffic, tall and straight, his chin held high, his vague eyes contemplating the hedgerows and hills. Two parishioners, one after another, stopped their cars to offer him a lift and he graciously refused. He didn't give his real reasons, of course. No one liked a pushy vicar, an evangelist. He assured them that the exercise was schcduled into his days.

The vicarage wasn't completely dark. The porch light was on, illuminating a stack of kindling and newspapers on one side and the bench on the other, where he sat to remove his outdoor shoes. In his socks, therefore, he unlocked the front door and pushed it open.

There, on the coir doormat, was a note, written in a shaky hand on a scrap of newspaper. At first, he thought nothing of it, picked it up from where it lay, one word visible, 'Vicar', and a single fold.

He hung up his mackintosh and took the note with him to the kitchen where his housekeeper had already set the table for his supper: a small crystal glass and a bottle of communion wine – 'as a tonic, you understand' – and something freshly baked from the Dancing Hare.

He hoped it was quiche. He was very partial to quiche.

***

At the same time, in her unsatisfactory cottage just up from the village green, Alice Spragg was considering the visit of the builder from Framlington. What was the man's name? Singer. She supposed she ought to ask around – find out if he was reliable, could be trusted around her few precious things. Hadn't Singer done work for Commander Kimmings, next door?

She looked round her austere home. There weren't many 'precious things'. Three pieces of Doulton china inherited from her mother. Two pieces of Wedgwood given to her by libraries in Chichester and Portsmouth where she had worked for seventeen and nineteen years respectively. Books, above all. A well-organised collection of socialist and communist literature, explaining inequality in Marxist terms – the inevitable fall of rampant, exploitative capitalism, 'red in tooth and claw', and the equally inevitable establishment of a workers' state. She touched the spine of her most treasured volume – a first edition in English of Karl Marx's *Capital*, dated 1887, twenty years after it came out in German, translated by Samuel Moore and Edward Aveling.

Yes, revolution was inevitable. But, these days, if she was honest, it didn't seem imminent.

She went to the front door and opened it just a few inches. There was a lovely moon looking very big, almost full, cresting the Down. The three lonely street lamps of Bunting were on, casting their orange glow on damp grass and tarmac.

Alice tutted. The street lamps really weren't necessary. Had anyone been out and about, the moon would have been enough. Waste, that's what it was, criminal waste. What was the point when there were children starving? Had nothing been learnt from the power cuts of the previous month when the striking miners – campaigning for the betterment of their own terms and conditions of employment but also for a more equitable division of wealth in all of society – had forced the government to turn off the lights?

Alice sighed. Kimmings' windows were dark. She had seen him go up the lane with Gordon Stock to the farmhouse after the evensong service. Clearly, he wasn't yet back.

***

Canon Dander was eating his quiche at the kitchen table, an electric bar fire close to his feet, almost scorching his trousers. Over his outdoor clothes, he had added an old-fashioned plaid dressing gown. Still, he wasn't quite comfortable. The Victorian vicarage seemed designed to take any warmth and funnel it up to the top of the house and out through the uninsulated roof.

Roll on spring, he thought.

He contemplated his quiche. It had a different taste. Perhaps Sumner had made it himself. Those made by Jenny Brook were the best. Dander had an idea that Sumner's diffident romance with the shopkeeper had stalled. If that meant that Jenny Brook would no longer help out baking for the pub, the food on offer would suffer and she, Jenny, would lose another strand of income. The loss of the shop would be damaging to the village community – perhaps even to the size of his congregation and the success of his parish.

Dander wondered if there was anything he could do to help bring more trade to the shop. Could he, for example, help her to set up a dry-cleaning service, collecting garments and taking them into town for a modest mark-up? Could Stock be persuaded to sell through her rather than – illegally, surely? – at his farm gate? Might it be possible to reinstate the sub-post office? There had to be something.

He took a second mouthful, cutting it away with the side of his fork, his left hand unfolding the handwritten note.

I know what you've done. Now you're going to pay.

He swallowed the quiche with difficulty, clumsily putting down his fork. It was horrid to receive a threatening, anonymous message. And, as heaven was his witness, he really didn't deserve it. Hadn't he given his best years in service to God and His community? Of course he had.

He put the note aside. A priest was a target for all kinds of foolishness.

Speaking of foolishness, Phyllis Pascal's idea for a respite home seemed disproportionate. Surely she couldn't be serious?

But yes, she was an extremely determined woman. And, of course, she had nothing else. What was her life? A shell. A foolish ageing spinster, casting around for something to give herself the impression that she mattered, beyond her money and her ostentatious 'good works'. Who would ever pay attention to her if she was poor?

Still, she had energy and drive. Might that be enough?

Dander poured a second small measure of communion wine into his crystal glass and drank.

He would oppose it, of course. Gordon Stock and Alice Spragg had given it no better than lukewarm approval, each wondering what they might trade for their votes, no doubt. Hopefully, the idea would fester for a while, then wither. The nature of the village could not be allowed to be altered in such a cavalier fashion. One could only imagine the kinds of people . . .

It would be tricky, obviously. The appeal to Christian charity was a strong one. He would have to find a way to counteract its persuasiveness.

An offence against an established community, a group of people with shared goals and values. Was there anything more valuable?

He toyed with his fork, took another bite of quiche.

Perhaps the recipe had been altered and he simply wasn't used to the different flavour? That was possible. Things sometimes tasted peculiar when the senses expect one thing yet receive another. He didn't want to wake up hungry in the night but, as he sipped his communion wine, he wasn't sure he would be able to finish his meal.

***

Alice was back in her low-ceilinged living room, looking out of her low-lintelled window.

Mrs Pascal was doing a 'good thing'. There was no doubt about it. It had been impossible to oppose her at the parish council meeting. Alice had questioned the project because it was important always to oppose the powerful, to serve as a check to the wealthy, to question their motives and intentions. Now, however, she was to have the builders in at no expense to her own depleted purse.

She felt a fault line open up in the edifice of her intellectual purity. Had her acquiescence been bought?

No. She had not yet acquiesced.

Through her net curtain, by the light of Bunting's three street lamps, she saw Kimmings coming along the green. She put on her faded overcoat to go and ask if he could vouch for Singer, the builder, then hesitated, her hand on the front door latch, thinking she would let him get home first. She waited but, unusually, she didn't hear the bang of his front door closing.

She stepped outside. The evening air was soft. The scent of spring was upon it – also the scent of Kimmings' flowers growing in his well-tended borders. Taking care not to slip on the slimy path, she went down to the road, then doubled back to her neighbour's front door.

Taking hold of the brass knocker, she was surprised to feel the timbers move beneath her hand. She put a hand on their glossy surface and gently pushed the door inwards.

'Hello?' she called.

There was a scrap of paper on the mat. Without thinking, she bent to pick it up.

VI

FAITH

THIRTY-ONE

In the kitchen at Bunting Manor, Maisie gave Jack a summary of her conversations with Ernest Sumner, Commander Kimmings, Gordon Stock and Jenny Brook. Phyl listened distractedly, having already been told.

'Oh,' said Maisie, 'but I also invited myself to go and speak to Alice Spragg at her cottage. Perhaps it's late, but I did promise . . .'

Phyl roused herself to tell them that she would like to be left alone to bathe and put out 'smart clothes' for her trip up to London the next day.

'In that case,' said Jack, 'I will walk down with Maisie.'

It was dark on the path through the woods, despite the moon being almost full. Maisie realised her cold symptoms had almost entirely evaporated.

'You're coming with me because you're worried for me?' she asked.

'About what?'

'Well, about murder and so on?' said Maisie, light-heartedly.

'What if I said I was using the threat of wild assailants in the undergrowth to spend more time with you?' he said, lightly. 'Would you admire my candour?'

'I suppose I would have to,' said Maisie, smiling.

He left a pause, then spoke in a more serious tone. 'You know I can't possibly approve of you provoking your aunt's neighbours.'

'A few innocent conversations—'

'You ought to have faith in the methods of the police – in my methods,' he told her.

'You know Gordon frightened Phyl,' Maisie insisted, 'but Jenny Brook was just sad for him. You remember who I mean? The rather limp shop woman, eminent maker of quiches and pies?'

'I know who you mean.'

Maisie stopped, feeling regret that she had told him so forcefully that they could, for the time being, only be friends. She almost hoped he could see the expression on her face, in the dusky moonlight beneath the trees, that he would take advantage of the solitude to kiss her.

'It's a lovely night,' she said, lightly.

But he just waited, a couple of paces ahead of her on the path, then asked: 'What did you hope to achieve?'

'To put them under pressure. I told you, Kimmings is awful and you know from your own experience that Dander is a snake.'

'I do.'

'And Sumner was just confusing. What do you think he meant about the homeless woman being two people?'

'I'm not sure.'

Maisie decided to share an idea that had been brewing. 'What if the dead woman isn't Phyl's lodger?'

'I've been wondering that myself, since the body we found was otherwise in good health and unlikely to have led a life of vagrancy for long. But Mrs Pascal identified her.'

'Say she was wrong,' said Maisie, with a pang of disloyalty. 'I'm not sure she looked properly.'

'I see,' said Jack, very non-committal. 'I will have to find someone else to confirm. But who else could it be?'

'That's exactly what Auntie Phyl said.' Maisie tutted at herself. 'I must remember not to say that. She hates it when I call her auntie.'

They walked on in silence.

'There are paths all through the woods round here,' said Jack after a while. 'When I was a kid, I used to come up and earn a few shillings as a beater for the pheasant shoots.'

'So did we, I mean Stephen and I.'

'Then you know there are quite a few shelters, too, hides for hunters, places someone can get out of the rain.'

Maisie frowned. She had been thinking about whether it would be possible to survive, living rough on the fringe of a downland village. The woman wasn't destitute, after all, according to the coroner, so that didn't really matter any more, but if there were places to hide . . .

'What are you pondering?' he asked gently. 'You know I don't like it when you get ideas.'

'What did you think,' she asked, changing the subject, 'of Phyl's plan to create a respite home for the homeless?'

Jack paused to weigh his words. 'I think it's something that requires a lot of thought and planning and I hope she isn't doing it on a whim.'

'Yes, so do I.'

They were almost at the green. Maisie stopped. He walked on a couple of paces then turned back to face her, a darkish shape with the moon behind him.

'Jack, I wish we could have met again under normal circumstances,' she said.

'You mean without bereavement and murder?'

She couldn't see the expression on his face. Was he being facetious and gently making fun of her?

'I feel like I'm existing outside of normal life,' she told him.

'That's grief,' he told her. 'Stephen only died a fortnight ago. You've been cut adrift from your family. And you live abroad, away from your own kind.'

He wasn't making fun of her. His voice was sincere.

'People like you, you mean?'

'Yes, that's exactly what I mean.'

She said nothing for a few seconds. She felt very strongly that she wanted him to embrace her, as he had done unexpectedly back at Church Lodge, when he had thought her in danger during her investigation into Stephen's murder. Why did he not do so now?

Because she had told him not to.

In the silence, an owl flew past behind him. Just as before, its white underside looked like a pale ghost against the dark sky. Then it screeched.

But no, that wasn't right. A screech owl didn't have a white underside.

Jack was already running, away from her, towards the sound.

She followed, out of the trees and along the road, past the green and up to Kimmings' front door. Alice Spragg was clinging to the jamb, her cries coming in short sharp bursts, like an animal. Her stricken face was cruelly illuminated by the bright bulb of Kimmings' porch light. Jack got to her first but Maisie was only a few seconds behind.

'Stay here,' he ordered. 'Try to calm her down.'

It was unnecessary. Alice Spragg's glance took them both in, she stopped screeching and her eyes rolled up. Maisie was just in time to catch her as she fainted, helping to lay her down on her side on the cold path in her faded overcoat.

'What's happened?' Maisie called.

She looked in the front door. Jack was standing very still, a couple of steps into the hall. Beyond him, she could just see Kimmings – the grey wool of his trousers and muddy outdoor shoes, lying on the carpeted floor.

'Stay where you are. Do as you're told this time, Maisie,' Jack said.

'What about Miss Spragg? She's fainted.'

'Get her inside. That's her, isn't it, next door?'

Maisie did as she was told. Alice was coming to, in any case, her malaise lasting only a few moments. All the same, Maisie supported her back down Kimmings' brick path and up her own slimy flagstones, into her austere, unrefurbished cottage. She sat her down in an upright wing-backed armchair, then went to fetch her a glass of water from the scrupulously clean and tidy kitchen.

'How do you feel, Miss Spragg? Should you put your head between your knees?'

'Please don't fuss. Please ask the policeman to come back and tell me . . .'

Usually grey-faced, Alice Spragg's complexion was almost white beneath her severe pageboy haircut, her eyes vague. Was she going to faint again?

'You're sure you're all right?' Maisie asked.

No answer came. Maisie went back to the kitchen for something sweet and found a packet of ginger nuts alongside a small loaf in the bread bin. She tipped three onto a side plate and brought them through.

'Eat these. You need sugar.'

'Yes, of course.'

'You screamed,' said Maisie. 'I thought at first it was an owl.'

'Is he dead?'

'Commander Kimmings?'

'When I got there, I mean. There was nothing I could have done?'

'Can you tell me what you saw?'

'He was on the floor.'

'Face up or face down?'

'Face down, and that awful thing was strung up.'

'What was strung up?'

'A game bird, a pheasant, strung up to his lampshade with wire, bleeding onto the carpet.'

This won't do, thought Maisie. *If I'm not careful she'll be sick.*

'Never mind now,' she said. 'I shouldn't have asked. I think it's time to pull ourselves together.'

Alice took a deep breath. 'Yes, you're right.'

Maisie saw the severe and systematic personality begin to reassert itself.

'Eat your ginger nuts,' she told her, smiling encouragement.

'Thank you.' Alice nibbled one of the biscuits to show willing. 'I will be fine. Please ask the sergeant to come back and tell me. I need to know, all the same.'

Maisie noticed Alice was holding a scrap of crumpled paper in her hand.

'What's that?'

'Just something silly.'

'You shouldn't have touched anything.'

'It was on his doormat.' Alice smoothed the paper on her knee. 'I expect it was a child.'

Maisie could see enough to recognise that the scrap came from the front page of the local newspaper, the white space above the masthead. Maisie recognised the tops of the letters spelling *Observer* where it had been torn away. And it was true, the writing was childish. The message, however, wasn't.

I know what you've done. Now you're going to pay.

'Can I take this?' Maisie asked, lightly. 'I ought to tell Sergeant Wingard.'

'Do so. I don't want it.'

Maisie held it by the very corner and went outside, almost skidding on Spragg's slippery front step, hopping over the flower border that separated the two front lawns. Kimmings' door was closed.

'Jack, are you there?' she called, knocking.

'Down here.'

She hadn't noticed him, standing by the white Ford Zephyr, the police radio in his hand, presumably waiting for a response. She showed him the note, a corner pinched between thumb and forefinger, and told him its story. He looked angry.

'Thank you,' he said shortly.

'She was in shock, Jack. She didn't know what she was doing.'

'I know, but this is direct evidence and she's . . . Never mind.'

He put down the radio receiver and reached into the cab. A case file was lying on the dashboard under the windscreen. He asked her to place the note inside. She did so. He closed the file and put it back.

'What's happened?'

'He may have fainted or, I suppose, he may have had a heart attack.'

'And he's dead?'

Jack frowned. 'No, who told you that?'

'Alice said he was face down on the floor.'

'She might have helped him then . . .' Jack began irritably. 'But no, he's not dead. I helped him onto his bed and called the doctor.'

'What about the pheasant?'

'How do you know about that?' he asked sharply.

'Alice told me. She saw it. She said it was strung up to his lampshade, bleeding on the carpet.' She frowned. 'Do you think it was deliberate, to shock him?'

'And give him a heart attack, you mean?' Jack shook his head. 'I'm not sure that's an inevitable cause and effect.'

For some reason, Maisie thought of Phyl's cut hand and her tatty, dirty bandage.

'Like the wire stretched across Phyl's drive?'

'Not the same wire,' said Jack. 'Much finer.'

'Any sign of a struggle?'

'I don't think anyone else was there. I think the dead bird was strung up and left there to shock him, to frighten him, but he was very fat, wasn't he? His complexion wasn't healthy. He came wheezing into the church earlier, as if that short walk had winded him.'

'So, anyone could have done it, even a child?' asked Maisie, quietly.

'I'm not speculating, Maisie. I'm accumulating evidence.'

'Yes, I know,' she replied. There was a pause. 'What should I do now?'

'I'll take you back to the house.'

'I can walk.'

'I will drive you and, please, you and Phyl will then lock yourselves in.'

'Yes, all right.' Maisie had a sudden thought. 'Zoe will be at the pub. She'll be walking home later.'

'I'll bring her. Or I'll get Barry to do it.'

'Good. Thank you,' said Maisie. She glanced back at Kimmings' closed front door. 'And he's definitely all right?'

'He is, I think. The doctor will have to confirm.'

She heard a call sign from the police radio. He picked up the receiver.

'Go ahead.'

Jack listened and Maisie couldn't hear what was being said. Eventually, he replied: 'Good, thank you.' Then he put the receiver back on its cradle on the dashboard. She waited for him to tell her what he had learnt, but he said nothing.

'You're freezing me out, aren't you?' she said.

He sighed. 'I'm behaving as any responsible officer must. I'm sorry it's irritating for you.'

'Fine.'

Maisie pursed her lips. It wasn't really Jack who was making her irritable. It was an idea that had bubbled up from her unconscious or out of her imagination. It might explain some of Phyl's behaviour – her changed mood and sense of guilt. But it seemed very far-fetched.

'Maisie,' said Jack. 'I need to take you home now. Then I'll have to come straight back. Will you trust me?'

Maisie thought about him asking her to have faith in the methods of the police. She reached for his hand and said quietly: 'Of course I trust you, Jack.'

'Thank you,' he told her, his face softening.

They both got in the car and they drove the short distance along the road and up the curving drive. Before she got out, she thanked him for his kindness.

'I appreciate this is hard for you.'

He smiled and put on a cockney accent: 'Just doing my job, miss.'

Before she knew why or what she meant by it, she leant across and briefly kissed him on the cheek.

'Thank you all the same.' He gently put his hand on her neck and it took all her strength of mind to pull away. 'No,' she told him. 'Let's not spoil it.'

THIRTY-TWO

Maisie opened the front door of Bunting Manor, thinking about the fact that there were two different types of wire to consider. She found Phyl standing in the centre of the hallway, her face drawn.

'I need to know who did it,' said her aunt, her face stern.

'How do you know about it?' asked Maisie, shocked that Phyl had already heard. 'Has someone come up from Kimmings' house?'

Phyl looked confused. 'What are you talking about?'

Maisie gestured in the direction of the path through the woods. 'The drama down there.'

'I mean being in my room, going through my things.'

'Oh,' said Maisie with a flush of guilt. 'You mean was it me or was it Zoe?'

'I do. It was you, wasn't it? What did you look at? What did you see?'

Maisie hesitated. Of course, she was going to tell the truth, but there was something she wanted to know first.

'Auntie Phyl, are you related to Zoe somehow? Is there more of a connection than just taking pity on her when you found her crying in the church porch?'

Phyl laughed but it was an unhappy sound.

'Is that what you've been thinking? Oh, God, this is all such a mess.'

'So, no?'

'Obviously, no. Can't you see?'

Maisie couldn't, but she had another theory she wanted to test.

'Auntie Phyl, did you cut your hand when you stretched the wire across your own drive?'

There was a moment of stillness.

'Have I already told you that you're a sharp one?'

'You have,' said Maisie. 'Yes.'

Phyl picked at a loose thread from her tatty bandage. 'How did you work it out?'

'I didn't. It just seemed to evolve in the back of my mind. I mean, the wire ends were sharp. It came from your tractor barn. No one else saw it, just you. And that story you told, of the bird sitting on the wire, the robin, so you noticed the bird and didn't drive into the wire . . .'

'Yes?'

'It didn't ring true. It was plausible but sort of poetic? But I can't imagine why you did it.'

'Can't you?'

'No, honestly.'

'Even though it was you who looked through my albums and things, not Zoe?'

Maisie frowned. How was that connected?

'Yes, it was me. I'm sorry.'

Phyl sighed, Maisie thought with relief rather than frustration or annoyance.

'You have every right, after all.'

Maisie didn't know what Phyl meant by that either, but she thought she'd take advantage of the moment to ask another question. 'Why didn't you share in your husband's racing triumphs? You like horses, don't you, and you know a lot about them?'

There was another moment of stillness, then Phyl turned and walked away.

'Auntie Phyl?'

'Will you please stop calling me that,' snapped Phyl, over her shoulder. 'Come with me and tell me what's been going on. What's this "drama" that's been going on down at Kimmings' cottage?'

Maisie followed her aunt into the library. While Phyl laid in a new fire, in as few words as she could manage, Maisie told her about finding Alice Spragg fainting on Kimmings' doorstep and the fact that Kimmings had collapsed and Jack had put him in his bed to await the doctor. She had so much to say that she almost forgot to tell Phyl about the note in the childish handwriting.

'It said: "I know what you've done. Now you're going to pay." And it was written on a corner of the *Chichester Observer*.'

'Recent?'

Maisie frowned again. 'I'm not certain there was a date.'

'The dead bird must have been strung up while we were all at the vespers service,' said Phyl. 'Before we went past when we came back here.'

'Jack and I heard Alice Spragg scream just as we were emerging from the path through the woods.'

'How long was that altogether, do you think?'

'I'm not sure. An hour, maybe more. I waited a while for you in the church before that. You went after Kimmings and Dander into the vestry. What was that about, by the way?'

'I was reminding them both of the duty of their Christian faith,' said Phyl forcefully. 'They have to support me in my endeavour.'

Maisie nodded. 'How would someone have got hold of the pheasant?' she asked. 'From the shoot Archie organised today?'

'Perhaps. Not all the shooters take their kills home.'

'What happens to any leftover birds?'

'Archie hangs them in the tractor barn for the game butcher in Chichester to come out and collect.'

'Will you ask Archie if one has been taken?'

'I will, but the timing is still important, isn't it? It must have been done while we were all at church and accounted for.'

'Do you know if he locks his doors?'

'Kimmings?' Phyl put a match to the scrunched-up newspaper. 'Probably not. Maybe the front door but he'd have left a window open somewhere. People do.' Phyl fed the fire some more paper. 'He said he was going up to Gordon's after the service. Someone could have left vespers and still had time to slip in there before he got home. He doesn't exactly move quickly.'

'No, he doesn't,' said Maisie. 'Zoe left well before us,' she said carefully.

Phyl replied in a tight, tense voice: 'Zoe wouldn't hurt a fly.'

'I was just asking for her own safety.'

'She'll come back from the pub later, about nine o'clock, I expect. There won't be a big crowd, midweek. Ernest Sumner will cash up on his own.' Phyl looked round at the furniture in the library, frowning. 'Did you move this chair?'

'I did.'

'Why?'

'I was worried about someone getting into the house through the cellar. The outside door doesn't seem to have a lock.'

'You should have more faith. I'm not a complete fool. The trap doesn't open from below. When you pull the rings in the timbers, they release a catch.'

'Oh, I didn't realise.'

Phyl looked Maisie in the eye. Her expression was different – calculating but also apologetic.

'I need a drink, Maisie. Then, perhaps I'll tell you more of my story. Before that, though, will you promise me something?'

'Of course.'

'When you know, please don't hate me.'

'What does that mean?' asked Maisie. 'Why would I ever hate you?'

'Don't lose faith. That's all I ask.' Phyl drew a bit of old string from around her neck. On it was the key to the glass-fronted cabinet in her bedroom. 'Here, go upstairs and fetch the albums and scrapbooks on the bottom shelf.'

***

Maisie did as she was told, feeling rather ashamed. When she got back, Phyl had returned the armchair to its position, parallel to the hearth.

'Give me a hand with this. I find it awkward to pull equally on both sides and, if there aren't two people, the catches sometimes stick.'

Together they opened the trapdoor. This time, Maisie thought she did hear the mechanism release. As Phyl went down into the cellar to fetch more wine, Maisie tapped the timbers. They weren't thick. Anyone down in the cellar would be able to eavesdrop on anything said in the library above.

The kindling settled and Maisie added two logs. She wondered what Jack was doing. Routine things, she supposed, following up on the circumstances around Kimmings' heart attack – the part of the investigation that she would have to rely on him for.

Or perhaps not, she thought.

Phyl climbed back up with two dusty bottles and went to the kitchen for glasses. Maisie shut the trap. Tomorrow, she decided, she would undertake her own inquiries in Old Portsmouth, with a visit to Mr and Mrs Beck.

Thinking about knocking at a stranger's door reminded her of her father, selling insurance and cleaning products. He used to talk about having 'good leads', the details of customers likely to buy. The memory gave her a kind of tingle at the back of her neck. The Becks, surely, were her most important lead. Sumner had seen Mrs Beck with Phyl's lodger only days ago.

Phyl bustled back in, the cork already drawn and two tumblers in her other hand. When she put them down, Maisie could see thumbprints on the insides of the glass. She used her clean handkerchief to polish them, reminding herself of Zoe behind the bar at the Dancing Hare.

'The other day, when I was still in Framlington, I saw Zoe,' she told her aunt. 'I had no idea who she was then. But after, once I'd met her and, of course, she's very distinctive, well . . .'

'What?' said Phyl, pouring.

'I thought back and I recognised her, in my memory I mean. Above all her Afghan coat.' Maisie hesitated, then decided she might as well just come out with it. 'She was drinking with Maurice Ryan.'

'The solicitor? In the Fox-in-Flight?'

'Yes.'

'Drinking alcohol?'

'I didn't see.'

'I hope not. She's only sixteen but these village pubs . . .' Phyl filled the two tumblers close to their brims. It reminded Maisie of her Paris friends who often drank wine from their leftover mustard pots once the condiment had all been used up. 'You didn't go in?'

'No.'

'And this bothers you because . . . ?'

259

'Well, I've been wondering what legal issue Zoe would need a solicitor for.'

'I put them in touch.'

'You did what?' asked Maisie, annoyed that here was another important piece of information Phyl had held back.

'I asked Maurice Ryan to talk to her and let her get it out of her system.'

Maisie was struggling to keep up. 'To get what out of her system?'

'To talk through everything that's happened in her life and find out what her rights are. You know Kimmings hit her one day?'

'He didn't?' said Maisie, putting a hand to her mouth. 'How awful.'

'He did,' said Phyl, shaking her head. 'And Dander was there and did nothing about it.'

'And she's angry with her foster parents,' asked Maisie, frowning, 'for not protecting her, too?'

'That's not the point, Maisie. The point is, I asked Maurice Ryan to talk to her, and Zoe's got some idea of going after one or other of them in law. It was Maurice Ryan that Zoe was going to see when you gave her a lift into Chichester on your first evening here. She pretended to me that she had a clandestine rendezvous out of a kind of devilment and she didn't want to say what she was doing out loud in front of you, a total stranger. She told me through her sobs when you got back having told her about the wire – when she was terrified I was going to be murdered.' Phyl sighed and pushed her untidy grey hair off her face. 'I've made a lot of bad decisions.'

'Okay,' said Maisie, taking it all in. 'That reminds me – the wire holding the pheasant from Kimmings' lamp was much finer than the one in your drive.'

'The sort you might use to catch a rabbit?' mused Phyl.

'Maybe,' said Maisie. 'But what was Maurice's answer about going to law?'

'She says he wasn't encouraging.'

Maisie paused. 'No one saw Kimmings hit her except Dander?'

'I don't know. I suppose not. Drink,' commanded Phyl, draining her own glass and refilling it.

Maisie took a sip. Zoe's motive for revenge was still there, wasn't it? In fact, was the motive even stronger, if the law wouldn't help?

How many people had failed to protect the young woman? Maisie thought about the look on the social worker's face, clearly aware of aspects of Zoe's life in foster care that weren't seemly to share. But, of course, she was a stranger as far as he was concerned.

She thought about the ferocity with which Zoe had said, staring angrily at the vestry door: '*I'm going to get him.*'

Did she mean 'get him' through the operation of the law or in some other way? And did she mean Dander or Kimmings?

'To answer your earlier question,' said Phyl, interrupting Maisie's train of thought, 'I never went horse racing with Pierre because he didn't want me there because I was unfaithful to him. I had an affair. I was having the affair before we were married and persisted, despite common sense and propriety, after we wed.'

Maisie remembered Phyl saying that she had 'found love elsewhere'. Why not, after all, if her husband was unkind?

'And Pierre found out?'

'He used a shabby private detective. Would you believe that? Like in a cheap B-feature at the Granada cinema. Of course, later on, I was grateful that he had given me the example. I did the same, putting a seedy-looking man in a dirty mackintosh on his trail and that was how I managed to pressure him into an advantageous financial settlement when we separated. Plus, he was unable to divorce.'

'But you said he was as rich as Croesus?'

Phyl drained her small glass tumbler a second time. 'His people are very strong Catholics from a rather austere tradition. He came into his rights quite late, at twenty-five. Had he divorced, he wouldn't have been allowed his inheritance.'

'So, you couldn't divorce but you could separate and you both had reason never to see one another again?'

'Exactly.'

'Is he dead?'

Telling her story, Phyl's gaze had become a little vague with the alcohol. But now, her attention sharpened. 'You're wondering if Pierre is the one with murderous intent, aren't you?'

'Well, he might harbour ill will towards you. If he's still alive, he might have festered all this time and—'

'But I was the one who strung the wire,' Phyl interrupted.

Oh, yes, thought Maisie. *That's a point.*

'And Zoe actually heard you doing it, Phyl,' she remembered. 'She wanted to know, on that first afternoon, why you were "up at the bang of dawn, rummaging about in the barn". But what about the mushrooms? The death caps?'

'That was me as well,' Phyl admitted. 'Last autumn, I knew there was a place where they were growing close to the path, you know, the old pilgrim trail over the tops of the Downs. So, doing my civic duty, I plucked them up so no passing idiot might do themselves a damage by eating them and left them on the window ledge in my bedroom. They lay there drying until a few days ago when I scooped them up and placed them by the fire up at my lodger's encampment.'

'But why?' asked Maisie, completely baffled.

'The same as the wire. Because of you.'

'Because of me? But . . .' The pieces suddenly aligned in Maisie's imagination. 'You strung the wire and placed the poisonous mushrooms in order to have a reason to get in touch with me.'

'Yes,' said Phyl. 'It was all a pretext to draw you into my life, against a promise I made to three people, to Pierre and Eric and Irene. And now I'm worried that I've given someone ideas and . . .' She stopped and took another pull at her wine while Maisie tried to understand what it was that her aunt was leading up to. 'Actually,' Phyl resumed, 'thinking back, there would have been death caps growing when my lodger came the first time, on Guy Fawkes Night. She would have known. She was a country woman. She could skin a rabbit. But it seems pretty clear that everything's my fault in the end.'

'You mean you're worried you've given the idea of murder to someone?' said Maisie carefully. 'But that isn't true. You didn't smother and stab the sheep, did you?'

'No, of course not.'

'Well, that's nothing to do with you then. Neither is the body in the stream, stabbed in the heart in the same way. And the Kimmings wire, used to string up the dead pheasant in his living room.' Maisie frowned, searching for the correct phrase. 'If it wasn't the same . . . ?'

'You want to say *modus operandi*,' said Phyl. 'I've been reading books on poisons and things. You may have seen them by my bed.'

'I did,' said Maisie, baffled. 'But this doesn't explain why you couldn't just get in touch in a normal way.'

'Because I didn't think you would come and . . .' Phyl pushed away her third glass, sitting up straighter, looking Maisie in the eyes. 'I needed something to keep you here while I got up the courage to tell you. And, then, a reason for you to stay once you knew.'

'Tell me what?'

Phyl didn't answer but there was a look of yearning in her eyes. Maisie glanced at the albums and scrapbooks on the occasional table, next to Phyl's armchair. There was something else Phyl couldn't bring herself to share – the truth of the affair that had driven Phyl and Pierre 'Blaise' Pascal apart.

THIRTY-THREE

There was a loud knocking on the front door.

'Oh, what is it now?' cried Phyl.

She went to answer it and Maisie stayed where she was, her mind surprisingly calm, despite her confusion. But she felt adrift, unable to trust the people around her. What had Charity said?

'*Tu as beaucoup encaissé, ces derniers temps. Tu dois prendre soin de toi.*'

You've taken a lot of hits recently. You must look after yourself.

Eventually, Phyl came back from the hall.

'It was that awful police constable bringing Zoe home, banging like he was trying to wake the dead. I told her about what happened to Kimmings. I thought it better that she knows.'

Maisie didn't answer. She felt quite detached in her bookcase-armchair, watching the flames licking the firestones at the back of the hearth – and desperate for her bed. Phyl stayed where she was, irresolute, watching her.

'You take tranquillisers?' Maisie asked. 'Benzodiazepine? Is that what they are?'

'Yes,' said Phyl. 'For anxiety.'

'But prescribed by a doctor? I'm not going to find there's some other drug thing going on as well, am I?'

'No, of course not.'

'And you've not been overdoing it?' she asked, gently. 'I mean, this is all true, not some crazy hallucination?'

'No,' said Phyl. 'Of course not.' She picked up one of the scrapbooks. 'It's all true. Let me just finish what I was saying—'

Maisie stood up. 'I'm sorry, Phyl. I'm dog-tired. It's late and you said you have to be up very early in the morning to go to London. Did Zoe go straight upstairs?'

'She did, yes, but—'

'You know she's got a beautiful singing voice?' Maisie interrupted. Despite all she had to think about, she wanted to help the girl find a pathway to a new life – as she had done when she had fled her parents' deaths and gone to live in Paris.

'Of course. She used to sing in the choir. Kimmings wanted her to do the solos at Christmas but she refused—'

'She could be somebody,' Maisie insisted. 'You know she wants above all to escape this dead-end backwater?'

'Well, of course,' said Phyl, looking pained. 'I will help her in any way I can.'

'Good. But now, please,' said Maisie, wearily, 'can we close up properly, every door, every window?'

'Yes, of course,' said Phyl. 'And tomorrow, after I get back, we'll talk again?'

Maisie thought there was desperation in her aunt's eyes but she was too exhausted to ask why. Might it be more half-truths, in any case?

'Fine.'

In awkward silence, they locked the back door to the kitchen garden and the front door to the drive, then stood for a moment in the silent, chilly hallway. Maisie reached out a hand and turned off the light. The moon had moved across the sky but it was still quite high, its cold radiance illuminating Phyl's face through the diamond panes of one of the tall narrow windows.

'In the morning, I'll give you a lift to the station,' said Maisie, 'then take the Land Rover on, if you don't mind. There's something I have to do.'

266

Phyl looked like she wanted to argue, but she said: 'I'll be back by lunchtime. I'm just going up to London and back. There's an Intercity train at six-thirty-eight from Havant.'

'Then I'll set my alarm for five-thirty,' Maisie told her. 'You go up. I'll just put the fireguard across.'

'But there's more I wanted to tell you,' Phyl began.

'Tomorrow's another day,' said Maisie firmly.

'But . . .' Phyl began, then she nodded briefly and trudged away up the stairs.

Maisie went back to the library, illuminated by the dying fire. As promised, she carefully set the fireguard and stood in silence, listening for Phyl's door closing on the landing, then the floorboards creaking as her relative moved around her room. Finally, the house was quiet and Maisie went up herself.

She didn't immediately get into bed in the chilly room. Instead, she put on her overcoat and looked out of the window at the moon through the skeleton of bare branches, a few early spring leaves just discernible as fine detail on the twigs.

Finally, she undressed and climbed under the covers, her mind churning, not yet aware that her subconscious mind was rummaging through the pattern of her own life, reconfiguring her memories to mean something different from what she had always believed, changing her understanding of who she was.

***

The next morning when the alarm on her travel clock sounded, it felt to Maisie – swaddled in thick cotton sheets beneath warm woollen blankets and a heavy eiderdown – that the night had been very brief. Inevitably, the clock having been her father's, she woke thinking about him – his betrayal

267

– and the way in which the kaleidoscope of her memories had taken on a new pattern in the moments before she slept.

How had it happened, she wondered? How had Eric looked from Irene, his wife, to Phyl, his sister-in-law, and thought: 'That's what I want'?

From all she had learnt, it seemed clear that Phyl was the less academic but sprightlier, more vivacious sister. Eric and Irene already had Stephen. She knew it was common for women to lose interest in their husbands after childbirth – or was that just a story people told to excuse men's infidelity? She was convinced that her parents had loved one another, deeply and sincerely. Their Christian faith gave their marriage vows deep and lasting meaning. That being the case, once the affair was over, had Phyl done the right thing, distancing herself from their lives – at considerable cost to her own happiness, perhaps – allowing the space for Eric and Irene to heal, for Irene to forgive and for Eric, perhaps, to make amends?

Maisie dressed in her room and went along the corridor to the bathroom. She brushed her teeth and her short curly hair, wetting it slightly to push it back off her face. When she got downstairs, Phyl was in the hallway, offering her a cup of tea.

'I put sugar in it how you like it.'

'Thank you.'

Maisie took the cup and drank. Phyl had dressed up, no longer in moleskin trousers and waxed jacket. She was wearing a lime green blouse with a ruched front and a matching woollen jacket and skirt over thick grey tights. On her large feet were flat but dressy shoes.

'You look very professional,' Maisie said, letting the tea warm her hands.

'Thank you,' Phyl replied, looking as though she was biting back what she really wanted to say.

Once she had finished, Maisie put the cup and saucer in the big chipped kitchen sink. They went outside to find the morning was overcast and the air mild. Maisie got into the Land Rover on the driver's side, wiping the inside of the windscreen with her handkerchief to remove the condensation. Phyl got in on the passenger side and Maisie spread her hanky on the dashboard to dry.

'Out of the village through Harden,' said Phyl, 'then down towards the Common Road.'

'I know the way,' said Maisie, then realised she sounded rather brusque and softened her tone. 'These hills are home to me, too.'

She pulled away, crunching the gears. They descended the curving driveway and turned left onto the winding country lane, away from Bunting, seeing no other people or cars in the three-quarters of a mile to Harden where Maisie slowed, looking out of her window at an ambulance, parked outside a substantial Edwardian house, its lights on and the front door open.

'That's Dander's vicarage,' said Phyl, looking shocked.

Maisie brought the Land Rover to a halt just as an ambulance team emerged, carrying a stretcher. Maisie wound down the window. 'What's happened?'

'Are you a relative?'

'Just a neighbour. We were with him at church yesterday afternoon. Is he all right?'

'Some kind of food poisoning,' said the ambulanceman. 'He called in himself.'

On the stretcher, Dander pushed himself up on one elbow.

'Talk to Sumner,' he said in a weak voice, his face very drawn. 'You must tell him—'

He stopped and leant over the side of the stretcher, retching.

'Now, then, sir, let's get you to St Richard's Hospital.'

The paramedics lifted the stretcher into the back of the ambulance. Maisie forced the awkward Land Rover into gear and drove on.

'Why do we have to talk to Ernest Sumner?' Maisie asked. 'Could that be another assault? Or, if it's food poisoning, might it be something from Sumner's kitchen?'

'Lots of people take home pies and things from his kitchen,' Phyl replied.

'Prepared by him?' said Maisie.

'And by Jenny Brook. I think Dander's housekeeper comes to collect. I sometimes see her.'

'And also prepared by Zoe, perhaps with ingredients from Gordon's farm?'

'How do you mean?'

'I mean ingredients that are unregulated, untested by Trading Standards or anything like that.'

'I hadn't thought of that,' said Phyl, quickly. 'Zoe said the kitchen was a mess, yesterday evening, after vespers, when she arrived for work. She thought perhaps Ernest and Jenny had been arguing and left it untidied, which would be very unusual. Or as if someone had been in who didn't know what they were doing.'

'Then there's the death caps. Jack said he was going to get them cleared away . . .'

Maisie frowned, distracted by what she about to do – defying Jack and going to talk to the Becks.

But I'm involved, aren't I? she thought. *Why does Jack have so little faith in me?*

'Just so you know,' said Phyl, unexpectedly, 'I'm going to London to speak to the executive and trustees of Every One Counts, to tell them that I can no longer support their work.'

Maisie thought of the notes she had snooped on in Phyl's 'day book'.

'I imagine they will be disappointed.'

'I sent them a major contribution not long ago but this will be my final board meeting. I need to tell them in person that I'm going to put all my energy and resources into the transformation of Bunting Manor.'

'Do you mind me asking about your income?' Maisie wondered aloud. 'It must be expensive keeping up the estate.'

'There's plenty of income across the land and property – forestry, tenants, tenant farmers, the pub, our own sheep. Old Archie works for me but there's a dozen others under him.'

Fair enough, thought Maisie, *but what about the tranquillisers you're already relying on?*

'Have you thought this through?' she asked. 'It's your home and it's bound to be much harder than you imagine.'

'I'm not stupid, Maisie,' retorted Phyl. 'I'm so bored with people talking to me as if I'm an idiot – Maurice Ryan, Canon Dander, Archie. But I'm not an idiot. Yes, I have thought it through. I've had all kinds of meetings with what they call "the relevant agencies". Zoe's social worker has been surprisingly helpful.'

'Steve-the-Sneak? Zoe doesn't like him.'

'Zoe doesn't know who to like. She doesn't dare like anyone, for fear they'll abuse her faith and let her down.'

That wasn't a problem Maisie had ever had to face. Her parents had instilled her with confidence and self-assurance, making sure she believed that she could achieve anything she put her mind to, as long as she worked hard enough and long enough.

Maisie pulled out onto the Common Road and picked up speed, clunking past the recalcitrant third gear, jumping from second into fourth. They met more traffic as they entered the outskirts of Havant, through the industrial estate, past the Lec fridge plant and the Goodmans speaker

271

factory. After a sharp right-hand turn, they pulled up not far from the barrier on the northbound platform.

'Good luck,' Maisie said.

'Thank you,' said Phyl, opening the passenger door. 'I'll take a taxi when I get in. There's no need to come back. But can we talk again later? There's more that you don't yet know.'

'Of course. Don't hang about, though. You don't want to miss your train.'

'I'm so sorry, Maisie,' said Phyl, inexplicably, then she got out of the car, ran up the little ramp to the barrier and disappeared.

***

Maisie was torn. Part of her felt she should drive back to Harden or into Chichester to find out what had happened to Canon Dander. Perhaps even speak to Jack? Would he have been told? Eventually, she supposed.

But, if she did that, she would lose this golden opportunity to confront Zoe's foster parents in Portsmouth and it was still very early, before seven.

Determined to show faith in her own judgement, she drove on, out of Havant, onto the main road, the busy A27, past the IBM complex and west towards Portsmouth. In her rear-view mirror, the sky was light.

Soon she came to the left turn onto the Eastern Road, one of the main approaches to the island city. She took it and made her way through Fratton, past the rundown football stadium, into Southsea and along the seafront, seeing a big car ferry setting out for France and a smaller commuter service coming across the Solent from the Isle of Wight.

She parked all the way down in Old Portsmouth, the original heart of the city, in a car park behind an old greasy-spoon café close to the water – the Dolphin Café. It was still too early for her to confront the Becks so she went inside and ordered a full English breakfast with tea and toast.

She sat down at a table in the window. Like the Land Rover windscreen, it was drenched in condensation. She wiped a paper napkin across it to make a kind of letterbox to look out of.

What time was it? It felt like it was just after seven. She looked at her watch. Twenty past, in fact. When could one reasonably knock on a stranger's door? Eight o'clock? Would that be more or less civilised?

The waitress brought her breakfast. She picked up her knife and fork and began with a piece of inferior sausage, dipped in the yolk of her nicely cooked poached egg. As she ate, she wondered about the possible reasons for – and consequences of – the ambulance they had seen outside Dander's vicarage. Then she moved on to what had happened to Kimmings last night and the fact that Alice Spragg had been the one to find him. Didn't they say that the perpetrator was, very often, the person who claimed to have discovered the crime?

After the egg, the rest of her breakfast was slimy and salty and disappointing. She ate only half then put down her knife and fork, sitting back, picking up her drab green teacup. It was hot and strong, almost stewed.

Her mind became blank, a combination of the early hour, the lack of sleep and the stresses and strains of her drifting existence: waiting for closure with the trial that would finally settle Stephen's murder; money worries; a sense of responsibility for poor Zoe; the fact that she was betraying Jack's trust; her father's affair with her aunt.

She drained her cup, paid at the counter and went outside. The sun was up but still low, dazzling just above the rooftops. She walked towards it, keeping her eyes half closed, along the seafront fortifications left over from the Napoleonic Wars, and watched the bright sea, allowing time to pass. A church bell began to ring. She made her way to the high street, the very beginning of the A3 on the line of the old Roman road that led all the way up through Sussex and Surrey to London Bridge.

The cathedral was on the left, huge but squat. A few parishioners were going in, presumably for an eight-o'clock service. Maisie walked past them, into a quiet, narrow street that led to the boat pound.

There it was, a small terraced house, with a small chalkboard by the front door.

'We love our home.'

That may be true, Maisie thought. *But you didn't love Zoe. At least, you didn't love her enough.*

The cathedral bells were tolling their final call to prayer, promising consolation to those who kept the faith, a peal of three descending notes – '*ding, daing, dong*' as the French nursery rhyme had it.

Maisie knocked and a voice called out: 'Just a minute.'

The triple peal ended, becoming a single bell, tolled over and over.

Final warning, it seemed to say. *Now or never.*

She heard two bolts being drawn, top and bottom, and the voice once more from behind the door: 'I'm sorry, Sergeant Wingard. I expected you a bit later.'

The door opened, revealing a medium-sized man in his mid-forties, thin and dark-haired, unshaven, wearing grey slacks with an elasticated waistband, a thin blue jumper tucked into them. Behind him, Maisie could just see into the kitchen at the back of the house where two bored-looking children were eating cereal from a variety pack while reading the small boxes.

'I'm sorry, can I help you?'

'You were expecting Sergeant Wingard?' she asked.

'Yes, I mean . . . Who are you?'

'I'm associated with Sergeant Wingard's investigation,' Maisie lied. 'Can I come in?'

'Oh, God, you've found her, haven't you? Is she all right? Is she . . . ?' He dropped his voice and crumpled against the doorjamb. 'Is she dead?'

THIRTY-FOUR

While Maisie was eating her unsatisfactory breakfast in the Dolphin Café in Old Portsmouth, Jack was already at his desk, reading a routine missing persons briefing. There, in black and white, was a potentially crucial connection to the goings-on in Bunting.

He had a moment of anxiety, imagining what Maisie might do if she had come to the same conclusion that he had.

Speaking of conclusions, he wondered if Maisie had remembered the story Mrs Pascal had shared about her lodger trapping rabbits with fine wire.

Jack moved on to the notes from Constable Barry Goodbody, regarding the halfway house in the village of West Dean, just a few miles away from Bunting on the pilgrim trail across the Downs. It had closed just two weeks ago due to budget cuts across the local health authority. A small number of long-term residents had been evicted, finding themselves cut adrift from support. It confirmed his suspicions in relation to the rash of petty thefts he had been looking into.

Barry's notes were, Jack was pleased to see, coherently organised and – apart from a few spelling mistakes – professionally expressed. He called Barry over.

'This is good, thorough work. Well done.'

'Thank you, Sergeant,' said Barry, shifting from foot to foot. 'I did my best.'

'Your best is all anyone asks,' said Jack. 'Now, tell me, what should one deduce from it?'

'In relation to the Bunting business?' said Barry.

'Yes.'

'Well, it gets us a bit closer, doesn't it, to your idea?'

'Yes, it does.' Jack sat back. 'What do you think our next step should be?'

'You had it in mind to talk to the Becks, didn't you? Maybe get on to the social worker who got the sack, as well?'

'Right again, Barry.'

Constable Goodbody smiled sheepishly. 'Thank you, Sergeant. I'm sorry I've let you down previous, sir.'

'Never mind that now. Tell me, which do you want to follow up on?'

Barry frowned. 'Shall I go for the social worker, Sergeant? He's just down the road in Apuldram and I can take my bike. Then you can have the Zephyr to get over to Pompey – I mean Portsmouth.'

'Good. I called Mr Beck yesterday. He's expecting me. Before you go, type up these notes and we'll show them to Inspector Nairn when I get back.'

'Thank you, Sergeant.'

Constable Goodbody returned to his desk, put a fresh report form, carbon paper and coloured copy sheets in his typewriter and began, laboriously, to pick out the letters. Jack watched him for half a minute, feeling pleased that his faith in Barry was finally being rewarded.

Then he went outside and jumped in the car to shoot over to 'Pompey'.

THIRTY-FIVE

In Old Portsmouth, it was, luckily, time for the Becks' two younger foster children to get off to school. Maisie waited while Mr Beck helped them tie their lace-up shoes and push their arms into the sleeves of their anoraks. Then he sent them out of the front door with leather satchels on long straps over their shoulders, calling out a few brief words of affection and kindness.

Maisie found herself feeling rather sorry for them, one blond and frail-looking, the other dark-haired and more robust, of Indian heritage, perhaps – maybe an orphaned refugee from the Bangladesh civil war that Florence Wingard had mentioned. They gave an impression of living their childish lives as if they were tiny grown-ups, rather serious and frowning, on their way to work – not looking forward to learning and playing with their friends.

Mr Beck watched them from the front door, a vague smile on his lips, until they were out of sight, then returned to the kitchen and put water in the electric kettle. Maisie assumed he hadn't told them that their foster mother was missing.

'I'm sorry I shocked you,' she improvised. 'I'm afraid I have no news of your wife. I just came to ask you one or two questions. I take it she hasn't been in touch?'

Mr Beck sighed. 'I can't tell you how relieved I am,' he began. 'When I saw you, I honestly thought it was bad news.'

'I quite understand,' she told him.

'No news is good news, perhaps? Isn't that what we're supposed to believe? But what's happened to her? That's what I don't understand? It's completely out of character for Nicola to go off on her own, for her to be away from home for any length of time. I really can't remember the last time we were apart – just her appendix op and that was five years ago. We're never apart.'

Inevitably, he asked Maisie if she wanted 'a nice cup of tea'. She told him that she didn't need any kind of refreshment. He sat down and she followed suit at the smoked-glass kitchen table, the remains of the children's breakfast between them – homogenised milk in a tall glass bottle, the foil cap discarded to one side, empty boxes from the variety pack of cereals, uneaten toast crusts. Maisie's mind was working quickly, trying to fit Mrs Beck's disappearance into the pattern.

'You must love her very much,' said Maisie, encouragingly. 'I'm sorry to put you through this, but could you take me through the sequence of events?'

'But I told Sergeant Wingard.'

'Would you mind telling me, too?' Maisie gave him a bright smile. 'Would that be all right?'

Mr Beck nodded, wearily.

'It started with a phone call. I didn't take it. I was out. Nicola must have picked up and then left me a note. She didn't say who it was from. That's one of the things Sergeant Wingard promised he'd be looking into – you know, when he called to ask to speak to me. He said it might be possible to know from the exchange what number it was we were called from.'

'When was this?'

'Oh, a few days ago. Let me look.'

He went to fetch a calendar from its hook on the wall. Alongside it, inscribed on the door frame, were marks in pen on the paintwork, keeping track of children's heights at different ages. Maisie felt glad. Didn't that mean there was at least some kind of emotional connection between the Becks and their foster children? Then she realised that didn't add up.

He put the calendar on the table, pushing the cereal bowls aside to make room. She saw a rather splendid photograph of Nelson's flagship, the *Victory*, on the top sheet, then the month divided into little boxes on the bottom sheet. There were notes and reminders in most of the boxes.

'You have busy lives,' said Maisie.

'You have to keep track,' said Mr Beck. 'There's always something with children. It does them good to have lots going on.' He smiled and shook his head. 'But it's not always good news. We've had the inoculations and then the headlice and then there was ringworm in the school, but Bruce and Arif didn't bring that home at least.' His fingers traced the days. 'Then there's homework and the swimming pool and social worker visits—'

'Would that be Steve?' interrupted Maisie.

'Yes, Mr Weiss. Do you know him?'

'I've interviewed him,' said Maisie, not completely untruthfully.

'Steve Weiss. "Call-me-Steve", he says. Nicola used to call him "that hippy" . . .'

Maisie heard Mr Beck's voice beginning to crack. She felt bad. The man was obviously extremely concerned, utterly unable to explain his wife's absence. She felt cruel, persisting in her lie. What did she know, after all?

'This phone call?' she prompted.

He pointed to a little box on the calendar – Saturday, the day Maisie had eaten roast brisket with Jack and Florence Wingard.

'I think it was then, and she went straight out and I've not seen her since.'

'What was she wearing that day?'

'Her pale blue twinset. And she took her winter coat, the one with all the zips and poppers.'

'What did her note say?'

'That she was getting the train into Havant. I'd taken the Hillman to get the boys to their football over in Fratton. Then, I don't know.'

'Could she have gone on to Bunting?'

Mr Beck frowned. 'You did say you were working with Sergeant Wingard?' he asked. 'Will he not be coming over like he said?'

'It never hurts to go over things more than once,' Maisie improvised. 'You'd be surprised what can be missed the first time.'

Mr Beck accepted her lie with a sigh. His unshaven face was rather slack, his eyes lifeless. The nails on both hands were bitten down close to the quick.

'The train goes from the Hard,' he told her. 'That's what we call Portsmouth Harbour.'

'I know. I'm local.'

'Well, from there to Havant you don't have to change. Then, the bus station's right next to the train station. Could have gone to Bunting. There's a bus that goes out through the Downs.'

'How often does it run?'

'Three or four returns each day,' said Mr Beck, his finger still planted on the little box on the calendar. 'Then on Sunday, when she still wasn't back, I wondered if it was a sick relative. Nicola's sister Yvonne is in Leigh Park – you know, the big council estate? She doesn't have a phone so I went over myself, but no joy.'

'Then what happened?'

'The next morning was the day the school does extra reading before assembly. I got the boys up on my own and went in with them to help out.'

Again, Maisie found this rather touching, that Mr Beck took such an interest in the boys. She wondered how much it paid, taking in foster children. Enough to live on? Surely not. Enough to round out a pension or an inheritance of some kind? Probably.

'Tell me about Zoe,' she prompted. 'Would she take your name in the end?'

'No, they all have their own names, although that can happen, with some couples, if you have them long enough and you get on and so on.'

'She was a foundling. Isn't that correct?'

'That's right, given the name Richards because of the hospital in Chichester, St Richard's, where she was left.'

'And no one has ever known who by?'

'No, never.' He raised his head, looking more alert. 'Is it something to do with Zoe?'

'How do you mean?'

'My Nicola. Is this to do with her and Zoe? Has something happened between them?'

'Inquiries are on-going,' Maisie prevaricated. 'Why do you ask?'

'I have a right, haven't I?'

'They never did get on?' Maisie hazarded.

'They did not.' Mr Beck sighed. 'I don't know where the fault lay.'

'It must be easier with the babies, the little ones,' said Maisie, hating herself for manipulating him.

'They need you more,' he agreed, nodding. 'The older ones, they want their independence and something to kick against.'

'And Zoe kicked against your wife, above all.'

'They never hit it off.'

'Even when you first had her?'

'Even then.'

'How old would she have been?'

'Nine, just after we came to Bunting.'

'So quite little.'

'Yes.'

'And where had she been, before that, I mean?'

'Bounced around.'

'And what was the problem?'

'We had two others younger than her and Nicola was run off her feet. I'd just had an operation to my ingrowing toenail and it was septic and that laid me up and she and Zoe, they just couldn't see eye to eye . . .' His voice trailed off.

'Did she beat her?'

'Nicola? Never, she wouldn't never have touched her.'

Maisie could hear the note of authenticity in the man's voice.

'But your wife was harsh with Zoe?'

'Nicola can be sharp. She doesn't mean anything by it.'

He was trying to hold her gaze but failing, his eyes shifting guiltily away to look at the pen marks on the wall. Maisie shared what she had deduced.

'That's not your children, is it? You've only been here a short time. That celebration of growing up is from the previous occupants of this house, isn't it?'

'I never said any different, did I?'

He stood up and put the dirty things – the bowls and side plates and cutlery – in the sink, running the tap, adding washing-up liquid. He stood there, turned away from her, hiding from her.

'Your wife was unsympathetic to Zoe. You'll admit that?'

He turned back to face her.

'It's Nicola who's gone, isn't it – disappeared? Isn't that what you're supposed to be investigating, not whether Nicola had a struggle to keep Zoe in line, to stop her carryings-on?'

'What carryings-on?'

'I liked young Zoe. She was a handful, but there was no malice in her, none at all. But Nicola couldn't see it.' Mr Beck's eyes looked pained and sad. 'You're not a mother, are you? Nicola prefers the boys. She says the girls are manipulative, that they're not all "sugar and spice and all things nice". I tried to make her see reason.' He stopped. 'You don't think it was Zoe on the phone, do you, getting Nicola back out to Bunting? Is that why you were asking about the Downland buses? You don't suppose they got into a bust-up, do you, and Zoe did my Nicola a mischief?'

'No, I do not,' said Maisie firmly, though she wasn't entirely sure. 'One other thing. You and your wife told Zoe that Nicola was ill, that she had cancer.'

His expression became closed and he folded his arms. 'That was for a kindness.'

'A what?'

'To soften the blow, so she wouldn't think we were abandoning her.'

'Just to be clear, your wife doesn't have cancer, never did have cancer?'

'No, of course she didn't.'

'And you told Zoe this lie when you left her homeless, under age—'

'She was sixteen,' he interrupted.

'Only just.'

'But she was all right. She had a job with Ernest Sumner. He's got a spare room, too.'

'Zoe might not have felt comfortable moving in with a man old enough to be her father.'

'No,' accepted Mr Beck. 'I don't suppose she would.'

'If you don't mind me saying so, I think that was very cruel. And it was purely good luck that Mrs Pascal took her in,' persisted Maisie.

'She's a fine lady, Mrs Pascal,' said Mr Beck, grasping at the change of subject. 'She does a lot of good work. Everyone knows that.' He sighed again, hanging the calendar back on its hook. When he turned back to her, his eyes were sharper, more focused. 'I've been talking, but you've not said much. Why did you come over?'

Maisie stood up, too. 'As I said, just to compare information. You've been very helpful. Thank you.'

'But what about my Nicola?' he whined with a mixture of frustration and worry. 'What's next? Haven't you got anything to tell me?'

'The police are doing all they can. Goodbye, Mr Beck.'

Maisie turned away and walked down the narrow hallway to the front door. He followed and put a hand on her shoulder. 'Here, I thought you said that you were the police?'

'That's right.' Maisie shook him off, opened the front door and stepped out into the street. He let her go and she turned back to face him, carefully out of reach. She had an idea he might have manhandled her further if she hadn't moved out into the public space. He really did seem quite desperate. 'I'll talk to Sergeant Wingard for you,' she assured him. 'I hope Mrs Beck comes back very soon.'

As she walked away, she felt his eyes on her back.

But I would be very surprised, she thought, *if Nicola Beck ever came home again.*

THIRTY-SIX

Maisie stood still for a few seconds, round the corner from the Becks' house with its touching blackboard sign, 'We love our home', deep in thought. She had learnt a lot that was new and unexpected, plus a number of depressing elements that seemed entirely predictable. Eventually, she walked away, her eyes on the pavement in front of her feet. She had much to think through and try to connect, but the timeline of events was becoming clearer.

Her shoulder brushed another pedestrian, going the other way.

'Excuse me,' she said, then realised who it was, a stringy-looking man with long hair and an earnest unshaven face. 'Oh, Mr Weiss, isn't it?'

'Yes?'

'Maisie Cooper. We met in Bunting.'

Steve Weiss's eyes remained vague.

'I'm not sure . . .'

'I've been staying with Mrs Pascal, my relative, the lady who took in Zoe Beck – I mean Zoe Richards.'

'Oh, yeah, Songbird Zoe. Of course. What a coincidence. I'm here to speak to her foster parents.'

For a second, Maisie wondered if she should lie, then decided not to.

'Not a coincidence. I came to speak to them myself. Did you know Mrs Beck is missing?'

'Missing? Like, left home?'

'Mr Beck doesn't know. He's worried about her.'

'He would be. You saw his fingernails? He's an anxious one.' He put his head on one side. 'So, you've been talking to him, have you?'

Maisie hesitated. Weiss seemed willing to talk, though she supposed he must be sworn to some kind of professional secrecy.

'Why did you call her "Songbird Zoe"?'

'Beautiful voice. I heard her one day and got her to join the church choir, but she wouldn't let it go – let it fly. Do you know what I mean?'

'She wouldn't sing out strongly?'

'She was embarrassed. They usually are. They don't want to stand out.'

'You mean children in care?'

'Yeah.'

'You encouraged her to join the choir. Were you aware of the reputation of the organist, Commander Kimmings?'

'Not then, but . . .' He sighed. 'There's a lot of freaks out there, Miss Pascal.'

'Miss Cooper.'

'Anyway . . .' He looked like he was about to say goodbye, then changed his mind. 'Did you say you're related? Is it a family thing? You were singing that Cat Stevens song, weren't you?'

'No, I wasn't,' Maisie admitted, hoping the truth might help get Weiss on her side. 'That was Zoe. I covered for her. She didn't want to speak to you.'

He seemed to take the news of her deceit with complete equanimity.

'Yeah, that was what I thought. Faith and trust, that's what you need, but she hasn't got any.'

'You know her quite well, don't you?'

'I'm good at reading people.'

'There's something else,' said Maisie. 'Can we speak in confidence?'

'Try me,' he said, not entirely reassuringly.

'Perhaps she mentioned it to you? She's been speaking to a solicitor about her rights. You know Kimmings hit her? The vicar was there and saw it happen and did nothing about it.'

Weiss nodded again. It was very characteristic of him, even when expressing a negative thought. 'She'll do well to make that stick.'

He seemed sympathetic, though. Maisie seized her chance.

'Mr Weiss, do you have time for a cup of tea? I really would be very grateful. There's the Dolphin Café round the corner.'

'I'm not sure—'

'Mrs Pascal wants to do the best for Zoe. It would be helpful to have a little more background, anything you can share.'

'You shouldn't have lied to me before,' he drawled, nodding some more. 'That wasn't cool.'

'I'm sorry. I'll make it up to you. I'll buy you a nice poached egg.' Maisie gave him her brightest smile, the one that she knew was almost guaranteed to open doors or obtain a table in crowded restaurants.

Steve-the-Sneak pulled a wristwatch with a broken strap out of a fob pocket in his embroidered waistcoat. 'Yeah, go on then.'

VII

COURAGE

THIRTY-SEVEN

The Dolphin Café was crowded with builders and delivery-men, having a bit of a sit-down for some kind of hybrid of late breakfast and early lunch, having probably begun their days before the sun. Most of them were smoking. Packets of Senior Service and Woodbines lay by choked ashtrays. The atmosphere was jovial, damp and noisy. The same window table that Maisie had sat at earlier was available. She and Steve Weiss took it, facing one another across the stained Formica as a bored waitress came to take their order. Steve-the-Sneak Weiss turned out to be 'almost vegetarian' and didn't want a poached egg unless they could be guaranteed to be free range from 'happy birds'. They couldn't so he ordered black tea with a side order of toast and margarine and jam. Zoe asked for a glass of water. It came almost immediately, well before the rest, in a smudged glass. She didn't touch it.

'So?' she prompted.

'So, what?'

'Tell me about her?'

He grinned. 'Is she still wearing the coat I gave her?'

Maisie took a moment to catch up. 'Her Afghan coat? Yes.' She smiled. 'She wears it every day.'

There was something oddly appealing about Steve Weiss – his regular nodding, as if he approved of whatever you had to say, understood it, respected it, even if he disagreed.

'I got it when I was in India,' said Steve. 'I went, you know, to open my eyes.' Inevitably, he nodded at his own reminiscence. 'India's an incredible journey. Life's a journey, right, but there's no destination so you've got to be brave. That's a good way to think of it, right?'

'Yes, it is,' said Maisie, not sure she agreed.

'I'm glad,' he said, 'that she likes the coat. She's not my responsibility of course.'

'Because she's sixteen?'

'Yeah. I hope she's settled where she is. You said it was your aunt's house?'

'I did.'

Maisie thought he was fishing, wanting to know why she had invited him to this smoky café to ask him questions. If he was suspicious of her reasons, did that mean he had something to hide himself? He had encouraged Zoe to join the choir – pushed her towards the awful Kimmings, in fact.

'When did you find out that Mr and Mrs Beck upped and left Zoe, abandoning her?'

'Not straight away. It's not like I'm in the village every other day,' he said, dismissively.

'Did you know that they told her a story about Mrs Beck having cancer and having to move to Portsmouth to be closer to the hospital – that she still believes it?'

'Maybe she does, maybe she doesn't.' He yawned. 'Kids believe stuff to protect themselves. Everyone's always telling them to be brave. They need a kind of shield – but the shield has to be their own courage.'

'Be that as it may,' said Maisie curtly, impatient with his moralising, 'you do realise that Mrs Pascal found her in the porch of the church, alone and crying with all her worldly possessions in a suitcase at her feet?'

'No, man,' he told her. 'I had no idea. It's sad but what can you do?'

Maisie was becoming frustrated. 'Doesn't any of this mean anything to you, if not as a professional, at least as a human being?'

Steve wiped the condensation from the window with the side of his hand and looked out. He seemed completely at ease. Maisie wondered what she might have to do or say to throw him off balance. Then, abruptly, he spoke.

'When I met you at the house, I was just coming with some papers to sign her off. There's a lot of paperwork. I'm really behind. That's why I'm here today – to officially get her off my books. She's not my responsibility any longer. Never was really.'

The waitress brought his tea and toast. He ate it in small bites, nibbling at the edge. Maisie found it strange that he seemed so unashamed, so unconcerned with Zoe's predicament and distress.

'You don't care?'

'No, I care,' he said with crumbs on his lips. 'But you can't do everything. People have to make their own way. You can't expect us all to walk in step.'

It sounded like a pat phrase, something he might repeat often.

'What are you talking about?'

He swallowed, sipped his tea and grimaced. 'Stewed,' he told her.

'Please, Mr Weiss.'

'Okay, it's like this. I'm there to do what I can, and the welfare state is . . .' He made a vague gesture, turning his hand in a circle above his head. 'The welfare state is like absolutely not everything. It's not there to give you a frame to live your life. It's the thing that might catch you if you fall but, like, if it's a net, a safety net, you know, it's incomplete, there's gaps.'

'Isn't it your job to plug those gaps?'

'Trust me, I do what I can. But I'm just one man, you know?'

There was a note of sincerity in his voice. Maisie tried to get back to the point.

'Do you think that Mrs Beck ever hit Zoe?'

'It isn't in the file.'

Maisie tried again. 'What if it was very recent?'

'Someone might have told me. A neighbour could have spilled, but I've only been on the case for a few months.'

'Oh, I didn't know that. Why?'

'Someone retired. Sacked, actually, for sharing confidential information with their clients, not keeping proper records.'

'Sharing information with the people they were looking after?'

'They like us to call them clients. Yeah. I picked up the caseload. I'm drowning,' he said, complacently. 'You know there was a mental health ward closed just last October? Where do you think those people are now? And the halfway house in West Dean? They've been looked after so long, some of them, that they've no family or homes to go to any more.' He slurped his tea and grimaced again. 'Maybe some sugar.'

He turned the dispenser upside down, allowing at least three spoonsful to cascade into his cup. Maisie wondered if Jack knew about the possible West Dean connection. It was only a few miles on the pilgrim trail over the Downs.

'So, you barely knew the Becks or the other people,' said Maisie. 'In Bunting, I mean.'

'I'm more Bognor, Littlehampton, you know? Not so much the villages.'

He was listing the more working-class neighbourhoods in south-west Sussex. And, she remembered, he was only here in Portsmouth because he was 'signing off' the Becks.

'I'm sorry I didn't realise you'd taken on someone else's caseload. Would you mind telling me what you were going to say to Mr Beck?'

'I can't tell you that.'

'Would you agree,' asked Maisie, fishing, 'that the Becks are more suited to smaller children than teenagers?' Then she added, remembering something Mr Beck had said: 'Or to boys rather than girls?'

'You're a nice person,' said Steve-the-Sneak, unexpectedly. 'I can see that. You're on a journey, too. Not an easy one.'

'I beg your pardon?'

'I can see it in your eyes, you know? Something's happened in your life.'

'We aren't talking about me,' said Maisie, defensively.

'Don't want to share?' said Weiss. Maisie kept her expression bland. 'Okay,' he went on. 'That's cool. You don't have to. You're asking me to share, though. Do you see that?'

He gave her a funny little half-smile and Maisie couldn't help laughing.

'Yes, I do see that.'

He leant in close, making sure only she could hear.

'I'm telling you this because it might help Zoe's case, you know?'

'Go ahead.'

'I'd say they're not suited to fostering at all. I'm going to tell them that, and I'm going to tell the Portsmouth social services to look for a new home for those two kids.' He fished in an inside pocket of his embroidered waistcoat, pulling out an official letter. He unfolded it. 'Bruce and Arif,' he read. 'Maybe it's not Mr and Mrs Beck's fault. Maybe they've just been doing it too long, you know, they've given too much love away? Everyone's got, like, only so much to share.'

Maisie didn't reply. She wished she could find Jack and tell him all she had learnt – not least, the discovery that Steve-the-Sneak was intelligent, perceptive and trying to do the right thing.

'Why did you give Zoe the Afghan coat?' she asked.

'I wanted her to have something of her own. I don't think they ever let her choose anything for herself.'

'That was very nice of you.'

'It was too small on me, anyway. I work out,' Steve added, implausibly. 'And she delivers pies and things round the village and even up the road to the next one, Harden, in all weathers, so I gave it to her.' He drained his tea. 'Mind you, it stinks when it's wet.'

While Steve was speaking, Maisie had been thinking about Mrs Beck's 'winter coat', but she had to admit that, if Zoe delivered food, could she have taken something round to Dander yesterday – something that had made him so ill that he had to call an ambulance? What personal resources would it have taken the girl to do such a thing? Courage, no doubt, and desperation. She tried to work out if there had been time. Wasn't every minute of Zoe's day accounted for?

No, not quite. She could have cooked the tainted food during the lunch service while Ernest Sumner was too drunk to notice, then delivered it immediately after the sung vespers. She had left alone and the last thing she had said was: '*I'm going to get him.*'

Maisie racked her brains for something else to ask – anything that might lead her to a murderer. Potentially, a double murderer – first Phyl's lodger and now maybe even Mrs Beck. Should she say out loud that was why she was talking to him?

'The previous social worker who was sacked,' she asked. 'What sort of information did they share?'

'Who's who and what's what and where people might have come from. Do you know what I mean, doll?' he asked with a wink.

Maisie forced herself not to bridle at being called 'doll'.

'I don't follow.'

'Look, I have to go. I have things to do and I need this job, you know, so I can't be talking about all this. I don't want to get sacked like the other guy.' The café was much quieter so he was speaking almost in a whisper. 'You're on the right track but you can't ask me anything else.' He put away the official letter and stood up. 'Thanks for this.'

'No, thank you for talking to me,' said Maisie, half-standing, but he was already walking away.

Taken by surprise at the speed of his departure, Maisie watched him go, an odd, jaunty figure, sure of himself and of his place in the world, of the limitations on what he could be expected to achieve.

Yes, she thought, *he doesn't think he can fix the whole world, but he might try and fix the thing closest to hand – finding a new foster home for the two boys.*

That, however, was no use to her at all.

THIRTY-EIGHT

Maisie paid and left the Dolphin Café, down by the water in the heart of Old Portsmouth, an incipient headache behind her eyes from the noise and the fug. She walked down to the sea, through an archway in the fortifications, and looked out at the grey water. The tide, she thought, was running in. Beyond the water was the rather forbidding naval coastline of Gosport.

What next, she wondered?

She checked her watch. She didn't need to hang around. Phyl had told her she would pick up a taxi from Havant to bring her back to Bunting Manor. When would that be? '*Lunchtime*,' she had said. What did that mean, twelve o'clock or two o'clock? Probably the latter.

Maisie walked back through the arch in the fortifications and saw a white Ford Zephyr driving slowly along the road. She hung back in the shadows to watch it pass. Sure enough, it was Jack. While she had been talking to Steve Weiss, he must have been to see Mr Beck and found out that she, Maisie, had been there before him. Now, he was looking for her.

Jack drove on out of sight, behind the last houses, towards the dead end of the water and the turning circle and the car park where she had left the Land Rover.

Maisie felt herself crumble, her self-confidence ebbing away. That morning, she had felt brave. Now, she wanted to run out into the street and call out to him, but she couldn't face his disapproval.

What had she done? She had got involved. She had interfered. Defied him, possibly broken the law, exactly what he had asked her not to. She had decided that she knew best and come looking for clues, ahead of him, when he already had an appointment to question Mr Beck, no doubt armed with much more pertinent information than she possessed.

Had Jack also briefly met Steve Weiss at the Becks' door, the social worker going in as he, Jack, came out? And would Steve have said anything to him? That would be even worse.

She stayed where she was, hidden in the shadow of the archway. The police car came back past. She was on the point of stepping out and hailing him when she saw through the windscreen that his face was angry and set, so she stayed where she was and watched him drive away.

As soon as he was out of sight, Maisie emerged from her hiding place and almost ran back to the car park. There was a piece of paper folded under one of the windscreen wipers of the Land Rover. She took it out and unfolded it. The message was terse and unsigned, no gesture of familiarity or affection to soften the blow.

What the hell do you think you are doing?

***

Maisie climbed into the Land Rover, started the engine and tried to engage first gear. It stuck, just like Phyl had warned her that third gear would do. She struggled, then managed to get the car into second and pulled away with a lot of revs to make sure she didn't stall.

The road out of Portsmouth was busy with traffic from a car ferry that had recently docked – lots of haulage trucks and vehicles with foreign number plates and European letter codes on bright white stickers. She struggled along in second, following them onto the A27, heading east towards Chichester, then jumped up into fourth. The main road would be better than picking her way across country back to Bunting, having to navigate with only even-numbered gears and she hoped to catch Jack at the police station and come clean.

She now regretted avoiding him. She should have come out of hiding and faced him, told him what she knew, what she was thinking. Hanging back in the shadows of the fortifications would make things worse. Hiding only ever made things worse.

In the back of her mind was something Mr Beck had said about Zoe being able to get work in the village if she wanted it. By an odd mental process, it made her think about the André Malraux novel she had brought with her and was failing to read, *Les Chênes qu'on abat.* The possible explanations she kept coming up with were like the oak trees in the title, felled by contradictory facts.

Was Zoe capable of murder? The question made Maisie think of the famous quotation from *A Midsummer Night's Dream*: 'Though she be but little, she is fierce.' That was a pretty good description of Zoe. In the play, Helena says it about Hermia, a rare strong Shakespearean woman who rebels against her father's law. But Zoe had no father, just Mr Beck, a kind of sympathetic but disengaged caretaker. And Mr Beck was still alive. No one had come after him.

Dander could easily have been given a poisoned pie or quiche or something from the pub kitchen. It might even be death caps. What had Phyl said? They were 'thermostable'. Cooking didn't make them safe. But that wasn't necessarily Zoe. The girl had told Phyl that someone had been in the kitchen at the pub when everyone was at the sung vespers and whoever it was had left a mess, as if they didn't really know what they were doing.

300

But perhaps they did know what they were doing? Perhaps they had simply been obliged to move fast and didn't have time to clear up? But how would a poisoned pie end up on Dander's table? That was absurd, like a fairy tale or something, wasn't it? No, the vicar's housekeeper sometimes fetched his tea for him so anyone could have left it.

Then there was Kimmings, an assault by stealth, stringing up the dead pheasant from his lampshade to shock him when he got home and turned on the light. The dead bird came from Phyl's barn. How much muscle did that need? Not much, just a strong stomach. Would it have been deliberate, in the hope that it might bring on a heart attack? But wasn't that rather far-fetched? Could it have simply been a vengeful prank?

Looking ahead, up the road, Maisie caught a first glimpse of the spire of Chichester cathedral in the distance. That made her think of Maurice Ryan's solicitor's office, almost next door, and her first re-meeting with Phyllis Pascal, badly parked, barking orders, an almost-cartoonish 'loud country woman'. What had she said, when Maisie probed about having seen so little of 'Auntie Phyllis' during her childhood?

'*Yes, I regret all that very much.*'

'*What do you regret?*' she had asked. '*What do you mean by "all that"?*'

Phyl hadn't properly replied.

Since then, of course, time and their shared experiences had peeled away more layers to reveal who Phyl really was – someone who felt things deeply, who supported multiple charities in order to make up for a wrong that, apparently, no one else knew she had committed. And a lonely woman, too. What was Zoe, if not some kind of surrogate? Her lodger, too?

Maisie remembered looking at the photographs of Phyl's austere wedding day at the wartime registrar's office. She remembered thinking that she, Maisie, resembled Phyl in her wedding dress. She had rationalised it as a shared facial expression, revealing a shared attitude to life – a sort of reserved amusement or tolerant detachment. But it wasn't just that. It was a close family resemblance.

She felt her heart skip a beat. Perhaps, the closest family resemblance?

Maisie forced the gearbox from fourth to second as she entered the city of Chichester from the south, past the canal basin, heading for the police station, trying to imagine a timeline for everything she knew, just to make sure it was straight in her own head. Then, perhaps, she would be able to explain to Jack and he would understand why she had felt the need to defy him.

She parked at the side of the road and sat, with her hands still grasping the steering wheel, thinking about what Steve Weiss had said, lamenting his caseload. He'd mentioned that a mental health ward had just closed, and a halfway house in West Dean.

Where were those people now? And one in particular? And what knowledge had that person obtained from Steve's predecessor, the one who was sacked for failing to keep professional secrets? But how did that connect to Zoe?

And in that moment, the pieces of the kaleidoscope all shifted and formed a bright new pattern into which she thought absolutely everything might fit, at last.

THIRTY-NINE

Maisie ran into the police station, desperate to share her thoughts with Jack Wingard. There was an elderly sergeant on duty, an officer she didn't recognise, overweight in a rather worn but otherwise immaculate uniform. He knew who she was, however.

'Miss Cooper, isn't it?'

'Yes.'

'I'm Sergeant Dodd. Sergeant Wingard asked me to look out for you.'

'Has he left word?'

'He has, to the effect that, should you drop in, might you see your way clear to waiting for him, here, at the station?'

'Oh, yes. Of course. Can you tell me where he is? I might go and find him.'

'I couldn't say, miss, no.'

Maisie wasn't sure if that meant 'no, he didn't know' or 'no, he couldn't tell her'.

'Never mind.'

She sat down on a bench, her eyes sliding across the official notices on a crowded corkboard. A feeling of impatience grew inside her. This was ridiculous. More bad things might be happening at that very moment and she thought she knew where and why. She stood up again.

'You really have no idea where he is, when he might return? I saw him in Old Portsmouth and he left before me.'

'No, miss,' came the stolid reply.

Maisie frowned, tapping her fingernails on the counter. Would he try to stop her – to detain her – if she left? There was only one way to find out.

'I can't stay here doing nothing. Tell him I've gone to speak to Ernest Sumner, would you? He'll know what I mean.'

'He really was very particular—' Sergeant Dodd began.

Maisie ignored him, his voice fading out of earshot as she left the imposing police building and ran across the car park. Would he follow her?

She climbed into the Land Rover, turned the key and started the engine. First gear again refused, so she pulled away with an angry whine in second. In her wing mirror, she just caught a glimpse of a miniature Sergeant Dodd, standing on the front step, watching her go.

***

Navigating the narrow roads out of Chichester, Maisie worried that she was becoming melodramatic. What was she doing, fleeing the police station?

No, she told herself. A woman was dead, Dander had been poisoned and others might be at risk – more rotten oak trees in danger of being felled.

But were they rotten?

She had decided that the ambulance at Dander's Edwardian vicarage was too much of a coincidence. There was no way it could be simple food poisoning. How often did that become a reason to call an ambulance? More or less never.

She remembered the description of death cap poisoning from the book on Phyl's nightstand. The first symptoms were pain, vomiting and diarrhoea from six hours or more after ingestion, continuing for a day or two, then an apparent recovery, followed by jaundice and kidney failure, coma and death.

She wondered if prompt medical attention might save him? Perhaps. On the other hand, some natural toxins couldn't be counteracted. Death caps were possibly among them.

She found she didn't care. Dander was, as she had reminded Jack, 'a snake' and didn't deserve her sympathy.

Her thoughts changed tack. Sympathy was important. It had changed Phyl's life, so she said, taking in first Zoe and then her 'lodger'. And Zoe had been sympathetic, too, helping the newcomer. What had she said, exactly?

'*She was a nice woman, but she always looked like she was about to cry. I gave her leftovers, in the afternoon, when she came to the back of the pub at closing time. I used to talk to her.*'

'*The homeless woman?*'

'*She wasn't homeless. She just . . .*'

Maisie had waited for clarification, getting the distinct impression that Zoe was holding something back.

The Land Rover spluttered as she swung through Framlington, turning right just after the pub and the forge, heading up into the Downs. Rain began to fall, heavy vertical rain, falling straight down out of the clouds with no wind, running down the windscreen in determined rivulets.

Maisie put on the wipers and crunched the gears from fourth to second at the little junction where she had first seen Old Archie, riding his tractor, when he had let Phyl go first. There was loyalty there, wasn't there. Was it blind loyalty? That was an interesting idea, one that she hadn't considered before now. But what did Archie actually know? He seemed, like his brother Bert in Maisie's investigation of Stephen's murder, to keep himself at arm's length from what he would doubtless refer to as 'the goings-on'. But might he have become involved – intimately involved?

Maisie drove on, taking the right turn into the lonely valley, signposted for Harden and Bunting. As she came level with

Dander's vicarage, she saw a woman in a pale-blue house-coat, shaking dust out of a rug in the shelter of the porch.

Maisie stood hard on the brakes and pulled over, causing the Land Rover to skid in the wet gravel at the side of the road. She jumped out, ran round and darted up the path. As soon as she too was under cover from the downpour, she introduced herself, said she had seen the ambulance leaving early that morning and asked if the woman knew how Dander was now doing.

'I'm sure I couldn't say. Police told me they'd finished their business and that I could come in and clear up. And what a mess it was.' The woman had a bottle of Domestos bleach in her hand. 'If you don't mind me speaking out of turn.'

She wrinkled her nose. Maisie supposed it was vomit or diarrhoea that had needed clearing up.

'You're Canon Dander's housekeeper, I suppose?'

'Not exactly, but I come in.'

'Can I ask you who fetched his supper from the pub last night? I understand he used to have something from the Dancing Hare most evenings?'

'Well, it used to be the girl.'

'Zoe Richards?'

'Yes.' The woman left a pause and Maisie waited her out. Eventually, her natural garrulousness made her go on. 'I don't like Dander and there's not many who do, but I've got to make a living, haven't I, and he pays on time, on the kitchen table, every Thursday, regular as clockwork.'

'Are you aware,' said Maisie carefully, 'that Zoe has been speaking to a solicitor about making a complaint to the police?'

'Good for her.'

'Would you be able to support her?'

'No, I wouldn't want to be talking to no police.'

'Never mind,' said Maisie, exasperated. 'You say it "used to be" Zoe who delivered the vicar's suppers?'

306

'He didn't often fetch them himself. I reckon he thought it beneath him to be walking home with a pie in his hand. Some days, it was Ernest Sumner out for his afternoon exercise. It's only three-quarters of a mile. Sometimes Miss Brook from the shop. I might, if I was going that way.'

'And yesterday?'

'I can't say. It was on the table when I came in to put his electric heater on ready, his glass and plate and his knife and fork.'

'And Ernest Sumner or Jenny Brook would be able to get in?'

'Vicar wasn't much of a one for locking up. Folks aren't, as a rule, round here.'

No, thought Maisie. *I know.*

'And you didn't stay and speak to him?'

'Went back to my own fire.' She gave a shiver. 'It's a terrible cold house, the vicarage.'

'You didn't notice what it was, did you, his bit of supper on the table?'

'It was quiche.'

Maisie nodded and dropped her gaze, her mind whirring. There was a pile of newspapers under the bench seat in the porch, presumably set aside for lighting fires. It made Maisie think about the second dark chamber in Phyl's wine cellar, the one that the unlocked door opened into, with newspapers strewn across the beaten-earth floor like a rudimentary mattress as if someone had been sleeping down there.

Something clicked.

Phyl's lodger had been in there, listening to Phyl's conversations in the library above. That's why she had abandoned her encampment. When was that? Last Friday or Saturday? And down in the wine cellar, through the thinnish timbers of the trapdoor, she had overheard all

307

kinds of conversations, enumerating all the accusations and injustices Zoe had suffered. Put that alongside Zoe talking to the woman after hours at the back door of the pub . . .

'Thank you,' said Maisie, abruptly, and left the housekeeper standing with the dusty rug still in her hand.

The rain was heavier still, splashing on the brick path in great fat drops. Maisie ran back to the Land Rover, almost stumbling as she went round to the driver's side. Her hair felt wet through as she climbed into the cab. She turned the key in the ignition and tried to engage first gear. No go. She tried second. The gear lever wouldn't move. Third was out of the question. Nothing would take. The lever was like a bar of metal, caught in concrete.

'Oh, come on,' she said aloud, exasperated.

She let out the clutch, depressed it and tried again, managing to get the gearstick through neutral and into the notch for fourth. She trod down hard on the accelerator, bringing the revs up very high and feathering out the clutch, infinitely carefully. Unsurprisingly, the engine stalled. When she tried to restart it, she found there was no response, no ignition at all. She had flooded the carburettor.

'Damn it,' Maisie shouted, banging her hands on the steering wheel.

She got out, looking for passing traffic to thumb a lift, but there was no one. The rain continued to fall.

It wasn't far from Harden to Bunting, was it? What had Dander's housekeeper just said? 'Three-quarters of a mile.' That sounded right.

She decided to run through the downpour. As she set off, the soles of her shoes slapping against the wet tarmac, she was aware of the woman watching her go with undisguised interest.

FORTY

Years before, at Westbrook College, their minor public school, and later in the army, Maisie and Stephen had both been keen pentathletes. Stephen had been selected for important competitions while Maisie, as a girl, had only been allowed to take part recreationally. But she retained the skills and attributes she had trained for: horse riding, fencing, pistol shooting, swimming and – most importantly at this moment – cross-country running.

She arrived, therefore, sodden but not entirely out of breath at the Dancing Hare, having run all the way along the road from Canon Dander's Edwardian vicarage in Harden. As she went to bang on the door of the pub, she noticed there were three or four chickens on the village green, pecking about in the wet grass.

Poor Gordon's left the gate open, she thought, *up at the farm.*

She knocked and called out: 'Are you there, Mr Sumner?'

It was Jenny Brook who opened the door.

'Oh, what do you want?' the shopkeeper asked.

'Where's Mr Sumner?'

'He's here but he can't be disturbed.'

'I need to talk to him.' Rain was running down Maisie's neck. 'Let me in.'

She pushed her way in and found Ernest Sumner sitting close to the fire in the public bar, a mug of coffee on the table in front of him. In his right hand, rather incongruously, he held a frying pan. Both Ernest and Jenny looked white with shock.

'What's happened?' asked Maisie, quickly.

'He was attacked,' said Jenny, a tremble in her voice. 'Just five minutes ago.'

'Who by?' Maisie demanded. 'Did anyone see?'

'He's hurt,' said Jenny, her eyes wide.

Ernest held up his right hand, the one that was holding the frying pan. His sleeve was pulled up and there was a nasty gash in the fleshy part of his forearm. Blood was dripping from the wound, making a puddle on the table.

'Go and get me a tea towel,' Maisie ordered. 'And one of those cloth mats you put on the bar – a clean one.'

Jenny shook her head. 'They're all in the kitchen. I'm not going in there. They might come back.'

Jenny was wearing a chiffon scarf.

'Take that off,' Maisie insisted, 'and give it to me. Mr Sumner, do you have a handkerchief?'

For a second, he looked vague. Was he drunk? No, this was different. Definitely shock.

'Yes, of course,' he replied.

He fetched one out of his left-hand trouser pocket. Luckily, it was clean.

'Put down that frying pan and tell me what happened,' said Maisie. 'Why have you got it?'

'I just picked it up. I didn't know what else to do.'

He let go of the frying pan and Maisie applied the handkerchief in a dense pad to the wound, binding it tight with Jenny's chiffon scarf. She didn't think it was serious but she took Sumner's left hand and placed it over the top.

'Keep applying pressure, firm pressure.'

'Yes, thank you, Miss . . . You say we've met?'

'Yes, we have. Yesterday, the day of the shoot, when Mrs Pascal came in to help you and Zoe. And the day before, at lunch. My name is Maisie Cooper.'

'Did you come upstairs with me?' he asked, the vague memory visible in his eyes.

'I did.'

'And I was rather the worse for . . .' His face reddened and he averted his gaze. 'I'm sorry. I may not, on any of these occasions, have been the best version of myself.'

'Never mind that now,' Maisie interrupted, needing to confirm her own suspicions – the pattern she thought could explain everything. 'Please, tell me. What did you mean when you told me that the homeless woman was two women?'

'I'm not sure.' He hesitated then raised his head, his eyes bloodshot, his face drawn, no longer the dapper, jovial landlord. 'Did I say that, though? God, I say a lot of foolish things.'

'You mustn't browbeat him, Miss Cooper,' said Jenny. 'He's had a shock. What do you want, anyway?'

Maisie was very aware of the puddle of water around her feet, dripping from her sodden clothes. She must look a sight. No wonder the shopkeeper was wary. And, while Sumner seemed defeated, Jenny seemed different, too, but in a different direction – less limp, more alert and purposeful.

'Miss Brook, Jenny,' she said firmly, 'this is important. It's to do with what's happened to Mrs Pascal's lodger and to Kimmings and Canon Dander.'

'What about Canon Dander?' said Jenny.

Maisie shook her head in frustration. There was no time. She turned back to the publican, determined to get her answer.

'Mr Sumner, what did you mean when you told me that the homeless woman who set up camp at Bunting Manor was two women?'

'I suppose just that? Or perhaps I should have said: "the same woman".'

'The same woman as on Bonfire Night?' guessed Maisie. 'And then, more recently, when Zoe would give her food at the rear of the pub? That was the same woman.'

'Yes, it was.'

'But then she came again, in different clothes, more ordinary clothes? That was the same woman?'

'That's right.'

'And that was just a couple of days ago, wasn't it?' said Maisie, sharing some of the timeline she had worked out in her head but told no one. 'Can you confirm exactly when?'

'I can't,' said Ernest, his eyes sad, his mouth turned down. His eyes wandered to the bar and the row of optics attached to the upside-down bottles of spirits. 'This is a poor show, I know . . .'

Jenny made a movement. 'Just one wouldn't hurt,' she said. 'You've had a shock—'

'No,' interrupted Ernest. 'Not one. I'm done with all that.' He picked up his mug and drank.

'But in the kitchen?' Maisie insisted. 'There was some kind of confrontation, just now?' Maisie turned to Jenny. 'And you were here?'

'Everything was normal. We were making coffee at the filter machine behind the bar. Ernie went through into the kitchen because he thought the back door was banging in the wind. Then he called out and I said, "What's that?" but he wasn't talking to me and then I heard a crash of things falling on the floor and I followed him through and he was bleeding.'

Ernest put down his mug. 'Someone was in there. Miss Brook and I had just been for a walk, up the hill behind the pub. We were back no later than eleven. What time is it?'

Maisie glanced at her watch. 'Half past.'

'Perhaps you shouldn't open for lunch today, Ernest,' said Jenny.

'Yes, perhaps.'

'Go on,' ordered Maisie. 'Someone was in there.'

'There's a path into the pheasant woods. I had something I wanted to say to this lady.' He gave Jenny a grateful glance. 'When we got back, we came round and in through the front door from the road, so . . .' He took a deep breath and that seemed to steady him. 'Excuse me, would you?' He drank a mouthful of coffee. 'We went behind the bar to put the water through the Melitta filter and I heard someone in the kitchen. I thought perhaps it might be Zoe, come to get ahead with lunches.'

'Just a moment. Did you have any difficulties with Zoe?' asked Maisie.

'Never, never.' He turned to Jenny. 'She was hard-working and honest.'

'Nicola Beck,' said the shopkeeper, 'told me that I should look out for her pinching things off my shelves. She told Alice Spragg that Zoe wasn't to be trusted, too, but I never saw any reason to believe it.' She paused. 'There was one odd thing.'

'Yes?'

'Gordon told me one day – I think he'd been drinking for courage – that he was going to ask Mrs Pascal for permission to propose to Zoe.'

Maisie saw again, in her mind's eye, Gordon's chickens on the village green. She felt a surge of inexplicable anxiety, far more perhaps than was warranted by some escaped poultry.

'I drink too much,' said Ernest, apologetically, following his own train of thought. 'This lady has consented to help me.'

Jenny was standing very close to him and he leant his head against her side. Clearly, he had persuaded Jenny that he had determined to go on the wagon.

'Never mind that now,' said Maisie. 'Did you see who it was, clearly, to recognise?'

'They were cooking, would you believe?' he asked her.

Yes, thought Maisie, *I would.*

'Go on. Tell me. Who was it?' she demanded.

313

'Er, well, I didn't see them clearly. They were on the other side of the extractor hood, you know? And when I came in, they snatched up a knife and threw it at me and it did me a bit of damage, as you have seen, and – at the same time – I was snatching up that frying pan to defend myself. I think the knife was thrown in panic . . .' He hesitated. 'I am not a brave man.'

'Go on.'

'It struck my arm and I fled.'

'You fled – back into the bar, you mean?'

'And then we heard them,' Jenny interrupted, 'moments later, banging out the back door.'

'Man or woman?' Maisie insisted.

'It was all a blur, but I would say woman,' said Ernest.

Without hesitation, Maisie went behind the bar and through into the kitchen and stood at the foot of the narrow stair that led up to Sumner's apartment. For a few seconds, she stayed very quiet and still, listening, trying to sense another's presence. But no, there was no one.

She moved round to the far side of the extractor hood. On the stainless-steel counter, someone had been preparing pastry and filling. Alongside the diced carrots and onions and minced beef, there was a little heap of chopped mushrooms, dry and unappetising, grey with a hint of yellow.

Maisie found a glass bowl on a shelf and put it upturned over the mushrooms, weighting it down with a tin of chopped tomatoes. She looked around on the floor for the knife that had wounded Ernest Sumner, but couldn't find it. She went back to the bar, her wet clothes chafing against her skin.

'You must call the police. When they come, tell them there's a small pile of death cap mushrooms under a glass bowl on the food-prep counter. Tell them that the person who broke in may be armed with your chopping knife, probably the one they threw at you and then picked up after you ran out. Tell them that she has killed with a knife before. Tell them, if they don't already know, that Canon Dander is more than likely suffering from death cap poisoning. Tell them that someone should remain with you, because you may be in danger.'

'I don't . . .' Sumner began. 'Forgive me, this is a lot very fast.'

'I have it,' said Jenny. 'Poisonous mushrooms in the kitchen. Canon Dander a victim. Beware knife. Stay here and keep safe.'

Maisie gave her a glance of recognition. Jenny Brook had not been found wanting in a crisis.

'Call the police straight away. Do it now. When they get here, tell them I've gone to Gordon Stock's farm. Do you have a coat I can borrow?'

'By the door,' said Ernest, waving his good hand.

Jenny went to the phone behind the bar. Maisie peeled off her borrowed anorak and put it down, the sodden fabric slapping against the seat of the chair. Just inside the front door were some coat hooks. On one of them was a yellow oilskin. She put it on, pushing her arms into the overbig sleeves, doing up the zip and poppers. She had a flashback to Jack and his forensic technician, showing her the remains of the coat that had been burnt on the fire at Phyl's lodger's encampment.

Nicola Beck's coat, obviously.

FORTY-ONE

Maisie pulled open the door of the Dancing Hare and went out into the rain. It was falling just as heavily, drenching the verges, filling the potholes at the edge of the broken tarmac and pooling out onto the road.

Maisie hesitated under the shallow porch, wondering if Phyl was back yet. She might be, a taxi bringing her home from the railway station in Havant, after her flying visit to London. She wanted to run up to Bunting Manor and find out – and to make sure that Zoe was safe.

Then she noticed that there were now at least two dozen hens pecking about in the sodden grass of the village green and, of course, there was really only one explanation. Something had happened at Gordon's farm.

Maisie took a deep breath and sprinted the hundred yards to the heart of the village, her feet rubbing raw in her drenched socks. Alice Spragg appeared in her doorway wearing a lime green Pac-a-Mac raincoat. At the same time, Archie Close came rattling along on his tractor. Maisie waved him to a stop and bellowed at him over the noise of the diesel engine.

'Archie, collect up these hens before someone comes through and runs over them or has an accident trying to avoid them. Can you do that?'

'I'm your man,' he shouted back.

'Then follow me up to Gordon's.'

'I get it. They must have come down from up-along.'

Maisie couldn't help smiling at Archie's idiosyncratic country speech. Then someone was tapping her on the shoulder. It was Alice Spragg, tying a see-through plastic headscarf over her severe pageboy haircut.

'I'll help you,' she shouted. 'I mean, I'll help with the chickens.'

'Thank you,' said Maisie, nodding her approval.

She left them to it and ran on to the edge of the village, nearly to the bonfire field, then left, up the rutted lane towards Gordon's farmhouse in the valley. Three fastidious chickens were picking their way between the puddles in the chalk and flint, while she stuck to the verge. Halfway up, she slipped and almost fell avoiding another hen, wiping the rain from her eyes. Finally, she reached the five-bar gate where she had seen the failing farmer giving Kimmings his fresh milk and eggs.

The gate was open, the chain lying untidily on the ground. Warily, Maisie went through into the filthy yard. She heard squawking and turned, noticing a gap in the fence to the chicken run where it had been pulled open. The last few hens were tentatively investigating the opening, wary of leaving their wire prison.

Maisie was about to turn away and cross the filthy yard to the house, the front door hanging open, when she saw movement behind the haphazard chicken coops. She went closer. Four hens came skittering and squawking round her feet, thinking they were about to be fed. Then she caught a glimpse of someone trying to hide. For a split second, there was a fringe of a leather coat with drab yellowing fur.

An Afghan coat.

Maisie slipped into the chicken run.

'Zoe,' she hissed, 'it's me, Maisie. Don't move. Don't say anything.' She crept forward. 'It's going to be all right. Everything's going to be all right.'

She put a hand on the edge of the jerry-built coops, on a length of loose timber only held in place by the fact that one of the tarpaulins was tied onto it.

'Trust me,' she whispered. 'I'll look after you.'

Zoe was sitting on the ground, her knees pulled up tight to her chest, her arms round her shins, her hands curled tight into fists. Her hair was plastered against her head and it was impossible to tell what was rain, running down her face, and what were tears. Maisie crouched beside her, putting a hand on her shoulder. The girl looked up.

'I didn't do anything wrong,' she said.

'I know,' Maisie reassured her. 'Tell me what happened.'

'I was at Bunting Manor. I was upstairs, in my room, and the phone rang for ages. Then it rang again and it just kept going and the third time I went down and answered it.'

'It was Gordon, wasn't it?' said Maisie.

'He sounded really worried about me all alone. I told him that I would have to be at the pub soon but he said it wasn't safe with a murderer about. I think he really meant it – he wasn't just trying to get me on my own. We used to be proper friends.'

'I understand. And then?'

'I got here and there was shouting from the farmhouse and I was frightened. What Gordon had told me on the phone – I began believing it.' Zoe unclasped her hands and Maisie saw that she had torn her palm on some sharp edge. 'I did that on the chicken wire.'

'Never mind. Keep your hand tight shut until help comes. Go on.'

Zoe balled up her fist. 'Then I just hid and I thought about what Mrs Pascal said when I got back last night – that she was going to London and could I look after you.'

'She said that?'

'She said I should remind you that you weren't to leave before she got home.' Zoe wiped her nose with the back of her hand. 'Are you leaving? I don't want you to leave.'

'Never mind that,' said Maisie. 'What happened then?'

'The chickens were getting out but I was too frightened to move. Then I saw them.'

'Saw who?'

'Gordon ran out of the farmhouse over to the barn and she was just there in the doorway, watching him go, with a knife in her hand.' Zoe looked Maisie in the eye. A flash of understanding passed between them. 'You know,' said the girl. 'Don't you?'

'I think I do,' said Maisie. 'What sort of knife?'

'It looked like one from the kitchen at the pub.' She stopped. 'Is Ernie all right?'

'Mr Sumner is quite safe. Go on,' Maisie prompted. 'What did she do then?'

'She went back inside.'

FORTY-TWO

Maisie approached the open door of the farmhouse, indifferent to the mud and animal mess all over her shoes. In her right hand, she held a piece of timber, the loose length from the chicken coop that she had put her hand on. She carried it as a deterrent, hoping she wouldn't have to hurt anyone.

She came to the open front door and peered round the frame into a sombre hallway: a dirty rug on the floor; a side table for bills, all of them unopened; shabby coats on hooks all along one wall; heavy boots and muddy wellingtons by the skirting board. There were two doors, one straight ahead, one to her left. Both were closed.

She went to the left-hand door and pressed her ear to the timber.

Nothing.

She went to the end of the hall and did the same. Then she smelt it – smoke.

She took hold of the Bakelite handle and turned it, gently pushing the door open into a filthy living room with a wide French window, standing ajar, giving access to a drenched and untidy vegetable garden and the valley beyond. She took in a grimy low sofa with a scruffy valance, a footstool, a side table and a small shaded lamp. There was a scorched hearth rug and a fire burning in the hearth.

The woman was kneeling in front of it, wet with rain and smudged with dust and dirt. She was leaning in, across the fire dogs, grasping a smouldering log in heavy tongs, an expression of great concentration on her face, as if she was working out some kind of difficult puzzle. Maisie could see moss on the dark bark and the wood seemed rather damp, but it was burning, beginning to fill the room with acrid fumes.

'What are you doing?' Maisie heard herself ask.

Without looking up, the woman replied: 'I'm going to burn farmer's house down.'

Next to the fireplace was an occasional table covered by a dirty lace cloth. The woman adjusted her position and held the smouldering log to the edge. The lace tried to catch, becoming black then developing a little orange ember. The woman canted over, blowing gently on it to encourage the flame. The lace began to smoke as well, grey wisps rising the length of the drape of cloth.

'But why?' Maisie asked.

'Because he won't leave her alone, my sweet, beautiful Zoe, chiding and chasing her. I heard what Mrs Pascal told you, too, when I was hiding down in that old cellar, that he was angry and dangerous.'

'I don't think that's true,' said Maisie.

With the woman's breath encouraging them, a few narrow flames snaked up the drape of lace to the level of the table, flickering and weaving, their tips reaching the fringe of the shade on the small table lamp – a ring of balls of some synthetic fibre that hissed and spat as they shrank and melted.

'You don't want to do this,' said Maisie. 'This just makes everything worse.'

'People got to pay for what they do,' said the woman. For the first time she looked round and Maisie saw her clearly – very pale skin, good bone structure and wide-set brown eyes, but aged and saddened by life and by difficult circumstances. 'I chased him out.' She gestured towards the hallway and the front door with the smouldering log. An ember fell and began burning its way into the filthy hearth rug. 'He ran like a rabbit.'

Maisie wondered what she should do. She wasn't worried for her own safety. She knew she was strong and agile enough to protect herself, but she couldn't let the woman burn down the farmhouse. In the brief silence, she thought she heard sirens, vague and distant.

'The police are coming,' she said. 'You don't want them to find you doing this.'

'I don't care what anybody finds me doing. People got to pay.'

Suddenly, Gordon was framed in the open French window, a hatchet for chopping kindling in his hand.

'No, you won't be burning down my mum and dad's house,' he shouted.

'Stop, Gordon,' said Maisie, stepping in front of him.

In his fury, he swept the head of the hatchet backhand, left to right. Maisie avoided the blow, swaying away, then parried the return with the length of timber from the chicken coop when he tried to strike her from the other side. A protruding nail caught his knuckles, tearing the flesh. He cried out and clasped the wound with his other hand as the hatchet fell to the floor.

'She mustn't,' he cried out, his face crumpled in distress.

He kicked at the side table, knocking it out of the woman's reach. The lamp fell to the floor and the burning lace fell against the valance of a grimy low sofa. He stamped on it to put out the flames.

'Gordon, control yourself.'

'I've got no call to control myself. Look what she's doing.'

Maisie could see. The woman was using the tongs to rake the burning firewood out of the hearth onto the rug.

Gordon barged into Maisie's shoulder, sending her tripping over the footstool, landing square on her back, all the air knocked out of her lungs. As she struggled to get her breath, she saw Gordon snatch up the fallen hatchet and raise it above his head, the blood from the gash across his knuckles dripping on the side of his face. The woman cowered, raising her thin hands ineffectually to protect herself. Masie could do nothing, not even speak. It wasn't her courage that failed. All the wind had been knocked out of her.

She saw that Gordon was undecided, that he didn't really want to do the woman any harm. But, just then, Zoe came barrelling across the room in her sodden Afghan coat, ducking under Gordon's arm and striking him with her shoulder just above the waist, like a rugby tackle, bending him in half. Gordon stumbled back and toppled over the arm of the sofa, landing with a crash in a heap on the floor behind it.

'Come,' said Zoe quickly to the woman, breathlessly standing up. 'Come with me.' She almost had to drag the woman to her feet. Meanwhile, the air grew more and more difficult to breathe. 'It's over,' said the girl, her kind eyes never leaving the woman's face. 'Come outside, now. Let's get away from all this smoke and upset.'

Maisie could clearly hear the siren of a police car not far away, perhaps even coming up the lane to the farm gate.

'Take her outside.'

Zoe did so and Maisie used the fallen tongs to put the burning logs back on the fire. Gordon levered himself to his feet, his hands on the back of the sofa, watching her. He looked sad, defeated.

'A man's got a right to protect himself, hasn't he?' Gordon asked, sounding like an abandoned child. 'It's my home, isn't it?'

'Yes, Gordon, it is,' said Maisie, quietly. She smothered the burning valance with a cushion and transferred the smouldering lace tablecloth to the hearth where it could safely be consumed. When that was done, she faced him, her eyes running from the smoke. 'You wouldn't have hurt her, would you?'

'No, I wouldn't. I just wanted her to stop what she was doing.'

'I know,' Maisie told him. 'It's all just a terrible misunderstanding and everything's going to be all right.'

FORTY-THREE

Maisie left Gordon in his filthy living room, making sure the small fires were fully out, and followed Zoe and Phyl's lodger outside. It was Jack who arrived first, of course, driving the white Ford Zephyr. The tyres slewed sideways in the filth of the farmyard as he trod on the brakes, leaping out and running towards her. Maisie allowed herself to be wrapped in his arms, her wet head on his shoulder, feeling the cold insignia of his uniform epaulettes against her cheek.

'I'm sorry, Jack. I thought I could stop anything else bad happening—'

'Never mind now—'

'No, but I shouldn't have—'

'It's easy to say after the fact what we should or shouldn't have done—'

'And I saw you driving away in Portsmouth and I read your note—'

'Never mind that now, I tell you.' He took a step back, his hands on her shoulders. 'Are you all right – physically, I mean. You're not injured? The ambulance is coming.'

'I'm fine,' she assured him. 'Quite all right. But I've made a mess of everything, haven't I?'

'Maybe not. Maybe you've stopped something far worse.'

Jack looked round the dirty yard and Maisie followed his gaze. Barry Goodbody had got out of the rear seat of the Zephyr and was moving quickly towards the farmhouse. Another officer – a prematurely balding man in plain clothes who had been riding in front – was attending to Zoe and helping the woman by wrapping a warm blanket across her back. And there was the ambulance, creeping carefully up the lane.

'The rain's stopping, at last,' said Maisie. She felt herself weaken. 'I have so much to tell you, Jack, but I'm sorry I went and talked to Mr Beck and . . .' What could she say? 'Will you be able to forgive me?'

'I won't ever forgive myself,' said Jack. 'I should have told you what was happening on my side, what I'd been learning. Then it might have all come clear sooner. And I didn't believe you when you first came to me. I told you it was fanciful – and I was wrong.'

'No, Jack, you weren't wrong,' she told him, thinking of Phyl's deceptions with the wire and mushrooms. 'But neither was I, in the end,' she added, in a small voice. 'I know I shouldn't have let Mr Beck think I was a police officer. You must have worked that out when you talked to him right after me—'

'Don't worry, Maisie,' he interrupted. 'You're safe. That's all that matters. It'll all come right.'

He pulled her to him again and, for a few seconds that felt like much longer, neither of them moved or spoke.

'We'd better be getting away, don't you think, Jack?' called the balding plain-clothes officer. 'This woman needs some proper care and attention.'

'All right, Fred,' Jack replied, too quietly to be heard, except by Maisie, his arms tight around her shoulders.

Maisie remembered Florence Wingard talking about her grandson's contemporary who had been promoted above him to inspector. What was his name? Fred Nairn.

'You should do as he says,' she whispered.

'Yes, I should, but I don't want to.'

'Jack,' called the other man, urgently.

Maisie pulled away, not wanting to make things any worse than they already were, not wanting him to see the expression on her face. Once he knew about all of Phyl's deceptions, what would he say?

The rain had stopped. Jack went and spoke to Inspector Nairn by the open rear doors of the ambulance.

'You'll take Miss Tinker back to the station, will you, Fred?'

'I will.'

'I want to go back to West Dean,' said the woman. 'Why can't I go back-along there?'

'The West Dean house is closed down, Alberta,' said Jack, kindly. 'You know that. I'm sorry. You'll have to live somewhere else now.'

'Somewhere else? It'll be prison then, will it?'

'Yes, Alberta,' said Jack. 'I expect it will.'

The woman's face relaxed and she gave a small smile, adjusting the blanket over her shoulders. 'Then I'll get a bit of peace and quiet, I suppose?'

'I hope you do,' said Jack.

'I'll have someone check her over at the station,' said the inspector, 'and speak to social services and find an appropriate lawyer.'

'I want to go with her,' said Zoe.

'No,' said Jack. 'You can't do that.'

'But she's not well,' Zoe insisted.

'She's under arrest for the murder of Mrs Beck,' said Jack. 'You do understand that, don't you?'

'I don't know anything,' said Zoe. Her eyes were desperate and her face drawn. 'No one tells me what's going on.'

'Zoe,' said Maisie, kindly. 'I promise I'll tell you everything. I can, can't I, Jack?'

'Yes, but I think it might be better if I'm there, too,' said Jack. 'We need to get everything straight.'

'You mustn't go questioning Alberta, though,' Zoe insisted. 'She didn't know what she was doing.'

'Yes, I did, lass,' said Alberta Tinker. She sat down on the step between the open ambulance doors. 'I knew what I was doing. Old social worker told me where I could find you and I come over Bonfire Night and I saw what I saw and I didn't like it.'

'But you didn't come back again until just ten days ago?' said Maisie, unable to stay quiet. 'Why was that?'

'I had to think it all out, didn't I?' said Alberta. 'And it was dreadful cold all winter and then the lights were out with the power cuts and everyone was better off indoors, waiting for the spring. But then the West Dean house closed down and I couldn't wait no longer. I was out and I didn't know what else to do or where else to go so I slept in a shed a couple of nights and found an old tent in there and pinched some things off a clothes line and got an old trolley from the Co-op supermarket to put it all together and come up here.'

They made an odd grouping, Maisie thought, Alberta seated on the back step of the ambulance and the others in a semicircle round her. Maisie glanced at Jack and he gave her a small nod that she took as permission to continue.

'And you took a tarpaulin from Gordon's chicken run, didn't you?' Maisie asked.

'I did, and it weren't so bad up-along from the Big House where I had my fire and my rabbits and clean water from the stream and a bit of something from the pub every afternoon. That was a kindness.'

She held out her hand towards Zoe but Jack stopped the girl from approaching and taking it.

'One moment,' he said kindly to Zoe. 'Then what, Alberta?' he asked.

'Then I done what I done and I thought I should stay out of sight.'

'What do you mean,' said Fred Nairn, 'by "I done what I done"?'

'I practised on that old lamb and then I pushed my knife up under her ribs, too, and left her face down in the stream, but below where I used to take my drink so as not to spoil the water. I'm not making no secret of it.'

'How did you get the phone number to call?' asked Maisie.

'Call who?' demanded Zoe.

'Mrs Beck,' said Maisie.

'There was a note on the front door of their old house telling their telephone, wasn't there? I can read numbers all right so I slipped into the back of the pub one day after the lass had gone home and that old landlord was nodding in his chair by the fire with his whisky glass in his hand and I made a phone call from the kitchen. I told that Mrs Beck that she should come out here and speak to me or I'd be down there and on to social services about what she was like and she said yes but she'd have to get the bus.' Alberta shook her head. She seemed resigned – glad even that it was all over. 'You all know she was cruel to the lass and hadn't she taken her away from me?'

'No,' said Maisie. 'She didn't take her away from you. You gave her up when she was a baby and then later – much later – Mrs Beck became her foster mother. And she may not have been very good at it, but I think she tried her best.'

On the back step of the ambulance, Alberta Tinker began to look agitated.

'Never mind "her best". I heard what was said, round the village. I listened from down in the cellar in the Big House. I know all that went on.'

'What about Commander Kimmings?' asked Jack.

'I got a pheasant from the tractor barn at Bunting Manor while everyone was in church and strung it up to his lamp with my rabbit wire.'

'That's what I thought,' said Jack, smoothly. 'That'll do for now. Alberta, my friend Fred will make sure you're looked after. He'll make sure you're warm and find you a bit of peace and quiet.'

The woman's face softened.

'Like back at the West Dean house?'

'Not exactly like that, but everyone will do their best.'

Maisie wondered if this was what the woman had needed all along – somewhere safe and peaceful to live out her days. Then she reminded herself that she had done some terrible things.

Alberta reached out her hand to Zoe. This time, Jack let the girl step closer and take it.

'You stopped that farmer from doing me a damage.'

'He wasn't really going to hurt you,' said Maisie.

'You're a brave little thing,' Alberta told Zoe.

'Thank you.'

'You want to watch out, though. You don't want to turn out like me.'

Zoe put her hands to her face, stifling her tears. Maisie put an arm round her thin shoulders, thinking about her own family and what she had learnt from Phyl's tentative conversation and the mysterious scrapbook.

How, she wondered, *will I ever manage to make sense of that?*

FORTY-FOUR

As the ambulance pulled slowly away, Barry Goodbody and Gordon Stock emerged from the farmhouse, the constable's hand on the farmer's arm. Gordon had changed out of his wet clothes into a beige suit with wide velvet lapels, a ragged cardigan and a black T-shirt underneath.

'Perhaps we can bend the rules and go back to Bunting Manor to dry out and warm up,' said Jack. 'Barry can take Gordon into Chichester in the car and get his statement.'

'Yes, please,' said Maisie. Then she added: 'Everyone needs to know how brave you were, Zoe.'

'I agree,' said Jack. 'You showed great courage and real kindness. You should be very proud.'

Then his face fell as he realised he had said the wrong thing. Zoe burst into a flood of tears, releasing a tide of pent-up emotion, lurching into Maisie and clinging to her as if she was afraid of falling and would never let her go.

★★★

A little later, they were all four in the library at Bunting Manor: Maisie, Jack, Phyl and Zoe. They had found Phyl on the front doorstep, back from London, unaware of all that had happened.

'I saw the Land Rover parked at the pub. Ernest Sumner told me he was attacked and that Maisie had gone after whoever did it. I've been desperately worried.' Her eyes were wide. 'Zoe, what's happened?'

'We'll tell you everything,' said Maisie. 'But Zoe and I must put on some dry clothes.'

They ran upstairs to do so. When they came back down, Jack was crouching beside the hearth in the library, lighting the fire, using pages from the *Chichester Observer*. Feeling suddenly exhausted, Maisie flopped down in one of the bookcase-armchairs. Phyl subsided into the other one. Zoe sat on the Persian rug at Maisie's feet. As the kindling began to burn up, Jack added two logs and stood up.

'How did it begin?' asked Zoe in a small voice. 'Will you tell me that?'

'Of course,' said Maisie.

She took a moment, though, feeling that she had been running along behind events, unable to catch up. Thanks to Zoe's courage, the worst had been averted, but there was something else she knew she needed to confront – a shadow from her own past that would have to wait until she spoke to Phyl alone.

'It began when my friend Charity – you know, Maurice Ryan's wife – introduced me to Phyl who asked me to come to Bunting Manor and investigate a mystery. She had seen my name in the paper for helping to solve my brother's murder. But she knew me from when I was a baby.'

Maisie told the story of Phyl's subterfuge with the wire, creating a pretext for getting Maisie to come and stay, then Phyl's worry that she had actually put the idea of murder into someone's mind.

'That was a very foolish thing to do,' said Jack, 'but thankfully no one actually did get caught by a wire strung between trees.'

'And it never was strung between the trees, was it?' said Maisie. 'Phyl tied it round the trunks, making it look like it had been. That was all.'

'Yes,' said Phyl, looking uneasy.

'At that point,' Maisie went on, 'Phyl's lodger, Alberta Tinker, had disappeared so, when the body was found in the stream, everyone believed it was her.'

'Until the post-mortem showed it was a woman in good health and so on,' said Jack.

'But Alberta wasn't actually homeless herself,' Maisie said, realising this as she said it.

'Well,' said Jack, 'not for very long. And there was also the difference in age. Mrs Beck was forty-five while Mrs Pascal thought her lodger was significantly younger.' He turned to Phyl. 'Isn't that right?'

'It is,' said Phyl, not meeting his eye.

'The timeline is this,' Jack continued. 'In October last year, the social worker responsible for the halfway house in West Dean was sacked for lack of professionalism, poor record-keeping and sharing confidential information – including with Alberta Tinker, causing her to get herself wrapped up in some old coats and rags and trek the few miles over the Downs on the pilgrim trail on Guy Fawkes Night to Bunting.'

'To see me on my sixteenth birthday,' said Zoe quietly.

'That may have been the reason for choosing that date,' said Maisie.

'Of course,' said Phyl, nodding. 'The Guy Fawkes Night bonfire, when the village was full of visitors.'

'And that evening,' said Zoe, as if Phyl hadn't spoken, 'after the bonfire, the Becks told me they were leaving and I couldn't go with them. She doesn't have cancer, does she?'

'No,' said Maisie. 'She doesn't.'

'And the next morning,' said Phyl, 'I found you in the church porch and went and gave them a piece of my mind, but—'

'I'm sorry I've been such a pain, Mrs Pascal,' interrupted Zoe. 'I really am grateful, for everything you've done.'

'Call me Phyl,' she replied, gruffly.

'As Alberta told us,' Maisie continued, 'last winter was very harsh and she stayed where she was, biding her time, until the halfway house was closed down two weeks ago and she was out on the street.'

Jack told them a little more detail of how Alberta had then managed, based on the petty thefts and the shed break-in that he and Barry had investigated.

'Then,' Maisie resumed, 'she decided to come back and set up camp in the clearing above Bunting Manor.'

'But,' protested Phyl, 'you didn't know all this yesterday? What's happened to get everything out in the open?'

Maisie gave them all a summary of what she had done that morning – her conversations with Mr Beck and Steve Weiss.

'The key thing was, Steve had only had Zoe on his case-load since last October, but he's no fool and he told me something very interesting, in his odd way, without wanting to take responsibility himself, but giving me the hint.'

'He ought to have spoken to me,' said Jack.

'Obviously,' said Maisie, 'but I don't think he has great confidence in what I bet he would call "the machinery of the state". He's a hippy, isn't he? Anyway, he told me about the closure of a mental health ward and a halfway house and he asked me: "Where do you think those people are now?" And that made me think about how everything revolved around Zoe but none of it was her fault. In fact, it was the opposite. It was someone trying to protect her, someone with a burden of guilt, perhaps. Put that together with Mrs Beck being cruel to Zoe from more or less the first moment they fostered her and then disappearing . . .'

Maisie looked at Jack and he continued.

'We don't yet know the circumstances of her having to give up her baby sixteen years ago, but we will. Then, poor thing, she found herself ill-equipped to cope with the modern world, evicted from the halfway house into what must have seemed a very shocking and alien society—'

'Then,' Phyl interrupted, her face full of sympathy and anguish, 'ten or eleven days ago, she came back and built her encampment up behind my house because she, Alberta Tinker, is Zoe's birth mother.' She turned to the girl. 'I'm so sorry.'

Zoe nodded, her expression surprisingly calm.

'I think she thought it would be the perfect way to be close to her daughter,' said Maisie. 'And her daughter was kind to her, giving her food from the back door of the pub at the end of each lunchtime service.' Maisie put a hand on Zoe's shoulder. 'When did you know?'

Zoe spoke in a matter-of-fact voice. 'She told me, in her funny way, without ever spelling it out. She said things like: "I didn't have no choice but to leave you," and "That was how it was in them days." But it's all right. You don't all have to look at me like I'm going to break. I never really knew her. You understand that? I'm sad for her, but the family connection's just like an accident. It doesn't really mean anything.'

'You might not think that later on,' said Maisie carefully.

'Maybe,' said Zoe. 'But there's no point making it out to be more than it is. Your real parents are the people who bring you up, aren't they, and I never had any.'

'Stop it,' said Phyl, with a gasp. 'It's too much.'

'Really, it's fine.' Zoe frowned. 'But does anyone know who my father might have been?'

Jack took it upon himself to reply. 'We can ask social services for a copy of your birth certificate, but it might just say "unknown".'

'Oh yeah, of course,' said Zoe. 'And really, all of you, I'm all right.' She frowned. 'I suppose I'll be able to visit her in prison?'

Jack nodded. 'Of course.'

From her position on the rug, Zoe looked up at Maisie.

'Tell me more about how you worked it out.'

To spare Zoe, Maisie didn't repeat the details of the lamb that Archie had discovered, dead in the field, and how Alberta had practised for the murder of Mrs Beck.

'The body in the stream was your foster mother, Mrs Beck. I learnt from Mr Beck this morning that someone rang his wife – he didn't know it was Alberta calling from the pub, like she admitted just now –and got her to come out to Bunting on Saturday. Ernest Sumner saw them together but he was drunk, of course, and didn't entirely understand what he had seen. That was because Alberta had changed out of her dirty clothes and was wearing things she found in the cellar of Bunting Manor. And that was so that she wouldn't attract attention and so she could kill Mrs Beck and then dress her in her own rags and leave her face down in the stream, as she told us. Then she burnt Mrs Beck's clothes on her fire but Jack's team found the poppers and zips in the embers.'

'Alberta has confessed, in any case,' Jack reminded her.

'It's all my fault,' interrupted Phyl in a desperate voice. 'It was Mrs Beck in the stream. Oh, God, that's on me as well. I couldn't bear to look and I told you—'

'We don't take the testimony of one distressed witness at face value,' said Jack, giving Maisie a look that meant that he wouldn't be taking the matter any further. 'We always look for corroboration. One of the reasons I was in Portsmouth this morning was to arrange for Mr Beck to view the body. Missing persons reports are a matter of routine police briefing and, of course, I immediately saw the potential connection to Bunting.'

As economically as she could, Maisie told the story of the difficult drive back from Portsmouth in the failing Land Rover, via the police station and Dander's housekeeper.

'It was seeing the newspapers in Dander's porch made me think about Alberta hiding down in Phyl's cellar and how she would have overheard all that was said in the library above, reinforcing her idea that everyone was against her daughter.'

'But that wasn't true,' said Zoe. 'It was all just stupid gossip.'

'Kimmings did slap you, didn't he,' insisted Maisie, 'when you refused to rehearse with him for the Christmas carols?'

'Yes, in the church, back on Guy Fawkes Night. And she was there so she saw me run into Dander and he sort of grabbed hold of me but he didn't do anything about it – didn't stand up for me.'

Zoe stopped, her face reddening. To move things on, Maisie asked Jack about the two other men.

'Kimmings is quite well and will soon be up and about. It was just a panic attack after seeing the dead pheasant, not a heart attack. Dander did eat death caps concealed in his quiche, but it didn't agree with him and he was sick shortly after, so the dose he consumed was small. He did feel unwell, however, and fretted all night long before finally calling an ambulance just before you went past this morning. The doctors at St Richard's aren't worried.'

Maisie told Zoe and Phyl what she had discovered at the Dancing Hare.

'I think Alberta intended to poison Gordon as well, but she was disturbed by Ernest and Jenny coming in from their walk before she had time to finish. Then there was something Jack said to me about all the old tracks across the fields and through the woods, that it's easy to sneak about from place to place without being seen. Alberta must have taken the poisoned quiche to Dander's vicarage by one of the hunting paths.'

'Do you think I'll go mad as well, then?' said Zoe suddenly. 'Is that what you're worried about, that it's in my blood?'

'No, of course we aren't,' said Phyl.

'Not at all,' said Jack.

'Good,' said Zoe, firmly. 'Neither do I.'

'And it isn't madness to want to protect your own daughter,' said Maisie. 'She just misunderstood. She had no experience of the world, not really. The things she did, well, they made sense to her, even if they couldn't make sense to anyone else.' She turned to Jack. 'I don't think you know that Zoe was speaking to Maurice Ryan about her rights. Do you think she could bring an assault charge against Kimmings or pursue the Becks for neglect?'

'I don't know—' Jack began carefully but Zoe interrupted.

'I don't want to do that any more. It doesn't matter now. It's all over and done with.'

The adults didn't reply. Maisie looked from Jack's face to Phyl's and knew they were thinking the same thing she was.

Nothing was ever really 'over and done with'.

EPILOGUE

Jack left soon after, saying there was plenty for him to be getting on with at the station. But he promised to return the next morning to take their statements in the dubious comfort of Bunting Manor. Before leaving, he briefly took Maisie's hand.

'We should talk, too,' he told her.

Maisie, Phyl and Zoe stayed up just long enough to have something to eat – pasties from the Framlington farm shop warmed on the shovel over the flames. To pass the time, Maisie told Phyl and Zoe stories from her life in Paris.

'Is it hard learning French?' Zoe asked, at last.

'Not if you have the right brain for it,' Maisie told her. 'It's luck really. Some people have it and others don't.'

'Might I have it, do you think?'

'It's possible. Musical people often find languages easier.'

Finally, they went to bed, having locked up every door and window. Maisie fell instantly into deep sleep and woke, refreshed, with the morning sun on her bedroom window. She got up and padded over to the glass, seeing the early leaves beginning to unfurl on the trees, happy that she had contributed to solving the mystery, both pleased and sad for Zoe, deeply torn about her fractured relationship with Jack.

Having washed and dressed and brushed her teeth, she went downstairs to the kitchen where Zoe was cooking bacon while Phyl was burning toast under the ferocious grill of her Calor gas stove. Jack arrived and tea was drunk. Then he said: 'Perhaps this would be a good moment for me to start taking your statements?'

Phyl and Zoe put on their coats – a waxed jacket and an Afghan fur – to walk down to the pub and find out how Ernest Sumner was getting on. Maisie went first, learning for the first time about the page Alberta had copied out of Phyl's book on phytotoxicology.

'You kept that from me,' she complained, with a smile.

'I did,' said Jack. 'I'm sorry.'

'And you didn't tell me why the dead woman being in good health was important. You let me work that out for myself.'

'I hoped it might slow you down,' replied Jack, apologetically.

'But it was actually Ernest Sumner's drunken recollection of "two women" that put me on Mrs Beck's trail.'

Half an hour later, they were done and Phyl and Zoe returned with good news. Ernie had managed not to drink and was on 'day two of a new regime'.

Phyl went next and Maisie and Zoe waited in the library. Zoe had thought of several dozen more questions she wanted to ask about how Maisie had worked everything out. By the end, Maisie was convinced that the girl wasn't pretending when she said she would be fine. Despite her experiences, Zoe seemed much more self-assured than the fragile young woman Maisie had met just a few days before.

'Are you sure you're feeling up to giving your statement?' she asked. 'It might be painful.'

'It's fine,' said Zoe. 'Sergeant Wingard is a nice man and what you know is nowhere near as scary as what you don't.'

That's very true, Maisie thought.

Jack came to ask Zoe to sit with him at the kitchen table and give her version of events while Phyl joined Maisie by the library fire.

'On the inside cover of that photo album,' Maisie said, 'the one with all the pictures of me, there's a message in pencil.'

'There is,' said Phyl, quietly.

'When I saw it, I remember wondering what it could mean. I thought perhaps you had found the album when Mum and Dad died?'

'No, it's always been mine.'

'The message says: "Because you couldn't be there." It's dedicated to you, isn't it? You're the one who couldn't be there.'

'Yes.'

'And it's Dad's handwriting, isn't it?'

'Yes.'

Maisie paused, trying to find the correct neutral words. 'It's an album of photos that he prepared for you, so that you could see me growing up, even though you never came to visit us, not birthdays or Christmas or anything.'

'We agreed it would be for the best,' said Phyl. There were tears on her cheeks. 'I'm so sorry.'

'And all that because you were in love with Dad and that was who you were having an affair with before you got married to Pierre, but you wouldn't break up my parents' marriage.'

'It was a mistake. They already had Stephen—'

'And you became pregnant,' Maisie interrupted, 'and your husband, Mr Pascal, found out—'

'No, that was later.'

Maisie started with surprise.

'The affair that broke up your marriage was with someone else?'

'Yes, an American airman at the base in Tangmere. That has nothing to do with my album of photographs of you.'

'So,' said Maisie, 'back before I was born, Mum finds out about you and Dad—'

'It was just after New Year when she saw that I was pregnant. She knew, of course, that it couldn't be Pierre's because he and I hadn't . . . Well, you know.'

'And then what?'

'She was with me when I went into labour and I couldn't help myself. I told her the truth, that you were Eric's child. She was my sister – I had to. Then your birth was so traumatic I had to remain in hospital. There was no way I could look after you. Eric came to the hospital and took the baby away.'

'Took me away.'

'Yes.'

'Mum agreed to raise me as her own but made you promise to—'

'To "never darken our door again". That was what she asked of me.'

'And you agreed?'

'Of course, I did. Now and then, I tried to get them to let me back into your life, so you did see me once or twice, but . . . Eric sided with Irene, as he was always bound to. He regretted it as well. I was in the wrong. We were both in the wrong.'

'Stephen wasn't my brother.'

'Your half-brother.'

'My mother wasn't my mother.'

'No.'

'But you were.'

'I am.'

There was a moment's pause.

'Was it you who named me?' asked Maisie.

'It was, yes. Irene let me. Maisie comes from the Greek meaning "pearl".'

'That was why you started that odd conversation about Greek-inspired names, when we first met.'

'Yes.'

Maisie stood up. Phyl was out of her chair in a flash.

'Please don't leave. I know I've been very stupid and I may have had a part in the awful things that have happened, but I wanted to see you and it seemed such a good idea finally to bring you into my life.'

Maisie looked down at the Persian rug. 'You've said that.'

'There was a truly terrible day,' Phyl resumed, 'when Pierre found my album of photographs of you, the one with the blank pages with all the photos pulled out. He burnt them, all the precious pictures of you as a baby and a toddler that Eric had been sending me, without Irene knowing, in this hearth, right here in this library. That was why Eric put together the other one, having copies made from the negatives behind Irene's back, and sent it to me with the inscription. I promise you, Maisie, I kept my word. That's the only contact I had with your father after we broke it off.' Phyl hesitated then said: 'Please, I wanted to tell you and I didn't know what else to do, how else to start.'

Maisie went to stand at the rear window, looking up the lane towards the clearing and Alberta's encampment. Outside the cold glass were the damp woods with their myriad paths, worn by sheep and deer and human feet, pilgrimage trails and desire lines and simple shortcuts to water.

And she, Maisie, felt utterly lost in amongst them.

Was Phyl's story true? Obviously, yes. Maisie had worked it out for herself. It all hung together, especially the touching inscription, exactly the sort of thing her father would have written – simple, understated, but imbued with deep emotion.

Because you couldn't be there.

Because Phyl couldn't be there to watch her own child – the child she had been allowed to name and then seen taken from her – grow up. Phyllis, the dynamic sister, the enterprising sister, the wild sister. Perhaps the sister that her father should have married?

No, that was unfair and disloyal and wrong. Eric and Irene had been happy, always. At least from the point at which she, Maisie, had begun to form her own memories of family life when, she supposed, the trauma had subsided and forgiveness had been forthcoming.

'That's why you've been getting so angry when I call you "auntie",' she said, without turning round.

'I'm sorry.'

'Please stop saying you're sorry. And you're sure that it was a mistake, your affair with my father?'

'It was, definitely. I regretted it deeply.'

'I see.'

'We both did. Poor Irene. It took her a long time to get over it, to trust and be happy. But, in the end, your parents were perfectly suited. I was the foolish one who didn't know what I wanted and made unfortunate choices. I thought my American airman was going to take me home to Iowa or Kansas or wherever it was and . . . Oh, I've been such a fool in so many ways.'

Neither of them spoke for a couple of minutes. Then, all of a sudden, Jack came in, followed by Zoe, full of energy and enthusiasm from having unburdened herself.

'Sergeant Wingard is my absolute favourite policeman,' Zoe said, happily. 'You could do a lot worse.'

Maisie felt herself blushing. 'Really, Zoe . . .'

Kindly, to cover her embarrassment, Jack changed the subject.

'I have other news, too, Maisie,' he said. 'I found out this morning. A date has been set for the trial.'

'What's that?' asked Zoe.

'My brother Stephen's murder,' replied Maisie, simply. 'When will it begin, Jack?'

'Monday, April third.'

'That's barely a fortnight,' said Phyl. 'Maisie, there's no point going back to Paris. You must stay here with us.'

Maisie dropped her gaze. Would she? Should she?

'Please do,' said Zoe. 'Don't leave quite yet.'

Jack didn't speak, but she knew he was thinking the same thing. She raised her head and looked from one to the other. There was a similar expression on each of their kind, attentive faces. For their different reasons, they all wanted her close at hand.

For Zoe, Maisie thought, it was the fact that she had helped solve the mystery, but also the glamour of the stranger who lived in Paris, who had a life of her own, far away from the rural dead end of Bunting Manor. And, perhaps, the girl thought that Maisie might provide some of the affection and guidance she would never receive from her mother.

For Phyl, it was the desire finally to mend some of the damage from the mistake she had made thirty-five years before. Also, perhaps, the hope of establishing a relationship of honesty and trust in the present – not by pretending that Maisie could ever become truly her daughter, as she had been Irene's daughter, but something close to that, at least.

Finally, for Jack, it was different again. He had persuaded himself that he loved her, despite her wilfulness and fluctuating emotions. Was it possible that she could move past her grief and accept his offer and begin to explore what they might eventually mean to one another?

It was hard, though. They all knew what they wanted, but her life had been brutally turned upside down for the second time in just a few weeks. What did she want?

She gave them an uncertain smile.

'I'll have to think about it,' she said.

The End

345

ACKNOWLEDGEMENTS

Thanks to my literary agent Luigi Bonomi whose idea it was that I should write cosy crime, and to the team at LBA; to my supremely gifted editor Beth Wickington and all at Hodder & Stoughton; to the booksellers, festival co-ordinators, podcasters and all the others whose dedication and enthusiasm are so essential to a flourishing book industry; to all the generous writers who have supported this playwright's unexpected transition to novel writing.

And, of course, to the person from whom I learnt to write books - the best and only Kate Mosse.

Read on for a sneak peek
at Maisie's next sleuthing
adventure in *Murder at the
Theatre*, coming in 2024.

PROLOGUE

In her dream, Maisie Cooper was back at school. It was a warm summer's day and the sixth-form boys and girls had been brought together to read a play, *The Beggar's Opera*. She could smell the fresh cut grass and hear the persistent hum of the groundsman's mower on the playing fields outside the open windows. She could hear the voice of Jack Wingard, the boy chosen to read the lead, sitting two rows ahead of her in the stuffy classroom.

Then the dream-time went by in a kind of woozy surge and she and Jack were facing one another on stage, with an intimidating audience of teachers, parents and grandparents, brothers and sisters, aunts and uncles and friends. Under the lights, in full eighteenth-century costume, Jack tentatively took her face in his hands and kissed her.

The dream flipped for a second time, to a damp gravel drive and Jack, now grown up, clasping her in his strong arms, angry that he had allowed her to put herself in danger.

The confused memory lasted only for a moment. Straight away, she was back on stage at Westbrook College and Jack was being led up the steps to the scaffold. Another boy, with a canvas hood over his adolescent acne, placed a noose around Jack's neck ...

Maisie spoke without waking: 'No!'

She turned over, her face to the wall. For a time, she slept soundly, though her subconscious still roamed the world of the play: her role, Polly Peachum, in love with Jack Wingard's role, the highwayman Macheath.

Then, cross-fading like a film, her woozy memories found her at the end-of-term afternoon summer party on the cricket lawn, enfolded in a moment of unexpected intimacy in the shadows behind the pavilion, when Jack had kissed her in real life, not in the play, with no one watching, their teenage destinies becoming entwined – perhaps for all of time – only for circumstances, good and bad, to rip them apart once more.

Then, she was back in the play, competing with another girl, in old-fashioned dialogue, for Macheath's affections – for Jack's affections. Then, suddenly, they were allies, desperate to save him from hanging.

Maisie woke in a tangle of bedclothes, her strong limbs constrained by the narrow single bed, her eyes reluctant to open. She could hear faint night-time sounds from the streets of the cathedral city outside the narrow window of her poky hotel room.

At last, she opened her eyes and sat up, wearily rearranging her lumpy pillows, the image of a lithe and youthful Jack Wingard still vivid in her mind. She heaved an unhappy sigh.

How long ago was all that? Sixteen years? And now we have a chance to be together, properly.

Did she want to? Was she ready to?

The truth was, she didn't know.

On the bedside table were her three birthday gifts, touchingly wrapped in identical patterned paper. In the gap between her flimsy curtains, she had a view of the backs of other buildings and a grey sky with no hint of dawn, despite the lengthening of the days as April finally drew to a close.

Maisie groped for the light switch and turned on the table lamp – a weak forty-watt bulb beneath a fussy beaded shade.

Why do I feel so trapped in the past? Why don't I yet feel free? It isn't fair.

The trial arising from her brother's murder was over, taking much longer than she had anticipated, with the defence

lawyer cruelly undermining Maisie's actions by contemptu-
ously referring to her as an 'interfering amateur detective'.
She had found it exhausting and upsetting, though guilty
verdicts were finally pronounced by the jury and appropriate
sentences handed down by the judge.

The trouble was, she had yet to face the repercussions
of what the local paper, the *Chichester Observer*, called 'the
murder at Bunting Manor'. While she wished – almost to the
exclusion of everything else – to finally to feel properly free
to grieve her brother's death, her heart seemed numb.

She got out of bed and went to stand at the north-facing
window. Was there a little lightness in the sky?

No. And there was no lightness in her heart.

When did everything get so complicated?

★★★

When, finally, Maisie climbed back into bed, having washed
her hands and face in the unfriendly shared bathroom on the
corridor outside her room, the cathedral bells were chiming
half-past-two. The immemorial peal drifted over the Roman
walls to a park at the northern edge of the city, where the
impressive Chichester Festival Theatre sat, incongruous, like
a concrete-and-glass spaceship.

Keith Sadler, a porter at the Dolphin & Anchor Hotel,
had a second job at the theatre as nightwatchman. He didn't
hear the bells because – burning the candle at both ends –
he was asleep, neglecting his duties, his head upon his arms
in the green room, the space where the cast and crew of
The Beggar's Opera went to relax and eat and drink at the
management's expense.

He ought to have been alone in the enormous 1200-seat
building. The actors, creatives, technicians and management
were all supposed to be in their respective accommodation;

their homes, their hotel rooms or their bed-and-breakfast digs.

One of them, though, had contrived a makeshift bed out of a pile of dusty curtains in a neglected storage space, deep in the theatre basement, and lay awake, thinking bitter thoughts of avarice, unlikely prosperity and revenge.

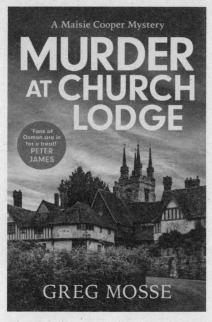